THE TRAIL OF THE BEAST

Book Two of The Deschembine Trilogy

BY

MATT SPENCER

BACK ROADS CARNIVAL BOOKS,
BRATTLEBORO, VERMONT

BACK ROADS CARNIVAL BOOKS
mattspencerauthor.wordpress.com

Digital ISBN: 978-0-578-62803-5
Print ISBN: 978-0-578-62802-8

ALSO BY MATT SPENCER:

THE DESCHEMBINE TRILOGY
The Night and the Land
The Blazing Chief (forthcoming)

TALES OF OLD DESCHEMB
Changing of the Guards
The Renegade God

OTHERS
Story Time with Crazy Uncle Matt
Cult of the Stars
Chapel of the Falcon
Summer Reaping on the Fields of Nowhere
The Drifting Soul

For Bill and Syd,
who believed all along

Well, well, well, here we are, back for more. First off, I can't express enough love and appreciation for everyone who read the first book, responded so enthusiastically, and demanded a sequel (if you're reading this, chances are, that includes you)…which, lucky for everyone, I'd already written, along with the third volume, pretty much back to back to back, years before landing a publishing deal on the first one.

I wouldn't have made it this far without Bill Hilburn, Dan Seitz, Jesse Cross-Nickerson, Kate Barry, Stephen Seitz, and Sydney Isle. Mad props also go out to Alyse Landis, Cyndal Ellis, Luke Burke, Ian Bigelow, Lissa Weinmann, Luz Elena Morey, and Laura Janisieski. My life and these books just plain wouldn't be the same without having known you.

AUTHOR'S NOTE

In the first edition of this book (Damnation Books, 2015), many of the most major rewrites were done very quickly, at the eleventh hour, prior to publication. Long story short, the writing/publishing world is sometimes screwy like that. To be honest, once all was said and done, the final results never quite sat right with me. Hence, I took the opportunity with this re-release to give the prose a bit more refining than I normally allow me-now to impose his sensibilities on my younger self's previously published work A lot of fat has been peeled from the bones, plus some moments previously relegated to footnotes have been allowed more breathing room, allowing them to shine in the overall tapestry like they always deserved. As with the previous volume in this series, The Night and the Land, *I took the opportunity to correct a few minor continuity errors, since I've written quite a bit more about the Deschembines and their history/lore since writing this first trilogy, and I know a lot more about all that now. Also as with that previous volume, I've done away with some of the previous publisher's house-style editorial impositions, as well as having it subjected to a fresh round of proofreading. Beyond that, the essence of the tale remains the same. Enjoy the ride, folks!*

THE TRAIL OF
THE BEAST

"There were giants in the earth in those days; and also after that, when the sons of God came in unto the daughters of men, and they bare children to them, the same became mighty men which were of old, men of renown." —Genesis, 6:4

~

"Livin' on the road my friend, is gonna keep you free and clean Now you wear your skin like iron Your breath as hard as kerosene" — "Pancho And Lefty" by Townes Van Zandt

PART ONE:

SEARCH

POSTVILLE, FLORIDA

ONE

Nose cartilage strained and crackled. Rob's scars puffed and pulsed. He rolled with the punch, but still felt every inch of those knuckles, as if that part of his face hadn't felt anything since a set of talons had opened it five years ago. The scars forked up Rob's right cheek, streaking both sides of his eye and up his forehead.

Everyone's got a plan 'til you punch 'em in the nose. Pretty funny, how a solid strike slowed down time, making room for such thoughts.

Staggering, he sensed the ropes near his back. He planted his feet and willed his eyes to clear—*quick*—before the pale, black-haired drifter could step in to finish him off like a pissed-off tornado with arms. Except—no, wait—now the guy was doing that stupid fucking blustering dance again, all over the ring, daring Rob back for more.

They'd been drunk getting into the ring. By now, they'd burned off most of it, but the drifter moved like he was drunker than ever.

Hell, Rob figured he must look like a hundred and eighty pounds of chewed-up raw steak by now. He sure felt like it. Either way, he launched into what started as a looming overhead flail. The drifter's right came to meet him. Rob bobbed under it. His right uppercut came like Edgar Allan Poe's razor pendulum and scraped chin and cheek. The drifter's neck lashed backwards. As Rob's left circled, his back foot shifted so his waist swung just right. The clock to the guy's crown thumped with just the right special something. The black-haired man's head snapped sideways, and he fell flat on his ass. His skull bobbed and lulled like a bobble on a loose-coiled spring, then he sprawled limply.

Rob stared with hazy bewilderment, not quite grasping that the grueling ordeal had ended. He tried to lean forward for a better look, just to make sure the guy wasn't dead. Before he could topple forward onto the poor bastard, a set of big oil-musky hands got him by the shoulders and pulled him back. Whoever was on the other end of the arms let go. They must have stepped out of the way, because he fell against the ropes.

Somewhere in the roll of his eyes, Rob noticed that a world existed outside the ring. In it was Ryan—a bony, flat-faced, half-white, half-Hispanic boy—reclining and chuckling. "So…that it?"

Cliff, a heavy-set black man in his late thirties, helped Rob out of the ring. "Yeah, 'less you want me to haul both their asses up and knock 'em against each other for a while."

Ryan's toothy grin widened. "You could do that, couldn't you?"

Rob managed to fling up a middle finger in Ryan's general direction. Cliff's limp was back, Rob noticed.

Last New Year's Eve, they'd split a bottle of vodka between them, and decided to knock the snot out of each other, literally into next year. Rob was a lot more comfortable with his fists than his feet, but when Cliff started throwing kicks, he returned the favor. It turned out later that he'd been stomping repeatedly on an ancient leg injury. Cliff's limp came and went ever since.

Cliff climbed back into the ring, prodded and roused the drifter. From here, it looked like the guy was actually conscious. Rob fumbled out of his gloves and set them on the edge of the ring. Then he shambled towards the small wooden table where he'd set his wristwatch.

The rec-space felt bigger than usual. It even *looked* bigger. Cliff's bar had a dilapidated garage out back that came with the lease. Half the space was full of bar supplies, the other half cleared for Cliff's personal rec room, which included the boxing ring. The humid space smelled like old sweat and blood, absorbed in the concrete, in the foam of the ring, 'til it sputtered through the leaky pipes running across the ceiling. Rob liked to imagine customers tasting it in the tap water. In the ring, he knew only new sweat, new blood. He threw himself into the plastic lawn chair. At least now the concrete tortured his feet less. His breathing still came in low, hoarse, shuddering growls.

How long had they kept at it? He fumbled around and found his watch. It was edging towards three in the morning. *Shit!* Sally wouldn't be too pissed at him—this had actually been her idea, as nights like this frequently were.

"Hon, look, you've been busting your ass left and

right lately," she'd say patiently. "You're too wound up. Go. Now. Have your guy's night, before you drive me crazy."

She'd be asleep by the time he made it home, though, so he'd still be pissed at himself. For now, it was a dull awareness of a feeling that would bloom later, probably whenever he managed to shake his brain loose from the back of his skull.

The drifter had showed up around midnight. At the time, Rob had planned to leave within the half-hour. Everyone was gone except for him, Cliff, and Ryan. They hadn't expected anyone else, even though Cliff hadn't bothered to turn the sign. For Rob, that had been perfection, just him and his friends drinking the last of the evening dry. Couldn't Cliff have just told the guy he'd missed Last Call? Then Rob hit it off with the drifter, who started talking shit about boxing and martial arts. Once had a shot at the Golden Gloves, he claimed. Actually, he sounded more than a little like DeNiro in *Raging Bull* doing Brando's old '*I could'a been a contender*' bit. Rob let it slip—accidentally, yeah fuckin' right—that Cliff had an honest-to-God boxing ring in the back building.

Rob's breathing got halfway back to normal, now that he'd stretched out. The lean muscles in his racehorse build relaxed involuntarily. The drifter leaned on Cliff, mumbling something. Everyone flopped down but Cliff, who grabbed a fresh sixer of Yuengling from the cooler. He gave the first beer to the drifter, the second one to Rob, then popped one for himself. Ryan didn't drink, so he went to the cooler for a Mountain Dew. Cliff made a run to the ice machine.

"Where the fuck are my clothes?" The drifter had stripped to his shorts for the fight.

"No clue." As usual, Rob left on his jeans and wife-beater. Now there was blood on the shirt. "That was great, dude. You fought well."

"Huh? Oh, yeah, man…cool. Yeah, no shit yo, huh?"

Somehow, they managed to bump fists. Rob didn't look over, but figured Ryan was smirking. Cliff and Ryan were used to Rob saying shit like *You fought well* instead of *Hey man, good fight*. It never got old for them, the way it threw new people off.

Cliff came back with wet rags and plastic bags full of ice in one hand, the drifter's pants and shirt in the other. He tossed the latter at the drifter's feet, along with an ice pack, then tossed the other into Rob's lap. He threw the rags in their faces.

"Shit, man," said Rob, squirming so the ice pack slid off his crotch. "You tryin' to freeze my balls off?"

"Not right now. That's a good idea, though, if I ever decide I want Sally to kill me."

Rob grinned and set his beer aside long enough for another middle finger. He grabbed the bottle for a swig. Cliff's voice was sincere, which Rob liked. He loved reminders that folks around here knew his wife's fighting side was no joke.

Just think what they don't *know about that.*

With a little sinister smile, he rubbed the wet rag then the ice pack over his face and chest. A sting flashed through his bruises. Both the rag and the ice pack came away splotched red and deep, wet pink. His fingertips touched his face. A shallow cut ran parallel to the outer scar. He'd collected plenty of fresh scars in Cliff's ring, small ones most folks didn't notice. The two big ones got all the attention. When he ran his tongue across the inside of his cheek, he still felt where the talons had cut all the way through. Whenever he got hit hard enough, the edges of those inner scars still broke and bled a little.

He spotted the drifter fishing out a smoke. "I get one of those off you, dude?"

After getting his own smoke dangling between his swollen lips, the drifter passed one without looking. Rob leaned over with a light, then lifted his beer in a toast. The drifter figured out the gesture and they clinked bottles. As far as regular habit went, Rob had quit smoking five years ago. Some nights, though, the beer still didn't taste complete 'til it was washing down some nicotine. At the time, he hadn't even noticed himself dropping the full-on habit. Then again, there'd been plenty else on his mind, to put it mildly. It was after the night he got the scar…*the night of the Second Call.*

Not long after that, he'd lost track of a lot else, things he'd never quite convinced himself were bad habits, good riddance. So many promises and possibilities left behind…

Tonight, Rob didn't want to resent anything. It had been perfection up in the bar, perfection in the ring. It was still perfect, like it would be to get home and crawl into bed with Sally, even though she'd be asleep. Hey, it was lovely to watch her sleep, too. No good dwelling on how he paid his way on off-the-books day labor, couldn't even let wireless internet into the trailer, because he couldn't risk a paper trail—physical or electronic—leaking his whereabouts onto the grid, to the wrong places. No good thinking of the duster coat that never left the closet, of what hung from a leather belt on the same hanger…

For a second, Rob almost felt ready to get back in the ring. Maybe he could goad Cliff into it. Then he tasted smoke and beer, saw his friends, thought of his wife. Like that, he was happy to be used up, drunk, sore and silly in Postville, Florida.

Finally, Cliff started shooing everyone out. "You gonna make it home okay tonight, man?" he asked Rob.

"Sure." Yeah, Rob could probably manage the half-mile walk without falling dead in a ditch somewhere. This countryside would lend him the strength to get home in one piece. It always did.

The drifter looked for his shoes as Rob dragged himself towards the broken garage door held open right now by some bungee cords. Out in Florida's pulpy summer night, he glimpsed the shape perched on the power lines above. He almost dismissed it as some fat bird. Then he looked again. Yeah, there were those beady, glittering eyes, chasing the summer out of his body in a cold flush. Soon the cold was chased out by a rage hotter than any summer, even in Florida.

Before Rob could shout at the creature, there came another rush, on the air from far away, charging his body and soul with something that made his boxing rage seem feeble, so he no longer felt all his fresh bruises. 'Til a second ago, he'd idly wondered if some of his joints would ever work right again. Now they became tiny drops of fuel for this new fire. It would have been the most exquisite ravening hunger, if it weren't for the fear. He might not have been scared, if the energy rush hadn't come from the direction of home.

Later, Rob would remember footsteps clapping across the concrete behind him. Ryan shouted something like "Hey dude, wanna stick around, help clean up?"

It was the last time Rob ever heard Ryan's voice, and he didn't stay to answer. Instead, he bolted down the dirt road, through the Florida countryside that had assured him over and over that he would never feel that rush as long as he and Sally stayed within the county limits—

Oh yeah, the rush…even still out of reach, he already tasted its source, sweet as ever. The years folded shut between now and the last time he'd tasted it.

Two

When Sally woke up, Rob still wasn't there next to her. *Son of a bitch!*

She'd had the kind of day where the summer gets inside your soul. While it lasted, she'd genuinely loved this scattered, rotting little town of theirs. She would have, even if she hadn't made twice her usual tips at the diner. So naturally, she'd felt like ending it with some great sex. She fell asleep waiting for Rob to get home. Now Rob had missed his chance, because *guy's night* ran late. Hell, it wasn't like she couldn't have sought him out. Sometimes the antics he got up to with Cliff and Ryan were her thing too.

Why not, right? She wasn't disappointed or annoyed now, though. She felt disturbed. Something had woken her, and she had no idea what. One moment, she'd slept curled soundly on their little mattress. Then her eyes snapped open in the muddy darkness, instantly lucid.

You're being silly, she tried to tell herself. There were no sounds that didn't belong out there, in the orange grove in front of the camper or in the swamp behind it, nothing she hadn't gotten used to, grown fond of even. If Rob were here, those noises might tell him something useful. Not that he ever said what.

The only light came from the house at other end of the grove, filtering through waxy leaves and the window overhead. She couldn't see the clock, but she knew it was way too late for that light to be on, for the Carters to still be awake.

Sally always awoke so instantly, not constantly with the unease she felt now, but with the ghost of it. Why fall out of practice, right? It had been her way for a long time before she'd met Rob. When they'd first met, she'd wound up in his bed way too soon. She'd fallen asleep in his arms and had her first morning in years of slogging languidly and comfortably from a peaceful slumber. As it turned out, it had also been the last chance either of them had for such a sleep for over a year.

Eventually, they'd found this town. Rob had found the Carters with their orange grove and their old family camper for rent at the far end. Best of all, the Carters didn't ask many questions. Rob made some of his money tending Chet Carter's crop, some on the other local farms, occasionally bartending or bouncing at Cliff's. For all the ways their life was a constant pain in the ass, Sally never quite shook the itchy feeling that it was too good to be true. Like it fell together with some unnatural serendipity, like Rob was some Old World Schomite sorcerer who'd told these lands to conjure the town just so. Even the squalid aspects of it seemed to appeal to something in him, so she'd always wondered. After a while, he got comfortable kicking back after a hard day's work, with Chet on the porch or the boys at the bar, like he might get too comfortable and let something slip. That never stopped worrying her, either.

She'd never worried about herself like that, even when she got to carousing *like one of the guys* as some Earth-line saying went. She was an old hand at keeping quiet, at leaving places of the past in their own black void where they belonged. Rob was more into shooting the shit with random people, often in loud, friendly pissing contests. The funny thing was when it came his turn to tell anecdotes. He was so smooth at leaving out the real clincher details, smoothing it over with more mundane implications people could buy into. Sally might half-listen to the tale of something she'd been part of and not recognize it at first.

After the first few months in Postville, he was sleeping deeply, waking up as relaxed and groggy as he pleased. It was one more thing about settling here that pissed her off, one more thing for which she'd mostly forgiven him by now. There was always his rabid protectiveness, but he could have stayed sharper to real dangers. If she'd woken up and found him with her, would he even sense anything wrong out there?

She slipped out of bed. The first thing she found was her pocketknife, then some jeans and a shirt. She'd gone through some trouble to hunt down a knife that was so much like the one her dad had trained her on, the one she'd carried through the years spent wandering alone. She'd lost that one around the time she met Rob. It was far from sentimental, but when keeping up her weapon skills, feeling the familiar haft and weight made things flow more naturally. With any luck, she wouldn't have to use it tonight.

Something out there circled closer and closer…something bad. The wrong random noises often gave her that idea, but why was it so intense now? Never had dread been this palpable, almost specific, on nothing but an intuition, because…what? Because the lights at the other end of the orange grove were on later than usual?

Sally thought of the duster coat pushed far to the back of the closet, of what it concealed. No matter what Rob told her, she knew how often he thought of it. Crazily enough, she wished he'd stayed less cut off from it, kept that horrid, ancient prowess of his a little sharper.

He'd just say "Why bother?" They were in Postville, Florida, and Postville told him he wouldn't need it here. At least he'd kept his bare-handed martial arts abilities sharp, but she knew damn well that that wasn't the same…not at all.

Sally stepped outside, not bothering with shoes.

Even if the ground hadn't been so soft with early dew, she knew her way around. Besides, she'd go more quietly, stepping free and limber on the balls of her bare feet. Nothing happened by the time the house came into view. That didn't stop every tree and slope and shadow from looking like a possible hiding place for lurking threats. What had caused the Carters to snap on the kitchen and back porch lights?

For that matter, where were the Carters? They would probably call her paranoid. So what? Paranoia was a word that belonged in the Earth-line languages, to that false sense of security they created and the civilized hypocrisies that festered there. What night sounds could have gotten the Carters' attention, especially after four years of Rob and Sally's irregular hours? Obviously, something had woken up either Chet or Flo. One of them had come out for a look, but they weren't out here now, and there were no lights in the bedroom window, so…

Sally's fingers dropped to the pocket holding her knife. In the grass at the foot of the porch steps stretched a dark lump that wasn't an earth mound or a series of garden rocks. It was long and narrow, so she knew it was Chet, not Flo.

Sally rushed forward. "Chet! Oh Christ, Chet!"

Her alarm was real, but not the panic. The panic was a show for the dark shape she'd spotted in the shadows to her left. She spun as it sprang. Her elbow struck a grasping palm, right before her slender fist cracked her attacker across the jaw. The man hadn't even gotten a full blow in, but she already knew his method.

She'd been trained in it from age six up, after all. She also knew that first punch wouldn't stun him for long. Her next set of strikes would have fractured his ribs, pelvis, and nose, but a sharp, gagging cry came from the house. It was the cry of a dying old woman, one who may or may not realize her husband was already dead. The killer must have watched through some window with the lights still off. Sally snarled off the distraction. Something sharp jabbed her stomach.

Metal sank into the meat of her abdomen. Her next strikes flew wild. So, this new cloud in her brain must be the fade-out of death. When the point drew free, she realized the cut was less than an inch deep. Then she wasn't aware of anything.

THREE

The old Earth-line woman's body shuddered to a stop around the kitchen knife. The handle quivered in Ashwin's grip with the heart's last sputters. He wiped his prints from it with a rag from his pocket, some of that special Secret Police fabric woven and chemically treated to obliterate DNA traces, or at least the best homespun approximation Vencie could come up with. Ashwin wore clothes of the same material. He left the blade in the body and glanced out the window. His brother-in-law disappeared into the murk between the orange trees with the girl.

Yep, they knew for sure by now. It really was Sally

Fucking Wildfire. Ashwin had let the old woman scream once, right on Vencie's signal. The old bag had done her part great.

In the living room, Luna and Sevrin watched the driveway through the window.

"Vencie got her," Ashwin informed his brother and sister.

"You don't have to whisper right now." Sevrin paused. "Good job with the old bitch."

They weren't a family of the Spirelight Secret Police—Ashwin, Sevrin, Luna, and Luna's husband Vencie—but they conducted themselves as one while working. At least this was how Vencie told them a Secret Police family conducted itself. It hadn't gotten them killed yet. The main difference—so far as they knew— was that they never reported to any Tribunal except to collect rewards. They confined their business strictly to a few choice homesteads throughout the South where Tribunal representatives rewarded them discreetly.

So here stood Ashwin, Sevrin, and Luna, waiting for a Crimbone who'd slaughtered one of the meanest families of the Secret Police, minutes after he picked up his black blade for the first time...the blade that materialized for each Crimbone fledgling from their infernal corner of the ephemeral realms.

That was just how some stories went, Ashwin reminded himself. So was the one that Rob Coscan had received *blades*, plural. Still, when dealing with a guy who inspired stories like that, a little over-caution never hurt, even in a neutral state.

Florida had at some point become neutral territory

by default of neglect. The Schomites controlled it for as long as most remembered—up to and through prohibition. Those were good business days for the Cabinet, and crops were good for Schomites, who preferred farming to whiskey running. The Florida Crimbone did mostly peacekeeping work back then, making sure Earth-line gangsters weren't manipulated into warfare by the Spirelight Secret Police Tribunals, puppeteering their competitors in Georgia and Louisiana as they did. Illinois and New York had already been shaken up badly by this, which was probably what the Tribunals had in mind when their hands in Congress had pushed prohibition.

The Schomites also mixed with all the Earth-line races, which meant a lot of them were black, so the Crimbone had stretched themselves even thinner in these parts, fighting Klan activity and such. Vencie always told the family how that would ultimately be the beasts' undoing, letting themselves get distracted by such Earth-line affairs, straining their ability to blend in. That's what the beasts got, for letting their men mate with Earth-line women who they let live afterwards.

Then alcohol had turned back into a legitimate stateside Earth-line business, and the Cabinet had relaxed too soon. Spirelight fingers pushed new markets, shoving bit by bit against Schomite interests, which were always invested more deeply in the land's concerns than Earth-line legitimacy. In the cities, disputes were settled in urban furnaces where Earth-line thug warfare made good camouflage. Out in the country, blood spilled in patches of swamp where Earth-line boats neither rowed on oars nor chugged on motors.

Finally, the Spirelights came to hold the state 'til their resources dried up. The Schomite Cabinets might have reclaimed the territory at that point, but the Crimbone remained wary of the land's fickle spirit. So, the state was left to the Earth-liners, typically none the wiser that it had ever been otherwise.

If you believed all that crazy Crimbone shit, you might say the Spirelights had fallen from favor with the land of Florida. Maybe the state hadn't approved of bootlegging after all. Did all the Schomites really believe that, or did they just humor the Crimbone to avoid an uprising? Ashwin wasn't sure.

When Rob Coscan showed up, he wouldn't be carrying any blade. None of the descriptions around here mentioned any, or a duster coat under which to hide them in public. Only the earlier sightings mentioned the duster, all far upstate or out of state, dating back four years. Then again, they'd found Rob Coscan and Sally Wildfire by following the stories. The yarns started in the east coast neutral territories, getting thicker the further south you went. Old barflies and waitresses, shelter volunteers and cheap, shady laborer supervisors...They remembered the man with the devil-crown scars who always seemed to be having a conversation with someone or something no one else could see or hear. Just something *off* about the way he answered you, they all said, the way a person speaks after turning and asking a trusted companion for advice. Other people said he wasn't so subtle. In fact, they were convinced he was a schizophrenic, the dangerous kind. When Ashwin, Luna,

Sevrin and Vencie heard about all this, they knew they were hearing about a Crimbone. Except most Crimbone knew how to be subtle, if they had to be.

The hunted animal, folks called the woman with him. She acted sweet, except you always got the feeling she was sizing you up, figuring out if you were one of the hunters. What if she decided you were? Only the uglier stories offered answers.

The weird part was how Ashwin's family had first heard about the couple. Ashwin's family had known this territory—what would become the celebrity couple's territory—well before the Wildfires were even killed. Then, like anyone else who mattered, they'd heard of the fugitives. Yet they never managed to pick up a solid trail 'til a few weeks ago. That trail led to Postville.

Sally Wildfire and Rob Coscan, hiding in this shitty little Florida town all these years, and neither the Crimbone nor the Spirelight Secret Police had caught so much as a whiff…but Vencie's family had.

Ashwin's gaze returned to the black front yard outside. Throughout the bushes and mossy willows, a thousand night critters chirped and rustled. Somewhere up in one of those willows, one critter rustled louder than the rest. Its out-of-rhythm sound shook an evil chill from the trees. The chill floated across the yard, through the window, to the three Spirelights who watched and waited.

"How long did Vencie say he was gonna take?" asked Sevrin.

"However long it takes to get the girl back through the woods, to the van," said Luna. "Weren't you listening?"

"Quiet," hissed Ashwin. His eyes went back to the window.

The willows painted most of the yard the color of char, with only a few scattered shards of moonlight. At the far end, a man came running along the lonely dirt road. His slight crouch didn't hide his menacing height. His hair was clipped short, close to the scalp, so the moon bathed his sharp, scarred face as white as the skull beneath, save for his small, dark beard. At the end of his long, slender, gnarled arms, the fingers half curled, tensed to grab and rip flesh. Either hand looked like it should be holding a black-bladed knife. There were already fresh stains on his shirt, maybe blood. Spirelight eyes were sharp enough to catch little details like that, yet strained to follow him once he darted into the blackness of the yard.

"Get down," hissed Luna. "Get out of the path of the window!"

When Ashwin didn't obey straight off, she yanked him to the floor. His shoulder smacked the floor hard enough to bruise.

FOUR

Near home, Rob slowed and forced himself to gather some wits.

"You lied," he growled. "You let them find their way here. You let them in."

A wind picked up at his back, hard enough to press him faster onward. He glanced around at the trees. They didn't move. So yeah, it was just him the wind was interested in.

Folks sometimes had to say to each other, *It's not all about you.* For Rob, that had been an especially comforting life-lesson to learn. Whenever it was all about him, it always sucked.

Across the yard, flames poured out of the Carter's front window. There was no actual fire, of course, no light but the back porchlights outlining the structure. Yet that's more or less how Rob's senses processed it, as an explosive, billowing flame.

The Spirelight glow…He'd learned its meaning on the heels of first experiencing it, the garish life energy of his kind's oldest natural enemies. It always came first as a smell, like steam wafting up from clear, bitter liquid that never blended right with anything else on the air. It overwhelmed the Crimbone brain 'til it blazed through the optic nerves in a unique way. It awoke a whole new set of senses, too, for which there are no words in the Earth-line languages. With it came the instinctive compulsion to defend his kind, as decimator and devourer of their enemies.

Now Rob remembered how it felt, to drink that glow as it spilled with their blood, as it changed from the living essence of their tyrannical gods to the fire on which a Crimbone grows strong and flourishes. His first encounter with it had caused a different effect, though…a need not to destroy, but to take to himself and give himself entirely unto, as if the gods had found a way to take him as a willing hostage after all. Her name was Sally. Everyone else—on both sides—called her *the tainted Spirelight.*

For their first year together, hell was everywhere. Then they'd found this town, so he'd stayed here for her. The enemy would never find them here, but neither would the glory for which he'd been made. At least that's what the spirit of the place had said, in how the warm air wrapped itself around him, in the rhythm of the bird songs, breeze rustles, and swamp chitters. All the same, now the enemy was here. Rob knew this naturally, as though they stood two feet in front of him. He raced towards them and his wife.

One of them watched him from the window, trying to track his silhouette through the dark yard. Did the fucker really expect to surprise him? Did these jackasses not know the first thing about Crimbone? What kind of amateurs was he dealing with here?

He slipped alongside the willow at the center of the yard, then skulked through a weave of shadows, towards Chet's shed. There he would find instruments with which to chop through flesh and deflect weapons. In the camper, in the back of a closet he hadn't gone into in years, there hung the only two such instruments he ever wanted to use for such work. There wasn't time to reach the camper now, though. Only minutes ago, at Cliff's, he'd hoped to be drawn home by the pull of Sally's glow. He wouldn't find her there now. She wasn't anywhere nearby. He knew because he couldn't smell her. The implications froze his blood. The glow he *did* feel pulsed and shifted, from those who'd created this terror.

By the Old Lords, he would make them scream!

He reached the shed and set to searching, stepping cautiously and stealthily, over and around cobweb-fettered boxes and rusty farm equipment. He reached the wall he wanted, decked in tools that hung on hooks. His fingers slid across the right handle, long and crescent-curved like the blade that extended from it. Rob's palm ran across the smooth flat, brushing the deeply notched teeth. Often enough, he'd used it to prune Chet's orange trees.

Sometimes afterwards as the sun set, he and Chet would sit down together with beer on the porch, or in folding chairs outside the camper, or right here in this shed. Rob would tell Chet about his nightlife exploits and listen to Chet talk rugged old-timer's philosophy.

Now Rob flicked the top of the blade. The metal hummed supply. He closed both fists around the handle. It was made for slow sawing. With the right coordination and power in the strikes, though, it would work fast enough on flesh and bone.

Rob listened to be sure the Spirelights hadn't moved from the window, hadn't stopped trying to spot him in the yard. Then he slipped out of the shed and around the side of the house. The only sound he made was the low rumbling growl of his breathing. He peered around the corner, smelled death, and came further out of the shadows. Chet lay face down in the back yard. A trail in the dirt showed he'd been killed neither instantly nor where he lay. One of the Spirelights had struck him on the porch or indoors, then dragged him thrashing across the backyard while he bled out.

With that image in mind, Rob sprang over the porch railing, ablaze to add more corpses to the heap. His feet thundered on the boards. He didn't care. If these Spirelights were worth piss, they'd expect him to attack from this direction anyway.

He flung open the back door. The glowing shapes entered the black hallway. Rob didn't need to turn on the light to see the first one reach the kitchen. Something heavy and wooden dragged across the counter top…*Damnit, that was the problem with the fucking glow!* It painted Spirelights clear as day in any darkness, yet somehow didn't illuminate their surroundings—including any weapons they brought or found—like they were cut and pasted there from someplace else. Whatever it was, the Spirelight chucked it at him.

Pain exploded in his knee. He staggered and pitched forward, holding just enough footing to keep moving towards the Spirelight.

The faintest air rush brushed his cheek, from a fist that barely missed. His blade's stainless steel teeth bit deep into a thick, leathery neck. Rob tightened his arms, pressed hard, and dragged the edge through living tissue. The blade's teeth ripped meat and gristle before scraping the collarbone. He opened his mouth to taste the arterial spray raining on him, along with the glow's final flare-up. The body crashed into the wall.

Flailing arms struck Rob's face, neck, and shoulders. He drove the blade like a spear through the Spirelight's gut, into sheetrock. The body spasmed, pinned upright. Rob jerked the blade free. A clump of entrails splashed on the floor, a second or so ahead of the corpse.

The fight couldn't have lasted long, because the other two Spirelights were still only halfway down the hall. Somehow, Rob sensed they were brother and sister, that it was their brother he'd just killed.

As he launched himself at them, the pain in his knee sang loud. His mind ignored it, but his body wouldn't. He crashed to the floor and flipped onto his back, in time to catch the glint of the woman's knife falling towards his face. A reflexive pivot of his neck and dumb luck saved him. The tip of a K-Bar caught his cheek right below the eye. The edge sheered along the bone, slicing his ear nearly in half.

He kicked with both legs. The Spirelight woman's knife rose and plunged towards his side. His fingers scrambled and fastened back on the pruning blade. He drove it straight up into her screaming mouth. It stopped against the back of her throat. He kept driving it, so viciously that it jutted out through the back of her skull. The blade snapped at the handle, splintering her teeth so bloody chips bounced off his face. Next thing Rob knew, he and the last Spirelight were shoving the corpse aside to get at each other. Had the hallway been only a little wider, this one would have joined the girl in the struggle and finished him off.

Once the corpse was out of the way, they met in a grapple. The attacker's arm shifted between them, obviously to pull a weapon. Rob snatched the wrist and wrestled 'til the weapon clattered between them. For a while, nothing existed but the raw strain of full-body strength against full-body strength, tumbling and twisting through crude holds and flailing punches. Rob was stronger, but he was also cut badly. The fiercer he fought, the faster he bled.

There was blood on the Spirelight that wasn't Rob's, but it wasn't the Spirelight's, either. Rob's teeth sank and tore into the neck. He tasted two spurts at once, one hot and coppery, the other twice as hot but of matter for which there's no frame of reference in the language of Earth-line thought. Whatever you called it, it fired his limbs to full power, stronger than he ever remembered them. His every nerve sang with ravening life—and really, who ever argued with that? He jerked loose, twisted up behind his enemy, and pressed the bastard against the floorboards with fists and elbows, 'til the shoulder blades and spine caved like rotted wood.

Rob might have expected himself to linger and feast. Instead, he threw himself off and scuttled backwards. The Spirelight still gurgled through its torn throat, somehow managing raspy, whistling squeals, maybe trying to scream. Eventually, it stopped fighting. Rob rolled off and sprawled on his back in the living room. His chest heaved. His breaths were no longer the eager growls of a beast stalking prey, but the scared, agonized shudders of a scruffy kid he'd lost touch with a long time ago.

He knew the last Spirelight was still alive, because he still tasted its glow on the air. That taste was cold comfort. The smell of death now saturated this whole house the strongest. Rob felt ready to choke on it, then he passed out.

FIVE

Vencie came out of the other end of the orange grove with Sally Coscan slung over his shoulder. He was the only member of the family who'd gotten her current name straight in his head. They wouldn't have seen how it made a difference. Neither did he, but you could never be aware of too many details. That's how he'd spotted the true value here, the difference between him and the people who'd served as his family since Grandpa died twenty years ago…the difference between all other descendants of Spiralla and the bloodlines of the Secret Police.

The others had actually thought it was a good strategy for them to deal with Rob while Vencie handled Sally. Vencie couldn't agree more. They'd be dead soon enough, and he'd be allowed to start a new family, among those he truly belonged with.

Rob Coscan might be rusty enough for the others to kill him, but he'd take them with him. Maybe Vencie could have taken the boy on, but he had the one he needed, to present to the Tribunal as proof of his worth in the eternal eyes of the Spirah Pantheon. Rob Coscan would show up eventually, if he survived. No doubt he'd have some serious physical recovery to do first, though. By then, the trail would be cold. If he found his way to Sally, Vencie would be waiting, with proper fighting companions.

Vencie crossed a wide, wooden bridge made from railroad beams, braided with sickly smelling vines. He crossed a smaller, less tended field, then veered left onto a narrow, jagged, bumpy forest trail that took him to the road. The van was parked as far into the brush as it would go without getting stuck.

It had originally been a Crimbone's van…though not a Crimbone who could have slaughtered one of the deadliest Secret Police families around on the same night he received his black blades. If things hadn't worked out this way, Vencie would have needed to kill the others before reaching the homestead. One less thing he'd have to explain. It had gone over well enough with the few representatives who'd turned blind eyes—people born outside the proper bloodlines, trained in the secrets of the coterie, and all that—but not anymore.

In the back of the van, he slung Sally Coscan down onto a steel sheet. Rectangular holes were cut through it, in two places at the center, then at all four corners, thick leather straps woven through each. Vencie's jaw throbbed where she'd landed one on him. He touched his fingers to it and winced. Then he set to binding her, glad the straps were so strong, even if the drugs he'd laced his knife with *would* keep her in a coma for the drive. This girl may no longer have a place among the Secret Police, among any Spirelight company beyond those who'd pay her bounty, but the prowess of her line was still alive in her.

On the floor by the steel sheet, there lay a thin iron pipe. From one end ran two feet of curved, tempered, razor-edged carbon steel. Vencie had forged the blade himself, then welded and bolted it to the beam. For two years since, he'd oiled and sharpened it regularly. It had won him this van. He would have brought the spear along tonight, but he needed Sally Coscan alive.

Vencie's grandfather had been one of the Secret Police—no one of any special renown, but a man of respect among fellow agents, to be sure. So was Vencie's father. His mother was a woman of respect, too. In his early training, Vencie had excelled at tactical training, and showed promise as a physical combatant. Seminary training always stumped him, though, except in the studies of sacred geography. Try as he might, his Tribunal judges had denied him passage to the next stage: a stint in the wilderness training camps. Instead, they left him with his grandfather while his parents and brothers went off for field work.

The only reason Vencie's grandfather hadn't still been in the field, was that he took a blow to the head sometime in middle-age that left him too loopy for the job. Otherwise, he'd remained a strict, cruel, effective teacher. He went on tutoring his castoff grandson while the rest of the family went out hunting. One day, word came home that the rest of the family had died in Richmond, Virginia, even though Richmond was supposed to be neutral territory. It had even made the TV news; *gang-related*, the reporters called it. Young Vencie requested an opportunity to retake the tests, to reenter the field and help fill the void left by his parents and siblings. The Tribunals denied his request.

Vencie's grandfather had died not long afterwards. That left the Tribunals with the chore of figuring out what to do with the brat. Before they made up their minds, he slipped their watch and hit the road, along with his childhood sweetheart and her two brothers. Without Vencie, those kids would have grown up civilians, without a drop of any fighting bloodline in them, bound for life on mountain homesteads and in Earth-line cities. They wouldn't have lasted a day on the road without Vencie as their leader. While he beat them into shape with basic survival training, he also imparted his unutilized Secret Police training…everything he once swore never to reveal to those outside the sacred warrior bloodlines. They agreed originally to his crazy ideas because it sounded exciting. They stayed with him through what followed out of fear and respect. Their home became the world and each other. They'd since held their own against many brutal, ugly Earth-line people, and more than a few Crimbone. Civilian Schomites, of course, were no danger at all.

As with many of their generation, Ashwin, Sevrin, and Luna didn't really think of Schomites as the demons they were supposed to be—demons that lived to profane the very existence of the Spirah gods, as the latter lived in the veins of all Spirelight people. The regular Schomites were more like arrogant degenerates, the Crimbone a subspecies of vermin. Vencie still held some of the ancestors' piety. It was a good thing he kept it at heart when he trained his family. Demons or vermin, the Crimbone would kill you if you weren't just as deadly.

Vencie finished securing Sally Coscan, then climbed up front and got the van on the road. He went left and circled the area for a time. After a mile and a half, he found his way to the road out of town. He passed only a few scattered houses before that, one with an orange grove behind it. That house would be full of death by now. Vencie barely noticed it when he passed.

SIX

Rob awoke to the sound of screechy, wheezing laughter. He'd forgotten about the fat, bird-like shape on the power lines outside Cliff's. Actually, it was more like a bat.

"Ah, fuck," he muttered.

"*Buuuzzz!* An' the answer is, *What* Ain't *Biter-Boy gonna get to do again anytime soon?*" The exaggerated cracker accent was replaced for a moment by the smug, nasal yuppie proclamation, "*Ding!* That is correct. *Fucking* is something we do not anticipate the Biter-Boy doing for quite a while. Puttergong collects five hundred dollars."

Rob went into a coughing, gagging fit, trying to belch out the death smell that soaked into his throat and lungs. He rolled halfway over. The cut in his side bit hard, like it had just torn wider. He clamped one palm to it. His hand didn't get as wet as he expected. So he wasn't bleeding out. That was good. He used his other hand to push himself up. His guts churned with vomit that wouldn't come, no matter how hard he retched.

"*Fuck, fuck, fuck...*" He was pretty sure he was shambling towards the front door.

"You keep goin' on 'bout that. Oh, what, you want me to fuck somethin'? I don't know, I ain't seen nothin' 'round these parts looks up to it. No offense, Biter-Boy, but you ain't my type. You're pretty disgustin' right now, too. Anyhow, you better find your way outside. Why hell, you're gettin' blood all over this here nice ol' carpet!"

Where the hell was the door? Rob forced his eyes open. They stung, and one of them was full of blood. The door was about two feet away. He tumbled towards it and caught the knob, lurched out into the cool air, sucked in a deep breath, then went back to retching. Puke finally shot up his throat as he leaned over the porch railing. He vomited four times. Each bout burned worse, closer to pure liquid. Finally, he leaned there shivering, spitting the last remnants over the railing, into the grass. When he wiped sweat from his face, his fingers touched raw wounds. A fresh explosion of pain brought him closer to coherence. He was pretty sure he'd just fingered his own cheekbone. Coherence brought more pain, but he kept pulling himself towards it anyway.

Wings beat through the doorway behind him and settled on the porch railing. Rob limped off the porch, slid down in the wet grass, stretched his legs, and leaned back beneath where the wings had settled. Oddly enough, it was a comforting spot.

"You done good in there, Biter-Boy."

"Bullshit," he rasped. "Look at me. I'm all fucked up…and Sally…I can't find—" He choked on the realization. Panic jolted his body, so all his wounds pulsed.

"Yeah, I's'a lookin' at you, Biter-Boy, an' you look *fuckin' great!* By which I mean not dead, considerin' how rusty you let yourself get. No offense or nothin'. Nah, you been all fucked up since you got to this wide spot in the road, a place so silly an' podunk, it was happy to let a Crimbone High Natural cower in a camper gettin' all pussified."

"This place…the town…it told me it wouldn't let them find us here."

"*Wah, wah, wah.* This place didn't break no faith with you, Biter-Boy. Just that the place weren't the only soul with a say in things."

"How'd they find us?"

"Don't even act like you don't know."

"You…" Rob twisted around. He started climbing the porch beam, ignoring his shrieking body, looking straight at the bulbous bat shape. "You fucking birdie. *You led them to us!*"

"I said quit playin' dumb." The beady eyes glittered down at him. "Y'know it don't work like that, Biter-Boy. Not to say that'd stop me from doin' so if I felt inclined, but that ain't my style."

"Fine. Where's Sally?"

"Sally-Poach? Hell, Biter-Boy, you got your glow-dar runnin' again. You taste her glow anywhere 'round these parts?"

Fury broke apart into despair. "She's dead, isn't she?"

"Hell, Biter Boy, your Sally-Poach was dead—that one smell, that one glow you know better than any other—don't you think you'd'a noticed by now, picked it out from all the other rottin' carcasses?"

"So, where is she?"

"Somewhere on the road by now, be my guess. Though I don't think she's exactly coherent to the journey, know what I mean?"

Rob felt the sweats creeping back. It didn't help that his eyes had adjusted, so he saw more and more of the creature perched above him. "How—"

The creature's mouth split like a wound into a grin full of straight, sharp saw teeth. "How you think? You *missed one*, Biter-Boy. Again."

Rob sank back into the grass. Sally had never believed him when he told her they were safe here. She'd never stopped feeling like he'd bullied her into settling, no matter what she said, no matter what he gave her since. Before they went on the run together, he'd promised her he wouldn't *miss one* again. Even if he convinced her, he was the one who'd driven them both crazy with his alienating over-vigilance, 'til she'd *demanded* he allow himself that weekly guys night out with Ryan and Cliff.

Earlier he'd come home through the usual recurring nightmare. Except this time, it hadn't turned out to be his imagination. Now Sally was on her way to pay for it. It didn't matter how he had or hadn't fucked up. Here he sat, beaten and cut to ribbons, as useless as he'd been all along.

"Hey, quit givin' yourself such a hard time. You done what you needed to for a while—hidin' out here I mean, even if it did leave you sorta pussified. Now you just sit there a lil' while an' let some more of that pussification bleed out. Then get up off your wet, bloody ass, patch yourself up, an' figure out what you gotta be doin' now."

Rob's eyes narrowed across the yard at the coming

dawn. "I already know."

Again came that screechy, wheezing laugh. "Like I keep sayin', you Crimbone boys an' your pussy. 'Course you got some different taste than most, but hey, that's fine with me. Once a Crimbone High Natural gets where he's goin', ain't no one gonna give ye no shit for your choice in women…or much else for that matter. Trust me."

Those last two words were about the most unnerving to ever pass the creature's horse-shaped snout, which was saying something. Still, the rest of the statement…

Rob kept his eyes on the brightening yard. "Puttergong, listen to me very carefully. I'm gonna get myself together. Then I'm gonna go find my wife. Then I'm gonna kill whoever's taken her, whoever's holding her, anyone who's hurt her, and pretty much anyone else who gets in my way, for any reason. That's it."

"Nice to hear you mean to keep things so small."

"My point is, I'm not jumping back into the old game. You still gonna help me?"

"You askin' me for help, Biter-Boy?"

"Just as long as we're on the same page."

"I think that's Page Thirty-Three. Anyhoot, sure, fine. Now you just rest up, then go walk whatever trail you gonna walk." Wings beat the air overhead.

When the sun was high enough to warm the world, Rob lurched up and limped back to the camper, towards the closet that held his old duster coat. By the time anyone found the bodies, he was long gone.

SEVEN

Gladys walked out of Cliff's without saying goodbye. Maybe she'd snapped at him more than she should have, even if he acted like a dumbass about answering simple questions. She might stop back by later, for a few drinks after closing up the diner, to wash that stress away while letting him know there were no hard feelings. If she vented right, maybe he'd give her a few on the house. Maybe she'd stay 'til he closed for some real stress relief. She was old enough to remember times when a white girl sleeping with a black man in this town would be as good as cutting his throat herself. Cliff was a generation behind her, but he was still old enough to remember those times.

Maybe Gladys would finally hunt down Sally and give the girl the chewing out she had coming. Then she'd go see Cliff anyway.

Good Lord, none of this would be such a problem if Rob or Sally just got a cell phone like everyone else these days! It was almost funny to Gladys, an old widow like herself, annoyed at a couple kids in this day and age, being so resistant to some basic modern technology.

She recalled saying to Sally, "Look, if it's about the money, you don't even need to get some big fancy monthly plan. I'll drive you right out to Walmart. Hell, I'll front it to you if you need it. You can get one of those cheap, basic little rinky-dink burner phones, where you can just buy a card for 'em every month to enter the minutes you need. My daughter has one, and they're just fine. You don't need to enter any personal information or nothin'. Rob doesn't even need to know you have it. You can just—"

"*No.*" Sally had stuck a finger in Gladys' face. "I already told Rob *no*, too, and now I'm telling you, so don't let me find out you went to him behind my back with the same idea."

Sally refused to say more about it than that. So, it wasn't about Rob being the abusively controlling asshole Gladys first took him for. That would have at least made sense.

On the bar's porch, Gladys stopped and put her hand to her brow against the sun's glare. Up the road, some sonofabitch thought he was a cowboy or something, wearing that long, heavy coat in this heat! She thought to wait 'til he passed by. Even from here, something about him made her not want to get too close, like the heat had already boiled his brain so he moved weird, so there was no telling what he might do. Then she realized it was the man she'd come here hoping to find.

Sally hadn't even called in sick. When Gladys called the camper, the home phone just rang and rang.

Gladys had once asked Sally why they felt okay with a landline but no cell phones. Sally said it was linked up with the Carter's landline.

"Hey, this is Rob and Sally," went Rob's sleepy, scratchy answering machine greeting. "What do you want?"

Gladys then called the Carters. Their answering

machine picked up too. She'd nearly gone over to check on things, but something brought her here first.

She noticed Rob limping. His right shoulder sagged like it couldn't take the coat's weight. Good God! Opposite the two scars she was used to, a fresh red line of stitches now ran across his cheek, nearly to the end of his ear. He looked pale, and his eyes were bloodshot and narrow. Sweat dripped from his eyebrows and the tip of his nose. Suddenly, there was her first impression of him, from years ago, painted back ten layers thicker.

Rob and Sally hadn't been properly married when they got here, hadn't gone that final step for about a year. It was a small matter at the courthouse, with only Gladys, Cliff, two of Sally's friends, and one of Rob and Cliff's drinking buddies whose name Gladys couldn't remember. That night, Gladys had brought Cliff home for the first time. By then, she'd gotten used to Rob, even liked him some. It wasn't as if the boy had ever *done* anything to put her off, not in front of her anyway. Far as she knew, he kept his rowdy side at the bar, where his reputation was no worse than any other regular who'd never lifted a hand against a woman. He didn't restrict his crazy knight-in-shining-armor streak to his wife, either. Any drunk asshole who felt like jerking or slapping a woman around in public better think twice about doing it in front of Rob.

The first time Rob and Sally ever came into the diner, the first thing Gladys noticed was that double scar on his face. It took weeks for the rest of the face to come into focus. So weird, to see such a boyish face, not yet toughened and tightened like sun-dried leather. There was also that look in his eyes that first time…the way he peered around, so it took her even longer to notice those eyes' sweeter feelings.

It was different with Sally. Gladys gave the girl a job the same day she'd announced she and Rob had decided to stay in Postville, obviously trying to sound happy about it. She never said anything terrible about Rob, nothing worse than any woman venting to another after a spat with her man. Usually when you saw them together, their eyes reflected some dreamer's romantic adventure of old, and you felt a little sad they only shared it with each other.

Sally had a scar on her face, too, though it never bothered Gladys like Rob's. It started just shy of her left eye, running back in a wide, pink, shallow fissure into her reddish blonde hair. Eventually, Gladys felt she knew Sally well enough to ask.

Sally told her, "When I first met Rob, I was trying to stay away from my family. They weren't nice people. They wouldn't leave me alone. My brother gave me this, same night Rob saved my life. From my own little brother. Get it now?"

Rob's overprotective streak hadn't stopped giving Gladys the shivers after that, but she held it against him less. Of course there were still things that never added up, like how Sally had no problem hanging out with Gladys and the rest of the girls, but flatly refused whenever they wanted to drive her past the county line for some real fun out of town. One night they were on their way to an out-of-town club, Sally had noticed them nearing those borders, and she'd thrown a fit, threatening to jump out of a moving car. Gladys jerked the car to the curb so they could argue about it. For a while, Sally had acted like Gladys had done some unforgivable betrayal, just by not mentioning the exact destination. Finally, Gladys drove Sally home before the rest of the girls went off to salvage some fun from the halted evening. It was so bad for everyone there that Gladys had thought about firing Sally for it.

Near as Gladys could figure, neither Sally nor Rob had gone a step beyond the county line since settling here. It was a relief to realize it wasn't something he'd forced on her, 'til you stopped to wonder what the *real* explanation was.

Rob reached the porch. "Hi, Gladys. You hear from Sally today?"

"No. What happened to your face, baby?"

"Almost forgot how that question sounded." He brushed absently at the old scars.

"Oh Rob, I'm sorry. But really, honey, look at you!"

He shrugged. "Nah, I was comin' home from here last night, got jumped by some good ol' boys. One of 'em smashed a whiskey bottle on something. I guess they drove over from Gainesville."

"Oh my God, has Sally seen this?"

"She must've when she woke up this morning, 'cause she was there sleeping when I finally crawled in and passed out. I woke up, found her gone, figured she went to work. I went to the diner earlier, figured I'd explain what happened, but no one there had seen her all day."

Gladys shook off the cold metallic sound of his

voice. He must be numb from stress. "You…you have any clue where she could've gone?"

"Yeah. Some." He walked past her.

"Hey!" She caught his sleeve, though she wasn't sure what else she had to say. He jerked free, glanced at her with a look that made her shrink back silently, and limped inside.

EIGHT

Cliff was wiping down the bar before opening when Rob came in. "Hey brother, Gladys was just in here lookin' for—*Holy fuck!* Man, did Chaz do all that to you last night?"

"Who's Chaz?"

"You an' him spent almost a whole damn hour straight beatin' the shit out of each other last night in the back building."

"Oh," said Rob. "No. Not him. No, I got jumped on the way home, by some punks from over in Gainesville. I think one of 'em might be some kid I had to throw out of here a few weeks ago. Look, man, Sally's taken off. I think some shit might be really wrong. Shit goin' back to the old days."

"What old days?" Cliff's eyes widened and he leaned forward a little over the bar.

"The ones I don't talk about."

"Shit. Look, brother, you call the cops or anything?"

"Nah, man, it ain't nothin' like that. I'm just

gonna—"

"I mean about the little punks from Gainesville."

"Nah. We can go on a beat-down hunt—you, me, a couple other guys—when I get back." Rob didn't say shit like that unless he meant it. Right now, though, he looked and talked like some alien zombie-robot wearing Rob Coscan's face, reciting a script.

"Back?"

"Yeah. Didn't you just hear me? I said Sally took off and it might be some bad shit."

For no reason that made sense, Cliff thought of times he and Ryan had let Rob in on the jam sessions of their two-man blues act. When you stuck him on the mic, his snarls and growls made Ray Charles sound like a choir boy, but somehow, *damn*, it was a voice that snared you on fangs and held you there 'til it had its say. He could slam out the lyrics…except one minute he'd be going on about ups and downs with his woman, drinkin', the usual woes of the blue-collar working stiff. Then he'd launch into some crazy tangent with all this weird imagery, like something out of Uriah Heap or Manowar, only more pissed off, bloody, and plain damn weird. His voice told no difference you could hear between reality and what should be obvious fantasy…words like *Crimbone, Schomite, Spirelight, Deschembine…Old World.*

Cliff had never heard that voice outside a song, 'til today. All he managed was, "Look, you say you don't know how long, how long are we talkin' 'bout?"

"That's just it. I don't know. Thought I'd better pay you back that cash you helped us out with a while ago, 'fore I take off. Say hi to Ryan for me, would you?" Rob dug out three crumpled twenties, passed them to Cliff, shook his hand, and walked out.

NINE

Rob had stitched his own face, ear, and side. That was something he'd learned how to do shortly after settling here. Once he and Sally had the camper, he'd hunted down medical texts and diagrams at the library, used the copy machine there, and took home what he needed to study. Funny enough, he only got a little practice, thanks to the boxing ring over the years, nothing compared to this morning's chaos. Stitching the ear was the worst. So far, he didn't seem to have lost much hearing, and the stitches hadn't split yet.

Into his injured ear sounded, "Hey Biter-Boy, c'n'ye hear me? *C'n'ye, C'n'ye, C'n'ye?*" Puttergong perched in the gentle mid-noon sun on a rusty old mailbox, a heat-stricken field of tall, tan grass swaying behind it.

"So, where next?" Rob had to admit, they fell right back into their old special back-and-forth, like five years hadn't passed without speaking.

"I'd say the bus station. Call me crazy   "

"No problem."

"With a face like that, I don't see you hitchin' many rides anytime soon."

Rob tapped the scabbard on his left hip through the duster coat. "Ever hear of a little thing called metal detectors?"

"Heh. Biter-Boy, the metal them doohickeys is programmed to pick up on, it ain't fit to lick the ass of no metal come from the Old World."

"Fine. Where should I buy a ticket to?"

"To the Armpit of the Burghs, as they originally thought to call it. The ordinances of pubic decency made 'em shorten it to Pittsburgh, though."

"Cut the shit, will you?"

"None to cut. I done my business 'fore we left. Word of advice: make sure you do yours 'fore we see who we gotta see in Pittsburgh. I ain't in the mood to clean up after you shittin' yer britches."

"That fucker didn't take her to Pittsburgh. That's Schomite territory. You think I called you for the first time last night?"

"Hell yeah, it's still run by the Schomites! An' they got stuff you gotta go pick up from 'em 'fore you go catch up with the lil' better-half."

"Look, just tell me where Sally is now, then tell me what stuff you think I need there, then we'll see if we need to go to Pittsburgh."

"Biter-Boy, here's the choices, just so's you never say I was the one to take 'em from ye. You take what help I have to give, or you don't. Decide you don't want it, then go see how many pieces you can find of your lil' Sally-Poach by the time you find her."

Rob drew a deep, slow, rumbling breath. His nostrils flared. "Fine," he said. "Pittsburgh it is."

BRATTLEBORO, VERMONT

ONE

A sixteen-year-old boy hiked towards the center of town, from the outskirts where his latest hitchhiked ride had dropped him off. Along the way, he thought about an eleven-year-old boy and a thirteen-year-old girl from five years ago. They'd huddled from the rain together, beneath the deep-set archway of an old stone tower on a hill in the woods.

The Bloody Tower, she'd called it. Somehow Brattleboro was the kind of small, rural Vermont town where a medieval watchtower looming above the trees on a high hill seemed normal.

While they sat up there together, he'd idly started plucking and casting pebbles. The girl saw him doing it, so she laughed and mimicked him. Then he remembered a superstitious game he used to play when he was much younger than that.

Pick a pebble, then look at a spot on the ground. On one side of that spot is whatever your heart most desires. On the other is everything else that might be now or what might be coming…everything the gods have other plans for. Flick your pebble at the earth spot and see which way it goes, and it'll tell you the future.

Just the sort of goofy shit children make up. Then they grow up and tell themselves they've learned better, 'til it turns out they haven't. By now, Sheldon rarely remembered being eleven years old, except whenever he thought of the tower. Then, without fail, he smelled the dust they'd kicked up on their walk uphill. He tasted the rain on the afternoon autumn air. There was a bare earth spot about six feet out from the archway, surrounded by gravel. The girl had sat to his left. He'd tried not to think of what lay the other way. When he tossed the pebble, it hit the left edge of the earth spot then bounced in the other direction.

Was that why this trip seemed like a good idea? Was he still that much of a stupid kid? He guessed he'd find out soon enough. Either way, it was the best explanation he could come up with right now.

He'd only survived his family's murder because he'd been upstairs sleeping off a head injury his dad had given him. He thought about that now and muttered, "Thanks, Dad."

Three nights later, he'd followed the beast's Familiar up another mountain. He still had no idea why he hadn't been killed instantly. The point was, there was life in him yet, so he'd held onto it. Eventually, he'd willed himself up, lurching against the shriek of sundered guts and muscles moving around inside him, and made it to where there was help. He gave the people at the hospital the phone number of the nearest homestead. Another family from the Secret Police came to collect him. Naturally, they'd arrived fixed up with the proper documentation to prove he was theirs. After that, he didn't see daylight for two years, either strapped to the examination tables, or locked in the small room after his innards were put back together, and the wound closed up.

All because I lived…just like Sally.

No one ever survived a wound like that, not from one of the beasts. Of course, the others had wanted to know what it meant, what he'd become, *tainted* as he was, by the beast's blade. Just like Mom had wanted to know how Sally was changed when they first got her back, after the first time she ran away. So, while he healed in the cellars of the homestead, Sheldon Wildfire's own people *tried to figure him out.*

Well, they obviously never managed it, any more than Mom had figured out Sally. Still, *he* sure figured out a thing or two during that time, as it turned out.

Now he passed a shady park area with a gazebo in the center. He was close to the middle of town now. A localized burning rumbled from his solar plexus, running through him in a sharp line that stopped just to the left of his spine. He felt it now because he was thinking about it—about the night on the mountain fighting the beast, about the beast's blade where the burn now ran, about the two years he'd spent rehabilitating himself as best he could, whenever they left him alone in that dark, wet, rancid little room. He hadn't been able to do much other than push-ups, crunches, and stretches in that room. For a long time, his gut didn't let him do many of those. At least they were smart enough not to let him have a pull-up bar of any kind. His meals were barely enough to rebuild a functional body, let alone muscle and coordination. Still, somehow, in the final analysis, he'd made good on what he had to work with.

On the last day, they found out just how well he'd retained the war teachings of his grandparents. Two Secret Police agents always accompanied the scientist and the cleric. On that final day, he broke the scientist's neck, right after gutting both agents with one of their own knives. The cleric he found cowering and sobbing, curled into a ball in a corner. The pious jerk had tried hiding in Sheldon's own cell, a fact to which the shimmering bastard probably died oblivious.

Now Sheldon wished he could remember the escape in better detail. Not just because it would be a nicer memory than two years of torture, but because by all reasoning, he shouldn't have been capable of it. It would be useful to know how you'd pulled something like that off. You could figure out everything you'd done right, or where you just got lucky, so you could improve on it next time.

In the end, he must have just given fewer fucks than them.

He looked out into the park at the gazebo. On a Saturday when he was eleven years old, he'd come here with the thirteen-year-old girl and her mother, after the mother had taken them to see a movie…the only time the boy had ever been to a movie theatre. They'd walked through the park for a while, then sat in the gazebo where the mother told stories and philosophy in her mud-thick voice, soothing him into pretending everything could stay that way.

He looked at the gazebo and its good memories, 'til the worst of the darkness receded. He walked on and met more of the town for the first time, all over again.

As he passed through Harmony Parking Lot, he tried not to look at the red brick building on his left. A high wooden fence now walled off the back stairway he'd once used to sneak out of there. On the adjacent sidewalk, a few high-school-aged hippie chicks sat smoking, watching a scraggly man, who was probably in his mid-twenties, play guitar. Sheldon almost stopped to listen. Instead, he headed up Elliot Street.

The sign in the window now read *Kipling's Irish Pub* instead of *Mike's*. There was a lot of green stained glass. Two corners of it seemed particularly interested in flashing the likeness of a stuffy, smug-eyed, balding gentleman lifting a pint.

Sheldon looked through the glass. *After this last stretch, a drink sure would be nice.* He dug out his falling-apart wallet and flipped through the wrinkly bills. There was a little less than two hundred dollars left. Finding quick work came easy to him, same as buying beer. Most of his jobs involved things no sane employer would trust a normal sixteen-year-old with. Not that Sheldon found work from many sane employers. The last under-the-table dirtbag had tried to stiff him, along with the rest of the guys. Considering how he'd helped sort that matter out, the others hadn't objected to him skimming a little extra.

As Sheldon stepped inside, the attitude of his whole

body altered. Two barflies sat at the counter to help feed his performance, without realizing it. He leaned on the bar and said, in the tone of someone well into their twenties, not even thinking about it, "Hey, I'll have a Bud."

Behind the bar, a well-preserved, full-figured, middle-aged woman looked him over. She saw—or at least felt the impression of—a man well past the legal drinking age. She set an icy mug in front of him and said in a husky voice, "Four dollars, hon."

Sheldon almost sat at the bar, then he happened to glance back. What he saw almost shook him right out of the zone with which he created his illusion. In a nearby green-upholstered booth, a beast sat looking at him. This one wore all black and kept his long, gray-streaked ebony hair tied back. It was small-boned and limber-framed enough to be younger than Sheldon, yet it was clearly much older.

Sheldon thought fast, then realized the beast's smile was conspiratorial. He blinked rapidly 'til he was sure he saw correctly. No, wait, it wasn't a beast, but it was definitely a Schomite with some beast's blood in there somewhere.

Sheldon thought, *One of those United Deschembines, or whatever they're called these days.*

During his years confined to the cellar, he'd heard the scientist and the cleric talk about the United Deschembines. Schomites and Spirelights trying to overcome the old hatreds, trying to live side by side with each other, operating out of something like hippie communes scattered all over what was left of the

American wilderness, not unlike the homesteads. These folks claimed to have divorced themselves from their coteries to create a new one between them. The movement hadn't gotten far, because fighters of both races set to hunting and killing any members they found. The scientist and the cleric had speculated that Sally and her beast might be connected with them. *That's a good one.* When Sheldon stopped hearing about the movement, he'd assumed it was stamped out.

He steeled his nerves and carried his beer to the booth. "Mind if I sit?" he said.

The Schomite—or whatever he was—sipped something hard, straight, on the rocks. Sheldon sniffed and recognized Tequila.

"Go right ahead," said the Schomite. "I was hoping you would. I don't like to sit at the bar when I can help it."

"Fine with me. Probably better that way. My name's Sheldon."

"Okay, yeah," said the Schomite, as if drawing some connection. "I'm Lou." He didn't shake hands. "That's a cool trick. I'd heard about it, but they said you guys didn't use it anymore."

"Trick?"

"On Jill over there, along with anyone else in here who's noticed you."

Sheldon shifted for a look at the bartender. That must be Jill, now busy setting beers in front of three dusty, sunburned toughs, none of whom noticed Sheldon or Lou.

"Even if she's listening," said Lou, "she won't hear

anything the spirit of this town doesn't want her to. Neither will anyone else. Talk about whatever the hell you want."

Up close, Sheldon saw for sure, Lou was one of the beasts all right, except…No, wait. Yeah, this man had been born a Crimbone, but that's not what he was now. There was something familiar in his eyes. Sheldon tried to place it, but some part of his brain kept him from it. He hadn't seen it in the eyes of other Schomites. Then again, he'd never sat down to look this closely at their eyes, nor seen one so relaxed.

He's been altered…not like Sally and I were, not even close, but he's not what he started out as, either. He hasn't become anything that anyone becomes on the natural course.

"Okay," Sheldon finally said. "So let's get the obvious bullshit out of the way first. Are you here to try to kill me?"

"If I were, I'd have gotten around to it already."

"Fair enough. Obviously, we've got a lot to talk about. Let's start by ordering a pitcher. What do you like?"

"Get whatever you want. I know you have things to go do, so we can't sit in here all night getting drunk, covering everything. You finish your drink, I'll finish mine, then we'll get that pitcher."

"You recognized the *trick* I pulled—"

"Still pulling," Lou corrected. "Don't slip. Brattleboro lets you, but you need to keep up your end."

"It doesn't have anything to do with any *spirit of the town*," said Sheldon. "I learned it from reading things my grandfather wrote down."

"Oh. Right. That makes sense. Like I said, I'd heard about that kind of thing. Word goes, though, the Spirelights had stopped using it since before either you or me were born. You say it's all you, that it doesn't have anything to do with the land this town is built on, and how that land feels about you. The Spirelights stopped believing all that a long time ago. Before they were Spirelights, as such, matter of fact. Now you just claim it's something the Crimbone made up, what you call their dark magic. Know what I think?"

Sheldon took a deep gulp of beer. "I guess you're gonna tell me."

"I think your Tribunals have always known what their ancestors led your people away from. They're afraid of what you'd all find waiting if you found your way back to it. If you did, it wouldn't be good for their hold on you. They realized on some level how close an aptitude like yours brings your spirit to the lands of this earth. That might've led you away from the sway of the gods. Can't have that. So they made sure the Spirelight Secret Police stopped teaching it to their children."

Sheldon knew he was no less an enemy of the Spirelight Tribunals than Lou. It had been that way since the black blade had plowed through his midsection. If the eyes of Spirah had really followed its people to this world, they'd turned their gaze from Sheldon on that night. Yet he still felt the old racial impulse, to pull his own knife, dive across the table and slit Lou's throat for such blasphemy. Instead, he drained his mug nearly dry. "Well, that's an interesting theory. You about done with that Tequila?"

"Sure. You don't mind picking up the tab, do you? I'm out of cash. Don't worry, I'll pay you back."

When Sheldon got the pitcher, he wasn't sure why Jill looked at him so weirdly when he asked for a fresh icy mug. He came back and filled Lou's glass first.

"Thanks." Lou sipped slowly, the way a man savors pleasure when he's gone too long without it and doesn't know when he'll next get to savor anything.

"No problem." Sheldon filled his own glass. "Look, what are you doing in this town?"

Lou shrugged. "I used to live around here."

"Moving back?"

"I never left, exactly. I've realized I won't be able to, not 'til I figure some things out and manage to do whatever I'm supposed to do here."

"Sounds familiar," Sheldon sighed. "Obviously the Schomites still control Vermont."

"Vermont controls Vermont. You're right, though, it still favors the Schomites. So why weren't you scared to come back?"

"I was. I still had to."

"Good man…except you don't need to be as scared around here as most Spirelights, do you?"

"What gives you that idea?"

"You don't have the Spirelight glow about you."

Sheldon drew up sharply. That's what the beasts called it, the divine essence that lived in all Spirelight people, the united soul of Spirah. Grandpa had always said it was a purity the demons possessing the Crimbone were drawn to destroy.

"Well," Lou went on, "I ain't saying there's none of

it left in you anywhere, but when you're around Crimbone, they don't notice it. It doesn't set them off."

"No." It was true, and it had taken Sheldon the better part of a year after escaping to piece it together. Part of his *alteration*…the gods of Spirah had taken their uniting glow back from him. Since then, there hadn't been much need to worry whose territory he was in. The Spirelights wanted to kill or recapture him, and most Crimbone still tried to kill him if they realized he was there, even if they were a little confused at first. No matter where you went, you might run into Earth-line people who wanted to kill you or fuck you up, for whatever reasons Earth-line people killed or fucked each other up. "I once got stabbed by a Crimbone, you know."

"That's strange, that you survived I mean. Why did he spare you?"

"He didn't. He thought he'd killed me."

Lou laughed. "Now that *is* a new one, even if he did think you were dead."

"How's that?"

"That he stopped at stabbing you, unless of course he had more than one of you at a time to deal with. Even then, you're lucky he didn't get back to you, just to rip your corpse to pieces, absorb whatever of your glow was still flickering."

Sheldon shifted and drank more beer. "So, I bet you think it was the land we were on at the time that saved me somehow, right?"

"There's not a doubt in my mind about it. You know, it's the Earth-line people who divorced themselves from the lands of this world more than any other race here, and they're the ones who convinced themselves the most that they're running the show. They were here first, no less! That's why it takes so little effort to keep them from noticing us, even keeping to all our old, wild ways as we do. It also helps, not getting sucked so deep into all that technology they think makes them masters of everything."

Sheldon couldn't help smiling, even if it was nothing but Schomite madness.

"You still don't believe me. How else can you explain that we're sitting here, having this conversation where anyone could hear if they started listening, but no one does?" Lou paused and saw that Sheldon couldn't find an answer. "You know, they stayed close to the lands for a lot longer than most of them realize. Every year, their society gets more strictly regulated, and the Earth-line governments keep making more and more decisions for them, and all that slick little technology just tugs 'em deeper down that hole.

"Eventually, they'll literally be part of a machine. Then they won't have any more chance of spotting us or the crazy shit we get up to, any more than those beer taps know that Jill's pumping them, or those cars and trucks going by outside know about the people driving or riding in them. Just look around at the other customers here! Here they are, in this nice, fun, friendly bar with good music playing, and half of them are zombied out on their little phones. You barely need your mind tricks to deflect their attention. I guess you know the stories from back when they were still settling this young nation?"

"Yeah." Sheldon's mouth twisted impatiently. "We learned all that at the homesteads growing up. The elders said we needed to understand how the Earth-line people understood history, so we could understand how they thought, so we could blend in."

"Yeah, because you were scared of what the Earth-line society would do to you if they knew you were there."

"No," said Sheldon, keeping his cool, "it wasn't that. It's because—"

"Because your clerics assumed the gods of Spirah were still right there behind you. When the day came that you saved this world from the Schomites and our beast warriors the Crimbone, so the gods could come through, from their pantheon, and give you this world as your reward. Yeah, I know that version. It's not too far off the mark, 'cept you were looking at it from the wrong direction." Lou shook his head and chuckled.

"What was I saying? Oh right, the settling of the nation. Y'know, back in those days, they had law enforcement, but it wasn't like they kept some fat, mean-eyed cop on every corner or cruising around looking tough, making sure everyone let the *Boys in Blue* settle their troubles for them. No, just miles of bare hills and forests and deserts for them to run around in, shooting each other over blood feuds that their own Scottish and Irish ancestors brought over on some boat. Sound familiar?"

"Sure, right, I see what you're saying." Sheldon took a few rapid glugs of beer, like it might wash away his impatience. "Except their conflicts aren't nearly as old, or as fierce. Our feud's stayed alive and well, longer than any of theirs have lasted. Ever watch the news, Lou? Y'know all those times the Earth-line nations seem a dick-twitch away from sending their big bombs flying at each other, so there'd be no one left on any smoking land mass to fight over 'em? Then that just somehow...doesn't happen? You think that's the Earth-liners actually being that good at settling their silly little differences? Think it means one spot of land has any say over what folks in another do? Bullshit! Obviously, you've got no idea how deeply the Spirelight Tribunals have worked themselves into governments all over the world."

"You know how to argue a point. That's a relief."

"My point is, we're the ones holding that leash."

"Except *we* doesn't exactly include you anymore, does it? Besides, if flexing that kind of muscle means so much, how come the Spirelights didn't settle it a long time ago...unless there's something even bigger flexing its muscles? Either way, to either side—in different languages of spirituality, religion, whatever you want to call it—the world we share keeps reminding us how we need that secrecy, along with the limits it places on our potential, as long as we keep up the fighting."

Lou poured the last of the pitcher into the mugs.

"This land lets us keep up the feuds because there's something it has to gain from it, in the final build-up. I have no idea what, except that it'll be in your lifetime."

"So, do you expect to live to see it?" said Sheldon.

"That's a good one!" Lou laughed again. "No, but whatever it is, it's already building up. I wouldn't be surprised if it has something to do with why you're back in town. Probably why I'm here, too."

"Who knows, Lou, maybe you're onto something. Your beast teachers ever tell you how Spirelights find and hold a Spirelight-controlled area?"

"Do tell."

Sheldon leaned back, nursed the last of his mug, and held Lou's gaze with easy defiance. "They study maps of whatever landmass the gods have set us to get for them. It starts with building the homestead, always atop a broad summit that lines up on the landmass approximately with the location of the house of one of the gods, where it sits within the Spirah Pantheon. Once the homestead's completed, they spread out from there—an inch or a mile at a time—taking control of the civilized infrastructure and redesigning it so it matches the anatomy—the circulatory system—of the god. So, the beasts can come 'round and call on your lands for help all you like, but the Spirah gods are the only spirits ruling those lands by then."

"Huh." Lou shrugged and nodded at the tabletop. "No, I didn't know that."

"You wouldn't." Sheldon held his fixed gaze 'til he caught Lou's eyes again. "Only those of the Secret Police coterie do. Ever hear of Michelangelo? Big in the Earth-line Renaissance."

"Sure."

"Michelangelo said about his art, *I saw the angel in the marble, and I carved 'til I set him free.* The great Spirelight Priest Kings of the Old World taught their agents how to see the Spirah gods in the lands. The agents will carve the lands 'til the gods are set free."

"Not exactly in your best interest to look forward to that anymore, though, is it?"

"Who said I ever did?" Sheldon drained the last of his glass and stood up. "Anyway, man, it's been…interesting talking to you. Right now, I've got places to be."

TWO

Places, when you return to them, always look so much more compact, self-unaware, *simply there*, than in your memories. You go somewhere, everywhere, through Armageddon, start over in some formless void, wait for the light at the end of some tunnel, and get a thousand supernovas. Then you end up back on the old ground, and realize it's stayed right there the whole time. Yet you've also taken it with you, not noticing what your mind did to it along the way. If you make it back, what you took with you and what you left behind don't match anymore. It's moved on without you, like it never noticed you there in the first place.

Sheldon knew no one recognized him. When people see a narrow-faced teenager with dirty blond hair, wearing jeans, cowboy boots, and a worn-out black leather jacket, they don't think of a round-faced eleven-year-old they might have seen around for a couple of days, five years ago. No, not even if they were punk kids themselves back then, and the eleven-year-old had hospitalized them for messing with a tall, dark-skinned beauty.

Sheldon recognized plenty of faces, though: old folks who looked the same, only older; young folks who were taller, harder, wilder looking; crazy people who'd wandered the streets, wanted to stop you and tell you their life stories, or just screamed at you because you glanced at them wrong. Some of those crazy people looked like they might still have some piss and vinegar left, so Sheldon passed them quickly. Others trudged sleepily, as if someone had finally put them on the right meds.

Near the corner of Washington Street, he almost reached for a pebble, to cast it and follow whichever direction it skittered in. Instead, he went straight to the second house on the right. Fewer weeds choked the yard and porch railings. Plots of vibrant, mile-tall sunflowers flanked the walkway to the porch. For a second, Sheldon thought, *Shit, maybe they don't even live here anymore. This could be awkward. How am I gonna find them now?*

Dusk turned the green from bright to muddy, but the gray door looked the same shade as it would in the afternoon. It had looked the same shade five years ago. Sheldon knocked. A chair creaked in the kitchen as someone got up. Sheldon took a deep breath. He was still exhaling when the door opened.

"Annie?"

The short, dark, tough, middle-aged woman normally had eyes full of mischief, or so he remembered. Now she stared, puzzled. The shadows spilled deep into every line in her face. "Yeah?"

"It's me." Yeah right, that narrowed it down. "Sheldon. I stayed here for a few days, a while back?"

Her face lit up. "Oh, Lord, not Janie's little friend. Damn, honey, must'a gotten so tall, my bad eyes can't see that high!" She hugged him tight, pulled herself up and planted a big kiss on his cheek. When had he last hugged anyone—hell, been around anyone he wanted to hug?

As she pulled him into the kitchen, he almost smelled that first bag of microwave popcorn Janie had made. So, where was Janie? Did she still live here? She'd be eighteen now. That was the age when Earth-line people were allowed to move out and live on their own. Most didn't, but then again Janie wasn't most Earth-line people. Neither was Annie, but Sheldon wondered, was that actually all she remembered about him? Her daughter's little friend?

Little brave, she used to call him, telling him all those wonderful stories and thoughts he guessed she couldn't tell most people. Maybe she thought he was too old to still be her *little brave*, to listen to the magic.

"Good Lord. Good Lord. Growin' up so good, just like I thought you would."

Sheldon smiled. "Yeah, I've been around, but I still found my way back here."

"Of course you did. You promised, remember? Take a seat, honey, take a seat. Tell me what you've been doin' with yourself. Janie's out with some friends, livin' up the summer. She just graduated high school last month, tryin' to decide what community college courses to start in the fall. I don't think she'll start that soon, though. Says she's lookin' forward to it, but I don't think her heart's in it. 'Tween you and me, girl needs to get a bit more wildness out of her system before she can handle all that serious stuff."

Sheldon sat. "Just as long as she does right when she actually starts, I guess."

"So, how old are you by now anyway, Sheldon?"

"Sixteen."

"How the hell you get so wise at sixteen?"

He shrugged. Most people Annie's age would ask him about his own education. He usually made something up. Sometimes he told the truth, which was that he hadn't had any kind of formal schooling since he was eleven. Unless you counted the college campus libraries and common rooms he stayed in, sometimes sleeping, sometimes partying with the students, sometimes reading books the students left lying around.

So, where to start with Annie—explaining what he really was, the things he needed her help figuring out? His gods had abandoned him, which left *the crazy old mom of one of his little friends*. He wasn't ready to ruin this perfect reunion, this first time in years he could just sit at someone's table and feel welcome without having to play mind-tricks to blend in.

The front doorknob rattled. "Oh, shoot." Annie got up and unlocked it.

The door opened. "You left the door locked again, Mom." The girl's voice was crisper, stronger than Sheldon remembered. There was annoyance there, but nothing that spoiled the good mood around it, nothing anyone would remember in ten seconds, least of all the speaker.

"Oh, that's enough out of you! Bet you left your key on your desk in your room, huh?" The mischief in Annie's voice thickened. "Why don't you just crawl in through your window, spare my achin' back a little?"

"I haven't done that since I was a—" She walked into the kitchen, saw Sheldon, and looked even more puzzled than Annie had.

Sheldon stood up and smiled. "Since you were about, what, thirteen?"

"Hi." Her eyes looked smaller and darker than he remembered, narrowing further as recognition danced on the tip of her brain. Her thin, angled face hadn't really changed. Still, it was so weird, the *idea* that this girl who'd walked in was Janie. Her black hair had gotten longer and fuller, her limbs longer and leaner. Her high jean shorts and sweat-darkened tank top showed the smoothness of her limbs, her fuller breasts. Sheldon tried not to gawk while her mom was in the room. Instead, he concentrated on her eyes. Oh yeah, that was still easy to do.

"*Sheldon?* Oh, my God, I didn't think you'd ever come back here!" She leapt forward and hugged him almost hard enough to knock him over.

He closed his eyes and swayed with her, running his hands through her hair. Her fingers trailed his back, pausing on the indentation of the exit-wound scar beneath his shirt. Their faces passed close as they drew apart. He almost kissed her, thought she maybe almost kissed him. *Not in front of her mom.* Hopefully his face didn't turn too red.

"Let's sit down." She pulled her chair closer to his. "You gotta tell me everything you've been doing! *Everything!*"

His eyes dropped, then rose shyly. "You know that extended family I told you I had? Well, I went and stayed with 'em for a couple years. I decided I didn't like it, so I ran off."

"Ran off? Where?"

"Wherever I felt like going, really."

She smiled. "Yeah, that sure sounds like you. So, you've been just bumming around, drifting like you were when you first came through here, doin' that for…five years?" She said it in a dry *now let me get this straight* tone.

"Three years, actually." Sheldon smiled brightly at her. "Yeah. Except I wasn't bumming around like this back then."

"You were on your own, though. I remember you telling me that."

"What I always tell you?" Annie said. "Tough little brave, all the way. Not so little now, though. See how tall and good lookin' he's gotten?"

Annie *did* remember! The title swelled Sheldon's heart, letting off something warm and airy through him. He was used to another kind of energy swelling out through him…that burning black trail through his core, running from one scar to the other.

"Mom." Janie groaned, but she couldn't press down her smile. "Sheldon, that's so cool! *This* is so cool! How long you gonna stay this time? You *gotta* stay for a while, longer than you did before. I mean, you just popped up out of nowhere. You were one of the most awesome people ever, then you were just…*gone!* That's just not fair, man, y'know?"

"I don't know yet," he said. "There's actually stuff I need your mom to help me with, if she can."

"Little brave," said Annie, "you know I'll help you out with whatever I can. You got anywhere to sleep around here?"

"You know, I hadn't figured that part out yet."

"Well, we got us a guest bedroom right upstairs, same as always."

"That'd be a great start," said Sheldon. "Thanks."

Janie looked hesitant. "So…did you come back all 'cause you need Mom's help?"

"I came back for lots of reasons, but yeah. That's the big reason."

Her face dimmed, so he wanted to kick himself. *No, you idiot, say you came back for her! Tell her about all the times you've huddled from the rain in shacks, or under doorways or bridges, casting pebbles at the chaos and seeing her face on the other side. Tell her how you think back to this town, how your life turned into a nightmare here…a nightmare that was all worth it, just for that time she meant to kiss your cheek but instead kissed your mouth. Then you went back into the nightmare, to the beast.*

Back then she'd said, *I don't think you'll come back, even if you make it…but I hope you do.*

Great, except how could that possibly turn out to be good for her? That's why he'd never strayed anywhere near Vermont in all those years.

Then the burn of the blade had come back, worse than ever. It damn sure wasn't just an old wound acting up from the weather. All he'd known for sure was that he'd needed answers. Like Lou had said, there was no known precedent for surviving such a wound from a Crimbone blade, and digging deeper through the lore of his own kind was no longer exactly an option either. So where better to look for answers than where it all started? Or so he told himself, 'till he got here.

"So, what've you been up to, Janie?" he asked.

"Same shit, pretty much. I'm hoping to be out of this town by next year. I just graduated high school, you know."

Sheldon tried to seem excited for her, to pretend he had a frame of reference for how much that must mean to her. He glanced to the window. "It's a nice night out. Anyone wanna go for a walk?"

Janie stood up. "I do, sure."

"Y'all have fun with that," said Annie. "After the day I just worked, I don't wanna walk any further than the bathroom if I can help it."

THREE

They walked close together. Whenever their hands brushed, did she feel the same flashes of electricity that kept tripping up his words?

Lemme get this straight. You've fought—and sometimes killed—how many people who should've by all reason been able to squash you like a bug, which is just the tip of everything you've survived…and now you can't even work up the guts to make a move on the girl of your dreams, now that you've finally got her alone right next to you.

Without thinking or talking about it, they headed for the high school. At the edge of the basketball court, they stopped for a moment. It was freshly paved, and he was pretty sure that was a new hoop, definitely not the same ragged old net where she'd taught him how to shoot.

She met his eyes and apparently forgot how to talk for a second herself. Then she said, "C'mon, let's keep walking. I don't like looking at that place now that I don't have to go there all the time."

Further on, he asked, "So you still go to the teen center?"

"Huh? Hell no! I got sick of dealing with all the assholes there. New people manage it now anyway."

"Those kids who were giving you shit that one day, they ever mess with you after I left?"

"Huh? Oh yeah, wow, I ain't thought of that in years." Something like a shudder quivered through her. She tried to hide it under a wider smile. "No, but other kids at the high school did. Some of 'em were friends of those kids you fucked up. They were like, *Hey, your little buddy ain't around to hide behind anymore, is he, little bitch?* I learned how to fight after that, you know. I mean *really* fight. I got so I could really fuck some bitches up if I wanted to." She smiled almost giddily, anticipating his approval.

He grinned awkwardly. "Never put anyone in the hospital, did you?"

"No, but I was a real little hellraiser there for a while. I finally had to cool it down, or they were gonna expel me. Then I'd *really* never get out of here, if I didn't get to finish school I mean. It was cool by then, 'cause everyone was scared of me, so they left me alone."

"Did you want them to be scared of you?"

"Not really, I just didn't want 'em bothering me. I had my friends I was always cool with, but…y'know? Yeah, I think for a while, I really *did* want to scare everyone. It was like no one understood me anyway. They all heard how my mom was strange and said I was strange too. Well, if no one likes you and they're all gonna say nasty shit about you no matter what, being scary feels better than being helpless, right?"

"Yeah."

"So, can you tell me now what you were mixed up in back then?" She walked a little closer, though not in an affectionate way, more like an interrogator leaning in on a prisoner. "I mean really? You kept talking like there was some big thing you had to do, like it was something dangerous and you were the only one who could handle it, like you might get killed—"

"Yeah. 'Cause that's how it was."

"What the fuck!" She stopped sharply and flared up so hot, he thought for a second she wanted to show him her new fighting skills personally. "Dude, you were just a kid!"

Why was she so surprised? She'd just spelled it all out herself, hadn't she? "You don't think I'm still a kid now?"

"I guess I don't know. You've been living on your own this whole time—well, since you left whoever you went to stay with. I couldn't do that, and I'm older than you."

"You don't think you could?"

"No. So, are you gonna tell me?" She studied his face. "What happened when you went to do…whatever it was?"

"It didn't work out like I'd hoped."

"You mean you got hurt, like bad?"

"Pretty bad. Yeah."

"Like you almost died or something?" She sounded almost sick.

"Yeah."

"Did the cops ever catch whoever did that to you?"

"No. It wasn't the kind of thing where the Ea…" He almost said *the Earth-line police*, "where the cops get involved."

"So, what kind of situation was it, then?" Before he could answer, she stated, "It has something to do with why you're back now, to see Mom."

The silent seconds felt longer and longer as he tried to form a response, 'til he could hear and feel the air moving against him, as though rushing him to answer. It was rattling, how sharp she'd gotten. Earth-line girls were never this sharp, at least at her age. "Yeah. Look, don't worry, I haven't put you guys in danger by coming here or anything."

She huffed. "That's not what I was worried about. What, should I be?"

"I just said, no."

"Fine. Good." Her eyes lowered. Her voice was glum, resigned… agonizingly distant. "I guess you still ain't gonna tell me, are you?"

He took a deep breath. "I wanna tell you, but…I don't know how yet."

"You mean you aren't comfortable talking about it yet."

"I guess not."

"You're gonna talk to Mom about it, though, aren't you?"

"I guess, but I'm not ready for that just yet, either."

They fell back into walking, quiet now. Finally, she said, softer, "Look, Sheldon…it's okay. You're an amazing guy. You'll figure it all out, whatever it is."

It made him want to dance and sing, hearing her say that, in that voice. "Thanks."

"Well, it's true."

"Right on. So, tell me more about these plans you have about getting out of here."

"Oh. Right. That. I'm sure Mom's already talked your ear off about the whole community college thing. I don't know…I mean, we don't have money for me to go to a real college. I could just stay here and work my ass off 'til I'd saved up the money to move someplace cooler, but I really do wanna get a better education, really learn more than I could at Brattleboro Fucking Union High School. I don't know, my boyfriend doesn't get it. He keeps telling me it's stupid, that I should just stay here and work 'til I have the money to go live on my own. He says that's what he's gonna do 'cause he ain't got a chance at college either. I think he's just afraid he'll never get to go anywhere else, so he hopes I'll hang back with him."

"Ah," Sheldon said. It came out sharper than he

intended. For the rest of the walk, the night air felt hotter and thicker between them. Every second of silence got longer and longer.

FOUR

He sat up reading, freshly showered for the first time in days—*Maybe Janie would've decided to forget about her idiot boyfriend if I'd smelled better*—now wearing his last clean T-shirt and boxers, in the last safe, clean place on earth. Other than the bed, the nightstand, and the lamp, the room was bare. Last time he'd slept here, it had still been full of the belongings of Janie's brother who'd died in a car wreck along with their dad, Annie's husband.

On the cover of the beat-up paperback, an emerald statuette of a Lovecraftian monster sat atop a half-collapsed purple curtain. It was a book Sheldon still liked to read whenever he found a place to lay his head and couldn't fall asleep right away.

He'd read most of these stories at least three times by now. In this one, some ungainly escaped convict tried to rape the lover of an early American pioneer narrator, then fled into the forest. The hero chased the villain into a haunted house where some formless, demonic apparition crushed the latter to death. Now the hero fought for his life against that apparition.

Hell, if Sheldon was that guy, he'd probably get back to camp and find out the Neanderthal villain hadn't died, and that the heroine had willingly taken up with the fucker. Because Earth-line people were stupid like that, seldom much like all those brave, noble, true-hearted lovers and adventurers they liked to write books about.

Someone knocked. Sheldon wanted it to be his heroine. Hell, he'd like to go knock on her door. He said, "Come in," and her mother opened the door instead.

"Hi, Annie." He dog-eared the page and set his book aside.

"You close to sleep, Sheldon?"

"Not really, for some reason."

She pointed to his backpack at the foot of the bed. "You got any laundry needs done?"

"Yeah, actually. Was gonna ask if I could use the machine in the morning."

"Oh, don't you bother none with that, kiddo. I've got some loads to do yet myself tonight, so I'll see to it along with the rest, if that's okay with you."

"Hey, thanks—" He reached for the pack.

"Leave it for now," she said. "Let's talk, you and me."

He sat back. "Okay."

"Now, you said you came here 'cause you thought I could help you with somethin'. I'm happy to help however I can, but first, you gotta be honest with me. You and me, we need to trust each other. You understand?"

"I guess I do. Okay. What do you want to know?"

"You could start with what you went and did that night five years ago."

"You want me to start there? *You want me to start there, Annie?*" He sprang up onto his knees and pulled his

T-shirt up to reveal the scar on the center of his torso—a straight, vertical line of pitch black, two inches tall, slightly sunken, gray rivulets spreading from it like withered, twisting flower petals. He always figured the blackness spread much further and thicker through his innards, like flame-scorched wood. "Can you imagine what it was like to actually get this, to live through it, to *actually recover?* No. Of course not. None of you could."

"Shhh, shhh, not so loud, honey." Annie peered at the scar. "Oh my. Now I know what I'm seein', or I have an idea. I never expected to."

"Wait a minute. You…know what this is?"

"You could say that."

"Then you know what I am! You knew back then, too, didn't you? Why'd you act like you didn't?"

"I know lots of things. Plus, there's a lot more I *don't* know, but I've got an idea. I've always had plenty ideas about you, and I always had even more ideas about people like you, and the kinds of lives you're all leadin' right under all our noses. That's still all I have straight about any of it, at least for sure. That's all I need as far as we're concerned, so don't trouble yourself tryin' to fit all the nuts and bolts of it together for me just yet. Take a few deep breaths, then keep speaking to me. All this actin' up doesn't do a thing for you." Once he settled down, she said, "Now how 'bout you tell me a little about the one who gave you that scar."

"I don't know what to say about him. He was hiding on Marlboro Mountain, and I went up there to kill him."

"*Kill him?* Sheldon, what in the world would make a

sweet young fella like you decide it was the right thing to do, to go *kill somebody?*"

Got a while? "I guess I thought he was the worst monster possible. I thought I could take him on…like I was supposed to be the one to take him on, like no one else had managed, so…I don't know."

"Yeah. Seems to me, all boys of your sort have your ultimate monsters, and none of you'll ever settle for anything less than bein' the only one who can take those monsters on. Most of you, you'll find plenty more than one monster like that, and whether you win through or not, you tend to come away with scars like that one you got there for your trouble."

"Your son, Janie's brother…was he a boy like that?"

"In his own sorta way. Yeah, you could say so. 'Cept it wasn't none of the monsters he could or couldn't've beat that done him in."

"I'm sorry. If I shouldn't have brought that up, I mean."

"Oh, it's okay, baby—" It looked like she'd slap his knee or something with her usual humor, then she turned away and curled up sobbing quietly, pressing the front knuckles of her fist between her eyes like she meant to punch her own face in. The sobs sounded like hiccups, sharp and violent enough to do internal damage. Sheldon put an arm around her. She patted his back 'til she got herself together.

"Yeah," she finally said, pulling away and straightening out, "I guess in lots of ways, he was like you, but at the same time, not at all. You're still a kid, Sheldon. But even an ol' fart like me can see how in lots of ways, you probably ain't never been allowed to be a kid. I'll bet you ain't got the first idea what a *childhood* is, at least not like Janie or any other kids you'll meet around here. My Larry, though…His problem was, he could never stop bein' a silly kid, no matter how old he got, except when he saw those other kids around him, the ones with worse demons than he ever known, and that's when…Well, you could say somethin' woke up in him, like he suddenly turned into the big, strong, righteous man they all needed someone to be in their lives. He changed a lot of young folks' lives like that, and not by thinkin' it was his place to go 'round fightin' anyone, neither, not unless he absolutely had to. Those kids, he got a lot of 'em off the drugs, talked 'em and helped 'em out of lots of other bad stuff, and he never asked himself once if it was his business doin' so. Trouble was, anytime he thought he hadn't done enough, or when someone just plain turned out to not want anyone's help…that sorta thing always pushed him a little further down his own bad road, just to escape what he thought were his failures. This monster you had to go fight, why'd you see him as such a bad guy?"

"He killed my family. He killed my mom and my dad and my sister. Then he took my other sister with him and corrupted her."

"Corrupted…*seduced her*, you're sayin'." For the first time ever, Sheldon saw Annie truly shocked. "Well now. That's just plain unexpected." Once she'd processed it better, she said, "I reckon you've thought about him plenty since, your sister, too."

"Only in my nightmares, 'til recently. Except now

something's happening with this scar he gave me, when he stabbed me. It'll start burning, like it's split back open somewhere in me, slowly spreading, leaking something of him…I've started having worse nightmares than ever. I…this is gonna sound really crazy, but—"

"I'd say we're past worryin' about that, little brave."

"I think…It's like, for a while, he must've been…asleep or something. Now he's awake. The blade he stabbed me with…I think wherever he is, he's…using it again."

"Usin' it to hurt more people, you mean. Like he hurt you."

Sheldon stared at the bed between them and nodded swiftly. "Yeah. I feel a little of it whenever he does, a little more every time."

Annie nodded as she listened, as though easily taking all this as matter-of-fact. "Could well be that. Sooner or later, seems clear to me, you're gonna run into him again. He ain't the last of those monsters you'll find that *you'll just have to be* the only one who can take 'em on, neither. He sure sounds like a bad man, but he probably ain't even the worst you'll meet. Like I was sayin', though, that night he gave you that scar, he also took something from you, didn't he?"

"He took my sister, like he took the rest of my family."

"But he'd already done that. Sounds to me like your sister made her own choice, just like you made yours to fight him, like Larry made his, along with all those kids he couldn't help. When the monster won that fight, he took something straight out of you, closer to the center of who you are than your family or your sister ever could be, and he didn't even know it. Wherever he is, he still has it, and he probably don't even know it."

"You sound like you feel sorry for him."

"Maybe I do." She watched his face. "Now Sheldon, you know I love you to death, and if anyone tried layin' a hand on you in my sight, they best be ready to see if they can outrun buckshot. Don't think that means I won't look at both sides of any story, though. I can read between the lines of what you're tellin' me, and it sounds like maybe your sister had some damn fine reasons for runnin' to the monster from your family. You won't ever hear me say it's okay to go around killin' people. Still, deep down, I'll bet this monster's nothin' but another silly young man like you. As he saw it, you and your family were the monsters he couldn't let anyone but him take on. My point is, though, when he took what he took, he also gave you something in return, whether he meant to or not. I reckon you're gonna cross paths with him again, probably sooner than you think. That's why things started actin' up inside you, and you figured you had to come back here to ask me about it. When you see him, you have to put the two together somehow. Don't ask me what you're supposed to do with what you get, 'cause no one knows that yet 'cept the one Creator."

"I don't want to find him." Sheldon looked away. His eyes settled on the book he'd set aside. He looked at the monster on the cover. That monster was make-believe. It was safe. There was nothing safe or make-believe about the monsters he and Annie were discussing. Annie talked like she didn't realize that, because of course she hadn't met his monsters. It made him want to tell her where she could shove all her sagely abstract wisdom. Instead, he said, "I wanna stay here with you and Janie."

"I already told you, you can stay here long as you need. Before long, though, life's gonna find a way to take you back to the monster. Maybe it'll be a choice you make, 'cause of somethin' you don't know about yet, or maybe it'll be somethin' comes to force your hand in the matter…or seems to. Lots of times, life'll leave us no choice in where it takes us, like there really is somethin' called fate. Lookin' back, though, we usually realize there were all sorts of other choices we could'a made, but it was always just ourselves who went and did what we wanted to do deep down all along…hopefully, 'cause it's what we knew was right. Either way, when that happens, you'll have to go, and I wouldn't be able to do a thing about it if I wanted to."

"So, that guy. The monster…*the beast*…you think I'm gonna have to fight him again?"

"Maybe. Just remember, I didn't say that part. You did."

Finally, he just threw himself forward and hugged her like some weak, silly Earth-line kid trying to hide in a mother's arms. He didn't cry as an Earth-line kid would, but he got as close as he ever did. He drew away. "Thanks. I'm more scared than before, but thanks." He laughed nervously.

"I'd be thinkin' you weren't right in the head if you weren't scared, little brave." She ruffled his hair. "I guess you'd better get to sleep now…or stay awake and read your book a while. Take your mind off your own troubles, but first…" She took a deep breath and couldn't look at him for a second. "First you gotta promise me somethin'."

"Yeah?"

"Janie's crazy about you. You know the way I'm talkin' about."

"Yeah, right. That's what I was hoping, but no. No, it's not like that for her."

"Oh, bull! I saw how she looked at you tonight. I'd know that look on another woman's face even if she weren't my own kid. I guess she told you about that idiot boy she's with right now, and no, she don't look at him that way, neither. Minute you came 'round, whatever she felt for that bozo turned into an act, and not a strong one, neither. Before this here talk we just had, I thought it was about the best thing I could've seen. Knowing what you an' I both know now, though, you see sure as I do, it wouldn't be right."

"What wouldn't be right?"

"You got your trail to walk. You were glued to it the minute that man took what he took and gave what he gave. Nothing can steer you off that trail, least of all whatever else you want. Anything you pull to yourself, it'll be glued to that trail, following you wherever it leads. I don't know for sure if you can call it destiny or some bull, or just the way a guy like you's wired, with nothin' to be done but doin' it. Either way, I won't see my daughter glued to it. I can't watch another of my babies get tangled up in somethin' like that. If you act on what you feel for Janie now, you'll be sealing her to a fate that ain't right for her. Let her keep to her silly little world long as she's meant to, then let her go off to wherever she takes herself from there. While she'll be doin' that, you'll have your own way to go. Don't you think it don't hurt like hell to say so. Promise me you won't make that move, or you can leave this house tonight."

Everything in Sheldon sank to someplace cold and gurgling, 'til all he had left to say was, "I promise, Annie."

THE HOMESTEAD

The mountain road widened and narrowed between the high trees, zigzagging and curling like a constipated snake. It forced Vencie to slow down, 'til he reached the inner roads of the final stretch. He'd driven faster than usual for most of the trip. Once his wheels rolled smoothly over proper Spirelight-etched pathways, he cruised along naturally at a comfortable speed.

In the back, the tainted girl was still unconscious. When Vencie had dosed her again, he'd injected at least three times as much as before. She'd been shifting and flexing for three hours, sounding more vital, right on time for their final pine-walled stretch alone together. She squirmed worse now, as though the energetic frequencies of sacred ground shook up the tainted blood in her veins like a poison sound-bath. Her binds were reinforced with stronger straps. Those ought to hold, but then again, she shouldn't have woken up before the Florida border, least of all enough to start bucking and snarling. She sure as hell shouldn't have broken one of the original straps.

When he'd pulled over and went to her with the

needle, her left arm had snapped free. Her hand had closed around his throat, her thumb jabbing the sore spot on his jaw, palm pressing his windpipe. Incoherence set in fast. With his last coordination, he jammed the needle hard into her neck. For what seemed like a long time, he thought he would die in that vice grip, stuck at the end of her limp arm. Finally, he heaved backwards, came free, and landed hard on his ass. Her arm fell next to the broken strap and her fingers curled shut like a carnivorous plant on a bug.

In the two days since the orange grove, Vencie found himself missing his wife. He almost mistook it for sentimentality, then he glanced back at how the tainted girl twisted and flexed against her restraints, so all her nicest angles stuck out. The hot van fumed with both their unwashed scents, and he remembered how her body had felt fighting against him.

Yeah, he knew what he really missed about Luna.

If he spent some time with Sally Coscan's body fighting his in another way, he would at least have that out of his system quickly enough…but no.

For one thing, he wasn't *that* confident in her restraints. For another, dealing with the Tribunal representatives would be delicate enough, without them seeing and smelling such activity. They might even decide she'd infected him with her unholy alteration, and they'd probably be right. A Crimbone had been there, after all. Vencie would be relieved to turn her over, but he couldn't let them see that, either. He didn't even know if today was a good time to show up, hadn't called to confirm in code-speak like he usually did. Even if the representatives' superiors were there, it wouldn't matter once they saw what he brought.

Back when it had just been the Wildfires hunting their tainted daughter, their reports registered as a concern to the Tribunal, but nothing they wouldn't leave in the family's hands. Then the Wildfires turned up dead, all save the son.

The Tribunal had heard the boy's story, and they put some of their best doctors in charge of figuring him out. Then he escaped. Everyone would like to write that off as a testament to the Wildfire family's reputation—the little shit taking out those guards, after barely surviving such injuries. Whatever the doctors' tests had yielded was kept very quiet…as were the gory details of the wake of the boy's escape. Vencie suspected it didn't much resemble anything you'd find in a Secret Police training manual.

What the daughter would be by then—given her own involvement with the Crimbone—was anyone's guess. Nor was Rob Coscan the first beast to go there. The first one had raped her years ago in New Orleans, before the local Schomite charge had performed the now fabled ritual. Rumors went that the Vermont Crimbone actually had an audio recording of her firsthand account. The beast who'd interviewed her hadn't even needed to torture it out of her. Vencie wasn't even going to try figuring out how that happened.

All agents sent to steal the recording came home by post in parcels, the contents partially eaten. Those were the sort of jobs that tended to fall into Vencie's lap, the ones still of interest, but not enough to justify the losses.

At that point, the Tribunals won either way. If he died trying, it rid them of an embarrassment like him. Whenever he came through for them—which was always, because he wasn't dead yet—they got to take the credit without losing more legitimate agents. He might have taken the recording job, if he hadn't hit the *big* jackpot. Ella Wildfire, the late lamented matriarch of the tainted girl's family, had never divulged her findings. No one was able to unearth her notes, either.

Vencie didn't know about any ritual, but he sure sensed the alterations from willingly fucking one of the beasts for all these years. It was scientifically known that the Schomites and the Spirelights couldn't create children between them, but some new creature had certainly grown from this union.

Finally, the Tennessee pines cleared, before a sprawling lump of field. The string of buildings looked like a budding colonial village, though the more or less triangular grid and skyline of jutting arches created the feeling of passing into far more ancient, alien surroundings.

The Spirelights had preserved the drab exterior quaintness, in solemn homage to those who'd fought for and held the space, so the present generation might inherit it. Earth-line maintenance crews were brought in periodically, on the dime of Earth-line businessmen in the Tribunal's pocket. It saved plenty of straining labor, but hadn't proved as profitable an investment as those Earth-line independent military contractors. These day laborers were made to sign strict confidentiality agreements on whatever they saw, to not even speak of it amongst each other. They had no idea just how quickly their employers would learn of it, should they break this confidence in the slightest.

Usually, what little they glimpsed was enough to shut them up. They never saw the central buildings' insides—which weren't quaint at all, were in fact lined pristinely in whatever luxuries the residents' whims inclined them towards. If workers crossed the threshold in curiosity or carelessness, they never came out. Only the Spirelight scientists knew exactly what happened to them. For an Earth-line person to intrude on Spirelight inner sanctuary was a blasphemy only atonable by serving the quest for better scientific knowledge.

Vencie parked behind the long structure at the far end. In a broad, fenced-in area, a gaggle of children played. The ones who looked up, he knew, belonged to Secret Police families. Only three of them did, but that didn't mean they were the only ones. Some were probably just about to enter the wilderness training program. At their age, Vencie would have spotted a conspicuous visitor like himself, and that visitor would never have known. From the back door came a tall man in a white suit.

"Good timing, Amos," Vencie said.

"I saw you driving up through the window. I decided it would be better to meet you out here. Considering the people I was just speaking with inside, it would be…awkward, were I to invite you in."

"So invite them outside. I have negotiations to make with them."

"Hey, and here I thought you'd outgrown that

fantasy."

"If I had, you wouldn't keep seeing me here."

"Good to know. So, what did you drag in to leave on my porch this time?"

Vencie started around the van. "The keys to the next phase."

"You get crazier every year, you know that? At this rate, you'll be batty as your grandfather before long. The Tribunal sure dodged a bullet with that one, didn't it?" Amos paused to search for Vencie's reaction. Finding none whatsoever, he tried to hide his own squirming. "So, if this is so damned important, why is this the first I'm hearing of it?"

"This one's a surprise…an extra special surprise."

Amos looked a little more sour. "By the way, where's that—heh— family of yours?"

"Dead."

"Let me guess, as the result of your latest little Red Indian game? I suppose the reason you don't seem so sad is because you think you really *can* buy your way in officially with this one."

"Well, now that you mention it…" Vencie threw open the rear van doors.

Amos didn't come to look. "I'll tell you what. Inside, I was busy discussing important tactical and financial matters with one of my superiors. In his company are two field agents. I'll call them out, and you can play *show and tell*. One of those field agents is a young woman, not yet married. She's…well, you'll see. If we're satisfied with the product, we'll talk about instating you. If that happens—heh—you can make your play for her, if you care to. If we're not satisfied, she'll be the one who gets to slit your throat, right next to your van. You can of course try to defend yourself, but then you'll have all of us to deal with. You'll fall in plain view of your captive if it's still alive, and you'll die in this mud behind your renegade van. The field agents will be given credit for your captive, and you'll be written off as the renegade you are, finally put down properly."

"I'm sure you'll have fun explaining why I came here in the first place, and why my face isn't exactly unknown to the witnesses around here. Sounds like a deal."

Amos started back inside, then stopped halfway up the steps. "Or you can always drive away now. If you do, though, consider all our arrangements forfeit. I know who your other connections are—yes, even the ones you trade information with—and I'll notify them accordingly. A proper hunt for you will begin, with instructions to kill you on sight."

Vencie watched Amos disappear inside. Of course the cocksucker had no plans to honor his end of the bet. Among the Spirelight Secret Police, honor was a privilege, expended no more on a renegade like Vencie than on a Schomite. Soon, though, Amos would be forced to rethink his values.

Vencie looked in on the tainted girl. He hadn't gagged her, but she stayed silent, except for a faint rumble in her breathing. There was something unmistakably Crimbone to the sound. She no longer bucked or thrashed, but her eyes peered with calm, dignified hatred...a Spirelight's hatred, which only made it worse to see and feel the Crimbone stain on her essence.

Out came Amos, with another man in a matching white suit. Behind them walked the two field agents, both wearing plain hemp suits, the same kind Vencie would soon wear. The woman was tall, lean, and smooth-faced. Her eyes were cold, gray, and sharp, but not as much as her movements. Yes, Vencie looked forward to making a play for her. She'd thrash and buck and claw at first, against the idea of a renegade like him, 'til he broke her into the merits of the idea. Just like Luna, when he'd first told her his plans, only better, because this lady was already trained to give a good fight. It was probably unwise, presuming so much. Soon he could take his pick, after all.

Vencie greeted Amos with the same unreadable look as before. Amos nodded. The other three walked by without acknowledging Vencie. The woman's pale blond hair was pulled tight over her round skull, falling to the small of her narrow back in a single whip-like braid. Vencie stepped up beside her as the party looked in. He felt the chill of the tainted girl's gaze spread through them.

It was the woman who spoke up first. "Is that who—*what*—I think it is?" She remained stoic, except her voice dropped to a hush.

Vencie smiled and nodded. "The stuff of the most disgusting legends to pollute our own lifetime, my dear…Sally Wildfire. Actually, Sally Coscan now, no less. Who wants to help me get her inside?"

PITTSBURGH

ONE

As the bus passed within the city's limits, Rob spotted a huge billboard for an *All You Can Eat* country-style buffet. The fat man in overalls with the pearly, shit-eating grin, and giant arms crossed proudly over his chest, was the restaurant founder dressed as some city-slicker's idea of a *country-style* kinda guy.

A bridge railing streaked in front of the billboard, and Rob spotted the red letters beneath the photo, *Maybe more than you can handle.*

Rob caught two more quick flashes of the billboard, before it fell away behind the bus. Somehow, though, part of his brain absorbed a lot in those flashes, as though from staring at the ad for minutes, up close. The fat man's jolly expression looked forced, especially considering the blood leaking between his teeth. The front of his overalls had split so his belly tumbled out, so swollen it was turning purple, like he'd eaten something not quite dead, and now it was growing like a fetus in there, ready to burst out. It didn't look so bad in the second glimpse. Nah, that weird shit must have been a trick of the light. If Pittsburgh advertised food like that, and it actually worked, Rob had done himself a grave disservice, not stopping here back in his hard-partying drifter days…but no, the guy was obviously just…shrugging.

What had the sign actually said?

Or maybe you can.

What's the difference in the big picture, anyway?

Good question, really. Right now, Rob was a lot busier trying to figure out whether or not this place liked him.

Don't you get it? That doesn't matter anymore. Something about the whole rhythm of this place just changed. Holy shit, did my arrival have something to do with that?

Rob really wasn't sure this was cause to smile, but he did. For the rest of the ride, he caught smoother little signs, in bird formations and glimpses of graffiti. One thing Pittsburgh was damn clear on: it sheltered many of his kind. The graffiti was the biggest give-away there. One of Rob's greatest gnawing regrets was his scanty education on his true ancestral cultural heritage. There was that single thick volume on photocopied computer paper, held together with bands through punched holes between card stock binding, the one Zane had given him long ago. Beyond that, circumstances had forced him to make do, reading between the lines of obscure, ancient Earth-line history and mythology. He still knew the strokes and shadings of Schomite art when he saw it…particularly Crimbone art. That was the sacrifice he'd made to be with Sally. Funny thing was, he really knew a lot more about Spirelights, just from listening to her. Whatever was about to happen here, though, it had better set him on course back to her.

As the bus pulled in, he flexed and bent his knee as much as the seat in front of him allowed. Only a faint ring of soreness remained, though the bruise would still be one colorful blotch under his jeans. The stitches had mostly held, though his gashed side had started bleeding several times during the ride. That had led to a few hunched shambles down the bus aisle to the bathroom. The other passengers must have thought he had a wicked case of the squirts. Good thing he wore a dark shirt. Oh well, one more reason to keep the duster's lapels tugged close. Last time he saw his face in a stopover bathroom, he'd still looked like hell. By the time this was over, it'd be a nice surprise if he ever *stopped* looking like hell.

There were no men with metal detectors when Rob stepped off the bus. There had been at a couple of the other stops, though. Puttergong was right, it turned out.

The first time, Rob had stood nervously somewhere in the middle of the line, as they went from person to person, closer to him. When the security guard finally ran that humming bar less than an inch away from him, he stood frozen in a cold sweat like he'd already been caught. Not that he'd go down easy, but the point was to get Sally back safe and quickly, keeping on the down-low for as long as possible. The metal detector didn't so much as blip when it passed his blades. The second time, he'd stood calmly through the procedure, like one more law-abiding traveler, downright bored. The guard still frowned at his mangled face.

As Rob walked out of the bus station, he realized he no longer gave a shit about all the uncomfortable eyes on him. After a block, he spotted a shape flap into an alleyway ahead, so he crossed a street and ducked in after it.

"Now why you still do that bullshit, Biter-Boy?" Puttergong perched on the lowest rack of a fire escape.

"What shit?"

"Actin' like some nervous lil' bitch, that's what. Think I didn't eat 'fore you got here? Flyin' ahead of them gray-growler hoppers'll build up your appetite, let me tell you."

It took Rob a second to realize *gray-growler hoppers* meant Greyhound buses. Out of the alley, across the street, a cluster of pigeons darted around an old man casting stale popcorn. Maybe they hoped that guy could protect them from Puttergong. Rob didn't spot any mangled pigeon guts, so maybe the critter had cleaned up better than usual.

"Okay, fine," he said. "Maybe you don't mind all these Earth-line idiots looking at you and seeing another fucking pigeon, but I ain't quite comfortable standing around with 'em watching me, thinking I'm carrying on a heated conversation with one."

"Okay, Biter-Boy, have it your own way. Just remember, them Earth-line bozos can't do shit to ye. Where we goin', there's bozos who'll do *plenty* shit to you, you ain't ready to look 'em in the eye an' show 'em who's boss."

"Not Spirelights. Don't bullshit me, birdie. Don't

think I'm a total moron."

"Biter-Boy, quit settin' me up for cheap shots or we'll be stuck in this here alley all day. Your lil' Sally girl wouldn't like it if you wasted too much time like that."

"Just tell me where I need to go and what I need to pick up, so we can get this over with."

"We ain't gettin' shit over with in this town. Naw, we's jus' gettin' it rollin'!"

"Puttergong—" Rob's right hand slid to the lapel of his duster.

"Fine! Get your hand away from that coat an' what you got in there, an' don't put it back 'til you walked three blocks. You'll spot a big ol' sky-scratcher, an' believe you me, you'll know the right one when ye see it."

"What do I do once I'm in?"

"Oh, don't worry none, Biter-Boy. It'll come so natural, *figurin' it out* ain't even the right wordin'."

Rob started out of the alley. He glanced back, thinking to remind Puttergong of their little understanding. The creature was already gone. After three blocks, he saw an office building paneled in solid black glass, narrowing in cubic angles that split as it rose. He had no idea how the glass was dyed so, but it was as black as the metal he carried beneath the duster. He wasn't sure it was tall enough to be a sky-scratcher— sky*scraper*. Damnit, he'd already spent too much time with no one but his Familiar to talk to. Either way, *tower* seemed like the best word. About when he stepped past the decorative fountain outside, people stopped giving him troubled looks.

As he reached the door, a voice said, "Now don't go botherin' with the elevator. It don't go to the floor you need. Take the mopper-man stairwell an' just climb that sucker up, up, up, 'til there ain't no more stairs to climb."

"What do I do once I'm there?"

When no one answered, Rob grumbled and walked into a polished marble lobby. A man behind the reception desk eyed him, not like he was out of place…more like he was off schedule.

Behind time and ahead of time popped in and out of his mind. Emboldened, he walked towards an unmarked doorway with a little wire-mesh glass window in the upper center. His bravado shrank as he stepped into the thin, high, solidly off-white janitorial stairwell. Halfway up, the sting in his knee seemed to sap his energy, like a combination of a black hole and some sadistically howling siren. His legs stiffened and wavered, while his side pulled at him from within, trying to double him up.

"*If you pussy out here,*" he hissed at himself, "*you'll die on your way out and Sally will die even worse, wherever she is.*"

He pulled himself upright and climbed faster, his knee and side screaming louder. At the top, he looked down through the stairwell. The bottom floor was a tiny, fractured rectangle, seemingly miles away. The light up here spilled naturally from an arching skylight, but it felt weirdly antiseptic in this close space, the bottomless stairwell gaping beneath him. Neither heights nor close spaces had ever bothered Rob, but this combination left him shaky and faint. The nag of his injuries didn't help.

The hallway he entered was wide, not

advantageously thin like the Carters'. The two men at the opposite end weren't Spirelights. No, they were Crimbone, like him.

No. Not like me. Who the fuck have I been kidding this whole time? Look at them! It's been decades since they made their Calls, and they sure as hell haven't spent that time hiding in Postville, Florida.

Yet all three of them knew each other, in the smallest twitch of any muscle in their bodies, a depth of nonverbal communication Rob had never found with any other kind of person, even Sally. They looked at him without surprise or confusion. They didn't wear duster coats as he did, so he saw the scabbards on their belts just fine. They were supposed to be here, were filling their place within the present scheme of this city as they understood it, and he wasn't. Didn't. In that understanding, here and now, the fact that they were of the same line stopped mattering. There was no hesitation or guilt as they started towards him and drew their knives...*their long, black knives.*

Rob hadn't opened his duster since taking it from the closet and threading on the belt that held his own scabbards. Even then, he hadn't drawn the blades. So now he saw nothing but the handles, wrapped in black cloth, capped in their little silver knobs. Those knobs were both stamped with two curved, vertical slash marks, serrated on the outer edges, with a crescent slash across the center. The restraint was hell.

New steel shot through his frame as the ancient blades of Magur Sevi sang free.

The two Crimbone guards rushed forward. There

was no giveaway calibration in either of their sword arms, but Rob had seen enough weapons in motion to know when the wielder meant to hit him with one. He sprang to return the favor, closing the distance so swiftly that blinding light rushed through his brain. Then his enemies spotted his blades. The lower halves were serrated and the upper halves curved, with edges honed sharper than razors. Each blade ran not quite the length of a machete.

The guards hitched at the sight. Rob didn't. Two clean arcs cleaved flesh and bone, splattering the walls. The floor reverberated as the corpses thudded.

Before he settled, Rob was already vaguely aware that he might have called them brothers under other circumstances. He was equally aware of the freezing that had nearly undone him before he drew the knives. Now his nostrils filled and flared with the pungent blood-smell, turning the last of that ice to fire. His eyes stayed forward, not sparing another glance at the dead.

At the end of the hall, he threw open the door on a huge corporate office, anchored in the center by an obscenely long conference table. Opposite this was a desk covered in business papers. Behind it sat the first non-Crimbone Schomite Rob had ever seen. The man said under his breath, "*Old Lords.*"

Rob acted calm now, except his low, rumbling growl came back. Absently he shook his blades, raining spatter that looked black on the blue carpet.

The man behind the desk gawked. "The twin blades of Magur Sevi!"

Rob gawked back, at this Schomite in a pressed

black Earth-line businessman's suit, like some weak, snotty Earth-line lawyer or accountant. This guy didn't command the city's Crimbone— not exactly, anyway— because only the spirit of the city could do that. Yet he was the man through whom the decrees of the city, of the land, of the Old Lords themselves maybe, were too often interpreted.

Rob really tried—wanted—to spot *something* in the man, of a master of the mysticism and racial memory of another realm—any trace of what a local Schomite charge was supposed to be, that hadn't been stamped out in the privilege of Earth-line decadence. The blasphemy of it set a fire in him, and he stormed forward, blades raised to shed more blood.

"Don't kill me," squeaked the man. "They'll kill you if you do."

"No, they won't," Rob rasped. "They'll see these blades I have, and they'll do the smart thing." *Which is to help me save Sally,* because they would recognize the blades and follow him. Except wasn't this exactly how he'd said over and over that he *wouldn't* handle things?

Sure, but he hadn't counted on this blazing elation. How could he, any more than he could shake it off now? He was hardly a master of the ancient Deschembine languages, and no Earth-line words captured this feeling. "Once they see these blades, they'll do whatever I tell them to—even if they don't remember the old stories. They don't know that I'm here, or that I have these. So, ain't there a little message you ought'a be sending out? No, really, go ahead, be my guest. I wanna see what you've got."

Steadily as he could manage, the little corporate piece of shit—this tool of Earth-line restraint passing for a Schomite—said, "Yes."

Rob smiled and nodded, then sheathed one blade, pulled over a chair, and sat next to the man. For the first time since the stairwell, he noticed that his knee and his side were still killing him. By now, it just fueled the fire, kept him awake and alert. He draped the injured leg over the other and smiled.

The man went rigid and blank like a shivering statue. When the windows rippled, Rob rolled his eyes. Finally, the man slumped like a sweat-soaked towel tossed across the chair.

"There, it's done. Soon the city will tell them, they will each receive the message in their own way, and they'll follow it here."

"Good. You really ought'a keep in better shape, you know that? So let's make sure I get this. The Crimbone of this city…short of the spirit of the city itself I mean…you're basically the one they take orders from, right?"

The man nodded.

"Shit, man. That just plain doesn't work." Rob stayed seated as his unsheathed blade flashed left.

He heard and felt the wet slice and crunch of muscle and bone. The head bounced on the desk and glanced off the edge of the conference table. Rob heard it roll onto the floor, but didn't look to see where. A long splat of red had hit the business papers strewn on the desk. Another, smaller splat glistened on the table's rim. Rob sat and watched the door.

TWO

They came in with their black blades drawn, which didn't surprise him. What surprised him was how calm they all acted. None of them moved like pumped-up thugs spoiling for a fight, but they were all sure as hell ready for one. They all stared at him with murder in their eyes, expecting that fight to come from him.

Because of course they are. Fuck you, Puttergong.

Rob kept expecting his nerves to give out. That didn't happen. Instead, he kept sitting relaxed like he had been. A wild, fluttery detachment settled through him as he looked them over. Not all of them bore blades. A few held what looked like hammers, or even cruder bludgeoning shapes. No two weapons of the black metal were alike, he now saw, any more than the Crimbone who wielded them. He had yet to spot another Crimbone sporting more than one weapon, nor any so ornately sculpted as his.

There weren't as many as he'd expected, either, not even enough to fill the conference table. Each stood proud and rugged, scarred and wild-haired, clothes tattered and slept-in. Most wore some long garment to hide their weapons in the streets, everything from black leather trench coats to old-time waistcoats, or dusters like his own. So, maybe the city out there was big enough to tolerate such eccentricities, even in the summer. Not that any of them let the heat bother them.

It wouldn't be their clothes that stood out, but the proud, fierce animal elegance of their movements. Alone, any one of them might have blended in, among whatever Earth-line rabble where they found a temporary home. Collectively, some primordial elegance pulsated throughout the pack, something not simply animalistic, but downright *other than human, something only the lands themselves could ever truly own.*

Rob felt that same essence pulsating throughout his own being, tickling his own human consciousness.

No one looked too surprised to see the milquetoast businessman slumped over his papers, minus a head. The eviscerated bodies in the hallway had probably set the wrong tone. Either way, they'd all dealt with that by the time they came through the door.

Rob stood and drew both blades. None of them were prepared for that sight. He felt less prepared for it than them. These were his kind. That was a fact. He'd never expected to see so many in one place. Their world was the life he'd missed out on for too many years. Their eyes told stories he couldn't read. Some of them cast glances at each other. How many silent signals might they be sending each other, about him, with just a look like that?

Once he opened his mouth, he would have five seconds or less to hook them with whatever he said. If he couldn't, they'd rush him in a single body and chop him to bits.

He didn't choose his words at all, or at least that's how it felt. "These are the same blades Magur Sevi wielded in the Old World. These lands have sent them to me. Take a good long look, then take a swim in the memories that live in your blood...*the deepest, oldest, truest memories*...and tell me otherwise!"

"*The oldest and the deepest*, huh," growled someone from the crowd. "Kid, I really hope you bullshittin'. Seriously, man, there's a reason they teach you to stay off trails such as you're—"

"*Who?* Who teaches you that bullshit? Not these lands, not to the Crimbone, I can guarantee you that. C'mon, you must've heard all the horror stories by now. Let me save you some trouble. They're all true. The lands of this world gave me the blades of Magur Sevi." He hardly recognized the voice coming out of his own mouth. It was like when he drew breath to speak, the air met something alien in his lungs, combusting in the core of him so it roared up his throat like a long dormant, freshly awoken volcano. The longer he stood to it, the quicker his frame adapted to it, and the more he liked it. "Now I'm on the trail the lands have opened before me, with my blades drawn. Nice to see so many of you showed up with yours drawn too."

Whatever was coming out of him with these words, it was as real as the blades in his fists. He saw in every eye present that they felt it too.

It hadn't cowed that first dissenting speaker, though. "You hold the blades of Magur Sevi. That doesn't tell me shit about how well you use them."

Rob met the eyes of a dark man in the back. The

guy wouldn't physically challenge him now, but he planned to at some point. *Wait, how did I just get all that, from just a look?* Anyway, he kept looking and said, "You all came through that hallway, saw what I left there. What do you think?"

"This city," said another, "the land on which this city stands, it spoke to us all, told us you were here, to come meet you. It even hinted, now I think about it, that you might be a High Natural. I didn't hear shit about the heir to Magur Sevi."

"The High Natural *is* the heir to Magur Sevi. Come on if you doubt it." Rob gave the challenger a silent minute. Then he growled, "I am the rightful bearer of these blades, as I am the rightful voice to you, the Crimbone, of the will of these lands, just as *we* must be the enforcers of that will! This headless, dickless fuck lying here, his sort feed you a diluted translation of that voice, and you've let them 'til now. My Crimbone brethren, you've been guided by the antiquated echo of a past voice, while Spirelights drug the lands that should be home to us all, so their gods can rape those lands in their sleep. Magur Sevi freed our ancient ancestors from the tyranny of the Spirelights. *I come to free you from the oppression you've placed on yourselves.* If you would hear and heed the land's true voice, the voice that would bring you freedom, then follow me. If you would challenge the blades of Magur Sevi, come take them from me now."

The feeling of their response had flowed back to him as he spoke, further igniting his oration. Veins bulged in his neck and forehead. He drew deep, growling breaths, trying to calm down. Their devastated silence, the fire he fanned in their eyes, only sent him higher.

From the pack walked a woman. Her weapon looked like a shimmering black meat hook, curved sharply in all the right places like her body, except hammered into straight lines everywhere else. At a glance the weapon didn't look practical for combat, but Rob suspected this had never been a problem for her. Dark, reddish brown hair hung like the shoots of a hanging basket plant around her bronzed face. Her green eyes were those of a hungry fox. She wore no long coat to hide her weapon, just black jeans and a black tank top that was too small on her. She'd been no less affected by him, he sensed—had maybe felt it the strongest, for those wild, almost alien eyes bespoke the strongest mind among them—but she bore it better. Hopefully he wouldn't have to kill her.

She slung herself into the chair at the head of the conference table and spun it to face him. If anyone else in the room had seen her smirk, Rob would probably have been dead. "Yep," she said, "those look like the blades of Magur Sevi all right, least from the pictures I've seen in the secret books. Sure, I'll follow the blades. I'll follow you, 'til you fuck up. So, what are we following you to?" She batted her eyelashes. "If you don't mind my asking, I mean."

Recalling how he'd ended up here, Rob wanted to strangle Puttergong. He'd tried that once, had the scars on his face to prove it. Still, he couldn't shake something the creature had said more recently. *Once a Crimbone High Natural gets where he's goin', ain't no one gonna give you shit for your choice in women. Trust me.*

Still thinking of Sally, he met his challenger's gorgeous green eyes like a brick wall. "Nah, sure, you can ask. You'll find out when we get there." *Soon as I find out myself,* he might have added. "What's your name, girl?"

"Remelea."

"Remelea, this pack will obey me as they would the will of the Old Lords themselves, and that includes you. When for whatever reason I can't be consulted, they'll obey you as they would me. If you ever abuse that honor, I'll kill you."

"So basically, I'm your second in command."

"Sure."

"And here I woke up figuring this'd be a dull day. Sounds fun. What's your name, by the way?"

"Rob."

Remelea's smile broadened. "Rob, I'll do whatever you tell me as long as you bear those blades well. The second I think I see you fumble with them, you'd best be ready to kill me."

"Like you said, sounds fun."

She grinned and turned back to the rest of the crowd. With the easy authority of someone with actual street-cred as a leader around here, she howled with berserk joy, "Hear that, boys and girls? I'm his second in command. Let's give the heir to Magur Sevi a shot in the dark, huh?" She moved right up next to Rob. He felt her fingers dance along his spine. She breathed in his ear, "Better be, handsome. In case you didn't notice, I just saved your ass."

NEW ORLEANS

ONE

A rusty red van parked on the side of a nighttime highway running through the Louisiana wilderness. Two bald giants climbed out, one white, one black. Both wore ragged brown duster coats and scruffy goatees. They were both scarred all over, not too conspicuously except for the puffy web that covered half of Jesse's neck.

Jesse, the white one, went off among the trees to take a piss. Zane, the black one, stood by the van and lit a cigarette.

Within the dusters, both bore weapons forged from the ancient ebony metal. Jesse had a long, thin, forward-curved, serrated blade. Zane carried a hammer with a spike-topped, funnel shaped head, and a long handle wrapped in leather. Zane hoped an empty bladder would leave Jesse a little less pain-in-the-ass edgy. He was halfway through his smoke when Jesse came out of the bushes.

"Y'know, those things cause cancer," said Jesse.

Zane snorted a big cloud out of his nose. *Okay, so much for that idea.* "They give the Earth-line people cancer."

"Zane, do you know what cancer is?"

"A disease Earth-line people get." He knew better than to hope that'd close the topic.

"Yeah. When part of the body feels threatened by something unnatural to its system, in defense, by some logic, it starts mass-producing cells to drive off the threat. Then those cells just keep expanding, taking over more and more. Eventually they can't stop with overwhelming the threat, the weakness. Instead, they keep bubbling out 'til they overwhelm and kill off the whole body."

"Why the hell are we talking about Earth-line diseases?"

"I don't know, I just thought of it while I was taking a piss and smelled your smoke."

"Jesse, what the hell's wrong with you?"

"Lots of shit." Jesse stared off up the road, like he expected to see something useful already in sight. "Right now, probably the fact I've been driving for two days straight."

"Man, fuck you." Zane ground his cigarette out on his boot-heel, field-stripped the butt before tossing it, and climbed back into the passenger's seat. "I keep offering to take over a while."

"And I keep telling you, I don't swing that way, brother." Jesse climbed into the driver's seat. "Nah, but still, we ought'a stop soon for food and a beer. It shouldn't be too long 'til the next roadhouse or wherever. We really should sleep before New Orleans." Jesse said it like he hadn't been the one acting so damn dead-set against the idea. His eyes stayed a little too wide, too constantly forward-fixed, like there was something wrong with that bull-neck of his, that kept it from turning every now and then. "It'll do us good to actually crash on real beds for a while, too."

"Yeah, a beer sure sounds good," said Zane. "So does a place with real beds, if we can find one."

Not far past a place called Crazy Al's Fireworks, they found not a roadhouse, but an Honest-to-Old-Lords steak house, with a real motel next door. A wrong turn had brought them here. That meant they should get right back on the interstate and wait for the next one. Zane might have brought it up, but he was too far past the point of *fuck it*. Besides, Louisiana probably wouldn't throw them any more such bones 'til New Orleans.

Since crossing the state line, Zane had felt how much this place automatically loved them because they were Schomites, twice as much for being Crimbone. He didn't need to make sure they were on the same page, because Jesse ominously pointed it out every chance he got. Neither of them had asked anything of the places they passed, and they accepted as few impromptu gifts as possible. If they turned down something as fine and blatant as this, though, the spirits of these lands might take it as an insult. It might not let them reach New Orleans, or even find their way out of this swampy countryside, without jumping through enough increasingly weird-ass hoops, depleting the energy reserves they would need once they got there. Those reserves were considerable, as they ought to be, having been honed side by side since the Civil War.

The smell of the Cajun cooking inside sealed the deal.

As they neared the front door, Jesse tapped Zane's arm. Zane looked over, saw Jesse peering up, and followed the gaze. From the roof's edge, two puffy, leathery gargoyles peered down at them.

Jesse whispered, "Brings back some fucked-up memories, huh?"

One of the gargoyles twitched with what might have been amusement or offense. Zane let himself chuckle and nod. Honestly, he didn't remember much about those days, apparently less than half of what Jesse recalled. A Cajun cowboy and his girl passed them on the way in. The sight of an Honest-to-Old-Lords genuine cowboy, nothing missing but a six-shooter…Now that brought back memories. There'd be no six-shooters inside, and Jesse and Zane weren't exactly the skinny fledglings they were back then. No one would try to throw them out for a white man having the gall to bring a nigger in with him. Probably. It had been a while since either of them had been this deep into the South. There'd be fledglings inside who belonged to the Familiars on the roof. Two fledglings in one place meant there'd be a mature Crimbone chaperoning.

"Just remember," said Jesse, "the fledglings here probably ain't much like we were."

Zane grinned. "So, when the hell's the last time we met a fledgling who was?"

"That ain't what I'm talking about."

Zane nodded, less humoring than he'd been the first goddamn hundred times Jesse got started like that. They knew all the same stories, by heart. Louisiana would entice a Crimbone in, all too free with its poison love, doing strange things to the brains of fledglings.

Zane had come prepared for it, and yeah, he'd felt it as they entered the state. From the minute the trail pointed them towards New Orleans, though, Jesse had gotten obsessed with keeping his guard up, which was a bad idea anywhere. A Crimbone needed to flow in time with local energies, no matter how hostile or weird, if he wanted to survive anywhere. Jesse had never been here, but he couldn't stop thinking about two fledglings that had. Zane knew this, because one of those fledglings was part of their reason for this visit.

The other was Jesse's son, who'd killed himself less than a year after his stint there as a castoff fledgling. Zane kept his mouth shut on a modern state of affairs where any Crimbone fledgling was allowed to take that trail out, out of respect and compassion for his oldest friend.

Inside the steak house, they went straight for the bar like they owned the place. Zane's Familiar used to tell him, *A Crimbone gotta walk this here world like he own the place, Thumpy-Bumpy. An' if he in tune with its places right, he do own it, sure as it own him an' ever'thing else.* Zane glanced to make sure Jesse was walking the right walk.

The place was as polished as a franchise restaurant, but the atmosphere was all laid-back country, from the music, to the crowd, to the service. At the bar sat the three Crimbone. The two fledglings flanked the chaperone. They looked just a little more out of place than Jesse and Zane, more like uptown city playboys who'd somehow picked up a rough edge or two somewhere. A full-fledged Crimbone doesn't stand out the way Earth-line minorities do around Earth-line majorities, more like a timber wolf in a kennel of lapdogs. A civilian Schomite stands out a little less, usually for different reasons.

When the fledglings saw Jesse and Zane, they lit up with a kindred recognition that wouldn't have surprised anyone who'd been eyeing them nervously. One of the fledglings stood out more awkwardly than the other, like he was trying too hard with some of the schooling, obliviously obstinate to the rest. His hair was an unruly black mess that looked like he'd never heard of a comb or a razor. He had a scrunched, grotesque face and dewy crescent moon eyes, like some kind of were-rodent who never managed to turn all the way back to human, but his shoulders held the right posture within his suit. His arms looked loose and limber in the proper, seemingly casual stance across the bar-top, better than his slicker counterpart on the other side of the chaperone, in fact. Everyone clasped hands and shoulders, rough enough to knock over anyone but a fellow Crimbone.

Introductions felt like an afterthought. "Nergal's the name," said the leader—a thick, slightly short man with slick black hair. "The boys here are Vic and Crawler." Both fledglings were taller than Nergal. Vic almost stood as high as Jesse and Zane. Crawler—the rat-faced one— looked almost as powerfully built. Both only had a few visible scars, so far.

When Jesse and Zane gave their names, Vic and Crawler leaned closer. "Not Jesse Karn and Zane Rochester, I guess," Crawler said, like he had no idea what an indoor voice was.

Zane glanced at Jesse as if to make sure, then said, "Yeah. Why?"

The fledglings looked at Nergal as if saying *You didn't tell us we'd be meeting Jesse Ripper-Man Karn or Zane Thumpy-Bumpy Fuckin' Rochester!*

"What," said Jesse, "you guys know someone who knows us?"

Crawler said, "Not that I know of, but…*shit, it's Jesse Ripper-Man Karn and Zane Fucking Rochester!*"

Zane was just glad neither fledgling had called him by his Familiar's old pet name. Jesse didn't seem to mind. Yeah right, easy for him.

"Hey," said the bar girl to Jesse and Zane, "what can I get you guys?"

"A pitcher of whatever they want, on my tab," said Nergal.

Zane glanced and spotted something blessed that they all too rarely saw on tap anywhere anymore. He glanced over and knew Jesse had spotted the same thing. They said in unison, "Heineken! A big, frothing fucking pitcher of Heineken!" They busted out laughing and slapped hands in a hard clasp. Damn, they needed a good time…but they both knew how the best and worst times were always the most closely connected. This meeting was no more disconnected from the rough days ahead than it was a coincidence.

Zane asked Nergal, "So, how you guys know our

names?"

Nergal let Vic answer, "You kiddin'? You guys are legends all over the South!"

"That'd explain it," said Jesse. "We've been mostly in Vermont for the last sixty years."

"Here's your pitcher," said the bar girl.

Zane filled his glass and watched her linger. Of course she'd assume she'd heard wrong, sure neither of them could possibly be over fifty, possibly still be in their late thirties. She looked like mid-thirties, but she might be forty. Either way, she had a full, sturdy figure, and hard, bright, blue eyes. Zane gave her a smile that had nothing to do with what she'd overheard, even though her eyes lingered more on Jesse. Jesse had damn well better be in tune enough to notice.

Jesse was busy pouring beer. "So, where you boys hailing from?"

"New Orleans," said Nergal. "Thought I'd get these kids out to some raw swamp for the weekend, see what kinda crazy shit we could find to cut their teeth on."

"You know," Jesse said with a weird sharpness, "a fledgling once told me New Orleans was really just a swamp letting the city stay there for the moment."

Nergal laughed. "Ain't that the truth! Hell, that's one thing I was hoping these boys would get in perspective, after some time in a naked swamp."

"Yeah," said Zane. "Y'know, for a while, after that big flood and all some years back, it looked like the swamp had served an eviction notice. Must've been some tough work you boys did, keeping that shit together."

Nergal nodded. "It waved an eviction notice at the

Earth-line people, that's for sure."

"Yeah." Crawler let out a big rolling laugh, that managed to fit even more nails on that imaginary chalkboard.

"Shut the fuck up, Crawler," said Vic.

"Ah, lay off the boy," Nergal said. He turned his attention back to Jesse and Zane. "All us Schomites stayed for the show. The swampland provided for us like always. Just changed the menu around for a while, you might say. For the Crimbone, it was better hunting than many of us could remember."

"What," said Zane, "you mean the glowsticks tried making an opening of it? Didn't hear about that shit. Not surprising, but still—"

"Nah," said Crawler, "fuck the glowsticks and fuck the Earth-liners—"

"Shut the fuck up, Crawler," said Vic.

Something flashed through Jesse's eyes. He cut in, "But not you, right, Nergal? Nah, you remember some of the best hunting there's been in this age, I'll bet."

"It does find its way into the swamp," said Nergal, "doesn't it now."

Zane knew that tone from Jesse. It never led anywhere good, especially when there was beer around. He shot in, "You didn't have any trouble from the Earth-line law, when they came in and started forcing folks out?"

"Oh, they came knocking," said Nergal. "I wouldn't call it trouble."

Zane smiled at the fledglings. "So, you boys have already gotten a good taste of the true ways of the swamp." Their faces, particularly Crawler's, lit up at this small commendation from one of their legendary heroes.

Nergal clapped both fledglings on the back. "True, but you know how these youngsters can be. They get used to life a certain way, then it changes, then it starts to drift back to how it was before. Some of 'em have a hard time keeping up. Gotta keep 'em on their toes, make sure they don't get too comfortable for their own good. You say a fledgling told you that, about New Orleans being a swamp?"

Zane nodded.

Crawler wouldn't quit butting in. "What fledgling?"

Jesse refilled his glass and topped off Zane's. He seemed oblivious to Crawler's grating voice, which must qualify him for what Earth-liners called a sainthood. His eyes met Nergal's again. "One who'd traveled a lot. But then…a fledgling ought to."

Nergal either missed or ignored the implied slight. "So, what brings you two living legends traveling this way?" he asked.

"Headed for New Orleans, funny enough." Jesse held onto Nergal's gaze.

"Funny enough," Nergal agreed.

"Yeah," Jesse went on, "we're actually trying to figure out whatever happened to one of our own, us northern Crimbone, that is. Ever hear of Metaiew Coscan? You might say we all came of age together. He's not a legend all through the South too, is he?" The fledglings didn't go back into fits like Earth-line fan girls, so apparently not.

"None I've heard of." Nergal held up his end of the

eye-contact. "Metaiew…Wow, an Old World name, no less."

"Yeah. Good man, that one. Not quite so Old World as his name, though."

"What do you mean?"

"Oh. You know. He got too into all that Earth-line shit at some point. Getting out of the fight. Starting a family. Got comfortable in a farmer's life. He let it soften him up. He sort of fell out of the game before his time, you might say."

"Who was the fledgling?" Crawler repeated.

"I told you to shut the fuck up, Crawler," said Vic.

Nergal ignored the kids. "Yeah, shame when that happens. Consequences for that shit ain't what they ought'a be anymore, if you ask me."

"Yeah, too bad." Jesse's gaze sharpened. "Consequences ain't what they should be for a lot of shit. Right?"

"Right," said Nergal, eyes still locked studiously on Jesse's.

Zane wasn't sure what he was watching, except he knew that his brain screamed, *Jesse, shut the fuck up. Just shut the fuck up, now.* He loosened himself up on his barstool, and let his limbs swing loose, just in case. *Motherfucker—*

"Still," Nergal went on, "better that than staying in without the edge, then fucking up when other Crimbone needed him to show it."

"The farmland he found to tend seemed to feel he made the right call," said Jesse, "enough for that to do pretty well by him while he stuck to it. At some point, though, he sort of went back into things on his own. Then he stopped reporting to the Cabinets. That was around ten years ago."

"So, what was this fledgling's name," asked Crawler for the third time, "the one who says New Orleans is just a swamp letting a city live there?"

"Crawler." Nergal cocked his elbow at the fledgling's skull. Crawler flinched a little and shut up.

"Funny you should ask, Crawler," said Jesse. "That fledgling just happens to be the son of the guy we're looking for. Thing is, Metaiew Coscan's disappearance was always a concern. Someone just let it slip to the back burner, 'til recently."

Nergal leaned forward. "So, why now?"

"Metaiew's son's been missing for five years, and, well, he's not the kind of fledgling the Cabinets are gonna ignore forever."

Nergal folded forward, staring. The air left him like Jesse had slugged him in the gut. He whispered, "Are you telling me the High Natural grew up in New Orleans?"

"Huh. You said *High Natural*, not me. Anyway, nah, he just lived there a while."

"His dad, too?"

"Nah." Jesse grinned. "The Cabinets we worked with together never dealt much with you guys. Still, someone on one of the New England Cabinets recently had the idea that it might be useful in the search— finding out whatever happened to crazy old Metaiew. We tracked down his second wife, an Earth-line woman. She gave us all his old papers so we'd go away."

"Probably a good thing I decided to play hackey-sack with her cell phone when she lipped off about calling the cops," Zane added.

"*Anyway*," Jesse grunted, "some of those papers gave us the idea he might be in New Orleans."

"Interesting." Nergal had his poker-face back on by now. "You spoken with the local charge there yet?"

"Nah, why bother?" Jesse's grin kept getting wider. His eyes got crazier. The rest of his body stayed perfectly relaxed. "Figured we'd drop on in and the city—oh, sorry, the swamp— would let us know soon enough what we had to gain there."

Nergal's posture wasn't so relaxed. "Yeah, good luck with that."

Everyone around them went deathly quiet.

Zane sighed and pushed Jesse's beer into his line of sight. "I don't know about you guys, but I figure I've got about six hours where I don't have to think about the damn investigation, so I aim to spend it getting drunk as hell."

Nergal settled down. Jesse shrugged. The fledglings tried not to sigh too loudly with relief. When the pitcher ran dry, Nergal insisted that Jesse and Zane try some local brew. Jesse stayed oblivious to the bar girl's attention, so Zane exchanged more smiles with her, 'til she went to see to some customers at the other end. He got the fledglings telling him about New Orleans these days, while Jesse and Nergal traded war stories. Zane made sure to keep an ear on Jesse's mouth.

When the conversation started back towards internal politics, Zane piped up, "You know, I think the one thing we can all agree on and toast to: the Late Great Sam Kinneson and the A-B-C technique!"

Everyone got it and howled laughter. Everyone but Jesse cheered, *"To Sam!"* and clinked glasses, as if crossing blades like the Three Musketeers.

Jesse muttered under his breath, "Yeah, that's a fun enough little fledgling trick."

Zane almost asked, *Remind me, brother, who's gotten more action between the two of us in the last, oh, what, twenty-five years?* He let that one slide.

Finally, last call sounded, and the last pitcher ran dry. On the way out, Zane asked, "So, where you guys off to now?"

"To sleep." Nergal thumbed over his shoulder into yonder trees.

"Right," said Jesse. "Like you said—a real taste of bare swamp. Don't get those nice leathers too messed up."

"There's plenty room at the camp if you guys wanna join us," said Crawler.

"I think we'll check out that motel there," Jesse said. "You might say we've gotten a little softened by Earth-line comforts in our old age."

"Not too much, though," Zane added. "You guys don't seem to be off to such bad starts yourselves." He watched the fledglings' faces and saw that he'd just made their night.

The young trio walked towards the woods. The two old heroes walked towards the shitty, cheap motel. A raspy Steppin Fetchit voice said from the steak house roof, "Good goin' in there, ol' Thumpy-Bumpy."

Zane looked up as the two fat, bat-like shapes beat the air with their wings and flew towards the trees. He half smiled, recalling days that were strange to think of pleasantly…strange enough to remember at all.

Two

They laid down on the twin beds with the lamp on. They were both in the habit of sleeping naked, without covers, their dusters and next day's clothes folded on the floor next to their beds, within quick reach. They each set their black metal weapons next to them on the mattresses.

"I like those guys." Zane stretched and kept his eyes closed. "Sure you should've talked so much business with 'em straight off like that?"

"Nah, you're right," said Jesse, "I went a little crazy with that play. You gotta admit, it paid off, though. See what I mean, now, though, about this state?"

"Right. I get it. We're walking into some weird shit, even for us, such as *not being able to trust a fellow Crimbone.*"

"That's weird to you? Huh. Anyway, I wanted an honest reaction, and I got it. Notice Nergal wasn't surprised like he should've been?"

Zane perked up, but still didn't open his eyes. "You think they knew to expect us."

"Yeah. Well, not *us* exactly—"

Zane tried not to grin. "*Legends all over the South.* You believe that shit…Ripper-Man?"

"Never call me that again. Anyhow, I don't think the fledglings are in on whatever's going on…whatever it is. I think Nergal was sent out to follow the voice of these lands to us, and he brought the fledglings along as cover."

"Makes sense. Either way, I guess you don't like those guys much."

"The fledglings are fine. I was thinking about ripping out Nergal's intestines, then using them to hang him from the ceiling by his ball sack."

Zane whistled. "Guess you really hated that Dixie beer he bought us."

"It was fine if you've got a thing for horse piss. I was just thinking about a time around nine years ago, when a couple of runaway teenage girls wandered into that town. They took up with Nergal and some of his pals, who showed 'em around the French Quarter, got 'em good and drunk. Then they got 'em into an old courtyard and gang raped 'em. Except Nergal kept one of the girls all to himself, then they took 'em both back to the local charge. Nergal gave his special lady to that charge, who…well, you know the rest."

For a second there, Zane had figured all the strange serpentine energy around here had fried Jesse's brain. Then it clicked. "Oh shit. You sure it's the same guy? I mean, *that* guy, from that tape you won't quit playing over and over?"

"Yeah. The charge he handed Sally Wildfire over to? The one who sent him out to find us? Same guy."

"Damn." Zane rolled that one over a little. "You keep saying that charge heard about us from the swamp.

The guy she described was *not* Crimbone, and I've never met a civilian Schomite with that kind of attunement…let alone enough to manipulate the roadsides to our eyes at night, this far out, for us to run into those guys, and for it to all seem like random chance."

"Ever heard of one performing a ritual like that guy performed on Sally Wildfire? That was Old World magic."

Zane squeezed his eyes shut tighter. It was one of those times when he'd appreciate it if Jesse would just shut the fuck up, so he could go to sleep. Any answer Zane gave would be asking for more punishment, but he still said, "What Rob's Spirelight girl described was some rich, degenerate asshole trying to make Old World magic, having no idea what kind of shit he was stirring up. We do, 'cause hey, look, here we are."

"No doubt. Still…hell, man, you met her, too. Sally, I mean."

"I know who the fuck you're talking about."

"Yeah? So, how come you never say her damn name?" When Zane didn't answer, Jesse went on, "Anyway, lots of people thought we'd never see a High Natural in this world. It's like I keep tellin' 'em, though: there are things still living in these lands that no one but the Old Lords ever even knew we brought over from the Old World. That's what's bubbling up now."

Zane squeezed his eyes even tighter. Yeah, Jesse was about due for one of his apocalyptic alarmist rants. At least he wasn't going off on that old theory that the Earth-line people had evolved from Lepods. "Yeah, whatever." Zane almost left it at that. Then something clicked. "You know what? While you've been blathering on and on with your fuckin' conspiracy theories and shit, I've been going over some dates in my head."

"I'm shit with dates," said Jesse.

"Yeah, that's why I make sure I ain't. Look, so that shit that happened to Rob's Spirelight girl—"

"Sally."

"Right. Anyway, that was, what, ten years ago?"

"Nine. Give or take." Jesse's voice lowered to a grim rasp.

"Right. So walk it back two years, you're right around when sheltered little wet-behind-the-ears Robbie Coscan first runs away from home, right?"

"Not straight to New Orleans, though. He didn't end up there 'til about a year before his First Call."

"Right, but after Rob runs off, obviously Metaiew tries to find him. It's only a matter of time before he thinks to check New Orleans, right? So that's the last place anyone hears Metaiew's headed…a little over a year after his son runs off."

"Good catch. Keep going."

"About a year after that, some New Orleans Crimbone capture a runaway Spirelight girl. The degenerate fuck they serve tries to work some Old World magic on her. It turns her into something no one of either race has been able to figure out since. Four years after that, her scared, zigzagging trail leads her to Brattleboro, Vermont. What happens? The first High Natural in ages—maybe the first genuine article in the history of this world—*just happens* to fall in love with the tainted Spirelight girl. They run off together. So, guess who that High Natural's dad is?" Zane opened his eyes, stared at the ceiling, and exhaled fiercely. He'd put a lot of that together as he spoke it. He looked over. Jesse's eyes had also opened, staring at the ceiling.

"You're right," said Jesse. "Good thing I keep you around."

The room went quiet, 'til knocking shook the door. On either bed, a hand gripped a weapon. Jesse and Zane looked over at each other, but didn't move yet. The knocking sounded again. They got up and went to the door. On the way, Zane paused to put his pants on. Jesse didn't.

Zane unlocked and opened the door. Outside, the fledgling called Crawler stood there. He stared at Jesse, shrank up and stepped back.

"I'll explain it to you when you're older, kid," said Jesse. "What do you want?"

The smell of the swamp was thick on Crawler. Since they'd last seen him, he'd replaced his bar-crawling clothes with wilderness friendly rags. He squeaked, "The others are asleep."

Zane said, "You sure?"

"Hey, I've been with these guys for two years. I know how to tell." Crawler said it with the usual youthful zeal of a guy who thinks he's the first to figure something out.

"You heard the man," Zane barked. "What the fuck do you want, kid?"

Crawler extended a jittery hand, with a slip of paper pinched between two fingers, like he wasn't sure which of them he was offering it to.

Zane grabbed it and squinted at the scrawl in the dim light. It looked like a street address, without a city or state or zip code. He put two and two together on his own, but still said, "What the fuck's this, kid?"

"Go to that street address in New Orleans on Wednesday night, after…uh, say…nine thirty. It's a big house in the garden district. You come into the city proper by the overpass and find your way onto the Avenue, and head away from the French Quarter. When you spot that street sign, go left. The house you want is about halfway down that street, on your left. It's set a little ways back from the other houses, with a big yard. The party should be raging pretty hard by then, so you can't miss it. Go to the front door and just…tell 'em who you are. They'll let you in."

"Got it." Zane smiled. "Good job, kid."

"The house belongs to a man named Talino."

"He the charge Nergal answers to?" asked Zane.

Crawler nodded.

"So, is it safe to say that Nergal's Talino's closest enforcer?"

Crawler nodded again.

"Cool," said Zane. "Thanks. You'd better get back to your pack, kid." He almost shut the door in the kid's face, then added, "So Crawler, about your Familiar—"

"Yeah?"

"What does it call you?"

Crawler winced. "Slinky-Shiver."

"Some motherfuckers have all the luck." Zane shut the door in Crawler's face and handed the slip of paper to Jesse.

Jesse read it, then met his eyes.

"Talino, huh," Zane said.

"Yeah, that name sure hits a bell or two, don't it?"

THREE

The air on Saint Charles Avenue smelled like Crawler's swampy clothes, except fresh and healthy, thick and free, beneath the setting sun.

Over the last two days, that air had gotten down into them, cleaned something out, making it impossible not to feel good. Even the scuzziest streets of the French Quarter held some new color, taste, or song. All over town, street musicians played old-time tunes Jesse and Zane hadn't thought anyone else alive remembered. To their old ears, it sounded as fresh and magic as the new tunes Jazz players improvised in Jackson Square.

Yesterday, Jesse had even pulled several women from the crowd and danced up a storm with them. Zane had to admit, the old cracker could still turn on the charm when he let himself loosen up a little. After the last dance, Jesse had sat and talked with a lady for a while. Damn, it almost looked like the ol' boy might actually get laid.

Outside the quarter, they'd found more shades of green than they'd ever imagined, short of somehow getting back to the Old World…certainly more than they'd ever expected to see again growing from this polluted world. Many buildings looked more ancient than they could possibly be. Ageless magic leaked from mossy porticoes and half-sunken stones.

The sun had already set by the time they climbed out of a streetcar, into the Garden District. They walked towards the address Crawler had given them. The grand old mansions still seemed not so much built, as sprouted from the earth like vine-streaked, nature-sculpted rocks. Behind them, something sparked and flashed, lighting up Pennistone Avenue in blue for a split instant. Jesse cast an edgy eye over his shoulder.

Zane slapped him on the back. "It's the streetcar wire, man. It does that every time."

Jesse shrugged and walked on, already scanning the house numbers for 2417. He'd suggested they case for the place when they'd first gotten to town. Zane convinced him this would only risk fucking things up, get them spotted too soon. They needed to spend time with the city first, so it could teach them to blend in at its own pace. That still meant leaving themselves open to being spotted and watched, but considering their encounter with Nergal and the boys, it was a little late to worry about that.

Crawler was right. The house and the party were hard to miss. Parked cars of every class, make and model choked the driveway and lined the block. Up on the white columned porch, a greenish-yellow light spilled through the windows. Neither Jesse nor Zane had seen such light in years, specifically since they'd left the South.

What year was that? Zane had given Jesse so much shit about keeping up with dates. Now he was the one who couldn't remember.

Civilian Schomites in America tended to keep to the East Coast or Crimbone-controlled Southern states. There were more civilians than Crimbone socializing on the front porch. Zane hadn't spent much time around civilian Schomites, even when he'd lived in the South. Whenever he met them, they rattled him a little—too many traces of Deschembine races who'd never come to this world, whose traits he recognized only by descriptions in the most ancient, hidden texts. He'd only happened to get a look at those texts because he once filled in as a Cabinet secretary for a year, while recovering from some nearly fatal injuries. Some of the races in those files were supposed to be extinct, wiped out by Magur Sevi in the final days of old Deschemb, for siding with the Spirelights and their gods.

There were no accurate words for the subtleties in feature difference, in any Earth-line language. Earth-liners might use terms like *exotic* or *glamorous*. Any Earth-liners at tonight's party might recognize faces from the entertainment industry, particularly the music business. Folks they called *celebrities*, Zane guessed, though fewer and fewer such faces and voices had become known to the general Earth-line public over the last twenty years, at least in song. It didn't bother him intellectually, not as much as the pure-blooded Schomite doorman, anyway.

"Mister Karn and Mister Rochester!" The doorman flung up his hands. Jesse and Zane shrugged past him. He scuttled at their heels like a jumpy Scotty dog. "You know, I never believed what they said, that you'd both long since taken on one heroic deed too many—"

"What," said Jesse, "you mean some people say we're dead?"

"I think that's what he means," said Zane.

"Hey, glad to disappoint, so far."

"Not a disappointment at all," said the doorman. "Your presence makes our little gathering the honor of all New Orleans."

"Yeah, cool," said Zane. "Don't announce us to the room, though. You might piss my buddy off. He's shy like that."

"Right, yes, of course. May I take your coats, gentlemen?"

They let their dusters slide off their shoulders, into the doorman's trembling hands. They left the weapons on their hips, in full view. They took a quick scan of the glittering, crimson ballroom, and immediately spotted at least a dozen fellow Crimbone scattered about, all wearing their weapons in plain view so that Jesse and Zane's wouldn't look too conspicuous. A Crimbone without his weapon was about the most conspicuous sight Zane could think of, other than a prowling family of the Spirelight Secret Police. Most of these Earth-line celebrants were dressed so eccentrically that they barely noticed the silent, otherworldly guardians striding among them…probably on enough weird drugs to mistake their unearthly, animalian body language for affectations like their own, the weapons on their belts for decorative pieces…*cosplayers*, as the kids called it today. Even here, though, Jesse and Zane would still stand out, not least of all for their tarnished trail clothes.

"Man, I swear," Zane muttered, "if we're gonna

have to listen to horseshit like that all night—"

An eternally girlish looking lady with wavy red hair and pale green eyes walked past them. She wore a slight, incandescent, rusty-golden dress. Her wise lips twisted mischievously when she spotted Zane looking, then she moved on.

"Man, is that who I think it is?" said Zane.

"I believe so." Jesse slapped Zane's arm. "Welcome to the world of the elite, brother. We're livin' the high life tonight, at least 'til shit goes crazy."

"Yeah," Zane sighed. "Man, I miss that gal."

"*What?*" said Jesse. "When the fuck did you meet her, and how did I never hear of it 'til—"

"No," Zane said sternly, "I mean I miss when we used to listen to her CDs while we were driving around, before you got obsessed with playing…" He scowled and lowered his voice. "Before you got obsessed with playing that Spirelight gal's tape about how these cats—"

"You honestly think monstrous behavior like that ain't known full well to all these highfalutin celebrity types?" He swatted Zane across the chest and bellowed cavalierly. "Right, now I remember."

The fey redhead approached a handsome couple. The civilian Schomite man with dark, tangled hair and gentle, sage eyes wore a simple black suit. At his side stood a lean, muscular female whose every tiny movement was like that of a dancing snake, even when she stood still. Her full mouth and gleaming teeth looked as sharp as her wild, dark eyes.

Over at the open bar, a few more vaguely familiar faces got wine, mixed drinks, and expensive liquor straight on the rocks.

Jesse and Zane approached the bar. Zane asked, "You guys got any Heineken?"

A barman in a red velvet vest fished two out of a silvery ice well and handed them over reverently. "Mister Talino usually doesn't serve beer at his parties, but yesterday he called his caterer and demanded a shipment on short notice. Now I see why."

They were about to ask the barman for the scoop, then they spotted the answer across the room: a Crimbone chatting with several civilians and a fledgling girl. Jesse shifted, about to head that way, when Nergal vanished into the crowd.

"Not who we need to chase down right now," Zane reminded Jesse in a growling whisper. That said, they strode through the party and got more curious looks. Zane leaned close again and sang in an exaggerated twang, "*Blame it all on them roots, I done shown up in boots—*"

Jesse grinned. "Let's find this Talino fuck. I'm in the mood to ruin someone's black-tie affair."

Thick vines streaked the walls and ceiling like a skeletal web. Fat glowing pods hung like chandeliers, bathing the party in that greenish-yellow light they'd seen from the streets. All the light in here came from those pods. The lack of conventional electrical wiring was no illusion.

"I thought the Spirelight girl said there were more vines," Zane whispered.

"There were. This is a different house. The other one was abandoned and rotted by the time her family found her, remember?"

Zane muttered, "I wonder how many of these places this fucktard has gone through."

"Too many," said Jesse.

* * * *

Back when Jesse had first played the recording of Sally's testimony for the Cabinet, he'd expected Talino, Nergal, and the others to be the next official order of business. In their eyes, though, the problem at hand had been Rob Coscan and Sally Wildfire. The interspecies lovebirds pulling a disappearing act didn't exactly close the case. Besides, the Cabinets had long since left the Louisiana factions to their own devices, because it kept them out of national matters. Over and over, Jesse advised against ignoring the degenerate mystic for too long. You'd think the matter of Sally Wildfire would show them his point, and he'd already had his suspicions about Hurricane Katrina. The disappearance of the High Natural stayed a priority, though. Only when Jesse suggested the High Natural's missing dad might shed some light on things had the search taken him and Zane here. Sometimes the lands had a sense of humor like that.

Jesse thought about all this while he looked at pretty girls in glittery, revealing evening wear. When Zane slugged his arm, he turned. From atop the giant staircase came a tall, hatchet-faced, beady-eyed man in a silky, dark green tuxedo, a high-class cigarette smoldering in one hand, a waifish, stoned-eyed brunette on his other arm. She looked half her companion's age, if that. As they descended, his effect on the crowd was almost as strong as Jesse and Zane's.

If Jesse wasn't mistaken, he'd spotted a well-known writer or two here. Their imaginations must be bouncing off the walls with weird ideas about their host. Some of those ideas might not be so far off. That probably had to do with why the host had invited them; either as a perverse ego boost or a private ironic joke. There was something wrong with the girl. Jesse and Zane glanced at each other and nodded in agreement. Only the Crimbone in the room would notice. Likely, Jesse and Zane were the only two Crimbone here who saw it as a problem. Jesse knew he'd never set eyes on her before, yet she was somehow familiar.

The only Earth-line soul of the household—except to look in her eyes, he wondered if she still had a soul.

Bad things have been done to her, but it's more than that. She's had Old World magic worked on her as it was worked on Sally, only different...worse. This girl isn't even Earth-line anymore, but she hasn't been turned into a Deschembine, either. Whatever she's become, it doesn't belong in this world or any other.

Jesse and Zane met the couple at the foot of the stairs.

"So this must be the man of the hour." Zane gave the man a Crimbone handshake. The guy's grip was strong enough to handle it. Zane hid his surprise.

"If you gentlemen are who I think you are," said the man in a strong, cultured voice, "the honor is mine."

Jesse gave the same handshake and hid the same surprise. "So we keep hearing. Might not wanna announce that to the room, though. You might piss my buddy off. He's shy like that."

"It's refreshing to hear a pair of legends speak so

unabashedly with the knowledge of what they are. Nothing bores me faster than false modesty. Did you get any of those scars by speaking that way before you'd earned the right?"

Jesse cocked an eyebrow and smiled. "Us? Nah, we've always known how to talk it. We earn our scars by learning how to walk it. That wasn't a bad entrance you made just now, by the way." He looked at the girl. "Can't say it would've been so slick without just the right woman on your arm, though. Ma'am?"

Looking at her eyes was somehow the most horrid task Jesse had endured so far on this trip. Her smile should have come with a blush, though she might be physically incapable of blushing.

"Mister Karn." Her voice didn't reveal much. She nodded at Zane just as mechanically. "Mister Rochester. I'm Kimberly."

When she put out her hand, Jesse took it delicately and kissed it, which wasn't as bad as looking in her eyes. Her skin felt and tasted more or less normal, though, a little too cold for this weather.

"Call us Jesse and Zane." Zane shook her hand gently but didn't kiss it. "So Mister Talino, I guess Crawler told you to expect us?"

"Eh? Oh right, the fledgling. No. Nergal told me." Talino held his cool, but didn't keep the edge out of his voice. "It shouldn't have surprised anyone. It's only fitting that you two come to our side at the beginning of these new times."

"New times, huh."

"Please tell me you're not really that confused. The

mask these lands have placed over us has been crumbling for years. Not quite enough yet for the Earth-line people to see through it, but it's happening. That won't really start 'til the Crimbone are strong enough that we no longer need the mask. Don't worry. The High Natural will take care of that soon enough." Talino's voice dropped to a passionate whisper. "Your own legends are already part of his. I'm afraid that story hasn't yet spread so widely through this swamp, though. It's true, right, that you two were the first he met after his First Call?"

"Yeah," said Jesse. "You know, your name came up in a conversation around that time."

Talino cocked an eyebrow. "The High Natural knows my name? That's funny. Back when he was here, I forced myself not to approach him. At that time, it was better to let him figure it all out at his own pace."

"Actually, it was his girlfriend mentioned you. I hear you and the boys left quite an impression on her." Jesse noticed Kimberly shift…the ghost of a squirm?

"Oh, right. They're the perfect couple in their way, aren't they?"

"You sound like you've kept up with 'em better than we have," said Zane.

"Me? Much as I'd have liked to, no. Just anticipating the inevitable. Come on, though, I know you both met them together. If it was enough time for them to get that close, I'd be disappointed in both of you if you didn't watch enough to agree with me."

Zane said, "Yeah, they sure smelled like they enjoyed each other a lot, now that you mention it."

"*Goes to show you never can tell,* as the saying goes."

Talino licked his lips. "Isn't that how times of great change always seem at first?"

"Saw that one coming, huh," said Zane.

"By now in life, friends, it takes a lot to surprise me. I'll put it this way for you. There's an old Earth-line saying, which is that there's a great woman behind every great man."

"You sure are full of sayings," said Jesse.

Zane was just relieved Jesse chose the word *sayings*.

"Only the best," said Talino. "From where I've watched, I can't think of a better woman for the High Natural than the Tainted Spirelight."

"You haven't actually heard from Rob." Jesse's voice tensed.

Talino chuckled. "No, but don't worry, we all will soon enough. He's made his first move already, you know, wherever he is. Otherwise, you wouldn't be here in New Orleans. Neither would half the Schomites in this room, Crimbone or civilian. Just look around. They've come from all over the world. The Earth-line ways have changed a lot about our people, but no small matter ever draws us to stray from the greater lands that raise us. It won't be long before our boy makes a bigger move…his first stab into the old mask."

Zane answered before Jesse could. "Well, be sure to point that out when it happens. Actually, we were more wondering if you'd heard from his dad any time in the last, oh, ten years."

Talino straightened like he hadn't just gone on his crazy, prophetic rant. "Metaiew Coscan. Ah, yes. Too bad he didn't show up with you two."

"Yeah, too bad," said Jesse. "Let's talk about him anyway."

"All due respect, friends, I don't think that's a topic for this festive evening. Care to join me in the courtyard out back, tomorrow for lunch? We can talk about Metaiew Coscan then."

"Sounds good to me," said Zane. "Jesse?"

Jesse studied Talino, nodded coldly. "Enjoy your party."

"By all means, do the same, sirs." Talino sounded unperturbed. Jesse had already started back towards the bar. Zane gave Talino an *excuse me, please* gesture and hurried after.

* * * *

"Ah, there you are, man!" Jesse turned back to the red-vested barman. "Heineken! Get us a big, frothing fucking pitcher of Heineken!" He looked dismayed when Zane didn't join in.

"I'm afraid we don't have *pitchers*, gentlemen." The barman blinked rapidly and tried to smile, offering two fresh bottles.

Once Jesse cooled his guts with a few deep swigs, Zane said, "Y'know, it's kinda fun, watching you try to piss off every asshole we run into."

"Huh? Oh hell, I'm just hittin' buttons at this point, seein' what happens. I'd say we've found some damn interesting buttons here."

"You do realize that Talino guy is a delusional rich weirdo. Right?"

"Hope so." Jesse's fingers twitched towards his knife.

Zane lit a smoke without bothering to look around to see if that was okay in here. "Y'know, when I said you had to learn to flow with the energies around here, I didn't mean go clown-shit insane at the drop of a hat like a cocky fledgling."

Before Jesse could answer, a voice said from his right, "Got any Dixie beer?"

"I'm afraid the only beer we have is Heineken," said the barman.

"Heineken's fine." *Nergal. Great.*

Jesse held his cool. "Glad to see you got back in time for the big bash, man! What's the name again?"

"Nergal."

Before Jesse could do something like make a joke about the sound of it—not his style, but neither was pretending to forget names—Zane said, "So, how are the fledglings?"

"Around here somewhere."

"That was some funny dramatics you pulled with the one," said Jesse. "Crawler, I mean. You could've just dropped the word at the bar, you know."

"Oh good, you picked up on that. It wasn't playacting from him, you know. He really thought he managed to sneak out of the camp without me realizing it. He's pretty star-struck over you guys—especially you, Zane. He never stops studying the stories of you two. Hell, a lot of times, he studies between the lines of old Earth-line news reports better than he listens to me."

"Hey, whatever works." Zane smiled and shook his head. "Those damn fledglings." He might have added, *and their Familiars.*

"Yeah." Nergal went formal. "My charge has asked that you stay the night. I can show you your rooms now, or we can wait 'til the party clears out."

Of course Talino had only instructed Nergal to give the second option as a formality, to avoid a disruption. Apparently, though, Nergal still had enough Crimbone honor left in him somewhere to pose both.

"Sounds good," said Jesse. "Let's sit and drink a few more beers first, though."

Zane could almost hear Jesse thinking about what fun it would be if they waited for everyone to be asleep, and then went around slitting some throats.

FOUR

Two high, dark hallways waited atop the great staircase, one at either corner of the balcony. Nergal led Jesse and Zane to the left. The same endoskeleton of vines covered these halls, though the only light was what leaked from downstairs. Midway down the hall, a couple who hadn't found their way into a room yet made out against the wall. Around the corner were no less than three more such couples, one on the right, two on the left. Couldn't anyone keep track of their damn room keys around here? At the far end, the spill of light told that it led back out to the top of the same staircase. Midway through, another hallway split off down in the opposite direction—wider, longer, darker. Jesse couldn't keep track of where the light was coming from. What was up with this layout? He felt a little dizzied by it, like he was lost in an Escher drawing.

Before losing sight of the bright room behind them, Jesse noticed the first pair of young lovers draw apart.

Nergal led them into that final, longest, darkest hallway. "The room at the end on the left is yours, Zane. The one right before it is yours, Jesse."

"Thanks," said Jesse. Back at the fork, another of the couples had wandered into view, still holding hands. "Actually, you know, with all this love in the air, I think I'll go back downstairs a while, see if I can find myself some company for that room."

Another of the couples, and the first one from the hall—the ones he saw draw apart—had weapons on their belts. In the third and fourth couples, only the women had weapons. The two men didn't need weapons. Their eyes and movements were telltale enough.

They're all Crimbone, and how the fuck did I miss that? Am I that drunk? Then Jesse saw how their eyes all smoldered. *No, it's because they were giving each other all that slow, sweet lovin', and not attacking each other with rough, wild Crimbone love. I'll bet none of them are even each other's type.*

Why the fuck hadn't he thought of something like that? Hadn't he and Zane been on enough missions of their own where that act was part of the game?

"Mister Talino wants to make sure you don't do anything that would force him to call off tomorrow's talk, and he wants to make sure the conversation will be on his preferred terms. You understand, of course."

"Jesse," said Zane, "I don't think these folks want us to get laid tonight."

"Well that's too bad." Jesse started forward. "'Cause I think I'm about to work myself up an appetite."

"You too, huh?"

"Just remember, I got dibs on the redhead if she's game for it."

"Fine by me. I'm pretty sure the brunette was eyeing me special, actually."

Nergal pressed a hand to Jesse's chest. "I don't think you've understood."

Jesse's first answer was a growl. His second was to grab the offending wrist, simultaneously twisting so the bones snapped, and throwing Nergal into the wall, making a giant Nergal-shaped dent. His third answer was to slam Nergal's head three times into the wall, while he bent the broken wrist at an impossible angle.

Three of the others crowded in on Zane. He picked two of them up, tossing one over his shoulder, and the other into the remaining opponent, sending them staggering six feet back. Another three trampled over the fallen ones, slinging punches and kicks from too many directions for Zane to duck and block them all.

Zane took shots to the face and stomach, while his foot hooked a kick midair. He crouched, brought it to the floor, and crushed a knee under his boot heel. The attacker howled and rolled side to side. Zane's other foot pulverized a groin, while his right hand caught a throat and yanked a body forward, his left palm shattering a jaw.

He lashed around snarling to face the one he'd tossed over his shoulder, still holding the other by the throat. Gathering herself, the former dove like a lioness.

Zane swung the latter around, so two skulls met and fractured against each other.

That left four standing, including the one Zane had kicked in the crotch. While that man came back for more, the other two took on Jesse. Jesse set to hammering on them, not noticing that Nergal had dragged himself out of his hole in the wall.

'Til now, no one had drawn weapons.

Jesse and Zane came of a generation where it was unheard of for any Crimbone to draw a weapon of the black metal against another. Either that particular corruption hadn't touched these young ones, or their veneration for Jesse and Zane kept them from it.

It didn't stop Nergal from drawing his snake-tongue fork of a knife and swinging the pommel down on Jesse's head. Jesse turned in time to see it, but not to block it.

Everyone froze when they saw Jesse fall, even Nergal. Nergal stared back and forth between his weapon and his target, like he thought of them as the two most fundamentally separate entities he'd ever known.

Zane hadn't seen his friend defeated since the earliest years after their Third Calls. Crimbone drawing blades on each other was something he'd only heard about, never quite believed. The sight of Jesse actually falling was enough to petrify the other four, even if it was their objective. Some of the fallen ones were still conscious. They also gaped, as close as possible to forgetting their own agony.

Everyone here was Crimbone, so the stillness didn't

hold for long.

Zane launched himself at Nergal, forgetting the others, hand dropping to his hammer. The taboo no longer existed, so he no longer remembered it. Once he smashed Nergal's remaining wrist—the one with the dishonored knife—he would smash the rest of the bones in the hand, one at a time.

A leg came into his path, and Zane crashed and sprawled. In front of him, Jesse's features hung slack in a glistening of blood. Someone kicked Zane's hammer away. He heard it spin down the hall and thump against the far wall.

Four heavy bodies dog-piled him. A set of arms shoved beneath his, then up around to the back of his skull, and gripped him in a choke hold. With a big enough explosion of strength and will, he could throw them all off at once.

Nergal dragged up Jesse's limp body, holding on with the elbow of his broken arm, the edge of his fork-tongued knife pressed to Jesse's throat.

"Go ahead, Zane," said Nergal through clenched teeth. His eyes bulged, face glistening with sweat. "Fuckin' big shot Crimbone legend! All I see's a rowdy, beaten down nigger."

It had been well over a century since the petty Earth-line slur had meant much to Zane, but that didn't make his snarl any less murderous.

Nergal continued, "You know, yeah, you could throw them off, no problem. If you didn't have that to deal with, maybe you could get hold of my knife hand before I opened Jesse's throat. Then again, maybe not.

You know how sharp the black metal is."

In the din, a trickle of blood ran down the center of Jesse's windpipe. Zane made himself settle down. Few were disciplined enough with the black metal to cut at all without going all the way, let alone in such agonized frenzy. If Nergal so much as flinched right now, Jesse was done.

"Good thinking," hissed Nergal. "Now, assuming both you boys got all the stupid knocked out of you, I figure you'll both pull through for tomorrow's nice little garden party. You feel like making something of it then, hey, that's just fine with me. Mister Talino, though, he really hopes you'll keep it all calm and friendly. Right now, just let these boys and girls get you up and show you to that nice room he's had prepared—Hey, Zane, the split instant I see you even twitch against 'em, though, Jesse's head comes clean off. Got it?"

Zane let them hustle him up.

The door stood open. They let go quickly and shoved him in. Then they slammed it behind him. He staggered, shook his head clear, and looked around.

Here, the vines covered the walls almost completely. Some of them were thick as tree trunks. The glowing pods were the only small things in here, dangling like stars from the ceiling. Slithering hisses came from several directions. Zane spun. Only the thickest, strongest vines moved, snapping like bullwhips around his wrists and ankles, pulling him spread-eagle. He fought like he'd been given another crack at his humanoid captors, but each vine was stronger than ten of those disgraceful excuses for Crimbone.

All night, Zane recalled what Jesse wanted to do to Nergal. If Jesse got his chance, he better let Zane help.

THE SPIRELIGHT SCIENTIST

Tennessee, someone had said. Not Virginia, but still sickeningly familiar.

Thick, sharp leather straps on her wrists and ankles, the cold steel of the examination table under her naked body.

All time and change dropped away, between Mom's examination table and this one. Sally was fourteen again, her soul emptied by fear and pain. She'd never escaped, never met Rob. Soon Mom would come in with a needle and a notebook. The only difference was, this time it would be some other Secret Police scientist. Mom had died five years ago. What the fuck did that change?

Except Sally had figured plenty else out between now and then, hadn't she? Hatred, for one thing. Yeah, that felt most relevant lately, especially for that pathetic piece of shit who'd abducted her. *Dickless fuck with his drugged blade, thought he belonged among the Secret Police!* The deeper her soul went there, the higher she climbed from fourteen.

No, she *wasn't* that confused little weakling anymore, who'd lain shivering and pleading in her own excrement. She'd escaped. She'd learned how to give what she got, and it hadn't killed her yet.

Somehow in all that, she'd found Rob. They'd spent the next five years figuring the rest of it out together.

She wasn't like other Spirelights, didn't belong among them. Why would she want to? It wasn't like she'd ever stopped trying to figure herself out, searching herself for what she'd become. When she found something, she decided to harbor it, save it up for a time like this. They were smart to keep her strapped down like this.

Damnit, Rob, you'd better have done the same.

Harsh light burned her eyes, circling her in a funnel, leaving the rest of the room black as starless space. She squinted but didn't close her eyes against that light. Soon, they would come and find her staring blazing death at them. 'Til the moment the pain killed her, she'd make them see and feel what they'd caught. Yeah, she'd find a way.

I was born a member of the Spirelight Secret Police, after all.

Gods, I never expected to want *to see a Crimbone—a* specific one, obviously, but still—*spring into a room, shredding his way through everyone, like…*

Wow, there was an image she hadn't bothered with in a while; the idea of Rob as some kind of savior knight, *who'd always kill all the monsters and save the girl.*

Somewhere, through the years in Postville, he'd seemed to outgrow that idea, too. None of that silliness compared to what they finally settled into.

Or was it the other way around?

Hell, at first, she'd thought they'd left such romantic illusions behind, during their year on the road, where raw survival was everything. They hadn't even been lovers at that point, so much as a pair of desperate, dragging troopers with no one else who gave a shit if they lived or died, vaguely aware that they'd first gotten into this mess over each other.

It had all come down to dancing with each other's strengths and weaknesses. She'd been best at immediately practical matters, like finding the food and shelter they stole or worked for. Meanwhile, he determined their routes, found the back roads and byways that steered them clear of the Crimbone and the Spirelight Secret Police.

Sure, some of that came from his hard-knocks learning, but it also had plenty to do with those Crimbone instincts of his, the ones she never got used to…from the spirit-voices of places that had or hadn't liked them, telling him things she couldn't hear.

Long before she'd met him, she'd gotten used to always running, always *just surviving*. She hadn't missed ideas like *actually living*. She hadn't noticed Rob doing otherwise, not 'til they'd spent half a day in Postville. She had to admit, there was an easier vibe there than most places. Florida was neutral territory, so maybe they could linger there a while, let their nerves settle. Even neutral territory never stayed safe for long, though.

Then out of nowhere, he said, "Yeah, this is the place. Long as we live here, they won't find us. Okay, let's find something to eat, then a place to stay."

The declaration wasn't so much out of character for him as a known trait, taken to a new extreme. It was one of the first things she'd fallen in love with about him— that decisiveness, an innate pragmatism that was so refined and extreme that it went full circle, bordering on raving lunacy.

It's what had let him embrace and pursue what they'd found in each other, willing to stare down ages of war and hatred. Ironic, considering this was a quintessentially Crimbone trait, from what she understood. Still, that one announcement was too much to deal with. When she asked what he meant, he just repeated himself like it was the simplest statement in the world. He had to be kidding, right?

"Nope," he'd said, "I've known for a long time the exact voice I'd hear from the right place when we found it, if we ever did, and here it is. This is it. Exactly it. What more do you need to hear?"

She'd never know which was worse, his inflexibility or his unshakable calm about it. She'd never seen him so calm, which might have been why she broke down screaming at him that he'd gone crazy. He snarled that she was suicidal for not accepting the idea. That's when it sank in. The whole time, he'd been so busy planning that he hadn't bothered to mention it to her. Had he assumed she didn't expect them to run forever?

More furious than ever, she'd wanted to scream, *Fine, you crazy sonofabitch, stay and cower in this little shithole for the rest of your life, 'til they find you and kill you when you're not looking, but I'm leaving.*

So, why did that idea jolt her worst of all? She'd survived years on the run on her own, and one year with him. Only in the beginning had it been any less hellish. In some ways, there'd been less to be scared of before she met him. Hell, with her family dead, wasn't he the biggest reason to watch herself so close and run so fast?

Yet he was Rob—*her Rob*—and, once upon a dream, they'd been worth it to each other. He still wanted to fix things so they could climb out of the shit. So damnit, there she went, thinking, *What if it's true? What if it's actually possible to be* Rob and Sally *again, alive and in love, just by staying in this little shithole town?*

They still stood fuming at each other—his teeth bared, her own head throbbing. She had to go off by herself for a while. He didn't try to stop her. Off the roadside, she found an abandoned shack and sat on the back porch that looked out over a dead field of stripped, rusted car and truck frames. Over and over she thought of running, of leaving him there. Maybe that would be best for him. Maybe he'd come after her. By the time he found her, he would be pissed off enough to kill her like his blood should have led him to do in the first place.

Maybe he'd stay there without her, or go back to Vermont, find Jesse and Zane or that ugly little monster Puttergong, see if they'd take him back, let him claim that glorious fucking birthright he'd given up for her.

Instead, she'd just sat and sobbed and stared at the field of rust. Maybe he found her by the sound of her sobs, or maybe the spirit of this town had led him to her, this town he kept saying loved them so much. More likely, he just picked up her trail and followed his nose. When he used to go on and on about how beautiful she was, how crazy she drove him, he always mentioned her natural scent as a big part of it. But no. Why would he need any of that to find her? There was always her *glow*, after all.

She heard him coming around the side of the shack, and knew right away that it was him. She didn't know what to do. It depended on him. He stood next to her for a long time, calm and very quiet. Finally, he sat down and put his arm around her.

"Sally?" he asked softly, timidly like a little kid. "Love?"

Then she turned and grabbed him hard, sobbing against his chest, and she'd felt his face press into her hair, and he was sobbing too. Her hands ran up and down his sides. His knives weren't there, against his hips beneath the coat. She'd learn later that he'd hidden them in a drain tunnel at the end of a ditch, a mile back up the road.

"Please, Sally. I don't want anything else. Just give this place a chance. With me." After that, they hadn't discussed it much, which maybe caused a lot of the problems ahead. Shortly after leaving the shack, they'd found Gladys' Diner.

Now Rob was probably dead because he'd taken the town's love for granted.

Far in front of Sally, a door creaked open. Footsteps echoed towards her. She thought she counted four sets. By now, she recognized the tread of the Tribunal representative who'd bartered with the renegade. Two customary field agents would be with him, maybe the same ones who'd taken her out of the van and brought her down here. They'd knocked her out with more drugs once they had her down here.

She'd woken up like this, naked and cold, with nothing but her fading hope for Rob, along with her terror and hatred of this place, for these people who'd once been her own. The renegade wasn't with them.

As they drew near, she strained to make out something—anything—of them through the glare. Her neck tilted a little; otherwise, she stayed absolutely still. Here came a tall, slender, ascetically mannered female shape in gray hospital scrubs, carrying a black leather bag: the Secret Police scientist.

It's Mom, went Sally's inner fourteen-year-old, *perfectly alive and right on time. So Rob lied about that, too.* She almost broke down, knowing what Mom would do once the others left.

The representative and field agents avoided looking at Sally as much as possible. "Yes, I can already see what you mean," said the scientist. "It must be her. I can't think of anyone else it *could be.*" Her voice was warm with, of all things, nerdy enthusiasm.

Sally blinked in confusion. Mom's zeal for her studies used to come out in all sorts of ways. Nerdy glee wasn't one of them.

"Just look at the places on the body where the veins and capillaries show. Come on, this light makes them stand out." She didn't seem to notice when no one moved forward to take her up on that. "Three times the normal spectrum of iridescent shades. Still, I'll run some tests to make absolutely sure. You say the renegade should be at the compound by now?"

"He is. I got the call a few minutes ago in my office."

"So he thinks we've taken the sight of her as confirmation?"

"According to them, he seems quite at ease."

"You can go back upstairs. I'll be up in a few minutes. Then you can call them back, tell them whether to reward him or execute him."

The representatives and the field agents nodded and left. Sally heard the door close after them. The scientist's feet echoed on the concrete, circling her. She reached for the lamp and turned a knob so it dimmed. Sally's eyes adjusted as the scientist leaned in to look her over. By now, Sally realized this wasn't Mom. Too many spots still danced through her vision for her to tell much else. One of the scientist's shoulders looked higher than the other. Sally stayed still. When the scientist neared her face, her whole body bolted against the bonds, and her jaws snapped within an inch of the woman's nose. The bitch must have jumped back five feet! While she stood there, shaking, Sally laughed her ass off.

"You really are her, aren't you?" the woman finally said, still hanging back.

If Sally hadn't known what the scientist was fixing to do, she'd have called the attitude respectful. Then she remembered that these were Spirelights. This woman may well feel a form of respect, finding no incongruity between that and her duty. Growing up, Sally was taught that all life was due some basic respect, even when it needed to be taken—everyone except those demonic Schomites, and their beasts the Crimbone; no, just eradicate those vermin, for the good of all.

Mom's experiments had shaken Sally's faith, to say the least. Falling in love with a Crimbone had sent the last of the dogmatic house of cards fluttering down.

Problem was, she'd never formed a solid belief structure to replace it, nothing but her devotion to Rob and what few solid friendships she'd built in Postville. She looked at the doctor, remembered looking at life the way this lady did, and her gut churned sicker.

"You can come on back," Sally hissed. "Come on. Get your needles ready. What do you want to start pumping through 'em first?"

"Sally Wildfire—" The scientist reached into her bag.

"It's Sally Coscan, you cunt! Get it straight."

"Um, apparently." The woman drew a short stack of papers from the bag. "These documents are signed by some of the highest medical officials of the Tribunals." She held the papers up. By now, Sally's eyes had adjusted better. One of the woman's shoulders actually did sit higher than the other, out of some kind of deformity, maybe from an old injury. "They give me authorization to determine whether or not you are, in fact, Sally— formerly of the Wildfire family of the Secret Police—and from there, to continue the research your mother began, and to figure out what exactly you've become. The woman to whom those scientists issued these papers got halfway here, in a van not unlike the one that brought you here. My associates and I met her on the way, acquired those papers, and drove the rest of the way here in her van."

Sally stared, not understanding. The scientist drew out a sheet from beneath the table and tossed it over Sally's body. She arranged it, careful not to touch her. It was comforting to see the lady was still cautious.

"I mean to inject you with a tranquilizer that will make you docile for several hours. I'm sorry, but that really will be necessary for this to work."

"For what to work?"

"Once the tranquilizer kicks in, I'll go back upstairs and tell them my tests were inconclusive, and I need to take you back with me to my own facility, where more accurate tests can be performed." She'd already fished out her needle, preparing the injection. Without taking her eyes from the syringe, she said, "You will be unbound and far away from here by the time this wears off. At that point, if you ever want to see your husband again, you'll follow my instructions, which include not killing me or my associates."

Sally hadn't breathed during this explanation. Now she took a deep breath and let the scientist—or whoever the hell she was—brush the sheet away from her arm and inject her. She felt little more choice or hope than before, but this was an improvement.

For what seemed like a few minutes, the scientist watched Sally attentively.

Several times Sally spoke, felt like she was forming coherent words, even *heard* them coming from her own mouth. Then she couldn't remember what she'd said. Probably asking more about who this woman was, or how long it would take the tranquilizer to kick in. The last couple of times she spoke, she thought the scientist smirked. Then the scientist turned back into a set of echoing feet in the darkness. Sally's head fell back. Those last moments, alone with the dimmed lamp, were the worst. Then the scientist came back with the two field agents, and two assistants Sally didn't recognize. Metal bars unlocked and slid back, then the table folded into a gurney.

After the basement's harsh light, the sun didn't sting so badly, even though she hadn't seen it in days. When her head rolled to the side, she saw some of the same kids in the fenced-in playground from the day she'd arrived. A few of them ran to the edge of the fence to gawk at her. The attendant parents looked up curiously, but didn't move to chastise their children. Sally didn't mind them now, maybe because she was being taken away from them.

Yeah, she was definitely feeling that tranquilizer. It reminded her a little of the few times she'd gotten falling down drunk at Cliff's, and Rob had needed to carry her home, except she didn't feel like her head was being dribbled around like a basketball. Physically, she actually felt pretty good. Only her immobility was uncomfortable, but she didn't feel like moving around a lot anyway.

As they slid her into the back of a new van, she glimpsed the driver up front. Something about him was out of place. He was dark-skinned with long, tangled hair. His street clothes hung a size or two too big on him. It must have been the drugs, but every pock and mark and angle of his skin looked like a separate particle floating through the soupy ether of the whole.

Sally thought of the scientist geeking out over the color spectrum of her veins and capillaries, and almost wanted to laugh. From back here, she couldn't see any of the driver's veins or capillaries. Outside, the scientist exchanged a few final words with the field agents. The van's rear doors closed. The two assistants strapped down the gurney, then they both sat back against the side of the van. The driver turned back. A pair of deep, grim, brown eyes flashed across her from a sharp face. Then he stared forward.

The scientist climbed into the front passenger seat, and off they went—into the woods and down the mountain. Before slipping out of consciousness, Sally realized why the driver's skin had so fascinated her. It wasn't because she was tripping balls. There was a subtle difference to the makeup of the pigmentation—different from just anyone of whatever color you saw on the street, certainly unlike these Spirelights they rode with. She was familiar enough with it, though it was usually accompanied by powerful, supple differences of movement, from a subtly different bone structure that this young man lacked.

The driver was a Schomite—a *civilian* Schomite.

WHEN THE MAN COMES AROUND

ONE

Rob heard nothing but the nighttime Tennessee forest noises. It was perfect, while it lasted.

Somewhere between here and the motel, someone's footsteps didn't miss all the leaves. Rob's nose told him it was a man, still far away. He left his blades sheathed and spread his coat across the earth patch he'd cleared to sleep on. The easy manual process relaxed him. That wasn't so great, it turned out, because all his latest scrapes and strains and bashed bits finally snuck up on him. The nastiest early injuries—the ones from the Carters' place—hardly bothered him anymore. You knitted quicker once the fire of the Crimbone trail blazed in your veins. He'd almost forgotten that in the last four years. Moments of soothing calm now seemed alien.

Sometimes, the other Crimbone spoke an ancient

Deschembine language he'd never heard or read, made of sounds he couldn't imagine his own vocal cords forming. Remelea understood all those languages, so of course she'd keep an ear out on his behalf.

The man stepped into the clearing, blade drawn.

"I was trying to talk with these woods before going to sleep," said Rob.

"Yeah," said the man. "*Trying.* You're a fledgling. That's all you can do is try…or talk to your Familiar." The man said it like he was the first to figure that out. He must be one of the new ones.

"*I was about to say,*" Rob went on, "it has a harder time squeezing words out around here. Too cramped. Doesn't like being cut off from what's supposed to be the rest of it—what's left, that is—like a series of balkanized islands, between all this zigzagging concrete and metal."

Rob said it through his teeth, holding the intruder's eyes like the forest's plight was the poor bastard's fault. He didn't reach for his knives yet. Instead, he let his breath out slowly, then relaxed and smiled. "So, what did the forest tell you, to come get your nuts sliced off? Or was that just some of the liquor back at the motel? Last little bit of advice, you wanna impress some bitch with your cock size, stay in bed and stick it where it belongs, and speak for—"

With a roar, the man shot at him like a bullet, knife aimed dead center. The blades of Magur Sevi shrieked free. The attacker's knife dipped under them, then up in a lethal maneuver. Old World metal clanged once, then Rob's left blade crunched through the man's breastbone.

The handle twisted, splitting the ribcage in two. Rob gave himself only a moment to feel the attacker's death shudders, then jerked and spun back, still snarling. His own kind's deaths were a pale glimmer of a Spirelight glow. It was still a sensation he didn't want to get too much of a taste for.

The man dropped to his knees, muttered, "A fucking fledgling..." then fell flat on his face.

Rob let the blood dry on the left blade before sheathing both. The blades were thirstier for Spirelights, but for now they drank whatever blood he left on them. By the time he next drew them, the metal would have absorbed the stains. For now, he whipped his coat up over his shoulder and walked further into the woods, away from the corpse. He got twenty feet, flung it down, and started clearing a new earth patch with his boot.

Through the trees were the faint lights of civilization, which no longer mattered any more than the leaky corpse. He'd have to strip it before setting out tomorrow, make it easier on all the scavenger critters who'd sniff it out. Hey, it was one way to tell the forest thanks, right?

Hey, us Crimbone…Say what you will about us, but no wild animal's ever claimed we weren't good eatin'.

Wait, who the hell had first said that? Not Jesse or Zane way back when, and no one in this pack now. Oh yeah, wait…*Scaling the botanicopolis of rich, pulpy vines that cascaded beneath the looming mountain peaks, jutting at such angles as the gravity of this world would have forbidden.*

He and Louis hadn't strictly needed to scale the vines. They could have just hiked another few miles northeast, then another two miles northwest, where the smooth forest trail led straight up the mountainside. They decided on this trail, though, because it was less dangerous than the mountain-rimals that hunted those woods. They could try to kill themselves on savage thrills another day. An outbreak threatened to get its hooks into the whole village. The blend-lady said medicine should be easy to whip up, except she was short on a rare liquid, the nearest known springs for which were atop the peaks of those mountain ranges. Rob and Louis weren't the only Crimbone who settled amongst those villagers, but they were the ones to look at each other, not exchange a word, and volunteer to make the run for the blend-lady.

Once they pulled themselves up onto the meadowy peak, Louis peered back at the forests down the slope, still wary of lurking menace. "Hey, say what you will about the Crimbone, no beast ever accused us of not being tasty."

Right. How long ago had he dreamed that? *Dream* was the right word for it, mostly. How else could Louis have been there so often, both of them back in ancient Deschemb? Except you didn't wake up from *dreams* with stretched, sore limbs like you'd actually just spent hours climbing through those vines.

Rob wasn't in Deschemb. He was in Tennessee. He tried to clear his head for the forest again.

Tomorrow he'd lead his pack to a nearby mountain of this world. The fighting would be good. The forest didn't mention the outcome, any more than his own body told him how long a given ache or stiffness would last. It didn't tell him if Sally would be there.

*Beyond approval or disapproval…*That's what he'd felt when Pittsburgh reacted to him, like he and the spirits spoke on some purified, naturally flowing level, opening up a new world of power and possibilities.

Tennessee had been hostile to the Crimbone when he'd passed through with Sally years back, still searching for what had turned out to be Postville, Florida. It hadn't been hostile to the pack. It didn't even seem to recognize him from back then. That was before Sally had told him about how the Tribunals held Spirelight lands, through geometry, geography, and infrastructural manipulation, from the homesteads. That's how Rob had gotten his pack this far through the state, after Puttergong had led him and the others to its borders.

If the Secret Police brought Sally to Tennessee, that's where they'll have taken her: to the homestead. Now they'd all but found the place. Tomorrow's mountain would surely be grateful for blood to drink, though Rob doubted it would care if it was Crimbone or Spirelight.

The Pittsburgh pack had followed him out of the city in a caravan of motorcycles, vans, and cheap, fast, souped-up cars. He recalled the cracked leather smell of Zane's jeep and Jesse's big red van—the *Big Red Beast*, they'd called the latter. Zane had explained a bit of what monsters he'd tricked those vehicles out to be in a pinch. How many of this pack's rides were similarly tricked out? No matter how battered the vehicles looked, most of them ran super quiet, and on something other than gasoline, by the strange smell of the exhaust. Remelea's beat-up black Camaro led the way with Rob riding shotgun, watching the skies and telling her where to turn when the black shape above veered one way or the other.

At the second rest stop, the first challengers had stepped forward. People noticed that the car in front followed a shape in the sky—a fat bat-like shape everyone knew from their own fledgling days. New ones had joined them at the first rest stop, and they might have guessed the Familiar was Remelea's. Everyone from Pittsburgh knew she was full-fledged, though, so some challengers lined up to see what their new leader had in him. Actually, you wouldn't exactly call what they did *lining up*. Rob couldn't remember who'd swung first, or at what point Remelea had leapt in. He'd looked forward to seeing her in action since meeting her. Once it happened, he was too busy with his end of the fight to watch. It was enough that someone fought at his side.

As they pulled out afterwards, he growled, "If they had a shot in hell at me, you should've helped them."

"Oh, don't be such a fucking martyr, just 'cause you didn't get to find out if you could have taken 'em all. I can tell you this, though, you couldn't've. You've kept in fighting shape, but…man, you really are rusty as shit with those blades."

He peered hard at her. "Thought you said you'd turn on me if you saw me fuck up with 'em."

"Uh-huh. That's what I said, and that's what I meant. You've got a style all your own, there's no denying that. It's a nasty one. Unpredictable as hell, too." She watched the road quietly for a moment, then shook her head. "A fucking fledgling…Hey, I hear you were trained by Jesse Karn and Zane Rochester."

"Not exactly. They were the first of us I got to know, once I found out what I am. That wasn't long enough to get anything you'd call *formal training*."

"Holy shit." All she could do for a second was gape.

"You're telling me you haven't even—*do you even know what's supposed to come next after your Second Call?*"

"You know, in all the learning I've gotten hold of, that's always been a real frustrating missing puzzle piece."

"*Yeah, and there's a reason for that, jackass!* Okay, let me put it in idiot-speak for you. Your life leading up to your First Call, then whatever your Familiar puts you through to bring you to your Second—that's all supposed to put you through a ringer so you *think* you're a ready-to-go Crimbone badass. That's when your big Crimbone brothers and sisters take you off to put you through the *real* ringer. We don't talk about that training—not 'til we've got you in front of it with no way out—and we sure as shit don't write anything down about it. The results should speak for themselves."

"Guess that's one way to keep an oral tradition alive."

She batted her eyelashes and grinned wickedly. "In more ways than one."

Rob tried to ignore the inuendo. He twisted his neck and shoulders 'til he got the crackles and pops he was looking for. "Hell, maybe that's what this is. It just came together kinda different for me. Hey, better late than never, right?"

She kept shaking her head, slowly. Her eyes were calmer now, though, deeper in thought. "It still doesn't make any sense…Some of your movements back there—"

"Where'd I learn 'em? I try answering that, you'll *really* call me crazy. Anyway, right now I need to be able to lead them, and it looks like I'm just gonna have more and more of 'em to lead. Sure, any pack can dog-pile any leader and slice him up. The trick is to keep them from figuring that out." He stopped talking and stared at his hands.

"Go ahead," she whispered. "I already told you how long I'll be here at your side—on those terms and nothing else. So just say it."

"I don't feel like I've earned this."

She shrugged. "Victory's something you earn after you get it."

"I'll have to turn that one over in my head a little."

Several hours after that first rest stop, he told Remelea about Sally. Yeah, he'd said she'd find out when they got there, but stringing her out like that was never gonna work. She was too smart, for one thing. Besides, she was one of his kind, and she was acting like a companion, not a suspicious underling or blind zealot, or worse, some kind of mentor. For lone companionship, she was a huge improvement over Puttergong.

"Yeah," she said, "I've heard of that girl, though some of the rumors say it's a boy. Weird. They're all scared of her, you know. Her own people, I mean. Some of 'em don't believe she exists. The believers think she's turning *into* a Crimbone or something, is gonna come back and bite them all in the ass somehow."

"That's what her family thought. Didn't realize my wife and I were such a popular couple."

"So, how many actual Crimbone women have you known?" When he didn't answer, she went on, "So she's been with you all these years, the two of you hiding out…Yeah, that makes perfect sense somehow."

"You don't think it's a horrible blasphemy, an abomination?"

"Maybe I would, if someone had just told me about it. Actually seeing it, seeing you…Hell, the world's changing, and I don't just mean the way time changes cultures and the people in 'em. Haven't you felt it? Over the last few years, the Old World energy that brought us here has been waking up and getting stronger, mixing with the energy of this world in new ways. Different people feel it differently. Don't ask me to explain what it means, but…it feels like there's a new *kind* of natural being created, like this and some other realm are blurring together little by little." She smiled at him. "Maybe that takes a new kind of High Natural."

"Might help if I had a better idea what the fuck a High Natural's supposed to be in the first place."

Remelea thought long and hard before answering. "That's the thing. There's no real *supposed to be* about it. You're not some prophesized messiah or any of that arrogant Earth-line bullshit, so get that out of your head right now. What you are is a mathematical evolutionary eventuality, something that blows in on a perfect storm. What you—what your existence—means for the rest of us…well, we'll see. It's as much cause to be scared shitless as it is for celebration."

"So why are you so set on helping me?"

"I told you, I was getting bored." She elbowed him in the ribs. "Plus, it turns out, I kinda like you."

"Thanks," he said. "Guess you're still disappointed, finding out how I just ran and hid for so long."

"You keep giving yourself shit like that, I'm gonna punch you in the head. Nah, I just think you're an insane fucking bastard."

"The kettle duly notes the pot's observation, ma'am."

After every stop, the motley caravan rolled out with more Crimbone sticking to it. Whenever they saw the twin blades, it seemed to renew everyone else's faith, at least 'til the next time some newer pack members started whispering about the lead car following a shape in the sky. Oh, that led to Rob working some rust from his blade-work, alright. More and more, though, he realized it wasn't his blades keeping them in line. It was what caught fire in his gut and came out in his voice like dragon fire when he spoke to them, more galvanizing each time, something greater than his slender frame should have held. That flame, it seemed, roared higher and brighter with every stretch of land that sent more Crimbone.

Their last stop before this one had been another dilapidated rest area, a mile from the state line. "You're takin' us into Tennessee?" one of the newer recruits had growled. "That's one of the nastiest, best-held Spirelight states in the South."

Technically, Puttergong's taking us into Tennessee. Rob said instead, "That's right." By then, the last of his Earth-line-instilled self-doubt was gone from his voice. He strode back and forth, sure to look every face in the eye. "That's why we're not taking this road in."

"Fine, then. What road?" It was that one upstart, again.

Rob stopped to meet the speaker's gaze. "I don't know yet. We got any history buffs around here?"

Behind him, Remelea had leaned against her Camaro, smirking with her arms folded across her chest. She shoved off and stepped up to his side. "What do you need to know?"

He lowered his voice a little. "When did Tennessee first become a Spirelight-controlled state?"

"Days of reconstruction, after the war between the states."

He looked back at the pack and spotted two younger ones— a guy and a girl—who'd started forward before Remelea claimed his attention. There was some special brightness in their eyes that he liked. "You two. Strike out and search around 'til you find the nearest library. Might wanna grab a current atlas somewhere on the way, but what I really need are old maps—with road and street names—of Tennessee before, during, and after the reconstruction. Don't use the internet. The library should have an archive of actual old maps—of this area and the surrounding states. Figure libraries still have photocopy machines, but if the old ink doesn't take with those, smuggle the originals out if you have to. You have five hours. Go." Once the kids left, he took another stroll back and forth in front of his pack. "I don't suppose anyone's got anything special to add about Spirelight homesteads?"

The one who answered was the dark man he'd first had pegged as the likeliest challenger back in Pittsburgh. "Why are you so curious about Spirelight homesteads?"

Rob looked out hard over all their faces. Now was

the time to say it. "Because we're gonna hit one, in Tennessee." He stepped up to the man, put a hand on his shoulder, and led him off towards a nearby building. "Remelea, keep this lot wrangled for me for a few minutes, will you?" Once he and the man were out of sight, he said, "Know something helpful about Spirelight homesteads, do you, friend?"

Now that they were alone, the man no longer seemed so confident or defiant. He kept shaking, like his answer might mean life or death. Finally, he nodded.

"Yeah, how's that?"

"'Cause I escaped from one once. You won't meet many Crimbone who can say that, fewer who'll talk about it."

"Well then," said Rob. "If you could pull that off, I bet you got out of there with all sorts of interesting information under your belt."

The man held the stare. "Yeah. Before I tell you, you wanna tell me what the Crimbone High Natural needs with a map...or how that's gonna get us through a state that hates us?"

"Here's a little secret. Those lands don't hate us. They're under the control of Spirelight magic, the divine power from their gods, the same gods who sent 'em to wipe us out, who fill 'em with the glow. What they've done to the place makes it a spiritual minefield for Schomites, Crimbone especially. Once we have those maps, we're gonna look at 'em side by side, figure out where the Spirelights have mucked with the land, its routes, all that, and we're gonna find a safe path through that minefield, to the homestead."

The man's face tightened and his back straightened. "How's this? If this works—if your wild idea gets us within ten miles of it—I'll tell you everything I know that might help about Spirelight homesteads."

Rob clapped the guy on the shoulder again. "Mister, I got a feeling you and me are gonna be pals."

Once the kids returned with the maps, it took Rob, Remelea and the dark man about two hours to chart the course they needed. It turned out the latter two had some topography experience, or it might have taken longer. Their grim faces kept telling him, *You'd better be right about this.*

Before getting the caravan back on the road, Remelea had announced that everyone had best keep a low profile throughout the journey 'til further notice. "If you feel or spot any Spirelight activity on the way," she said, "resist the urge to attack. Don't present a threat unless they do. On the way we're taking, they shouldn't…won't…until we want 'em to. We don't want them to 'til we hit their homestead."

It took three hours for the caravan to find its way to the point over the state line for the secret trail they needed, a network of back roads and lonely highways that dodged major cities and towns with populations larger than two thousand. They met no trouble, though the humid summer air thickened oppressively, the deeper they went.

As night fell, Remelea slowed down. "Hold up that map for me for a second."

He did, and almost reached up for the overhead light.

"I don't need the light," she said, eyes darting back and forth from him to the road, "and neither should you. Just point to the general radius we've narrowed the homestead location down to."

He pointed.

She nodded and fixed her eyes silently ahead again, 'til the next exit sign. "We're…within twenty miles of it." She no longer said *If you're right about this*. The fixated crackle in her eyes was telltale enough. She felt it too, closer and closer.

I've actually made it this far. I've pulled this off. We've pulled this off. It's gonna work. Hang on, Sally.

Since crossing the state line, there'd been no sign of Puttergong. Was that because of the poisoned lands they passed into? Thanks to the fancy trick with the maps, they no longer needed the creature as a guide, but its absence still made Rob nervous.

"You still haven't told them about her," Remelea said after miles of silence. "You're going to have to tell them something, you know, before we do this."

They didn't speak again 'til they stopped along with the rest of the pack and took over the roadside motel. As the pack gathered in the parking lot, the first thing Rob did was to seek out the dark man.

"I've brought us this far," he said to the man, again out of earshot of everyone.

"That you have…High Natural. There's no doubt about that."

"Wherever that homestead is, it's a stone's throw away. It won't be any trouble for a pack this size to find from here. Or to take it, if whatever you know is worth shit."

"It'll be up a pretty big hill."

"I was hoping for something a little more specific."

"You're the one with the fancy custom map. We all know the kinds of weird signs to look for. I can already feel this safe little secret trail of ours about to run out, so I damn well know so can you."

Rob's eyes burned into the other, scorching away any hint of challenge. "Cold feet, old man?"

The dark man sighed. "After a couple hundred feet, the ground will level out real fast—in a way that'll feel *really* unnatural, coming from any direction but the main drive. Like you'll be climbing a forest hill that feels like it's supposed to go up a few hundred more feet. Then all of a sudden it doesn't. Either like you stepped through a portal into someplace else, or like a big razor just came down from the sky and sliced the rest of it off. There'll be a big grassy clearing. In the middle, we'll find two strips of dwellings, single, long buildings like townhouses. The strips shoot off at odd angles that'll make your head feel…even funnier to look at. On either side, they'll be split into two, maybe three buildings. Down at the end of that, there'll be a large building, like a church or a courthouse, rolled into one with an indoor country club. All the local leaders and most of the fighters will be in there. Some of the fighters'll be patrolling the woods."

Rob visualized all this and nodded. "How many fighters are we talking?"

"Maybe less than a dozen, maybe a lot. Depends on the day, really. If they've gotten word about us—"

"They haven't. How much is a lot? Enough to outnumber us?"

"Maybe. They won't be scouting the main drive too closely. They expect intruders to sneak through the woods—"

"Right. But if we all take the driveway and one of those patrollers catches wind—"

"They wouldn't attack 'til they spread the word to the others, 'til they're all closed in. Once they surround us, they shadow in a held formation 'til we cross the best spot for them to swarm in and dog-pile us."

"No way could they sneak up on us! We'd smell their glows."

The twisting line of the dark man's mouth wasn't reassuring. "Not if they keep their circle spread wide, just out of range. Once they close it, we won't smell 'em fast enough for any initiative."

This startled Rob in a new way. How far was *out of range* for these guys? Back in Postville, he'd sensed the intruders at the Carters' house all the way from Cliff's. Now he peered out through the woods, nostrils flaring. No danger yet, but it wouldn't be long before—

"What's behind the dwellings?"

"Gardens and recreational areas."

"Walk out of there with any other information I ought'a know?"

"How 'bout a list of the locations of Spirelight homesteads all over the country?"

Rob grinned. He called the pack together. Remelea stood closest to him, watching expectantly. He figured it was time to take her advice. "If you've heard about me," he said, "you've heard the rumors of the *altered* one…the *tainted* one. A Spirelight girl who's not a Spirelight anymore, someone her own people are afraid of, because of what she's becoming. They should be scared of her…as they should be scared of me, of us, fellow Crimbone, of what we're about to become, all of us. But right now, they're keeping her captive. We're going to set her free, unharmed. Any Spirelights who get in our way won't be so lucky."

They didn't turn on him as one, so he knew he still had them. By now, he knew, there'd be no in-between, not over so radical a revelation. He wanted to keep going 'til they reached the homestead, make the siege tonight. Before he could signal the pack to get back on the road, though, the Familiar flapped down onto the hood of Remelea's car in front of everyone.

"No one's goin' no further tonight. Y'all's gettin' too pooped to take on a whole homestead of glowsticks, whether all your piss an' vinegar lets ye see it or not. An' seein' as I'm doin' the real trailblazin' here, I says y'all ain't seein' no more trail 'til you get some R&R. That, by the way, stands for Roughhousin' an' Ragin' 'til you pass out an' get a few hours' sleep."

The collective murmur was a strange mix of confusion and relief. Puttergong's idea of R&R quickly turned risky in the *staying under the radar* department— hopefully nothing too out of keeping with the local hillbilly hell-raising. Rob and Remelea went over a few more possible points of necessity, after which Rob slipped off alone into the woods. Hopefully tonight's intruder would be the only dissenter.

The blades felt heavier than ever on Rob's hips. Those blades had led Crimbone in the Old World, had cut the Schomites free, both from the Spirah Empire and the outer beings with which the Spirelights consorted. *A fledgling*, they called him, because there was still a Familiar to guide him, along with the voices of states and towns. Eventually, he'd make his Third Call. He knew what the First and Second Calls were, because he'd made them years ago, within nights of each other. Apparently, it took months for most fledglings, sometimes years.

Yards away, the last upstart's dead bowels were still emptying, stinking up the woods. Rob picked up his coat again and went further. Hopefully he wouldn't have to walk much more before he could get a night's sleep. He spread his coat again and tried not to think about the Third Call. He tried not to think about a lot of things, like tomorrow's fight, or what would come after.

He tried not to think about Remelea. Hopefully she was back at the motel, having her way with some wolf of a Crimbone man, after downing a bottle of bourbon and punching the shit out of several competitors. Now wasn't the time for her to think of the man she followed, of the killing she'd take part in tomorrow, to save the life of a Spirelight girl...how the bearer of the blades of Magur Sevi loved that Spirelight girl, and would lead Crimbone to their deaths for her.

Once a Crimbone High Natural gets where he's goin', ain't no one gonna give ye shit for your choice in women.

TWO

Before he got far, another set of feet sounded from the direction of the motel. This one didn't even bother to mask its steps. Rob's eyes narrowed. His hands wandered towards his blades. Didn't these bastards have the Old Lords-given sense to know when their High Natural needed some fucking space? The intruder drew nearer. Rob recognized their scent and his blood blazed a different shade of red.

She almost stepped on the dead guy. "Dude! Maybe try to not kill *too* many more of 'em, at least before tomorrow's fight?"

"So tell 'em to quit making me. That shit's getting old."

Remelea sighed heavily. "It might not be that simple."

"What the fuck are you talking about?"

"You found us a safe route through Spirelight-poisoned land, but we're still on Spirelight-poisoned land. The Spirelight glow *lives in the air we're breathing right now*, without any Spirelights around to cut it out of. The longer we're all here, the worse it'll make maggots writhe in everyone's brains."

"And now they all have booze. Great." That had been Puttergong's idea, hadn't it? Figured. "I could use a damn drink myself. You didn't happen to bring a bottle along, did you?"

"See one on me?" She splayed her long, smooth, toned bare arms. "Sorry, man. Hell, that was the best thing your Familiar could've done—having everyone throw a party, let off some steam."

"Yeah, well, don't worry; it'll all be over soon enough."

She moved towards him faster, quieter, like something closing in on its prey, as though they weren't already looking each other right in the eye. "You think so?"

"Yeah, soon as I have my wife back."

"So what then? You expect to just go back to Florida, leave all this behind?"

Rob almost said she could go wherever she wanted, and so could the others. Then he grimaced and squeezed his aching forehead. "I know! My family just got bigger, and they're all expecting Daddy to provide."

"You will…and you'll…you'll have Sally to help."

"Will I?"

"If she's as strong as you say, she'll come to accept this like you have. You're the High Natural, she's the Altered Spirelight, the Spirelight who's not a Spirelight, whatever we—whatever she decides to call herself."

"Or she'll decide it's not for her, and she'll split, and she'll be strong and survive whatever other trail she takes, for as long as she can. You think I haven't thought this might mean losing her, no matter what I do? I just gotta make sure she's safe!"

Something caught in Rob's throat. In all this excitement, he only now stopped to think what this would mean between him and Sally afterwards. Who knew what she'd been through since he last saw her, or where her mind would be when they next saw each other? Remelea was right. Everything he'd done to get this far wasn't going away, for anyone. This wouldn't be like Postville all over again. He couldn't pressure Sally into staying with something like this; not like he'd pressured her into staying in Florida. He knew she'd never completely forgiven him for that, and she knew he'd never forgiven himself, even if it had been their only shot at the time.

"Right," said Remelea. "So you can accept maybe losing her, if you know it means she's alive and safe somewhere. That's sweet man. Really. So, say you keep tabs on her, and it turns out she can't keep up with what this world's about to turn into? You gonna drag us all off on another trail to bail her ass out again?"

"Hey, what do you mean, *what this world's about to turn into?* Never mind. First thing's first, right?"

"Right," she whispered, her gaze drifting around.

"Uh, can we walk a little further and talk?" he asked. "That corpse back there is really starting to stink."

Yeah, great idea, walk further into the dark forest, with Remelea and the doubts in his head she'd just jabbed at. Maybe she thought the same thing when she nodded and moved past him. He followed, trying not to let her hear his rising breath. If she heard his hammering heart, he could lie, claim it was from the fight he'd just been in.

From the moment Rob met Sally, he'd barely looked at another woman. So far as he knew, that depth of true, instinctive, body and soul devotion was unheard of, maybe unnatural or even creepy, but there it was. Somehow, she'd just become the *only* woman to ever register to him as one, a creature to whom the man in him responded as a mate. In retrospect, all the girls before her seemed like strange physical beings with which he'd tried to feel less alone. Now they were apart for the first time in years, and all this tortured adrenaline left him horny. Sally was the first woman he'd met who was descended from the Old World like him, at least that he knew of. Remelea wasn't the only woman among the pack, just the one he couldn't stop looking at. It didn't help that she looked right back at him the same way, only a lot more comfortably…the first Schomite woman he met, the first *Crimbone* woman. Now their walk brought them closer together, side by side. Keeping his eyes off her didn't help, because of that maddening scent of hers.

So what? He'd known Remelea for a few days. What did she know about anything he and Sally had gone through together? He took a deep breath.

It felt good to have another Crimbone for a friend. He hadn't had one of those since Jesse and Zane. Before that, there was only Louis, who might still be alive if he'd just brought Rob up to speed on any of this when he had the chance. What would Louis say about all this? There was a time after his death when Rob would ask himself that question, and something in his head would answer in Louis' voice. It was so clear, he sometimes swore Louis was right next to him, hanging back just shy of the corner of his eye as they walked, shooting the shit like old times. Rob still asked for that voice sometimes. He hadn't gotten an answer since Brattleboro.

Shivering, he looked at Remelea. "So what's it like, growing up knowing about it?"

"That's a weird one to try answering. What would you like to know?"

"Well, how much were you allowed to know before you were cast off into the world?"

"The basics, I guess. Most of what I knew, I figured out by watching the grown-up Crimbone around me. I don't remember much except general facts, from being a kid I mean. Hell, I was twelve when I was cast off, and I barely remember the days between that and my First Call."

"What do you remember?"

"Enough to know I don't want to remember more. This far enough out for you?"

She moved forward 'til her breasts pressed against his chest. Okay, there went pretending. At least she hadn't pressed close enough to feel his raging boner. He smelled her arousal, though, and she probably smelled his. When he tasted her breath, he shoved her up against the nearest tree and pushed her mouth open with his. Their tongues met in a sloppy tangle.

Her legs wrapped around him. His crotch flexed against hers. He swore his dick was about to punch through both their jeans. He jerked her head back by the hair and bit her neck. She let out a high moan. This time, he forced a slower, deeper kiss on her. He clawed down her tank top and pinched a nipple. Her fingers scratched his scalp, then tightened around his short-clipped hair. Her other hand squeezed his ass. Her hands, the way they touched…how she tasted, how her body felt against him…

He broke it off and pushed himself back. She

growled, tried to lunge at him, but he held her in place at arm's length. Finally, she settled down. He let go, stepped back, and turned away.

"Sorry," he muttered, shaking his head, wanting to shake out everything that had happened since leaving Cliff's back building. "I shouldn't've gotten your hopes up like that."

"Don't be sorry yet," she whispered, poising dangerously.

Damnit, why did that have to sound so good? He bit back a snarl. "Please don't try. I like you. I really do. I don't wanna have to hurt you."

"You've been hurting me since you told me about her, you sonofabitch." She paused to chew on her lower lip. "You know…it wouldn't be untrue to her. When you're with her, there's no other world, no Schomites or Spirelights, none of the responsibilities you've been running away from this whole time. I get that. But she ain't here right now, and that other world, the world outside of what you two create for each other…well, it's real, and so is everything happening in it because of what you've started. I'm the one who's here facing it with you."

He'd have backhanded anyone else for a line like that…except it wasn't bullshit coming from her. For all he knew, it might be commonly accepted logic among their kind. It was for some Earth-liners. Not for him, though. "I know. Thanks."

"Yeah, and tomorrow you'll have her back, along with whatever's left of that world the two of you created, whatever there's still room for. She'll be there to help you deal with it."

"I'm not gonna just brush you aside, Remelea."

"Isn't that what you're doing now?"

"No, damnit! It's just…Ah, shit."

"All you wanna do tonight is dream of having her back."

I wanna do that, yeah, he thought. *I also wanna throw you on the ground and fuck you 'til you can't walk straight.* Instead, he asked, "So, will you still fight at my side tomorrow?"

She reached around to dust bits of bark off her back. She winced several times. "Of course." She squeezed his hand. "I'll see you in the morning, dude."

Once she vanished through the trees, he tried to clear his head. It wasn't happening. What the hell was wrong with him? Maybe what he really needed to do was just jerk off. He still tasted and smelled Remelea, still felt her, imagined letting her hands undo his jeans. As he reached for his belt buckle, a screechy, wheezy laugh sounded from the trees above.

Rob's crotch cooled off like someone had poured ice water on it. "Hi, Puttergong."

The Familiar laughed hysterically, 'til Rob scanned the ground for something to throw. "Y'know, I was startin' to enjoy the show down there, but I'm kinda glad you crazy kids broke it off when ye did."

"Why's that?"

"'Cause I sorta wanna stick around an' see what happens next."

"What the hell does one thing have to do with the other?"

"Oh, you'll see." Puttergong yodeled, "*Yooouuu'll*

seee…"

Rob peered up into the trees, fixed the Familiar in its beady, glittering eyes, and braced himself. "Tell me now, Puttergong," he said through his teeth. "Tell me honestly. Is Sally still alive?"

"Why you askin' stupid fuckin' questions like that for, Biter-Boy?"

"You have me where you wanted me, you piece of shit. I did everything you said, and ain't you fuckin' proud, even after I told you—"

"Biter-Boy, will you quit that shit? All that bitchin' an' moanin', after all I done for ye. Yeah, *you told me* what you wasn't gonna do. Then you wanted to know what you *had* to do to get done what ye wanted done. Just like always, you ain't done a damn thing since that weren't all you. Shit, boy, I can't help it if there ain't one without t'other, what ye want an' what you keep sayin' ye don't."

"So answer the fucking question."

"Yeah. Your Sally-Poach is alive, an' yeah, you'll see each other again, assumin' one of you don't get yer dumb selves killed first. That's the Old Lords' truth, an' even I don't swear in vain by them two cocksuckers. Hell, I'm 'bout the last dude to do that!"

"So, you are leading us to the right place."

"Oh, I'm leadin' ye to the right place. Now 'fore I go find me some R&R of my own, you got any more dumbshit questions?"

"Just one, then get lost so I can jerk off and get some sleep." Rob took a deep breath. "How did they find us? Why'd Postville betray us?"

"Postville didn't betray shit. Didn't I tell you that?

Nah, that lil' town never sent a damn thing your way you didn't want it to. Naw, you never said so, but the place heard ye screamin' it loud an' clear. Just like cute lil' Foxy-Girl back there knows how you wanna do every dirty thing you ever thought of to her—includin' all the shit you was always too sweet to do to your lil' Sally-Poach—then come up with a few new ones. You never said it to Postville, but Postville felt it bubblin' up, ready to explode, screamin' *git me the fuck out'a here so I can fuck some shit up an' be what I's s'posed to be!* An' Biter-Boy, don't even try tellin' me you thought for a minute you was gonna sit on yer ass in that shithole 'til ye got too old an' brittle to pop a boner.

"You needed out, but you wasn't gonna make your move, so long as Sally-Poach stayed safe an' sound. Hell, that town hadn't brung what ye really wanted, sooner or later, you'd'a flipped out and sliced up every livin' thing in sight. So the town let the word trickle out through the state, an' the state let it trickle out to everywhere else. An' well, it sent what you ordered. An' don't tell me it ain't felt great, swingin' an' hackin' with them blades again, grabbin' this world by the balls an' tellin' it what's what." Puttergong yodeled, "*He's got the whole world, by the balls, he's got the whooole world, by the balls…*"

"Fuckin' birdie—"

"Say what you want, Biter-Boy. The blood in your veins always tells what you really want. An' like I always tells ye…" Puttergong cackled, said in a high, sultry, mock-feminine voice, "*Aaahh'll seeee yeeeww in thuh mawnin', dewd,*" and flew off.

Standing still and alone, Rob muttered, "'Cause in

the end, blood writes the book."

THREE

Rob woke up to the sun's glare in his face. Old Lords, he could have picked a spot beneath thicker branches. He squeezed his eyes shut, though he was already pulling himself up. When he opened them, the light felt softer, probably because he was no longer staring directly at it. For a second, the forest looked still, dead, frozen, the yellowish coat of sunlight more like ice. Compared to his dreams, it looked dead, or at least in a coma.

Where had he gone in those dreams? What had he been doing? There'd been a lot of green. Other colors, all bright with life…but so much green, more shades than he could have imagined. The closest he could think of in this world was the first time he'd seen New Orleans, or northern Vermont in the summer. Neither compared. Everything in the dream forest had moved, or seemed to, because how could anything be still when the world was so alive, from soil to sky?

Back on the mountain in the Old World, in the doorway to the Spirelight temple…Rob shook himself and blinked. No, it hadn't been that old dream. Louis always showed up for that one. Anyway, now Rob was awake and looking for Sally. He stretched and flexed 'til he was fully awake, 'til *this* forest looked alive again. He was alive, and so was his wife. He'd see her soon.

He dusted leaves and dirt from his coat, slung it over his shoulder, and walked fast. The night before last, he'd slept in another forest and woken up stiff and sore as hell. There was some stiffness now, but it faded quickly.

Midway to the motel, a shape stretched on its side next to a tree. Rob kicked it lightly in the side. A young man rolled over, sat up, and nodded. The man was younger than Rob—probably the age Louis would be today—yet wore more scars. They were fainter and thinner than Rob's would ever be, more evenly scattered, worn more comfortably about the face, neck, and hands. The only really nasty ones covered the back of his right hand in a pale, puffy web. The kid was a full-fledged Crimbone—had made all three Calls, whatever the third entailed. Hell, if the kid survived the coming fight, maybe he could teach Rob a little of the ancient Crimbone language.

It was sad. Rob knew scattered bits of the civilian Schomite language, and there was an interracial language of ancient Deschembine, of which he knew a little more. Over the last four years, he'd learned the ancient Spirelight language the best. Sally had noticed his eagerness, to learn all he could of his heritage. She'd seen his frustration at how little was at his fingertips, so she'd taken to teaching him bit by bit. He'd absorbed it pretty well, better than any of the foreign language classes he'd barely passed in high school. The more he comprehended, though, the less he liked having it in his head.

The traditional Spirelight tongue was designed to

breed supremacist thinking in the speaker, to feed the old collective Spirelight god-complex. Teaching it to a non-Spirelight was the supreme blasphemy. You weren't even supposed to speak it around people not of the coterie. It was a language of *gods*, after all, passed down to their worldly acolytes. Growing up in the Wildfire household, there couldn't even be an Earth-line radio playing in the background while the family spoke to each other in the language of their race.

The kid stood up as straight as he could. He looked like he should be taller than Rob, but his spine hunched out halfway down his back. "Is it time, High Natural?"

"Call me Rob. What's your name?"

"Joel." Joel started pulling on his cheap, gray trench coat.

"Don't put your coat on yet," said Rob. "It's too hot to wear it when we don't need to."

Joel nodded and slung his coat over his shoulder the way Rob carried his, and they walked on. Rob tried to watch Joel's movements, get a sense of him, but the kid kept lagging behind. At first, Rob thought Joel wasn't as awake as he should be. Oh, right, it wouldn't be fitting to get ahead of the High Natural, or even to just walk and shoot the shit. Except, no, it wasn't etiquette or elitism. The Crimbone hadn't fallen *that* far.

Rob kept something Remelea had said close to his heart: *You're not some prophesized messiah or any of that arrogant Earth-line bullshit, so get that out of your head right now.*

Younger Crimbone like Joel seemed to feel differently. So how *were* you supposed to interact with someone—something—that galvanized your will, then swept it out along the trail in a tide of others, against all reason as you understood it? Either way, Rob dropped back and clapped Joel hard on the shoulder. Joel seemed to get the idea, and fell uneasily into line.

"So, where you from, Joel?"

"Abingdon."

"Abingdon, Virginia?"

Joel nodded.

"Shit, man, that's neutral territory."

Joel shrugged. "I have enough fun there 'til whenever the call of the trail draws me elsewhere."

"To where a Crimbone like you is needed, you mean."

"Yes, sir."

"Don't call me *sir*. You feel like you're needed here?"

"Abingdon set me towards Georgia, and Georgia brought me to you. Turned out, my scouting and map reading skills came in handy for you." This was one of the two youngsters who'd gone in search of the maps yesterday.

"Quite a little zigzag there," said Rob. "Do your instincts say this is what you should be doing, going off to risk your neck for a Spirelight girl?"

"I'm going to *risk my neck* for the High Natural—and not just any Spirelight girl, from all the stories I've heard."

"Do your instincts tell you to follow me? 'Cause a Crimbone going against his own instincts is useless to himself, useless to his pack, useless to the land. If your instincts tell you something that goes against what I tell you, just consider this a wrong turn you took and follow 'em somewhere else."

The second he said it, Rob saw that Joel had heard these words before, probably in his own fledgling days. That was funny, because Rob hadn't. Yet the knowledge felt at home in his heart and mind…like it was the *oldest* part of him. Through the trees and brush, he spotted the motel parking lot and the road beyond.

"Should we put our coats on yet?" asked Joel as their boots touched pavement.

"Might as well." Rob pulled on the duster. He didn't close it, but tugged it halfheartedly over the blades on his belt.

When he walked towards the motel's diner, Joel followed. There was more broken glass in the lot than Rob remembered, and plenty more banged-up cars. Along the nearest strip of rooms, a few windows were smashed. They found the diner almost empty. Joel moved towards a booth.

"C'mon, let's sit at the counter." Rob waited for the kid to come. "Guzzle some coffee, get your nerves going."

A waitress hurried over, said in an unnaturally small voice, "What can I get you boys?"

"Two coffees, and some biscuits an' gravy for me," said Rob. "The kid gets whatever he wants, too."

"I'll have biscuits an' gravy myself, ma'am," said Joel.

When the coffee came, Rob sniffed and added with his best smile, "I'll have one of your cigarettes while we're waiting, if you don't mind, darlin'."

The waitress handed him a cigarette and hurried off. It didn't take him long to gulp what must have been two pots of coffee. Breakfast tasted great, so Rob wished he could sit and savor it. After today, he and Sally could go and eat a big celebration breakfast, anywhere she wanted, except it had better be far from here. He saw the green from his dreams again. He had to remember how to get there. Sally would love that place.

When Rob and Joel walked out, the parking lot was filling up with Crimbone. None of them came within fifteen feet of Rob. Joel edged away, 'til he stood on the fringes of the crowd. Rob didn't look around for Puttergong. The creature would show up in the sky once Remelea's car was on the road, the others pulling out behind them.

Remelea was nowhere in sight, but Rob addressed the rest of them. "You assholes got any complaints left about what we're about to go do? 'Cause remember, I know the difference between the injuries done by Crimbone and those done by Spirelights. I find any Crimbone marks on the Altered Spirelight girl, whoever gave 'em goes up in the same flames as the pile of enemy corpses."

Out stepped the dark man. "These lands tell me to do no different than what you ask. Hell, things are changing. We've all known that for a while, felt the old energies mixing with the new, like it was creating some new kind of natural order. Maybe that just calls for a new kind of *High* Natural."

As if on cue, Remelea strutted from one of the rooms with broken windows. She stepped up to Rob's side and shot him a conspiratorial smile, which he shot right back. He went and pulled Joel back out of the crowd. The others held their ground when he drew near, but wouldn't make eye contact.

"Remelea, this is Joel. You two met?"

"I've seen the boy around," she said.

Something in her tone made Rob wonder if the two had fucked at some point. He looked at Joel and couldn't tell. "Well, he'll be riding with us today. You cool with that?"

Remelea's smirk widened. "No problem, boss."

In Remelea's car, Rob asked, "What happened at the motel last night?"

"Some hick didn't like the noise," said Remelea. "Turned into a pretty big fight and someone called the cops."

"Anyone get killed?"

"Crimbone or Earth-line?"

"I know none of ours got killed."

In some weird way, she looked reassured. "No, Rob, we didn't kill anyone. Probably not enough cops around here—Earth-line, anyway—to make that big a deal to us, even." She was quick from there with the details.

Rob imagined two or three cop cars showing up, saw the cops try to subdue the human wolves they found waiting, then all getting beaten into submission before anyone could call for backup. Some of those cops had gone for their guns, one or two maybe even clearing holsters. Then the strongest and fastest of the pack would have ahold of them. Later, the cops would swear that the nearest enemy had been yards away, just an instant ago. No way in hell anyone could've gotten in that close, that quick, but it happened.

Of course the cops couldn't tell their superiors down at the Sheriff's Office that the troublemakers at the motel had mopped the parking lot with them, then sent them crawling away, lucky to be alive. First off, they'd claim the motel trouble was a false alarm. Then they'd make something up about why they looked like two hundred pounds each of hamburger meat. None of them would speak, even amongst themselves, about how the human wolves were exactly that, of how those wolves had won thanks to something besides superior physical toughness…some agile, primordial drive fueling them, so they moved differently through time and space, like *something literally not of this world*. The motel staff now acted towards the Crimbone like medieval peasants under occupation.

Over time, more enforcers of Earth-line law would oppose the pack. An older, more powerful line had risen to overthrow them. They couldn't hide it forever. Rob saw the world at the top of that rise, green as his dreams. He and Sally could settle wherever they wanted in that world. Neither the Schomites nor the Spirelights would dare intrude. His hand curled around one of the knife handles in anticipation.

"So, are we almost there?" Joel asked from the back seat.

"Oh, yeah," Rob growled in a voice he'd never used before in this lifetime. "We're almost there."

FOUR

After several winding miles of a dirt road maze through the woods, they reached a wide spread of gravel that wasn't quite a parking lot. Off in the brush, a low wooden fence ran the length of the spread. On the other side, Rob heard the flow and tumble of a broad, deep creek. He got out, walked over, and found a break in the fence, past which a wooden bridge ran across to another dirt road. The way was made for large vehicles, like the vans some of the Crimbone drove. Rob heard the rest of the pack rumbling into the lot behind him. He stood watching the forest, listening to it. He turned as Remelea and Joel reached his side. The others gathered as near as they dared. Rob walked back and crossed the dirt road, into the sunlight.

Back up a stretch, there sat a small house where an old man toiled in a small garden. Rob crossed the yard. The little old man gaped dully up at him.

"Hey," Rob said, "hope me and my pals didn't scare you, when we all came blazing by like the Hell's Angels, I mean."

"No sir. You didn't stop to push into my business, so I ain't gonna push at yours."

"There folks 'round here like to push into your business?"

The man lowered his eyes and huddled smaller.

"Right," said Rob. "What can you tell me about those woods over there, up that trail past the creek?"

"Not much to tell. You won't see many of the folks who live 'round here goin' in there, not too far or high anyway. Sometimes hikers go in there. Sometimes they don't come out."

"Who owns the land?" Rob didn't like the taste of the phrase.

"Oh, some strange folks. City folks with city money, I guess. They like to own a stretch of woods and hills for 'emselves, you know, just for a place they can get away to. Mostly they keep to themselves."

Rob thanked the old man and walked back to the pack. "Joel, Remelea, you guys come with me. We're going straight up that trail. Four more of you come with us. Who here's got the best chops at playing hide an' seek with Spirelights in deep forest?"

Two women and one man snarled and smiled eagerly.

Rob signaled them in close. "Divide up the rest of the pack between you. Circle the foot of the hill, one group in either direction. You know that feeling of the pressure change, climbing to higher altitudes? You'll feel something like that before you even start to climb…except this'll feel weirder, like it's fucking with your heads, fogging up your brains so you can't hear the voice of the hill. You're probably already feeling it some. You'll reach a point where that feeling drops off. Just hold your groups strong. Whatever you do, don't start uphill 'til then. Then find the right paths uphill along those lines. Don't expect clear, physical paths. Watch for patrols, but don't go sniffing for them. If they find you, they won't expect you to catch their glow like most places, so they'll try to sneak up on you. Just let 'em think that 'til it's too late. If there's a lot of 'em, take the leaders out first. Everyone here knows how to sniff out and take out high-voltage electric fences, security sensors, shit like that?"

When everyone nodded, he went on, "Let their underlings see it, thrash the ones you don't kill straight off into a panic. That way, even if they do spot us headed up the trail, they won't be able to organize enough to outflank us. After that, find your way to the clearing from behind. Regroup there, find the three quickest routes to that main building with the least chance of civilians spotting you. Get inside the building and secure it. The woman we're here for will probably be hidden. Leave finding her to me, even if you feel the *altered glow* nearby. Find whoever's in charge and drag them out front. I'll be waiting." He indicated Remelea and Joel. "By then, we'll have taken care of whoever we run into on the main stretch up. I'll handle everything else 'til I say otherwise."

Old Lords, Rob hoped he was calling all this right! When he gripped his knife handles, he felt stronger. In the eyes of his fellow Crimbone, he saw that they would obey. He felt stronger still. He gave the others a head start, then crossed the bridge. Everyone headed on their ways. The rest of the pack had a longer trek than Rob and his companions. He fully expected everyone to pace themselves accordingly.

The road ran sometimes straight, sometimes winding, sometimes rocky, sometimes smoothly. It was so thickly shrouded in places, you'd think dusk had come early. Other times, it baked in the bare sun, which soaked Rob and his band in sweat beneath their coats. He stayed several paces ahead, this time on purpose so they wouldn't see his face.

His senses sharpened and widened, ready to sense any skulking Spirelights before anyone else did. With no sound but boots on gravel and dirt, his thoughts grew lucid.

In the last few days, he'd burned through more adrenaline than he imagined a body could produce. Now he ran on something brighter, purer, stronger than adrenaline, something that never stopped flowing, like it came with the air he breathed, replacing the blood in his veins. Soon he would push it to its own limits, through new heights of bright, blazing madness, blood, and chaos.

Hang on, Sally. Even if I get hacked to pieces, I won't go down, won't stop hacking back 'til I know you're safe.

Something on the air tickled him. The higher they climbed, the more he smelled and felt it envelope him. He grew more eager to taste its source. He almost let the others know how close they were. Then all around, they breathed low, deep, and eager, almost gurgling through watery mouths. Remelea sounded almost hornier for this than she'd been for him last night. If anyone in the pack had needed further reason to follow him, they had it now: a main nerve of the pulsing life from the ones who'd hounded the Crimbone and all Schomites from their native world, followed them here, then spent the last epoch still trying to beat them down so they could move on to the Earth-liners in earnest.

Rob walked faster, heard the others quicken behind him. All around him, the glow blazed thicker than he'd ever smelled it, pungent with fear. The others had made their move. Most of the homestead's population were probably still in their dwellings, hadn't even seen the pack yet, but they'd felt the danger enter their sanctuary.

When Rob saw the homestead, the whole place glowed so brightly, he thought at first it had been set ablaze. Maybe he and the others would do that later.

At the far end of the central stretch, there rose the municipal building. At its rear, Rob saw part of a fenced in area, where the brightest, strongest, *freshest* glows pulsed from the smallest Spirelight bodies. They halted in their play as they realized what was happening. Some of them stood up before freezing in terror.

Spirelight screams sounded within the municipal building, mingling with Crimbone howls. Rob caught himself listening masochistically for Sally. His blades were out before he realized it. Faces peered out of dwellings, before doors and windows slammed shut. More faces stared from upper windows. The mangled body of a Spirelight man crashed through one of the front windows of the municipal building. He landed on his back atop some manicured bushes. The leaves and the earth ran red beneath him as shattered glass rained and sprinkled. The front door splintered open from within. Out came the dark man, dragging a thrashing, whimpering Spirelight man in a plain white suit. Rob had an instant to wonder, was that it, the big fight they'd expected? He strode forward, met the dark man and the captive halfway.

"You break policy," cried the Spirelight Tribunal representative—Rob thought that was the word for him. "You violate the land barriers!"

"*Break? Violate?* You threw all that shit out the window when you sent your goons to fuck with me and mine."

"What are you talking about?"

Rob sheathed one blade so he could grab the representative by the throat, dragging him from the dark man's grasp. The representative thrashed and kicked up dust, then staggered to his knees. Holding him there, Rob spoke loud enough for any Spirelight within earshot to hear—in the ancient Spirelight language. "*There is a girl, one of your own, but different. Better. Your dogs took her and brought her here. She is worth more than any of your miserable lives. Give her over to me now, or I will show you all how much I mean that.*"

Silence shot through the entire homestead, even among the Crimbone, like all humanoid sound came through one big speaker, to which someone had just cut the power. Finally, the representative hissed, "Rob Coscan."

"Hey look, everybody," Rob shouted in English. "It knows how to do math!" He sheathed his other blade, so he could hit the representative in the face and still get words out of him. Once he got the back of his hand good and sore, he dragged the representative to his feet and yelled in Spirelight, "*Take me to her, now.*"

Even in his greatest physical and spiritual terror, the representative answered in English. "She's not here."

Rob punched the bastard in the nose. Cartilage

shattered, along with some facial bones behind it. Rob gave the representative a few seconds to spit out blood and teeth, then spoke again in Spirelight. *"Do not lie."*

"It's true! She was here, but she's not anymore!"

"Where then? Where'd you take her?"

"I didn't take her anywhere!" The representative kept trying to lift his hands to shield his face, like that would do any good. "We couldn't keep her here, not the way she is—"

Rob's fist crashed so hard into the man's cheek, that the whole side of the face sagged slightly. It looked like the representative might lose consciousness, so Rob shook him and slapped the other cheek. *"Where, then?"*

"I don't know," the representative blubbered, words slurred by his new deformity. "None of us here know. They came and took her—"

"Who?"

"I don't know who she was…a scientist! A scientist of the Secret Police! She…she said she needed to take her somewhere else, that she couldn't do her work here—"

Rob's arm sagged, though the hand stayed tight on its captive. A scientist of the Secret Police…a Spirelight doctor like Sally's mom, to experiment on her like that old bitch had, turning her sweet body into blazing hell from the center outward, all in a mad effort to figure out what none of them ever had a shot in hell at understanding. Rob's guts churned sickly. His whole body convulsed. From the way his face trembled, you'd think the representative was the one holding him in check, beating him senseless. He steeled himself and cocked back his fist.

"She was supposed to take her to one of the head compounds," blurted the representative, fast as he could with his shattered face, "but she took her somewhere else. We don't know where." He spat more blood, then stared more pleadingly than ever. "The woman had papers! She was a real scientist of the Secret Police! She *was!* I saw the damn signature! It was her! She took her…she took her—"

The representative stopped forming real words. Rob threw him to the ground and kicked him full force in the nuts. He watched the representative writhe and contort, mouth gaping in a silent wail. The representative was already beyond recovery, his glow flaring out to be sucked up. Rob dragged him back to his feet, drew one blade, and drove it so hard through the soft flesh beneath the chin that the tip jutted through the cap of the skull. The body spasmed, dangling airborne. Rob held it there, not noticing his straining arm 'til the twitching stopped and the glow ran dry.

When he yanked the blade loose, the body fell like a wet sack. It hadn't been enough, but…*Oh, there were so many more of them, from the faces staring in disbelief from the windows, to the smallest, brightest ones standing and huddling petrified…so eager to flow into him, to feed him.*

All around, the other Crimbone stared, unblinking. Rob spun to face them. *"Crimbone brethren. There's no one here we need. Draw your blades and feast on the Spirelight glow like never before. Drink this place dry and dead!"*

SHELDON

ONE

For hours, he followed Janie and her skater-asshole boyfriend around town. Neither of them suspected his presence. No one who glanced at the three of them would guess that Sheldon was paying any attention to the happy couple yards ahead. Hell, right now, Janie had probably forgotten he was back in town. When the couple parted ways, the guy still didn't notice the shadow, let alone how it was thinking of slashing his throat whenever there were no witnesses. Sheldon lost count of how many opportunities he barely resisted. The last one was right off Elliot Street. During his last stay in Brattleboro, he'd shadowed another punkass kid through these same streets. That one had boasted to his thug friends about his intentions to jump Janie, so Sheldon had left him stuffed in a dumpster near this same spot. All of that had happened around back of a crumbling, moldy tenement block, which had since been torn down and replaced by a parking garage. Now Sheldon spotted

Lou standing outside Kipling's.

"So, how you doin', man?" Sheldon walked up.

"Oh, just the usual…watching."

"Watching me, you mean."

"Sometimes, yeah. Other times, the news."

Sheldon cast an eye through the bar windows, to the television that hung from the wall in the corner. A basketball game was on.

"Nah," said Lou, "what I'm watching for won't show up on TV for a while."

"So, what else has been on your mind?"

"Worried about an old friend."

"Why's that?"

"It's a weird situation. There was a time, we were the sort of friends who'd watch each other's backs through anything, but I finally broke it off with him. Some people just get too painful to watch, you know? No matter how much you love 'em, they ain't gonna listen to you and will just drag you down with 'em if you're not careful. A lot of it had to do with this other dude he started hanging out with…bad influence, you could say. Shit, what was that short, stocky, nasty fucker's name again? Hell, I'm rambling, man. Anyway, you know how it goes."

"I guess I do." Sheldon cast a glance around. Janie's skater asshole was gone. "You wanna go inside, get a beer?"

"Sure, I'll have one, if you're buying."

"Still no cash?"

"Still no cash."

Sheldon checked his wallet and shrugged. Given his

current arrangement, food and shelter weren't a concern. He'd worry about it again when they were. "It's cool, man."

"Thanks. I'll have one or two with you, then I've gotta go check up on some shit."

Sheldon shifted into the proper posture, started projecting the right energy so he could get himself a drink, and not be asked for the identification he didn't have. When he ordered, Jill gave him a look like maybe she was onto him. She wouldn't say anything, though, because she'd be in just as deep trouble, for all the beers she'd already served him. He and Lou took their same old booth. Over two beers, Sheldon told Lou some stories about his travels.

Lou said, "You know, sometimes you sound a lot like that old friend I mentioned earlier."

"I hope that's not too much of a bad thing."

Lou sighed and smiled. "I don't know. It's a little early to tell."

They left the bar and walked to Main Street. Far off to the left, Janie approached, hand in hand with her asshole skater.

"Just a second," Sheldon said to Lou.

"Do what you gotta do, man. We probably won't get to talk for a while. Do me a favor, though?"

The last person who'd asked Sheldon a favor was Annie, about Janie. "Maybe."

Lou pulled a folded piece of paper from his pocket. "I drew this once, for that friend I told you about. I'd like you to give it to my dad if you see him." Lou handed Sheldon the paper.

Sheldon unfolded it. "What, your dad's somewhere around here?"

Lou smiled enigmatically. "Nah. Just, you know, in case. One of those weird feelings—the kind you and your people probably call blasphemy."

"Right. So, your dad, I guess he's a..." Sheldon almost said *beast*. "...Crimbone."

"Yeah. That doesn't mean he'll try to kill you, though, long as you don't start shit with him. He's a bit of a rarity like that, among us."

Sheldon almost answered, then he saw the drawing.

He didn't look long enough to absorb details, though there were many, intricately shaded in time-smudged pencil. Mainly, he caught impressions: the foggy, mountainous backdrop, the black shape looming in the center, the twin dripping shimmers in the shape's hands. He refolded it quickly, nearly ripping it. He looked again at Lou in bewildered, disgusted horror, wanted to shove the drawing back, or tear it to shreds and throw it in Lou's face. Except he'd already promised, hadn't he? It was turning into a bad habit.

"Sheldon!" Janie and her skater-asshole were less than half a block away.

Sheldon gave one more look to Lou, who only nodded. Then he walked towards Janie, stuffing the drawing in his pocket.

"Sheldon, this is my boyfriend, Allen."

"Hey, man." Sheldon shook hands with skater-asshole Allen. "Heard a lot about you."

"Tha's cool, man. So, you Janie's old friend from back in the day?" Skater-asshole Allen sounded pretty stoned, with the kind of sloppy, droning voice that usually didn't sound much different sober.

"That's me."

"Hey, tha's straight. So, how's it goin' findin' a job an' shit?"

"Still lookin'." He tried not to think of the drawing in his pocket.

"Tha's cool. You're, like, homeless an' shit, right?"

"Well, not really. I mean, Annie's pretty much given me the spare room."

"Annie? Who's that, like some bitch you fuckin'?"

Janie elbowed Allen. "That's my mom, dumbass!" She sounded a little stoned herself.

Allen gave Sheldon a gaping grin. "You fuckin' Janie's mom? Dude, that's fucked up!"

Janie punched Allen in the chest. "Shut up! You asshole!" There was a vapid inflection to her voice, one Sheldon didn't usually hear.

"Hey, hey!" Allen stumbled back, throwing up his hands defensively. "Lay off, bitch!"

Janie got him around the neck and pinched him in the crook of her elbow. "You'd better stop callin' me a bitch, and you'd *better* stop talkin' shit about my mom!"

"Okay, okay!" Allen caught his breath. "So, wha' you gonna do to me if I don't?"

She pulled him closer. "You'd better worry more 'bout what I'm gonna *stop* doin'."

Sheldon looked back up the street so he wouldn't rip Allen's head off. Lou wasn't there anymore.

They walked around and shot the shit for a while. To Sheldon, it didn't feel much different than earlier, except now they were theoretically aware of his presence. They wound up loitering in Harmony Parking Lot, leaning against what used to be the Common Ground, seated on a slab of sidewalk with lots of gears, cogs, and other mechanical bits and pieces artfully stuck in the concrete like fossils. Janie mentioned she was hungry. Allen told her she was always fuckin' hungry, said she could eat wherever she wanted. She mentioned Elliot Street Café might still be open, and Allen suddenly remembered some folks he had to go see about some shit. He asked Sheldon if he wanted to come along.

Sheldon figured Allen meant to head off, meet some friends, and sit around playing video games and getting stoned. The transit center at the bottom of the parking garage, where it came out on Flat Street, had become the local hangout spot for hippies, stoners, skaters, and runaway teenagers around here, since the old Common Ground had closed, and the Boys and Girls Club had apparently gotten too straight-laced for a lot of the rougher kids these days. Sheldon had ambled over there and talked to those kids earlier. Actually, he'd really liked a lot of them. Some of them were clearly Allen's close buddies. Sheldon didn't hold that against them. He might be tempted, if the offer had come from anyone but Allen. "No, that's cool, man. Good meeting you."

Allen kissed Janie goodbye, then headed off, casting back what might be a suspicious glance.

Janie led Sheldon past Kipling's. He didn't see Lou there.

The Elliot Street Café sat on a corner across from the fire station, right where the rest of the street faded and crumbled into more of a ghetto. The inside was a spacious, well-lit, open-kitchen diner, with tables and chairs facing the street windows. The rest of the space was devoted to comfy couches and an extensive bookshelf. Allen probably found the environment too intellectually challenging.

"I don't know if I can eat a whole meal," said Janie, as they scanned the chalkboard menu behind the counter. "Wanna split something?"

"Sure." It turned out the Seafood Benedict was pretty delicious, actually.

As they sat close on one of the couches, plate on the coffee table, Janie asked, "So who was that guy you were talking to?" Most of her vapid facade was gone.

"Huh?"

"When we ran into you. You were talkin' to some dude."

"You saw him?"

"Well, yeah. What was it he handed you?"

"Maybe nothing. He's a ghost, you know." He caught a few strange looks out of the corner of his eye. He remembered what Lou said about folks not overhearing his strange talk, and he cursed himself for relaxing so easily.

"Yeah, I know."

"So you've figured out how to see 'em, huh?"

"Ghosts? Yeah, sometimes." She leaned closer and lowered her voice. "So, what did this…guy have to say to you?"

"I'm not sure yet."

"So what, you expect Mom to explain it all to you

when you talk to her about it later?" When he looked at her strangely, she leaned away. "What, you think I'm the same stupid kid you knew back in the day? It's not like I haven't learned a few things on my own."

"I never thought you were stupid."

"No, but you act like it sometimes, like whatever it is you're really goin' through, you assume Mom's gonna understand but I won't." Now her raised voice was getting them looks.

Oh, she'd be able to handle it, he figured. She'd freak out at first, but she'd get her head around it just fine. That was the problem.

"Whatever," she said. "I gotta run to the bathroom."

While she was gone, the sight of the town through the window started getting to him. No one but normal Earth-line cops and firefighters ambled across the street at the fire station. They had no immediate interest in the café, or anyone in it. He could go out there right now and say hi. Hell, he could probably use his favorite mind trick to convince them they were talking to a fellow officer. He used to be one, after all. It wouldn't cross a one of their minds that they were talking to the culprit behind two five-year-old unsolved homicides.

A curvy, heavily tattooed, frizzy redhead with thick glasses worked the register in here. When her eyes caught Sheldon's, she smiled at him. Everyone around here smiled at him, it seemed. Nights ago, he'd gone with Janie and Annie to an all-ages music show at a spot called Equilibrium, right down a side street from here.

The place had a cheerful café in the front room,

which led into a consignment shop of homemade clothes, jewelry, incense, and musical instruments, and from there to a wide event space alive with song. He and Janie had danced up a storm to the folksy jam. Annie said the place reminded her of the old Common Ground. Sheldon lied and said he'd never been there.

Now he thought of that old place, locked and dark. He wondered if the bloodstains were still on the floor. For a crazy moment, he wanted to tell a few people about those bloodstains, how they really got there. No, he'd rather see them all keep smiling. He wasn't earnestly thinking about killing Allen, but he had earlier. His restraint had nothing to do with the fact that Janie had since introduced them, that they'd all hung out and shared a few laughs.

The guy was still a dumb hick, with a face like a rat and eyes like a lobotomy patient, and there was still Sheldon's promise to Annie. That didn't change any of the looks he caught from Janie, didn't change the face in his heart and mind that had gotten him through the years spent beneath the cleric's and scientist's needles. The bottom line was, news of the discovery of Allen's corpse would wipe the smiles back off these folks' faces.

Yeah, except now he had that drawing folded in his pocket.

In his midsection, the burning rose and flared. One hand clenched on the spot through his shirt, the other on the edge of the coffee table.

"Hey, man, you all right?" It was the tattooed, redheaded waitress. He hadn't noticed her come out from behind the counter. "The food too acidic or something?"

"Yeah, maybe. Can I have some water?"

"Sheldon?" Janie was somewhere behind him, to his left. "Sheldon, you okay?"

"Yeah, fine, I just—" When had he shambled to his feet? Either way, he noticed right before one of his legs gave out. He caught the coffee table, which moaned as it slid at an angle. Something fell and clattered. Hopefully that wasn't their plate.

Janie had an arm around him. "It's okay. I got this." She must be talking to the waitress and anyone else taking an interest in the scene.

The black trail pulsed and blazed through Sheldon's body. It felt impossibly wide, like it had split open bigger than ever. Any second, his guts would spill out of his shirt, leaving a bigger bloodstain than ever on this town.

The beast was here, stabbing him again and again with that black blade, not reopening the wound but creating it for the first time all over again…*over and over*…Sheldon felt his arms lash and strain, back on the mountain, deflecting those blades with his own in the fight's final minutes, and then—

Except, no, wait, his arms weren't lashing or straining, because they were holding onto Janie.

"Jesus, Sheldon, ease up! That hurts! I've got you!"

She got him outside, to a faded picnic table in a corner yard, to the left of the door. The fresh summer air was easier to breathe. He settled onto the bench, still feeling that other body around him in that other place, arms moving madly to deflect the blades—

No, not deflecting. Feel that other body, that other place. You only had one blade on the mountain against the beast's two. It's two blades you're wielding now, and they're the blades of a beast, and you're hacking and stabbing into many bodies.

Sheldon didn't see that other place, because his eyes were open to the little café parking lot. He kept them wide. If he closed them, he would see that other mountain, see and smell the bodies his beast's blades were at work on, hear their drawn out, dying shrieks. Even now, he knew some of those bodies fought him with their own weapons. Others died cowering, or in mid-dash, cut down from behind. Every time the blades found a mark, Sheldon felt his own wound open afresh. Blood spattered him as lives fled in energy waves that bombarded and filled him. It was that life energy that set his whole body afire. His other body chased that fire like sex.

It's your own fire, Sheldon, or what used to be yours…the living fire that makes your people who they are, given to them by the Spirah gods. It hurts so much because it's no longer yours to feel, because your gods have abandoned you.

Finally, Sheldon stopped convulsing, not because it had lessened or because he'd gotten used to it, but because he was out of his own energy. For a while, all he could do was hold onto Janie, try to feel her and the picnic bench beneath them.

When it died off, he whimpered, "I'm sorry."

"Don't say sorry."

He stretched out. Janie held on, kept cradling him. Instead of closing his eyes, he stared up weakly into hers. She wiped sweat from his brow, letting him hold onto her other arm. His hand ran down to hers. Her fingers slid between his.

"I'm sorry I scared you," he said, the strength already returning to his voice.

"I told you, quit apologizing."

For a long time, they were alone out there. Two teenage girls wandered into the parking lot. Sheldon rolled his eyes back and absently recognized friends of Janie's. He'd met them days earlier, but he couldn't remember their names. They didn't look concerned, so he guessed he looked better from his little outburst. He liked them a little more for that. He didn't want to see more concerned faces.

"Hi," he said with a sigh.

"Hi, Sheldon," one of the girls said. "So Janie, who *are* you going out with these days?"

Janie gave some noncommittal, inarticulate sound. Neither of the girls pressed the issue, so Sheldon liked them even more. They sat on the other side of the picnic table and struck up small talk with Janie, all local gossip that Sheldon didn't hear much of. When he finally stood, you'd never guess the state he was in moments ago.

"You ready to go?" Janie asked him.

He nodded then said to her friends, "Good seein' y'all again."

They walked a block before she took his hand and squeezed it. Sheldon wondered if her idiotic skater boyfriend would come around and spot them. Though no, that fuckhead was probably still on his ass getting blazed and playing video games somewhere. Sheldon sensed Janie didn't care much either way.

"Where you wanna go?" she asked.

"Let's walk up to the tower." That was about the

most dangerous answer he could give.

"The Bloody Tower?" She laughed in surprise. "Man, I haven't been up there in years! Yeah. Let's go up there."

They didn't speak again 'til they reached the edge of the woods. Sometimes she'd tug him onto one street then up another, as if to remind him of the way, as if he needed reminding.

On the steep, winding uphill forest trail, she said, "You're gonna have to leave soon, aren't you?"

He felt the folded drawing in his pocket. The ghost of his vision in the cafe flickered through his chest. "Yeah. Maybe today. How'd you know?"

"Same way you do, I guess. Is it because of what happened back at Elliot Street?"

"Yeah, that's part of it." More than the vision, more than the drawing, what clued him in was his sudden desire to see their old spot in the woods. He had to see it with her, before he was gone again, probably for the last time.

"See? I told you I'd picked up on some shit over the years." Resentment dampened the triumph in her voice. She said more gently, "So, do you even know what that was happening to you?"

"It had to do with where I have to go and what I have to do when I get there."

"Yeah, duh. So what is that?"

"I don't know." He stopped himself from saying more. Whatever she'd figured out, it was already more than was good for her.

They crossed onto the final narrow, upward path.

Then up the bank through the trees, there was that big, carved stone wall. It was strange to realize he'd only seen it up close once before. Returning to this town, so many of his memories had proved questionable at best. How could the reality of any one spot match up so perfectly with a single memory?

Janie stepped onto the gravel spread in front of the tower. "Man, this is such a cool old place. I'm surprised I haven't kept coming here."

"Did you ever see any of those ghosts you told me about up here?"

"I don't think so. Why?"

"Well, we know you can see ghosts now."

She shrugged. "I don't know. I don't think the tower ghosts come out for just anyone."

He walked across the gravel, eyes scanning for the old bare earth spot. He didn't see it, even when he sat down beneath the archway. He made sure to sit down first, so it would be her call how close they got.

She leaned against the tower wall and slumped down, leaving about a foot of space between them. "So before today's up, you think you're gonna know where you have to go next?"

"I don't think it'll be today. Sooner or later, though, someone or something'll show up to let me know."

"Something? Like what, another ghost?"

"*There are more things in heaven and earth, Janio…*"

"I think I'll leave that one alone. So, what about once it's over?"

An unexpected twitch ran through him. The obvious assumption was that there'd be no afterwards. It was probably best that he kept assuming that. "I think I'll come back here, to Brattleboro."

"Yeah, I'll bet. You'll come back because everyone comes back to Brattleboro. Then you'll run off again to do more crazy shit that you just *have* to be the one to go do, 'cause God forbid you just leave it to all the other crazy fuckers who come from wherever people like you come from."

Now that was weird: Janie speaking her mom's words, sort of. Had she listened in on that talk with Annie? Maybe she'd heard every word, was dead set on getting Sheldon to break his promise. Or maybe she meant to knock him off his high horse. Likely he was giving himself too much credit, not giving her enough. Either way, *wishful thinking*. Besides, his promise was now fresh in his mind, so he scooted slightly away. Still, he started smiling. The more he tried to pull the smile from his face, the wider it spread. He gazed across the gravel into the warm, green forest. There were no ghosts in these trees, no beasts with their black blades.

"Nah," he said dreamily. "Fuck it. Once it's done, I'm done. If something else gets itself started and wants me to be a part of it, that's just too damn bad I'm coming back here, and I'll stay as long as I want."

"Good." She sighed. "Too bad I probably won't still be here by then."

"Well, then I'll just have to go where you are instead. You wouldn't mind, would you?"

"You'd better."

Gravel shifted and ground as she moved, then he felt the warmth of her face close to his. Then, yeah, those were her lips brushing his temple, opening and closing softly. As his face tilted towards her, he tasted her breath.

The last of his pain was gone, and he was flooded with the same sweet, floating joy he'd felt when she'd first walked into the kitchen and recognized him. Hadn't he promised someone not to do this? He couldn't remember why, maybe from sudden lack of blood pressure through his brain. All he could think about was kissing Janie crazily, deep as he could, holding her and never letting go. He rose to his knees and almost lost balance, almost pulled them both crashing over, but he wrapped his arms around her and they didn't fall, and he didn't care that the gravel was grinding into his knees.

When they drew back for breath, he brushed a stray wisp of hair from her face. He almost suggested that they move over into the grass. *This is a stolen moment, and there's only so deep you'll be allowed to get lost in it.* It didn't matter that she wouldn't hang on to that creep Allen for long, because she'd leave this town and find other guys, nice guys she could fall in love with who weren't hell bound like Sheldon.

"You still look sad," she said, stroking his cheek and neck.

He buried his face in her shoulder and hugged her for a long time, then he kissed her some more. Oh well, she'd made the first move, and it wasn't like he'd be around long enough to do any damage to her life anyway.

They held hands all the way back into town. It wasn't 'til they reached Main Street that she pulled her hand free of his. Far off, he saw the gangly, ambling reason why. Janie gave Sheldon a look as if to say he could walk on with her, or he could go his own way now. He walked with her 'til they reached the intersection of Main and Elliot.

Sheldon almost made out whatever expression was on Allen's face, right before a tall shape stepped off Elliot Street into his and Janie's path. He looked up into the slender, gleaming pale, unreadable face of a woman of his own coterie. Sheldon looked at Janie. He saw that she recognized the woman as such, if not in so many words. The woman wore nondescript brown clothes that hugged her slender frame. The clothes were the only thing *nondescript* about her. She was only a little taller than Sheldon, yet she carried her petite frame in such a way that she seemed to tower over him. Her frosty blond hair cascaded down her back and over her shoulders, all the way to her waist. One of her shoulders dropped lower than the other, like it hadn't healed right from some bad break. Other than that blemish, she might have been an Elfin statue, with imperious, gleaming eyes that looked almost purple in the graying light, calm but not gentle. She obviously wasn't hostile, or she wouldn't approach them out in the open.

Before the Spirelight woman could speak, Sheldon said, "Okay, fine. Let's go."

The woman cocked an eyebrow, then looked at Janie and understood. When Sheldon looked at Janie, she was already holding back tears.

"So, this is where you leave," said Janie, "just like that."

"He won't be leaving right away, Janie," said the

woman. "Your safety's not being threatened, if that's what he's worried about. Well, not your immediate safety, anyway." The voice was oddly warm.

Janie's surprise that the woman knew her name was tempered by resigned disbelief of her words. She gave Sheldon's hand a quick squeeze then hurried past, towards Allen.

"We can't stay," the Spirelight woman said to Sheldon. "These streets might not be as safe for me as they are for you. They might not be as safe for you as you think."

"What about Janie?"

"Like I said, she's probably safe. She'll be safer once we're on our way."

Sheldon saw Janie and Allen reach each other and hug. He looked away and followed the woman up Elliot Street, still tasting Janie.

Two

Sheldon did his best to keep up with the woman. He wasn't used to people who walked faster than him. Then again, he was used to being the only Spirelight around. When they turned down Elm Street, Sheldon averted his eyes from the Elliot Street Café. Now that Janie wasn't around, he no longer felt so obliged to comply with the strange woman's demands. He'd get a better sense of things before he started a fight with her, though.

"So, how many of you are there?" he asked as they started up another hill, over a bridge towards Canal Street.

"How many of what?"

"How many did the Tribunal send?" Sheldon snarled.

"No Tribunal sent me, but since you ask, there are two others."

"So where are they?"

"Waiting for us in a motel room, about half a mile up this hill."

"Okay. If you're not from the Tribunal, who are you?"

"My name's Claudette."

"How'd you find me?"

"We didn't have to. We figured out a while ago that this is where you'd probably go, once things started."

"When what started?"

"The war."

"Heh. What, you mean whichever war the Earth-line people are fighting now?"

"The war between the descendants of Deschemb."

"Not sure how you missed it, lady, but that started a while ago."

"Not between the Crimbone and the Spirelight Secret Police. That hasn't been a *war* since it got to this world. Just a feud."

"What's the difference?"

Claudette smirked. "You'll see soon enough. How's that scar these days?"

As if on cue, the old wound pulsed. Sheldon braced

for another flare-up that didn't come. "What do you want from me?"

"It's not about what anyone wants. We need you to understand what's starting, why all this has happened, so you can make an educated decision about where you stand."

If Sheldon had complied so far out of fear—more for Janie than himself—he now felt silly for it. He'd just heard it in the woman's voice: he was the one holding all the cards. Claudette was the one sweating bullets, and her only prayer was that Sheldon agreed to hear her out.

Sheldon thought of Annie telling him what was what, then throwing him that ultimatum about not making a move on Janie. Well, Janie had called her own shots on that one. If Annie found out, there wasn't much she could say or do about it now. So what if Sheldon said he didn't stand anywhere? Why not tell Claudette right now to go fuck herself, then walk straight back to Main Street, to Janie? If Mister Skater-Asshole had a problem with that, Sheldon could kick his ass. He was sick of all these old farts telling him his business, never giving a single straight answer. They just kept talking like he was supposed to clean up the mess they'd made.

"Well," he said, "if your folks need me to understand, they sent the wrong old gal, 'cause bitch, seriously, you're confusing the fuck out of me."

"Wait 'til we get there."

They hiked all the way up Canal Street, past Price Chopper. Claudette led him into the parking lot of the Econo Lodge, towards the rear string of rooms. Sheldon stopped short.

"What is it?" Claudette asked.

"The Crimbone," Sheldon hissed.

"That's right. They've been here. They've had their own important dealings at this same place. You can relax. They're not here now. Come on."

Claudette opened the door. Inside sat two Schomite men watching TV, one in a chair, the other on the bed. In the dim orange light, he identified them by smell—not Crimbone, so it hadn't been their scent that had triggered him outside the room. His hand still went reflexively to his outer right jacket pocket, where he kept his knife.

A strong grip closed on his wrist and yanked it back. Sheldon spun and faced Claudette, twisting his wrist free. He could still pull the knife and use it before Claudette could counter again. He held Claudette's gaze long enough to let her know that, then he turned back and looked at the two Schomites. To Earth-line eyes, they'd look like a couple of average white boys, the kind he'd expect to find getting high and playing video games with Allen. The one on the bed stood and turned off the TV. The other stayed seated.

"It's him," said the one who'd switched off the TV, eyes wide.

"He's different than the other one, though," observed the one in the chair.

"This is him," said Claudette. "Sheldon, my friends here are Blix and Tiger."

"Your friends?"

"It's okay if you don't wanna shake hands right away," said Tiger, the one still seated. He was a square-faced man with a matching square, tough build, dark eyes, and uncombed dark hair, wearing a Green Lantern t-shirt and low hanging jean shorts.

"Any news?" Claudette asked.

"There has been now." Blix looked at Sheldon. His tough build so matched Tiger's that they might be twins, but his face was softer and beakier, his hair lighter and spikier. His eyes were too bright to hide secrets like Tiger's could. "So you're Sheldon Wildfire."

Claudette patted Sheldon's shoulder. "Starting to piece it together, Sheldon?"

"You're from the United Deschembines," said Sheldon.

Tiger laughed. "So that's what they call us! It's even lamer than I expected."

Claudette smiled with gentle amusement.

"I'd heard you guys got wiped out," Sheldon said.

"Good," said Tiger. "That's the best rumor possible."

"Better than some of the others," said Blix.

"Take a seat," said Claudette.

Sheldon pulled up a chair next to the door.

"For a while," Claudette continued, "we were pretty much wiped out. Our numbers have been building back up pretty well, but we've had to work on staying discreet. More and more Deschembines find their way to us these days. That makes discretion harder."

"Yeah, but…don't you want more people to join? Isn't that the point?"

"Hell no!" Tiger grinned. "Most of the rest of you guys we couldn't stand."

Claudette leaned against the wall. "It's not about

converting anyone. The others will realize the truth, or they won't. Our doors are always open to whoever finds us. Hopefully when things get rolling, there'll be enough of us to stand."

"Against what?" said Sheldon.

"The ones who haven't united, Schomite and Spirelight, who won't stop 'til everyone's dead. That's the war I was talking about: the war between those who'll destroy this world, and those who'll build something new from the ashes. For a while, we held out hope that war wouldn't be necessary. We keep our own peace between ourselves, so hopefully some of us survive to rebuild."

"So, where will the Earth-line people fit into all this?"

"There's no way to guess," said Blix. "Not 'til the Earth-line people know about us." He sat back down.

"Safe bet there won't be many of those left," Tiger added.

"Because these lands will stop hiding us from them," Sheldon finished, mostly to himself.

"That's the most Crimbone thing I've ever heard a Spirelight say," observed Claudette. "That's why you're needed among us."

"Well," Tiger started, "we're not sure yet that we need *him*, exactly—"

"Don't start with that yet," Claudette said sharply. Then to Sheldon, "You know that children can't be produced between Spirelights and Schomites, right?"

"Duh," said Sheldon. "Everyone knows that."

"Yeah, and everyone knows about you, to one degree or another, because you are such a union. You were born a Spirelight, but when you survived what should have been a death stroke from a Crimbone blade, something of the Crimbone remained and became part of you. I can't imagine the war this must have caused inside you. If it had destroyed you, if you'd gone insane and become a monster because of it, no one would have been surprised. The others need to see—to feel up close—what you've become instead."

By *others*, Sheldon guessed Claudette meant the rest of the United Deschembines, wherever they were hiding. "Yeah? So what's that gonna do for 'em?"

"It'll show them that we have a chance," said Claudette. "Now that we've found you, I feel a little more relaxed. You have business to settle here before we go, I believe."

"Go?" Sheldon looked around at their faces. Finally, he nodded. "Right. Yeah. Can I sit in here for a while first, though, alone, just to think?"

"Do what you gotta do, man," said Tiger.

THREE

They stepped out to give him space. He knew one of them would linger behind and call someone at the home base with the good news. It was Tiger. 'Til now, Sheldon couldn't figure out if Claudette was former Secret Police. The lady sure had a smoothness to her, an almost sexless aura of ethereal detachment Sheldon once associated exclusively with his old line of work.

Apparently not, he now decided. No Secret Policewoman would ever fall for the trick he'd just pulled. From his chair, Sheldon watched the numbers Tiger's fingers punched on the motel phone.

"Yeah, we found him," said Tiger. "No, he hasn't tried to kill us yet. There were a few tight spots on the ride up, but nothing got out of hand…right. So how's, uh, everything else working out back there? Yeah, *that'll* be interesting to watch." Sardonic mischief entered Tiger's tone. "Hey, he's right here if you want me to put him on."

Sheldon almost rose from his seat, then decided not to.

"Nah, just kidding." Tiger glanced uneasily at Sheldon. "Hey, c'mon, I'm not *that* much of an idiot…Yeah, love you too. See you in a day or so."

Tiger hung up and left the room. Sheldon found a pen and some scrap paper and wrote down the number Tiger's fingers had punched in. He only had to look once at the fresh prints on the keys for a reminder. He didn't leave immediately, because he really wasn't ready to make his goodbyes, to *settle his business* as Claudette put it. When he stepped outside, the others were nowhere in sight.

Sheldon headed straight to Washington Street, senses peeled all the way in case any of them tried to follow him. None of them did, not unless the Spirelight end of the United Deschembines had improved on Secret Police spy craft in ways he'd never imagined.

He reached the house on Washington Street and knocked. Annie opened the door. She peered out less certainly than she had when he first got back to town.

"Hi," he said, fighting to meet her eyes.

"Hi, Sheldon. Janie's not here."

"So, can I come in? Am I still welcome here?"

"Well, I guess you're about to leave anyway, so sure." She stepped aside, impersonal as a security guard granting clearance. "I folded your clothes and put them back in your bag after I washed 'em. Put your book in there, too."

He went straight to his room, sure he would break down crying the second he left her sight. Instead, he slung his pack over his shoulder and went back downstairs. Annie still stood where he'd left her.

"Can we still say goodbye as friends?" He kept his tone blank as possible. She looked at him like she'd just caught him in a trap. "Come on, Annie, I didn't break my promise. It was just…well…"

"No, I'm sure you held out like the tough little brave you are. But you still *let* that promise get broken, didn't you? You were the one took it on for safe keepin'. Doesn't matter if you kicked it or let it fall and smash, pretendin' you couldn't've caught it. It's still broke, ain't it?"

"No, it isn't. You know why?"

"Make a believer out of me, little brave."

"I know where I'm going now. Janie will still be here after I'm gone. That's all that really matters to you, right?"

"It don't matter, little brave. Me, I done my part in this story."

He stared, searching her eyes for a clue what to say.

A story, she called it. The story wouldn't be right if this was how they parted. There had to be some way to change that look on her face, to look into her eyes and see himself reflected as her little brave, one last time.

"I'm leaving tonight," he said. "I'll say goodbye to Janie if I can find her. Either way, she'll come back to this house and I won't. That's what you wanted, right? Once you see that I haven't lied about that, will you at least remember me as a friend?"

She shrugged. Sheldon waited for something else. Finally, he sneered and stormed out.

As he walked down South Main, he thought for sure the tears were about to break out full force. They didn't. He spotted Allen's gangly rat-ape shape ambling uphill from the darkening distance. By the time the distance closed, Sheldon's face was unreadable again.

"Hey, Allen," he said. "You seen Janie?"

"Huh? Wha' you wanna see her for?"

"I'm about to leave. I wanna say goodbye."

"Bullshit!" There was so little difference between Allen's civil stoned grunting and his angry stoned grunting, that it took Sheldon a second to recognize the hostility. "You dumb little faggot," said Allen, "think I don't know what you tryin' to do? You tryin' to fuck my bitch, ain't'cha? Faggot punk!"

Sheldon wrinkled his nose at Allen's nasty breath. "Yeah, Allen. I'm gonna fuck your girl. That's what I'm gonna go do now, as a matter of fact. She says you look like a rat and you have a dick the size of a rat's."

"Oh, you think you're cute, huh, punk?"

Sheldon let Allen shove him once, then he sent one

gunshot punch that snapped the prick's head backwards. As Allen fell, Sheldon restrained the urge to clock him once more on the way down for good measure. The fall seemed to take longer that way, so he spotted the back of Allen's skull about to strike the concrete in a way that might actually be fatal. He caught the limp bastard by the collar and slung him over into the grass, next to some tombstones.

He walked on, not bothering to check if anyone had seen. If they had, they didn't come to pester him over it, which was smart of them. Since leaving the motel, he'd interacted with two people. They'd both given him shit on account of Janie. It must be Brattleboro urging him on his way. Only later would he realize how at home this distinctly Crimbone thought felt in his head.

On Main Street, he ran into one of Janie's two friends from earlier today in the café. When he asked where she was, the girl suggested he check Mocha Joe's. When he got there, chairs were up on tables, and the lone barista was sweeping up. Much as Sheldon had come to love this town, he wouldn't miss how practically the whole place rolled up its mats at around six every evening. He headed to Harmony Parking Lot, eyes peeled.

"Hey there," said a soft voice.

Janie smiled and waved at him. She sat at a little metal table that was left out by the darkened back door of the Tulip Cafe. Her smile faded when she saw his backpack. He made himself smile for her as he went for the metal wire-mesh chair next to her. She bolted to her feet, grabbed him, and hugged him harder than she had at their first reunion. He held her just as tight, running a hand through her hair, eyes closed against the side of her face.

"I thought you'd gone already," she whispered. "I didn't think I'd ever see you again."

"You thought I'd leave without saying goodbye?"

"I didn't think you'd have a choice." Her voice trembled with the threat of sobs. "God, Sheldon, I felt like such a heartless bitch…such a weak, heartless, cowardly bitch."

"What do you mean?"

"That woman scared me. Just the sight of her, the way she came out of nowhere…I didn't know what she was gonna do to you and all I could do was—"

"Hey, hey!" He stroked her cheek. "You're not weak."

"Right. Just heartless and a coward and a bitch." They shared a good chuckle. She went somber again. "You do have to go, don't you?"

"Yeah. With that woman and some of her friends. I wish I could stay long enough to tell you everything. I wish I had when I could've. Hell, I wish you could come with me."

"I could, you know. I will if you let me."

He steeled himself for the self-inflicted wound. "I can't let you."

"I know."

"I'll find you once this is over."

"Oh yeah?"

"Yeah." Damnit, why couldn't he stay just one more night, so they could go somewhere and do nothing but kiss, and whatever else they felt like doing? His hand slid down over her breast. She grabbed it and pressed it there.

"You have to go," she said.

They shared one last goodbye kiss that didn't turn out to be quite that. Several times, one of them drew back to say, "Okay, now I really have to go," or "You really have to go." Then one would reach up to dry the other's tears, they'd both laugh, then they'd try for one last quick peck, as if they really thought it would stop there.

Finally, he pressed the number Tiger had called into her hand. "Only call if you absolutely have to."

"What, this gonna be your new number?"

"Sort of."

"How's it *sort of?*"

"I don't have time to explain, but…you can get in touch with the people I'll be with that way, I think, if it's an emergency."

She chilled and stiffened a little. "Hey, wait, what do you mean, *emergency?*"

"Probably nothing. Only in an emergency, okay?"

She looked at the number, then dug out her cell phone and punched it in to save it there. "Okay."

He saw her shiver and smile with some illicit, adventuresome, mysterious excitement. Considering what he knew that she didn't, he shouldn't have felt it with her, but he did. "I'll get in touch with you when I can," he said. "I love you."

"I love you."

He hurried around the corner. If he didn't hurry, if

he let himself so much as look back once more, he would never go. The blood was still trying to flow back into his brain when he walked into Kipling's. Four familiar shapes sat at the bar. Tiger sat closest. From there it ran Blix, Claudette, Lou.

"There's the man of the hour," said either Blix or Tiger.

"You guys expecting me here?" Sheldon said.

"Nah," said Tiger, "just taking bets on whether you were gonna bail or not."

Sheldon still tasted Janie on his lips. He almost said, *Still thinking about it, actually.*

From the far end of the bar, Lou fixed Sheldon in the eye, nodded with a dry smile, and saluted with his glass of tequila. Sheldon sat next to Tiger. Jill looked at him strangely, disapprovingly, like she didn't recognize him. Shit, he knew he forgot something.

Not missing a beat, he looked her straight in the eye and said in the same voice he always used to her, "It's my last night in town, Jill. How 'bout a bottle of Bud? Actually, nah, make that a tequila on the rocks." He shot Lou a wink. Lou winked back.

She glared, then got him his drink.

"You ready to hit the road after this?" asked Claudette.

"Oh yeah," Sheldon said, though of course he wasn't. "I hope you parked close by."

VENCIE

He stood on the porch and watched the courtyard for exactly three hours.

Some rumor was spreading, though he hadn't yet asked anyone what. Instead, he watched everyone's movements steadily sharpen and quicken with agitation, like they all had the same frayed wire under their asses.

When civilians asked Secret Police agents about it, the agents shook their heads, playing dumb. They hid their discomfort well, from the civilians, anyway. Vencie saw how holding it in made it worse, though. Some civilians asked him if it was true. He didn't point out that he hadn't been sworn in yet, just fed them the same denial.

They just assume by the sight of me that I'm one of the agents, even though I'm wearing civilian clothes.

He smiled, even though his main concern right now was what the Tribunal decided to do with him. Now that he had that anxiety contained, he wouldn't let these civilians get him worked up.

The more he watched, the more it made him a bit sick. Here he was, keeping himself contained in spite of it all, and there were the official agents, letting civilians rattle them! Was it the comfort of a legitimate station that had weakened them so? If that was so—

Is this what I've spent my life trying to get? I've been out of my mind. I could have—

Hey. Cool it. You know what you're after. They're the ones who forgot. Hold strong. This isn't the world your grandfather taught you to fight for. You'll get your chance to remind them what they've fallen short of.

It's only your third day here. Keep watching and learning.

He didn't know where exactly here was, because he'd made the second half of the trip blindfolded. The woman Amos had offered him had driven, while he sat in the back, sandwiched tight between two strapping male field agents. Today, whenever he strayed near the gates, she'd wander into sight, along with the male agents, their weapons in plain view. Her smile told him to walk somewhere else. No one would tell him the score, but he knew: they were open to the possibility of instating him. Still, he let himself feel more trepidatious than was warranted, because that's what they expected.

To present a proper illusion, his grandfather always taught him, *you have to convince a small part of yourself that it's true.*

How the hell else could he have pretended for so many years that Luna was his beloved wife, that the rest of her scraggly little family were more than parasites?

The problem was, his new employers weren't convinced of the actual truth, which was that he'd brought them the real Sally Coscan.

Finally, the acting Official came to him with the

news. The scientist had shown up at the Tennessee homestead, and had said she needed to transport Sally Coscan to better facilities to conduct the proper tests. The Official had naturally emphasized *better facilities* as though to add, *places* you *don't know about.*

Except it hadn't been the right scientist.

The one the Tribunal had sent was found dead in the woods several states over. The impostor had disappeared, along with Sally Coscan—if it was Sally Coscan, the Official made a point of noting. The only reason Vencie was still alive was because they couldn't disprove his claim. The Official didn't tell him the extent of the suspicion, that the impostor was another renegade, working some conspiracy with Vencie. Vencie knew how the Tribunals thought, though, far more than the Official could guess.

When the Official told him the score, Vencie replied only with his eyes. If any of these drones here were worth half as much as field agents as Vencie was as a renegade, they would see through such an impostor. Maybe that's why they were so eager to keep him underfoot.

The porch door opened behind him. The Official said, "Renegade."

Vencie turned in time for the back of a hand to strike his face. He spilled backwards and his head thudded against the porch beam. He slumped to the boards. Out of the corner of one stinging eye, he saw several agents throughout the yard tense up, waiting for him to retaliate. He disappointed them by pretending to be stunned.

"Get up," said the Official. "*Get up!*"

When Vencie didn't oblige quickly enough, the Official dragged him to his feet by the collar. He let the Official drag him inside, content in knowing he could kill this stiff, pathetic man before any of the agents reached them. After that, he could easily take out one or two of them before they killed him. That remained counterproductive, though.

Inside, two more agents stood still on either side of the drawing room. They were much closer and on the ready than the ones outside. He was still pretty sure he could kill the Official before they got to him. For now, he let the Official vent, let him honestly think himself in control. After that, they could talk business. The Official wasn't entirely closed to the possibility, or he'd have already ordered the agents to kill Vencie.

The Official slung Vencie ten feet across the room. Vencie crashed into a small glass-top coffee table. He relaxed and tensed his body at all the right points throughout the ordeal, absorbed the impact of splintering wood and glass with some discomfort, rolled so only his clothes got a bit cut up. When he stood, the Official barreled into him, collared him again and slammed him against a tall bookcase. Several volumes shook loose and thudded next to their feet.

Behind the Official, the two agents stayed still. "Get out," the Official shouted at them.

After they left, Vencie looked the Official in the eyes. "That a signal to make this a proper two-way fight?" When the Official didn't answer, Vencie went on, "You know, I bet they hope I kick your ass, the way you're shaming your rank, fuming and snorting like one of the Schomites' beasts."

The Official shoved away in disgust. "*Kick my ass.* Now you're the one talking like a beast…or some Earth-line thug. I'm not sure which is worse."

"You're the one acting like one. Not that you'd know, cooped up here like you've been."

"I know you're stupider than either."

Vencie dusted himself off and propped one arm on the nearest bookshelf. "Right. Stupid enough to bring us our greatest catch in years. You're the ones smart enough to let her slip."

"Renegade dog! You've fucked all of us over!"

Vencie sensed an opportunity. "Tell me what everyone's so concerned about, so I can be the judge of that?"

"Concerned? *You've murdered Tennessee!*"

"Huh?"

"What did you say about how you captured that tainted bitch? Let me see: you and those other renegades found her with her beast lover in Florida. You could capture her, but you wouldn't face her beast, so you left your fellow blasphemers behind to distract him, so he could kill them while you drove off with your catch."

"Pretty much."

"Except Rob Coscan's lust for our life force must not have been too overwhelming, because he showed up with enough restraint not to kill all of your followers, 'til he made one of them tell him where you planned to take the girl."

"I didn't tell anyone where I planned to take her."

"Yeah? Well, he figured it out somehow, asshole. He also figured out a way to get a whole pack—more beasts than the Schomites ever keep in one place—through Tennessee, to the southern homestead there!"

It was starting to make sense why the Official was so upset. The Crimbone raided Spirelight-controlled lands all the time, often out of desperation the Secret Police strategically pushed them to. Fighting in "lands that didn't favor them" seemed to demoralize them. It was good for Crimbone population control. It had been well over a hundred years since they dared attack a homestead.

"So, how many were killed?"

"All of them, Secret Police and civilian alike."

"So it's the Schomite Cabinets who've obviously gone insane, or just whichever one Coscan went and pleaded his case to."

"It doesn't matter who he *pleaded his fucking case to*. The point is, he knew how to pull it off. Bottom line: *Tennessee's not a Spirelight State anymore, and we haven't even been able to keep it out of the national news*. The Crimbone have been flooding the place, drinking any glow they can chase down butchering it, raping it, eating it, you name it, and I'm not even gonna start on what order. The Earth-liners are talking about calling in their National Guard, and we don't even know how long our contacts there can keep them from holding off that shitshow."

Vencie listened and faked disinterest. "So give them their shitshow. Have the Crimbone ever heard of a lovely little invention called fully automatic weapons?"

The Official backhanded Vencie again. "Have you

ever heard of the Earth-line people managing to do anything against the Crimbone with guns? Do you know who the Crimbone believe this guy is?" The Official's voice trembled.

"Sure. The Crimbone believe a lot of crazy shit."

The Official banged a fist on the nearest wall. "All this one seems to believe in is finding his little abomination of a Spirelight wife. All you seem to give a shit about is what you want. Do you care about what the Gods of Spirah want, renegade?"

"The gods need agents to keep their people safe, and the lands they've claimed secure. While you've been shrieking at me like a little bitch, I've been thinking about how to best accomplish that."

The Official studied Vencie, with less certainty in his eyes.

Vencie smiled. "Look, Coscan doesn't know where his woman was taken any more than we do. He just knows she was snatched out from under him and taken to one of our homesteads. He doesn't give a shit about customs or borders or treaties, just about finding her. His pack doesn't give a shit about anything but what he says. They'll do again what they did in Tennessee, over and over 'til they find that girl…and they probably will, which you don't have a shot in hell at doing. What do you want me to do about it?"

The Official took a deep breath. "Who said I wanted you for anything?"

"Why else would you bother telling me?"

"Maybe I just wanted to see your face when you found out what a worthless, blasphemous fuck-up you are, before I have you executed."

"Or you could do the smart thing, which is pool enough agents to beat Coscan and his pack before they turn into a real unmanageable problem."

"What in the blue fuck could be more unmanageable than this?"

"If he's making as big a mess as you say, trust me, the Schomite government isn't any happier with him than we are. With so many of their beasts abandoning them for him, they'll be desperate. An alliance might even become necessary. Not to mention the Earth-line martial authority when they all realize this isn't exactly just another gang problem…especially when you consider how many young fledglings they have amongst them, just twiddling their thumbs waiting for something to make them jump one way or another. Imagine having to come a little cleaner to some of those Earth-line politicians and bankers about whose pockets they're really in. On the scale of *blasphemy*, that really would make me the least of your worries, wouldn't it?"

The Official glared no less hatefully, though now in a way that showed Vencie's points landing home, hard. "So, how does it make you any more useful?"

"At the very least, when have you ever complained about one more body for the meat grinder? Let me start by finding Sally Coscan."

"Why the hell would we want to find her? She's caused enough trouble, just like you. I'd like to see you try something against Coscan on your own. Maybe I *should* send you out after him. I can't think of a better punishment than what he would do to you." The Official paused. "If you suggest we barter her back to him—"

"I didn't say we should recapture her. We should find where she is and make sure Rob Coscan finds out too. He'll go wherever she is, and we'll be ready."

The Official took several calming breaths. "Two sets of enemies fighting each other."

"Once they've whittled each other down, we swarm them both. You have to admit, it's better than having to make deals with any of them."

"Well. Not bad. So, how do you plan to find out who took the altered girl?"

"I already know. Ever heard of the United Deschembines?"

"Hopeless blasphemers like you, only worse."

"The only thing they have in common with me is that they're smarter than you stuff-coats sticking to some stagnant straight-and-narrow. That's your problem."

The Official leaned against the bookcase. "I'll tell you my problem with those blasphemers. Ever hear of the last time someone broke from the *stagnant straight-and-narrow* and started calling themselves the United Deschembines? No, of course you haven't. It's only talked about in archives few are allowed to see, and it goes all the way back to the Old World itself…to the earliest days of the Spirah Empire."

"But you're going to tell me anyway."

"If it gets back to me that you've repeated it, I'll have you castrated. It was a rebellion, started by some field scientist gone insane. A whole city-state was taken over. The Tribunal infighting it sparked nearly tore the Empire in half. It took centuries to recover, and by then, the Crimbone had shown up. These punk kids calling themselves the United Deschembines now, one of their founders was another ranking official gone insane…Claudette Gris, a high-clearance Old World scholar, with access to those old writings. Many of her theories made the wrong people nervous, so we set a Secret Police family to investigate her. She seduced the male head of that family. When we learned of his infidelity, we had him killed. She fled into hiding, along with many of her translations she hadn't yet committed to the records. By the time we caught wind of her whereabouts, she was among those United Deschembine vermin."

"So you're so scared of anyone who breaks your rules, you've forgotten how to think like those of us who do. So you never imagine just how far we'll go, or where. Like right back in among you, for example."

"You think the United Deschembines have spies among the Tribunals?"

"How else could they have known we had Sally Coscan? The impostor was a Spirelight, right? Why else would Spirelights want to steal from Spirelights? If this Claudette Gris was—or is—smart and charismatic enough to pull a movement like that together, you don't think she has insider contacts…like, say, among her old high-clearance scholar pals? While we're at it, think about what Sally Coscan is, or at least whatever half-ass ideas you have about it. Know anyone else who'd be so interested in her?"

"Fine. Let's say it's the United Deschembines. No one's been able to find their central base of operation since we learned they're still straggling on. What makes you think you can?"

"You couldn't find Rob or Sally Coscan, either."

"So let me guess, you're already churning up a plan in that slimy brain of yours. What is it?"

"Now, now. I can't have you stealing my ideas."

"I could have them tortured out of you."

Vencie's smile didn't waver. "Try it." When he saw that the Official had no intention of doing so, he said, "So, what do you have to lose?"

The Official agonized over it some. "This isn't an instatement. You're still the renegade."

"Then why should I help?"

"So I don't have you killed, for starters. Secondly…" The Official had to drop his eyes. "…Because you still might be instated, if you make good on your claims. As long as you work on this, though, you work alone. If you're caught by anyone on either side, say whatever you like. No one in any of the Tribunals will acknowledge you, least of all me."

Vencie stooped, picked up several of the fallen books, and slid them gingerly back onto the shelf. He paused meaninglessly on a book he recognized. "Before I start, I'll have to look over some old records."

"What for?"

Vencie waved one finger tauntingly. "The master chef doesn't give out his recipes."

"Fine. What do you want to see?"

An hour later, the Official handed Vencie photocopies of the requested records. Vencie didn't glance at a word 'til the Official provided him with keys to a van.

"Which way to the nearest Earth-line town?" Vencie asked.

"You say you'll find Sally Coscan on your own. So find the nearest civilization on your own."

It took Vencie roughly forty-five minutes to do so. In a corner restaurant in a border town, he read between the lines of the Tribunal records on Sally Wildfire—they hadn't updated their data to list her as Sally Coscan—and on her brother Sheldon. Vencie and the Official both knew, even if they nervously avoided addressing it: the foul magic of the Schomites ran through all of this, from end to end, which was a more appropriate way of putting it than the Official knew.

Of course, the dark Schomite magic that had infected Sally Coscan was at the center. Vencie wasn't so arrogant as to deny its hand in his initial great find. Now magic was astir everywhere. Soon all the Secret Police would be needed against it. Sally Coscan wasn't its only Spirelight conduit, though, and the Secret Police had experienced as little luck finding the other.

'Til recently, Vencie wouldn't have hoped for much more luck. He doubted the United Deschembines' chances were any better. Still, he had a better idea about Schomite magic than he usually liked, along with a vague notion of how it might be affecting Sheldon Wildfire. If Vencie's ideas were near the mark, Sheldon would be busy looking for answers these days. Where else would he start but back in the place of his fateful run-in?

While reading through the files, Vencie noticed some intriguing, long dismissed footnotes, concerning

Earth-line connections made by the three surviving parties of the Brattleboro incident. Rob and Sally's weren't much help. Sheldon's, on the other hand…

Had the Tribunals forgotten the most fabled history? Did they think Magur Sevi's legendary siege to the eight winds of Deschemb had all been one howling charge? No, Sevi had trained certain select packs to resist the compulsion of slaughter, to mask their very beast nature and go ahead of the others, to infiltrate the local law enforcement of Spirelight-controlled lands. Hence, they'd managed to reach the Officials there and break the leadership from within, so the organization had crumbled, making way for the full-on attacks. So you might say, for once in history, the Crimbone had their own Secret Police.

Now, apparently, so did the United Deschembines.

The Spirelights of ancient Deschemb would never have believed it, any more than they'd believed the end had come down to the moment the black metal cut or crushed out their life, and not because the Crimbone had so well masked their beast natures. They were children of Spirah, after all, the greatest of all pantheons, and it was too unthinkable that their gods would give them over to such lowly horrors. Maybe that arrogance was why the gods had left them to their fates. Vencie, on the other hand, listened to the brains with which his gods had blessed him.

The Wildfire family had always been one of the most formidable among the Secret Police, though they'd been increasingly known for their questionable field tactics. The Tribunal hadn't let Syless Wildfire know that they were aware of his indiscretions, because he and his family never pushed their luck too far, and they always brought home results that outweighed their ethical violations.

The Tribunal had also known how particularly unpredictable young Sheldon could be, though this also went unaddressed, so long as his father kept him in check. Apparently, no one stopped to speculate *just how* unpredictable Sheldon might get, once left to his own devices. Now Vencie thought about Sheldon Wildfire in broader terms. So had the United Deschembine spies, no doubt, when they'd read these same records. Circumstances had favored them with Sally. Now they knew, as Vencie did, that the time was right to go for Sheldon.

Naturally, by the time Vencie reached Vermont, the United Deschembines would have come and gone, taking Sheldon with them. Vencie was more than fine with that.

THE CASTLE

ONE

Sheldon slept for most of the trip so he could dream about Janie. That turned out to be a bad idea. In one dream, he was back in Brattleboro, but it wasn't his promised homecoming after all this was over. No, the trucker dropped him off at the edge of a town he hadn't seen in five years, all over again. This time after the walk, he didn't go to the bar and meet Lou. Instead, he went straight into the Common Ground, which was still up and running. Some of the same hippies were there. They recognized and talked with him, even though he hadn't known any of them when he was eleven. Two of them shouldn't have been there: the caustic, dark-haired manager and the bum who'd come out of the bathroom right before eleven-year-old Sheldon had started interrogating said manager.

The manager smiled and served Sheldon a bowl of chili that sure as hell wasn't vegan, and the bum sat next to him swilling a forty of Newcastle. The chili tasted like the blood that had filled Sheldon's mouth on Marlboro Mountain as he'd forced himself to walk back through the woods to the college campus, while holding his own guts in. When Janie wandered in, she was the only one who looked at him like he didn't belong there. When he called her over, she sat opposite him and talked a little, but he couldn't make her laugh.

Because she was the only one who knew the manager and the bum were dead.

Or maybe she knew they weren't, and she was the only one who knew Sheldon was supposed to be dead. He'd never killed those men, so his dad had never knocked his head against that counter. Maybe she just remembered him beating the shit out of three punk kids outside the teen center, giving one of them brain damage.

She wouldn't feel that way if he talked to her long enough, if he reminded her of enough good times past. *If I can make her laugh just once, I'll be able to fix everything else, too.*

It was because she was Earth-line, because of the weak Earth-line way of thought she'd grown up around. Damnit, Janie should be beyond that! She was so much stronger, so much smarter than any other Earth-line person he'd ever met, except maybe her mom. It was all these fucking hippies' fault, poisoning her with their self-righteous weakness. Two long knives, made from a black metal that was stronger and sharper than anything of this world, hung heavy in their scabbards from his belt. He wanted to draw those blades and kill all these weak, self-righteous people, make them scream louder than the manager had, then go outside and keep killing 'til there was no one left to poison Janie with their weakness.

Sheldon woke up and talked to Tiger a little, then went back to sleep so he could find a better dream. This time, Brattleboro was pretty much as he'd left it, except half the buildings had burned down, and the other half looked ready to be condemned. Janie was still there, and she wasn't with that rat-faced skater-asshole anymore. No, now she was with a lurching lop-faced fucker named Russ, too brain damaged to remember that Sheldon was the one who'd fractured his skull, broken both his legs, and stuffed him in a trash can when they were kids. Sheldon asked Janie how her mom was, and she looked at him like she had in the Common Ground during the first dream. He left her with her brain-damaged punk and went to the house on Washington Street. Annie sat on her front porch and looked at him like when he'd come for his backpack.

"Thought you'd already left, little brave."

He looked around at the burnt-out block. "Is this what I did, by coming back here?"

"Maybe…or it could be what'll happen either way."

"So, how can I keep this from happening?"

"Who said you could? If you can, you won't do it by stayin' here waitin'."

Sheldon was sick of this shit, so he woke up. Through the van's windows, the side of the highway dropped off sharply to the right. The treetops spread thick and smooth like the earth of a bare field, against a white-hot tin sky. Hundreds of feet out, the trees split for what looked like the white painted towers of a medieval castle. What the hell was a thing like that doing around here? He had no idea where they were, but somehow the sight didn't look so natural as the Bloody Tower looming from the hills of Brattleboro. Wouldn't it be funny if that's where the United Deschembines were hiding out?

"Are we in Virginia yet?" he asked.

"Yeah," said Claudette from the driver's seat. "Almost home, boy. Just sit tight."

"You missed the trip," Blix said from the front passenger seat. "I didn't think it was possible for someone to sleep that long."

"Yeah man." Tiger gave a dry grin. "We stopped at five different whorehouses! I tried wakin' you up. For a while, we figured you were dead. I even found the perfect girl for you, too, totally your type. This hot Native American girl, tall and slender with perfect skin. Brought her out to the van to see if she could wake you up. She said you were cute. I told her she could try sucking your cock, see if that'd wake you up, but she said she didn't feel right molesting a kid in his sleep."

"He's bullshitting you, man," said Blix, "just trying to make you feel better. Nah, we only stopped at one whorehouse."

From the driver's seat, Claudette scowled, then smirked and shook her head.

Sheldon rolled his eyes and half-grinned. "Hey, next time, if she's that pretty, slip her twenty extra bucks and say she can molest me all she likes. At least I'll probably have better dreams."

"Will do." Tiger shot him a thumbs-up.

Wait a second. Since when do these guys know my type?

Sheldon looked up front at Claudette. She just smirked and rolled her eyes again.

The van swerved onto a steep exit ramp that took them onto a country highway. They went half a mile before turning onto a paved driveway that wove through the trees, 'til they passed a gutted tollbooth with a broken beam, into a dilapidated parking lot. At the far end, past a string of turnstiles, rose the castle spires Sheldon had seen from the road. They drove through the checkpoint into what looked, all in all, like some four square blocks surrounding the mini-castle.

"Well, fuck me," Sheldon muttered. "Figures."

"What," Tiger asked, "that we're shacked up in what's left of a closed down Z-grade Disneyland knockoff?"

"Pretty much. I've slept in places like this. Got picked up for vagrancy in one of them."

"We have some under-the-table local permits," Claudette explained. "People who live around here know to keep clear."

"How'd you get that message across? Just beat the ass of whoever comes snooping?"

"Not usually," said Tiger. "Usually when they come around, just a few of us go out, say howdy, act so they think we must be like the hillbillies out of Deliverance or some shit. They usually leave in kind of a hurry after that."

"Yeah, pretty much," said Claudette.

Sheldon remembered how the castle towers had looked from the road. He doubted most people didn't find that eye-catching. "Some kind of *hide in plain sight* deal, huh?"

"Nah," said Tiger, "more of a *hide someplace so dogshit piss-poor, no one thinks to look there* deal."

"So, where is everyone?"

"Inside, mostly. Most folks 'round here like to sleep during the day."

Blix looked around nervously. "So is this a good time to spring it on him?"

Claudette sighed. "Well, no use beating around it forever, I suppose. Let's go see if she's still up."

They led Sheldon through the open castle doors. The inside was one broad, high hallway that led straight to the other end. It would look more like the hallway of an office block than that of a royal dwelling, if the walls hadn't been painted in images depicting ancient Earth-line myth, everything from Greek gods to Arthurian knights. On either side were a few sunken doorways. They reminded Sheldon of the padlocked door to the Bloody Tower.

Claudette led Sheldon through the last door on the left, then down a staircase into another hallway, this one dark and narrow, with walls, ceiling, and floor carved from stone. A string of chemical lights ran along the center of the ceiling, to the right and the left. This hallway must stretch further than the grounds above. It branched off in at least a dozen places, into darker passages that Sheldon didn't look down. They didn't walk far, but it seemed like a mile. Claudette knocked on a door with light spilling through the seams.

"Yeah?" said a male voice within, crisp with annoyance.

Claudette looked perturbed. "It's us. We're back."

"It okay if I take off?" Tiger whispered. "I need to check on everyone."

By *everyone*, Sheldon guessed he meant whomever he'd talked to on the motel phone back in Brattleboro.

Claudette nodded. "You've worked hard. Go home and see to yours."

Sheldon was glad to see Tiger go. He'd hit it off best with Tiger, but suspected the man's wit wouldn't help whatever was about to happen. When the door opened, the dark Schomite with long black hair didn't look happy to see Sheldon.

Claudette glared. "Didn't come at a bad time, did we?"

The man cocked an eyebrow. "Now why would you say that?"

"I don't know. What brings you here?"

When the man opened the door fully, Sheldon noticed his clothes were a size larger than his frame. Only Blix's face stayed neutral. However rank went around here, Claudette and this man were on equal footing. That put them both high above Blix, so the tension between them was none of his business. That was the most sense of rank Sheldon had gotten so far, beyond Claudette's natural sense of authority. Spotting it now might comfort him, if it hadn't been for the way this new guy eyed him.

Sheldon put out his hand, said unreadably, "I'm Sheldon Wildfire."

"I know who you are. My name's Deacon." Deacon shook Sheldon's hand. "Well, Claudette saw fit to bring you here. So, I guess that's that for the moment."

Everyone stepped aside. Sheldon realized he was meant to go first. Claudette stepped behind him. That was better than having Deacon at his back. The red-carpeted room within looked like it might actually belong in a castle. Curtains of every hue lined the walls. A puffy circular bed sat in the middle.

On the far end, a woman sat at a stained mahogany table, dressed in plain clothes, chin on her hand. She stood up and looked at Sheldon curiously. Recognition set in and she drew up sharply. One of her hips bumped the table so it shook behind her. "*What the hell is this?*"

Sheldon might have asked the same question. Sally had changed remarkably little since that night on Marlboro Mountain, except she was tanner and better fed. There was a new sharpness to her, telling him he wouldn't get the drop on her now like he had back then. It spoke well of her Secret Police upbringing, except something about it was too animalistic to be Spirelight. At first, he didn't even connect it with the Schomite *alterations*, as Mom used to call them, the old changes that had sent their lives spiraling towards this moment in the first place.

Because suddenly those alterations *don't feel so alien. Why* should *I notice them right off, any more than when I look in the mirror?*

Sheldon turned and hurried out of the room. No one tried to stop him.

It was Deacon who found him at the foot of the stairs, leaning on the railing. "So once you get yourself together, are you going back in there?"

"Do you want me to?"

"No."

"This is fucked."

"I agree. It went better than I expected, though not as well as Claudette hoped."

Sheldon looked up for the first time. "So you know…I guess she's told you…"

"How you tried to kill her, how gave her that scar next to her eye?"

"I did kill her," said Sheldon. "I killed her to myself. I guess I always assumed in the back of my mind that it was the best thing I could have done for her."

"Leaving her with *him?*"

"With the beast?" Sheldon saw how the slur offended Deacon. He felt pretty good about it. "So, where is he? You guys got a nice happy reunion with him, ready for me behind Door Number Two?"

"*What?*" Deacon's face wrinkled in disgusted confusion. "No one knows where *he* is. She thinks he's dead, but none of us believe that."

What the hell was going on here, anyway? Obviously, it was a lot bigger than this twisted little family reunion. Whatever the explanation, Sheldon didn't want to hear it from Deacon. "So what, she with you now or something?"

"No." From the hatred on Deacon's face, Sheldon guessed the guy had just now been in there trying to change that, without any luck. "We agreed not to tell her about you 'til you got here. I just expected better sense out of Claudette, a little more forewarning, or something. I guess she's back there right now—her and Blix trying to convince your sister of why you should be here."

Sheldon shrugged and looked around. Down the hall, in the light that spilled through Sally's door, Claudette watched impassively. For the first time since the walk to the motel, Sheldon actively disliked her. Did she see it as some test, standing back to see how Sheldon would deal with this prick? Deacon was Schomite, but Sheldon couldn't spot a drop of Crimbone blood in him. So it wasn't a horror that the guy was trying to get into Sally's pants, just an insult.

Sheldon said to Deacon, "What do you say we go outside and talk about it, huh?"

Right on cue, Claudette walked up. "Blix has told Sally the score. Sheldon, are you ready to talk to your sister?"

"Wanna tell *me* the score first?"

"I already have. She's here for the same reasons you are."

"Yeah, but how the hell did she get here?"

"Ask her yourself."

Sheldon huffed, then walked back to Sally's room as Blix headed out.

Sally had sat back down but looked more on edge, more ready to kill him than Deacon was. "Well hi, little brother."

He moved towards her. "I guess 'til a few minutes ago, you assumed I was dead."

"Not really."

He sat on the bed facing her. "So…what's your take on all this?"

"My take? What, you mean all this crazy shit about

how I'm—how *we're* both supposed to be some great symbols or leaders or some shit to these people? I have no idea. I just wish I knew if my husband's dead or not. Either way, I wish I was with him."

The word *husband* jolted Sheldon out of his maudlin state. So did her last words. Also in those words, he heard his sister—really heard her *as* his sister—for the first time in as long as he could remember. She'd called him *little brother.* He studied her face.

"How'd you get separated from him, then?" he asked. "How'd you get here?"

She gave him a short version.

"Well, I haven't decided what I think of it, either," he said. "'Til you find out what happened to…your husband, I don't guess we have anywhere else to go."

"No, I guess not. I'd leave now and go straight back to Florida if I thought he was still there. I know him, though. He's either dead or out looking for me, and there's no more way for me to find him than he has a shot in hell of finding this place."

"Florida, huh."

She gave a choked, surprised laugh. "Yeah. It was real nice for a while, 'til…I guess a week ago. I'm almost afraid to ask what you've been doing all this time."

"I think if I told you about the first two years, you'd find it pretty familiar."

She stared. As she realized what he meant, her eyes brightened with tears. For a moment, everything that was wrong between them slipped from her face.

He stood up. "I don't know if I can deal with this right now. I'm sorry."

"Same here, really."

"I meant…I'm sorry for everything."

"Yeah," she said. "Me too."

He walked out, passed Claudette, Blix, and Deacon at the stairs.

"Still care to step outside?" asked Deacon.

"I'm going out. Come on if you like."

Deacon might have obliged, but Claudette put a hand on his shoulder.

When Sheldon breathed fresh air, it seemed his head might clear enough to make sense of all this.

Soon Claudette came out. "Started picking up the pieces?"

"I guess we've made a start, if anyone could."

"Let me know if you need to talk. Also, please don't pick fights with Deacon. Whatever you believe about civilian Schomites, he's not someone you want to fuck with."

"That's fine. Neither am I."

"I'll let him know. Hopefully, he's less of a stubborn jackass about it than you are. You're both assholes, though, so who knows?"

Before Sheldon could answer, Tiger came hurrying across the grounds, suddenly not looking so ready with a joke. "You said you found Sally at the Tennessee homestead, right? Right? *Right?*"

"That's what I said and that's what I meant," said Claudette. "What?"

Tiger just kept sweating and shaking, getting paler and paler. "You guys ain't gonna like this."

Two

Night had barely fallen, but everyone was already awake. A great tent stood hoisted at the far end of the grounds, strung through the upper inner seams with lights. Sheldon stood next to Tiger and his wife Lilly, behind the long, high, wooden stage. Tiger had done well for himself, Sheldon had to admit—Lilly was an auburn-haired, round-hipped hippie with a belly-dancer's build, a freckled, heart-shaped face, doe-brown eyes, and a silver-bell voice. *Spritely* was a word he sensed usually described her. Tonight, she stood pensive and somber like most of the crowd. On the other side of the stage, he heard the residents bustling and murmuring.

He'd never known either Spirelights or Schomites to be so nervous. The old impulse was to assume they'd all let Earth-line weakness get hold of them. An older impulse was to assume that the intermingling had brought about the weakness. Still another impulse was to think that the Earth-line weakness had allowed the intermingling. Sheldon saw no such thing in either Tiger or Lilly, even when Tiger had come with the news.

Earth-line people would be rioting out there. Spirelights without a warlike bone in them would be attacking their Schomite friends, not like lions as warriors, but panicked apes. He was still trying to talk himself out of his prejudices—a petty Earth-line word for it—yet here he was with these people, standing as a friend with these two Schomites.

Claudette and Deacon approached. Between them strode a woman wearing a light summer dress made of fabric that shimmered even back here with barely any light to catch. The patterns of the fabric didn't seem woven *through* it, but *within* it, dancing like images in a crystal ball, like a window into the Old World. Sheldon had never realized how beautiful Sally was. Maybe it was easier to see, now that she was no longer with the beast. After today's news from Tennessee, how could she be? As he approached, he almost forgot the tension between them. He could tell she hadn't, but it wasn't her active concern.

Some cruel part of Sheldon wanted to ask, *So, what do you think of your beast now?* Instead, he took a deep breath. "I want us to be brother and sister again."

She tried to smile. "We were always brother and sister. Just, we were enemies for a while, too."

"So you're not—"

"That's all come and gone. We're a son and daughter of the Spirelight Secret Police."

Something pulsed and flickered through his midsection scar. "Not anymore. I don't even know if we're still Spirelights. We—"

She grabbed his shoulder hard enough to hurt and looked him dead in the eye. No one but their dad had ever laid so forceful a hand on him without meaning to fight. "We're still Spirelights, whatever else we've become. No, neither of us will ever do the work of the Secret Police again, but we still need to act *as* Secret

Police, in whatever we fight for."

What the fuck was that supposed to mean? To act as Spirelight Secret Police was to do the duty of the Spirelight coterie. "So, what are we fighting for now?" he said.

"To survive. What else is left?" The other four watched intently, none more so than Deacon. So Sally said, "Okay. I guess we should do this."

"Do what?" Sheldon asked.

"I need to speak to the crowd," Deacon cut in. "Then you two have to come up there so they can see you. I'll let Claudette explain you to them. Let's see if you have the effect she hopes for."

"We've gotta work on the whole *filling Sheldon in about important shit in advance* thing," Sheldon said.

"We'll do that," Sally said to Deacon. "Then I'm leaving."

Everyone's eyes widened. "What?" Deacon snapped. She threw him a dismissive glance then said to everyone, "Rob's out there looking for me. Once I find him, all this'll end."

"So, what about what he's already done?" Deacon barked.

"I don't care," said Sally. "I was at that place, remember? Those people…they took me and they…I'm glad they're all dead."

"You don't mean that," said Deacon, trying to sound comforting.

"What the hell do you care?" she spat, shivering more violently. "Any last one of them would have loved to kill you and anyone here, then piss on your corpses.

Yes, I damn well mean it!"

Tiger butted in, "Hold on! We don't even know for sure that it's the High Natural."

The last of Sally's pissed-off bravado slipped away. She hugged herself and whispered, "It's Rob. I know him. I know how far he'll go. I don't want it to go any further."

"He's gone further than you know," said Deacon. "Even if he still thinks he's trying to rescue you, he probably wouldn't even know you if he saw you by now. He'll kill you. He might have killed you if he found you at the homestead."

"You know, I seem to recall a lot of people telling me that when I first got together with him. They didn't know him any better than you do. They didn't know me, either. Guess what? Neither do you, asshole!"

"It's not just Rob," said Claudette, "and it won't stop with him. It's not just his pack going crazy anymore, either. This'll spread. And…well, what he did at the homestead…however he got through to it—" She studied everyone's faces. "It's too early to tell. There are things I shouldn't talk about 'til I've seen more." She put a hand on Deacon's shoulder. "You need to go speak to them now. They're getting restless."

Deacon sighed, eyes dropping. He looked at them all, pleading silently for support. With or without it, he straightened himself and walked up a small staircase. Sheldon craned to see. He didn't want to be up there, in front of all those people who'd willfully cast off their coteries, the sort of people he'd been raised to hunt, to persecute, to kill. For all he knew, there were people out there whose loved ones his parents had slaughtered or tortured. He started up the stairs.

Claudette caught his shoulder. "Not yet."

Meanwhile, Sally had started crying silently, trying to keep anyone else from noticing. Lilly noticed and went to her. The two young women hugged, one crying on the other's shoulder. Sheldon ambled away and paced alone.

On the stage, Deacon said in a strong, carrying voice, "Let me start by addressing you all as friends. That's what we are, and that's why we're here together. Why'd we first come together like this? Because our lineages had failed us? Because our coteries had failed us? No. We came together, not to abandon our heritage, but to move it forward, to understand and embrace what it's truly taught us, including our oldest mistakes. We came together to share with each other what we've learned, so it may continue into the future, so the descendants of the Old World might survive whatever this world is about to become, that we may finally have the right to truly be part of it." The crowd had gone silent. "Yes, we first came together for survival, because we realized there was no survival left on the old paths, though this new one often feels even harder. Still we *have* survived, because of the bonds we've forged through our struggle.

"Today, we learned that the great change of this world has started, the one we all saw coming. Some of you remember those you left behind, who weren't ready to follow you on this bold new path. Some of those loved ones died in Tennessee. You were never wrong to love them. You aren't wrong to grieve for them now. It's the friends who stand with you now, to your right and to your left, who need your attention, who need your love and your strength. To endure what's ahead, you'll need to forge that bond stronger than ever. Looking out at all your faces, I guess you already knew that. Now there's someone Claudette wants you all to meet."

Sheldon figured that was his cue. Deacon, a Schomite, had used the word coterie, and his voice sounded respectful and truthful. What did he understand about Spirelight heritage? Sheldon knew himself to be cut off from that heritage.

To be a Spirelight was to be the living embodiment of the light of Spirah, a light that was supposed to rule and guide whatever land through which it shone. The Schomites spat in the face of that light and sought to snuff it out. All things considered, he wasn't sure he blamed them anymore. These Spirelights here didn't seem interested in spreading the rule of their light. Sheldon spotted Claudette approaching the stage, followed by Sally. Sheldon hurried up and fell in beside her.

Claudette stepped aside. "You two go first," she whispered. "It's you they need to see now."

Sheldon ran a hand back through his hair. "I'll see what I can do. I don't know. That was a pretty tough act to follow."

Sally reached for his hand. "Come on, little brother."

He let her lead him up the stairs. For a moment, all he could think was, *Sally—my sister who I once tried to kill—just looked at me with love…and she means it. She just took my hand, and she means it.*

Before them spread the crowd, eyes falling one by one onto them. None of them could tell exactly what they were looking at. There must've been at least a hundred. He couldn't tell how many were Spirelights and how many were Schomites. There were no Crimbone, and no Secret Police except him and Sally.

Claudette stepped up beside them. "Friends, if there's a fracture in your hope or faith in what we strive for...I introduce to you Sheldon and Sally Wildfire. You've all heard their stories, how they were born into the Spirelight Secret Police, how the Tribunals would have you believe they've been tainted by the Crimbone essence. The Tribunals would tell you they represent the seeds of our destruction. It's true that they're no longer only Spirelights, but something both Spirelight and Schomite. It's also true, as many of you have learned firsthand, that children can't be born between the two races. Yet I tell you now, and let you see with your own hearts and souls, here are those children. Here is proof that you have a future...a future of unity, of redemption."

Now Sheldon wondered if he and Sally were supposed to say something. Looking at her, he saw she had no more of a clue than him. When he looked back at the crowd, he realized neither of them needed to say anything. For just right now, these people had forgotten to be afraid, because of something he wasn't even sure he could believe. It felt like all that fear had gone out of them into him...*almost like a Crimbone absorbing the glow*...except without hurting them. Plus, wasn't that experience supposed to be more enjoyable than this, for the Crimbone, anyway? His and Sally's hands squeezed tighter than ever.

"Can we leave this stage yet?" he whispered to her.

"I don't know, but I'm about to, either way."

"You're both tired," they heard Claudette say. "You've done all you have to do for them tonight. Thank you."

Sally and Sheldon thundered back down the stairs, pulling each other along. They kept going, into the woods, 'til they reached the fence surrounding the grounds. She let go of his hand and clutched the wire mesh.

"Jesus, this is fucked…" He spotted her strange look. "What?"

"Nothing," she said. "So what do you plan to do?"

"Right now, every muscle in my body is telling me to jump this fence and go straight back to Vermont."

"Wait, hold up," said Sally. "You went back to *Vermont?* To *Brattleboro?*"

Sheldon couldn't remember a funnier look on her face. Yeah, now that he thought about it, she was probably even further behind on things than he was. "Well, yeah."

"I'm afraid to ask—"

"Look, it's a long story. I don't even really know what your experience of the place was like, but…well, things seem good back there these days, for what it's worth. *Really* good, actually. I've got a girl back there, would you believe? An *Earth-line* girl…I wish I was still back there with her."

Sally took a moment to process this. "I hate to be

the one to say it, but—"

"I know. It's good for her that I'm not. With everything that's about to happen everywhere. Hell, at this point, I expect I'll get killed wherever I go. If I stay here, I'll probably live a little longer, and I'll give these folks some hope, just by walking around looking pretty. They seem cool, mostly. You've been around them longer. What do you think of 'em?"

She shrugged. "They're decent folks. I like the nocturnal schedule everyone keeps."

"So, what's up between you and that Deacon guy?"

"He started out as a cool friend. I still respect him in a lot of ways, but more and more, he just acts like a pushy creep."

"Okay, then. Anyway, yeah, I guess I'll stay here for now. If I manage anything other than symbolizing these folks' fairy-tale, so they die thinking it's all made two squirts of piss worth of difference, then I guess I didn't turn out too bad."

"You haven't, at all." She ruffled his hair. After some silence she said, "I still haven't decided what I'll do."

"So your…him…Rob. What'll he do if he finds this place?"

"I can't say. That's why I'm still thinking of leaving, to find him on my own. If I'm back with him, he won't give a shit about this place, or anyone else who doesn't try to fuck with us."

"Then you don't believe what Deacon said?"

"No."

"Sorry."

"He's a good man, Sheldon." She rested her head on his shoulder. "I know how that sounds to you, I really do, and I'm so sorry—"

"Believe it or not, I sort of understand. I think of that night…on Marlboro Mountain…what I did—"

"Dude, I told you, you don't have to—"

His face tightened and he stared out into the night. "I can't help it, and not just 'cause of what I did—what I almost did. Now I think about Janie…"

"That her? Your Vermont Earth-line girl?"

"Yeah. I think about if I saw someone attack her like that…You're right, she's better off. Sorry. I just can't see how some things could ever be fixed. I don't see how these people in their broke down fairy-tale land think they can fix what the Crimbone and the Secret Police have done for countless ages over two whole worlds. Things could go all sorts of ways from here, but I can't think of any where everything doesn't just get worse."

She buried her face in his sleeve. "Worse than it's always been?"

He had to think about that one. "Was it any better when you were with him?"

"Yeah. For a while, things were better than I ever imagined they could be."

How many years had his sister known that happiness? If he'd ever known anything close, it had lasted the total of an hour. Oh well. Time didn't matter, not in terms of what an experience had given you, or taken away. "You ever miss them?" he said. "Our folks? I mean…before what they did?"

"Sometimes, yeah. How 'bout you?"

"Hell no."

She sputtered laughter then cupped her mouth guiltily.

"Sometimes I try imagining what I'd be like by now," he went on, "if things had happened different. I just can't do it. All I know is, I've got nothing left in common with that guy."

"I don't know about that," she said. "I still recall that little guy who was the only one with the guts to disobey Mom, who stayed behind in that examination room…who loosened the straps and slipped me that knife on his way out…Seems to me, you've still got plenty in common with him."

"Thanks," he sighed. "Who I am now, though, *what* I am now, that's all I have left."

She squeezed his shoulder. "Not anymore."

Someone came through the trees. "Hey, you two."

Sheldon didn't stand but reached up and clasped hands with Tiger. "How's it going, jackass?"

"There's quite a party going now, thanks to you, you scuzzy little bastard!"

Sally smirked. "So, are our fans calling for us?"

"Nah. Right now they're just loving life more than I've seen in a long time. I'll bet there are Spirelight-Schomite couples half hoping to get pregnant tonight. Talk about *filling 'em with the glow*—oh, sorry, was that a little—"

"You callin' us glowsticks, you fuckin' dirt-worshipping Schomite hippie bastard?" Sheldon grinned, then said seriously, "I gotta hand it to him, that was a pretty good speech Deacon gave."

"Yeah. The fucker's shit with people, good with crowds."

"Hey, I'm shit with both," Sheldon said. "That why he makes the speeches and Claudette does the planning?"

"Hey, you're pretty sharp."

Sally asked, "So, what does Claudette have planned next?"

"No one's planned anything next. Tonight's a night to dance, get drunk, and fuck. Speaking of which, I'd better go find Lilly before she figures I've bailed and decides to switch to girls for the night. I just wanted to check on you two heroes."

Sheldon and Sally exchanged glances. The surreal chill was lost on neither of them.

"So, when's the planning start?" Sally asked.

"Soon as we have an idea what to plan for. Hate to say it, but that probably won't be 'til we get some even worse news."

ON THE RUN

ONE

Janie got up from the couch, where Rose and Becky both sat gaping in horrific disbelief at the national news. At least they wouldn't grill her anymore about Sheldon or Allen, or both. She knew it was callous, which was more self-honesty than she credited anyone else here with. Rose and Becky had visited her today at work, had told her to swing by Henry's party when she got off.

At first, she hadn't planned to go. Then Ashley had hurried panting into the shop and slipped quickly out of view of the window, as if she was hiding from someone. "That fat girl ain't been in here, has she?"

"The one you were with at the Spot yesterday? No, I ain't seen her." The Spot was what everyone called the grassy plot with graffitied stone benches, between a little bridge leading to the Brattleboro Food Co-op and the crumbling parking lot across from the transit center.

Ashley was short and brown, skin and bones, with a hawk's nose, sunken eyes, and a head of tangled hair that was badly dyed red and grown out dark brown halfway. She wore all black and always carried around a ratty backpack with a raggedy doll of Tigger from *Winnie the Pooh* sewn to the side. Tigger was full of safety pins that made him look like a heavily pierced punk rocker.

Today, Ashley's eyes were even wider, blearier, and twitchier than usual. "Sorry," she mumbled, edging along the wall.

"It's okay." Janie looked around. No customers were in.

"Sorry," Ashley repeated. "I'm jus' sick of that bitch—"

"Why, what's up? I thought you two were, um, getting close."

"She was gettin' close. I was desperate, so she said she'd give me drugs all week if I made out with her whenever she felt like it."

"Oh, my God!" Janie noticed fresh bruises on Ashley's neck and arms. Normally, she wouldn't have noticed at this distance, but now—

"I'm just avoiding the bitch is all." Ashley was still trying to sound tough. "Can I hang out here a while? I only got a few bucks, but I'll buy somethin' so I ain't loitering."

"No, it's cool. I'm gonna close up in a few minutes anyway. You can sit around and wait for me."

"Thanks. You ain't gonna make me make out with you, are you?"

"Didn't plan on it."

"I will if you want me to, you know. I ain't tryin' to bribe you or nothin'. I actually like you well enough,

Janie." Ashley's eyes twinkled a little.

"No, it's okay, really."

"That's cool. I wasn't tryin' to—"

"Ah, shit." Janie looked out the window.

"What?" Ashley perked up like a nervous rabbit.

"You might wanna go hide in the bathroom for a minute."

A moment after Ashley scurried out of sight, in trudged a shaven headed ball of pasty, pimply flesh, covered in bad tattoos and piercings that looked infected, shrink-wrapped in a black tank top and jeans. "Hey, you seen Ashley?" she asked in a deep, sleepy voice.

The eyes and voice made Janie think of her boyfriend—ex-boyfriend, she now guessed. Suddenly she felt dirty, about Allen, about her whole life lately. She wanted to kick the lardball's ass, more than she already had after Ashley's story. Instead, she just said, "No, sorry."

Janie was ready for trouble, for the whole song and dance: *Don't give me that, you skinny bitch. I kick your ass! I know she here. I saw her come in here, blah, blah fuckin' blah.* "Okay," it moaned instead and trudged out, slumping shoulders that looked like soggy slabs of rancid ham.

As Janie closed up shop, Ashley came out and said, "Is it okay if I hang out with you a while, jus' 'til I find some other folks who got my back?"

"That's cool. I hear there's a party a friend of mine's throwing."

"Henry's party?"

"Yeah. Wanna go there with me?"

"You don't think the bitch'll show up?"

"If she does, me, Henry, Liam, and my other guy friends there'll have your back."

On the way, Janie put her arm around Ashley. Hopefully she wasn't sending the wrong signal. Either way, it meant she'd ended up at the party after all. Allen showed up, drank one beer, then left after barely saying hi. That was good enough for Janie, more than she needed in fact. The more his face healed, the less he had to say to her, and he was down to a black eye. When she'd seen him the day after Sheldon left, he'd looked like half his face had turned into a giant, dark, juicy grape. At first, she'd wondered if Sheldon had neglected to tell her about the encounter on purpose. No, Sheldon wouldn't even consider a thing like that worth mentioning. More and more, she felt like she agreed with him. Maybe that made her a horrible person, even if Allen was a jerk who she'd been wasting her time with out of lack of self-respect anyway. By now, she only got mad at Sheldon whenever someone asked about him, for leaving her to answer for his bullshit.

Henry was a guy who'd had trouble at home, so he'd moved in with his older brother Mack, who was cool with Henry flooding the place with his friends all the time. Mack was usually too stoned himself to worry about all the underage drinking and weed smoking he was hosting. As Janie got another beer, she passed Mack's open bedroom door. Mack's face was glued more intently than usual to his big computer screen. Henry went in to ask if he could borrow the bigger bong, and Mack said, "Shut up, quiet, man. Come here, check this shit out."

One by one, Rose, Becky, and Ashley drifted into Mack's room to see what was taking Henry so long. Janie saw them all crowding each other to look at the computer screen, so she figured she might as well check out whatever was so fascinating. Probably the latest YouTube viral train wreck. Except no one was laughing. A video news feed showed two aerial views, divided by a split screen. Each showed a string of houses along with one or two larger buildings in the middle of a vast field. The one on the left sort of reminded her of Buddhist communes she'd seen up in northern Vermont. Mom used to go there to visit old friends, and would take Janie and Larry with her when they weren't in school. For some reason, the footage also reminded her of grainy photographs of pioneer settlements from the old west. Except that was a weird layout for the wild west, or a hippie commune. Janie got an odd feeling looking at it, like she might get dizzy if she gazed too long. From above, it sort of looked like a face.

The helicopter shot revealed many shapes sprawled in the grass, between and around the buildings. The earth around them was darker than mud. The place on the right had roughly the same layout, except it was scorched black, the smoke and soot still too thick to see what was left of the bodies. The clouds gave the face agonized eyes and a screaming mouth...*like the face of a screaming god.* The latter was discovered first because of the fire, though the one on the left had happened days earlier.

Rose and Becky took a couch to the left of the computer desk that still let them see the screen. Ashley had found a male friend, a skinny boy in a *Calvin and*

Hobbes-style striped T-shirt, and they cuddled close. She was shakier than ever, looked ready to cry at the screen. Janie noticed the newsfeed sidebar, links to more coverage of the massacre, as well as links for national weather forecasts and stories about the history of solar flares. That was a weird mix, she thought.

When someone knocked at the front door, Mack asked, "Who is it?" He spoke in a drawn out, wary voice like he was scared it was the cops, or maybe whoever had killed all those people down south, come to get him like the bogeyman.

"It's Liam," the door answered. When Mack shouted an okay, in walked an impossibly tall, thin, long-necked fellow made entirely of tight, knotted muscles. Shaggy hair hung past his shoulders, and his mustache twirled up at the corners like Snidely Whiplash above a long, pointy beard. He ambled into the bedroom and said, "Hey Mack, can I get that claw hammer back from you? Oh hey, guys, what'cha watching?" His voice and eyes were somehow eternally boyish, in a way that stood out funny from the rest of his eccentric, wild ruggedness.

"You heard about this shit down in Tennessee and Kentucky?" asked Mack.

"It ain't Kentucky," said Henry. "The second place is…New Mexico, I think. Hold up, they'll probably say it again in a second."

"Huh. Yeah." Liam's face slackened with melancholy. "This the first you guys have heard of this?"

"Yeah. Hey man, I think that hammer's somewhere on the kitchen table. You closed the door right, didn't let the cats out?"

"Yeah, cool, man, thanks. Say, you mind if I grab a beer?"

"Sure, help yourself," said Henry. "Hey, there might be a bowl on the table with a little somethin' in it if you like, too."

Liam looked disconcerted to hear the younger brother answer, then shrugged and headed back towards the kitchen. Janie, who hadn't sat down, drifted after him. The kitchen table was a shamble of random crap, so Mack hadn't been kidding when he said the hammer was *somewhere* on it. At least the half-smoked bowl was easy to find.

As he cracked a beer, Liam said, "Hey Janie, how you been?"

"Been better, but I'm okay today."

They sat at the table after clearing enough space for their beers and elbows. She watched his face and shoulders. He seemed to be sinking deep into sad reflection. Liam taught fencing up at Marlboro College, and kung-fu at the local Dojo. He rented the basement of this building and used it as a tool shed and workshop, where he did everything from fix furniture to craft medieval-style suits of armor and basic fencing equipment. Much of the year he was out of town, traveling extensively with various Renaissance Festival groups.

The reporters called those places communes— hippie communes, maybe—because they didn't know what else to call them, or who the people there were. Maybe they were involved in some of those renfests, so Janie asked, "You know anyone down there?"

"No. I never went to Tennessee." He sounded more numb than he looked.

"Only one of 'em's in Tennessee. I think the other one's in New Mexico or something."

"They're closer together than that…but no, I don't know who those people were."

"One of the reports said something about a survivor at one of the places."

Liam shook his head. "Yeah. Doesn't sound like they're gonna get any more out of that guy, though. He's in pretty bad shape, like he's gonna die soon. I sorta hope he does. I mean, like, I know how…you know, mean that sounds, but…after everything he's been through, for his sake, y'know? I read something really weird—they're not releasing too many details on this—about how nothing the doctors try to do for him does any good, like there's something unusual about his body chemistry they can't figure out. I don't know, maybe that's, like, just conspiracy theory wingnut horseshit. I mean, man, it must suck to be in that much pain, to have actually been there and seen whatever horrible shit went on." As usual, Liam had such an eye for subtlety.

"Sounds like you've been following this story pretty close."

"I've been listening to NPR while I work. It's all they've talked about today." He sparked the bowl. "It just broke this morning, I think, or at least that's the first I heard about it, but I'm pretty sure they knew about it longer—" He exhaled a blue smokestack cloud and held the pipe her way. "Here. I think you may be able to get a hit or two off this. I'm all set."

"Thanks." She managed a tasty, decent sized hit, but wasn't in the mood to get too baked, so she didn't try for more. "So is the government still trying to say it's terrorists?"

"No. They can't really find any evidence in the place that burned down—about who those people were, I mean—and they only found a few papers at the other. It's, I don't know, really weird, like the local realtors around both places have records of the lands being bought, but they can't trace the money back to any one source. It's like both paper trails go so far back then just…hit a dead end. They say it doesn't even read like business papers, more like some weird, cryptic American history that never happened. A lot of it's in some kind of code no one's ever seen."

"So who do they think did it?"

Liam shrugged. "They're still saying it was one of those biker gangs that have been tearing around down in those areas."

"The Hell's Angels or something?"

"No. This was a different bunch, and now no one can find 'em, either. The FBI says they think they've broken up and are hiding out, are gonna try to let shit settle down some before they regroup and, like, *strike again.*"

"Why?"

Liam shrugged again. "I guess 'cause they made a scene. They have to be discreet after something like that, or they'd get caught right away, y'know?"

"No, I mean why are they doing it?"

"You wanna know what I think? This is gonna

sound like some *way* out there conspiracy theory shit, but I think those people who got killed are part of some weird cult, and the biker gang or whatever you call 'em is, like, a rival cult or something, making war on 'em for some reason. That's what some people say, and it makes the most sense to me."

Janie shrugged. "I couldn't say. This is really the first I've heard of it."

"Huh. Yeah. So what's been up with you lately, Janie, huh?" His face brightened, eager for happier topics. "I guess you and Allen broke up."

"Yeah."

"So, how 'bout that other guy I've seen you around with? He seems like a nice young fellow."

"Oh. Right. No, he's not around anymore." Janie reminded herself not to hold the sting of the remark against Liam.

"That's too bad. He seemed...I don't know, something really earnest and stand-up about him. He reminded me a little of a guy I used to know, in a weird way—"

She smiled, a little sad, and not just 'cause she missed Sheldon. In that moment, Liam's natural big-brotherly tone reminded her of Larry, the way he used to be—not just with her but all the troubled kids around town he had taken under his wing.

Something more haunted crept back into Liam's face. "Janie...do you remember Jake?"

"Huh?" Then she realized who he was talking about. Wait a second, was Liam saying Sheldon had reminded him of that jerk? *Be nice, Janie. Be respectful of the dead.* "Oh, yeah. A little. I mean, I was just thirteen. I wasn't hanging out with you guys so much."

"Yeah, well, you remember those other murders that happened at the same time? Yeah, there were lots of really weird rumors going around Brattleboro back then—"

Weird rumors in Brattleboro…Yeah, that narrowed down the time frame a lot. Still, yeah, Janie remembered.

There was one Common Ground manager, one local girl, one bum, one cabdriver, and a married couple segmented and stuffed in bags in their own basement, along with the house's apparent new residents, a father, a mother, and a daughter. Obviously the parents had killed the house's owners, and were believed to be responsible for the three dead townies. Whoever had killed them and their daughter had also killed the cabdriver. No one could ever piece together who the family was—literally or figuratively. For some reason, a lot of people got the idea that they were part of some obscure cult, and their killer might be a rival.

"Well, there was someone else from out of town hanging around," Liam went on, "this girl…I can't think of her name, but she was kinda strange—" *Someone kinda strange in Brattleboro.* Liam's specificity skills just kept getting tighter. "No, I don't guess you'd remember her. You remember a guy who used to live around here named Rob Coscan?"

"I don't think I ever met him, but yeah. I remember the name. What about him?"

"He was only around for a short time, but he was kinda a buddy of mine. Had some mental problems I think—I'm not sure what, definitely some anger issues, and maybe he was a little schizophrenic—but he was a nice guy. We used to go up to the Marlboro campus and fence together. That was before I started teaching." Liam shook his head and smiled at fond memories. "Man, he was a scrapper. Something in his eyes when he picked up a weapon, the way he moved, though... almost like there was a completely different person in there you didn't see the rest of the time, someone you didn't want to know. He went missing at around the same time. I think he might've hooked up with that strange drifter girl and gotten into some trouble because of it. I don't know, Janie, just something about...Oh, never mind."

"Hey," called Henry from Mack's room, "someone out there grab me another beer?"

Janie would normally shout back, *Why don't you unglue your own ass?* Now she said, "Yeah, sure, be right there."

As she walked in, the computer was playing another news clip. This one showed the raving survivor. It was hard to tell what he said, so the news editors put yellow subtitles at the bottom of the screen. Some demon with an indecipherable name had come back from ancient times, to lead an army of monsters across the land. That demon had started with the survivor's people, and soon it would move on to everyone else. The weapons and governmental powers of this world wouldn't stop the demon, for the earth and the skies would open at his command to swallow and drown them, and the beasts and the birds and even the trees would rise to his side to crush and rend them. The only way to stop the demon was to give him something called the Tainted One. The survivor screamed to his own people, if they were listening, to please, give the Tainted One back to the demon before it was too late!

Yeah, sure, all very biblical. Before leaving, Janie went to make sure Ashley was okay. Ashley's Calvin look-alike had gone to the bathroom or somewhere.

"You okay, girl?" Janie said.

"Oh yeah, I'm fine now," Ashley said with a happier jitter in her voice. "I'm goin' home with that guy. I used to go out with him. He's real cool. Really good at anal sex."

"Uh…okay."

"Yeah, it's cool, though. He's bisexual so he knows how to do it right." A sloppy grin crossed Ashley's face.

Janie decided to take Ashley's word for it. She said goodbye to Liam, then left without looking at any more of the news. As she stepped outside, she tasted a storm on the air. The sky looked so thick, it was weird that it wasn't pouring already. Maybe she should go back in, let it break and pass while she had another beer, maybe a hit or two more of weed. No, she realized, the buzz she already had was more than enough, to where she looked forward to walking it off a little. It sure didn't leave her in a good place for more morbid news reports, or conversations about them. The rain might even be nice to get caught in. Too bad she didn't have anyone to get caught in the rain with. Sheldon had liked getting caught in the rain with her.

Hopefully Mom wouldn't have seen the news. For one thing, Mom would have something to say about it that wasn't bullshit, something that wasn't so easy for Janie to put out of her mind.

The first drops touched her right before she stepped onto her front porch. She fished for her key, then saw that the door was ajar. None of the lights were on when she went in. That wouldn't have made the kitchen so dark at this hour, except for the storm-thick day. There was still enough light to spill through the window, across the kitchen table and the chair on the far side. Mom sat facing Janie. Her head was thrown back, throat yawning between the edges of a clean slice. A lake of blood spread across the table. Otherwise, Mom sat so naturally that the reality of it didn't sink in 'til Janie walked halfway over. Then she started shaking and walked the rest of the way to Mom's side.

Janie reached out, almost touched Mom's face, and felt the warmth that hadn't fled yet. She looked around as if expecting to find someone who could help, as if anyone *could* help. She started several more actions, in several different directions—to the phone to dial 911, to her room, to the nearest corner to curl up in and hide. Then the chill that hadn't yet claimed the corpse claimed Janie's body. She turned and walked back outside. By now the downpour had broken. When Janie stumbled off the porch, it shocked her back to herself. Through the rain, she turned and looked back, into that darkness. She should go back inside, call an ambulance, call the police, try to stop the bleeding! The body had still been warm. Maybe there was still life in there. Maybe someone could—

Janie had her foot on the first porch step, when she

saw the dark doorway again, the door that had already been cracked when she got home. A morbid supposition hit her, a supposition that solidified into certainty: *Mom's killer was still in the house!* The instinct was as complete and weirdly physical as any revelations Mom's forest walk meditations had ever revealed. Hadn't Mom's always turned out to be right? The blackness of the doorway felt like the killer's eye staring Janie down. She was already soaked, chilled nearly to petrifaction, when it all built to an explosion in her brain. She forgot the rain, forgot the cold, and ran like hell.

Two

Vencie hadn't quite stood in plain view when the Indian girl came in and found her mother, even though there were no physical barriers between him and her line of sight. No, nothing but a matter of knowing just where to stand in the shadows, where to lean against just the right portion of wall in relation to where she'd go, where she might pause to look frantically around. Once or twice, her eyes had passed directly over him.

If he'd so much as breathed, she'd have spotted him. So he'd decided not to breathe for a few minutes. The calculation was no harder than his deductions based on Sheldon Wildfire's file. Of course, the latter had yet to be proven, strictly speaking, at least when it came to the Indian girl and her mother. He thought through all the usual variables, but he didn't expect to need them. Earth-liners were pathetically predictable, especially when you showed them an unexpected corpse. Yes, Sheldon Wildfire had been in town recently. Vencie wasn't sure how long it was since the United Deschembines had come, but yes, they'd clearly visited too. The Indian girl probably didn't know where they'd gone, but boys were boys, after all, be they Earth-line, Spirelight, Schomite, or even an oddity like Sheldon Wildfire. A boy wouldn't come back to his girl after so many years, then leave so soon without giving her some way of getting in touch with him. Any boy brought up as one of the Spirelight Secret Police would find a way, even if he wasn't supposed to have that information to give.

Sheldon Wildfire would surely find a way to leave her a trail of breadcrumbs. Vencie didn't know how much the girl knew, but surely she was perceptive enough to realize that her recent fortunes and misfortunes weren't unconnected. Whether she blamed Sheldon, wanted comfort or protection from him, just needed answers, or any combination thereof, she'd use whatever means he'd left of reaching him. If other forces detained her, like the Earth-line police, Vencie could still get to her through them, and extract the information directly. He'd rather not, though. If he tracked the United Deschembines too directly, he risked them becoming aware of him before everything was ready. For now, he would leave the work to her.

It was funny: the girl and her mother were descended from the same dark people who the light-skinned Earth-line people had found when they'd come to settle this country—much like the Spirelights had found the Schomites waiting when they first came to settle this world. The warriors of those darker people were as bloody, berserk, and cunning in heart and soul as any Crimbone, or at least as close as any Earth-line warrior could be to any Deschembine, and they'd given their own bright-skinned usurpers a similarly horrid time. Of course it didn't take the Earth-line people nearly as long to resolve their conflict, but then again, what Earth-line race could keep any such struggle up but so long? Still, the Spirelights would win this world, as the white Earth-line folk had won this corner of it. With the Indian girl's unwitting help, Vencie would have his chance to lead his people when that day came.

He stood on the porch 'til the rain let up. Then he went to catch up with the Indian girl.

THREE

Janie halted at the edge of the graveyard. A block away sat a police cruiser, barely visible through the heavy rain. Janie's first impulse was to run over, get the cop, and bring him to the house where Mom's killer waited. The cop could deal with it. Janie wouldn't even need to get near whoever had done it, except—

No, a cop can't do any good. He'll be killed too. Then the killer will come after you!

That was crazy. The killer had used a knife. Cops had guns. Yet the thought pulsed repeatedly through Janie's brain like someone yelling at her over and over from someplace hidden. She remembered the body's warmth registering to her fingers from an inch away in that silent house. Mom couldn't have been dead for a whole minute!

*Mom dead...*Tears stung Janie's eyes. She hurried through the cemetery, then through the woods. Something about all this was beyond wrong, beyond dangerous, beyond even sheer terror and grief. She stumbled and slid down the muddy hillside, past the last mossy gravestone and beneath the trees. Fewer raindrops hit her here, though those that fell were thicker, collected above 'til leaves got too heavy and spilled them, splashing and drenching her faster. She went deeper and deeper, as if hoping the growth would get thick enough that she wouldn't get any more soaked.

Through the trees ahead, down the last steep embankment, she spotted Vernon Road. She should get out of these woods, go to one of the old factory buildings across the road, and take shelter there. Something in her made her stay in the woods. These were Mom's woods, where Mom had always gone for quiet and solitude, to find herself, find the strength and the wisdom to get through the days. Janie looked around as if hoping to find Mom still out here. That was someone else's corpse in their house, at their kitchen table. Any second, Mom would come lumbering through the sop, irritated but still smiling.

Damn this weather! Even the skies above won't give me peace today, tryin' to turn my woods into an ocean. The nerve! Janikens, what you doin' out here?

"Mom," Janie sobbed.

Yeah, glad to hear you still remember who's who. Of all the days you could pick to finally try takin' my advice. C'mon, let's get inside and get warmed up!

"Where?"

Back to the damn house! Where else? Oh, right. Sorry. Still gettin' used to this ghost shit since someone cut me out of my body. What an asshole! I guess my mind's still a little shook up from that nasty ordeal.

"Mom," Janie whimpered, "is that really you?"

Sure it is. Didn't you just lately talk to our little brave about how you can sense ghosts too? Damn, good thing I at least taught you somethin' right, girl. Is that really me. Pffff…shit, you think that matters? Quit bellyachin' over whether I'm really here, and listen to what I have to say.

Janie heard herself laugh desperately. She kept looking around. What did she really expect to see? What had Mom seen out here, found out here? Was that what Janie was here looking for now? The woods didn't make her feel safe by a long shot, but she felt closer to safe here—closer to sane—than she would anywhere else. She needed to be able to think.

Thinking isn't what you should be doing. What you should do is get back up to South Main and find that cop, find any cop, not wander here trying to find Mom's ghost or whatever ghosts she came here to talk to.

That didn't sound like Mom's voice in her head.

'Course it don't. Come on, girl, I raised you better than that.

Janie's foot slipped. For an instant, she plummeted through the air. Then she slid through muddy water, caught a hanging branch, and pulled herself up into a sunken hollow. It wasn't dry, but it was rocky and covered enough that she could sit and at least start to dry off. She hugged herself 'til the shivers lessened. She stared out at the road below.

"Why are you dead, Mom?" She shuddered.

Come on, girl, you know the answer to that, well as I do.

"No I don't! So why don't you fucking tell me?"

Watch your damn language, young lady. You think I know any more of those details any better than you do? Sorry, honey, turnin' into a ghost don't work like that. The tone in Janie's head softened, 'til she could almost feel Mom giving her a hug. *Hey, hey…c'mon now, baby, I know…I know…it's rough. You can still get through it, though, so long as you stay smart and on your toes. Now quit your blubberin', and think. Think back, through recent times. Put it together on your own. You can do it. Don't worry, baby girl, I'm still here with you for it.*

Janie took one deep, slow breath after another. Steadily her mind cleared. The first image she got was the tall, pale, narrow-faced woman she and Sheldon had met on Main Street, the one who'd led Sheldon away. Janie had no idea who or what that woman was, except that she was some kind of authority figure unlike any Janie had known—a representative of something known only to Sheldon. She'd *moved* like Sheldon, seemed to come out of nowhere the way only Sheldon sometimes would. Just like Mom's killer must have moved, so he could—

The thought of Mom's phantom killer almost sent Janie back into a panic.

Oh no you don't, girl. No more time for that silly crybaby shit, anymore, ever, remember? Didn't that fretful state you last saw me in get that through your skull? Go on, keep thinkin' it through. You're on the right track.

"Whatever Sheldon was running from, it tracked him to this town, just like that weird, tall woman with purple eyes and the deformed shoulder did…the one who took him away."

So far, so good. Keep goin'. It's called instinct for a reason, girl. You got it. Use it.

Janie's shivering hand slid into her pocket. She found her phone. *Only call if you absolutely have to,* Sheldon had said.

The inside of her pocket was already waterlogged. *Oh no, no, no, no.* Slippery fingers got hold of the slipperier plastic casing, and she yanked it out. The screen was black. She held the button down, waiting for the screen to light up. Her eyes sharpened on the blank screen. Liquid rolled around through the edges under the glass like oil in water. *Oh shit-fuck-shit-fuck, no, no, no, not now! Come on, you sonofabitch piece-of-shit phone; why you gotta do this to me now?*

Don't panic. That was Janie's own voice talking to her, to her relief. *He gave you the number on a slip of paper, right? It could be still on you. Take a few deep breaths. Maybe you didn't do anything stupid like throw it away.*

She dug through the loose change and detritus of her pants pockets. The first thing to come out between her fingers was a ruined, twisted scrap of something that left white flecks on her fingertips. *Thank fuck for grabbing pants from the still-clean-enough-to-wear pile this morning.*

Her heart sank like it wanted to melt through her guts and fall out of her ass. As the rain washed the ruined scrap away, her left hand shook so bad that she didn't notice her right slip out of her pocket at first. Then she looked down and saw something pinched between the latter's thumb and forefingers. Of course! What she'd pulled out first was just a stray old receipt she hadn't thrown away. This new find was folded tight and hadn't been *completely* soaked. Hunching so more rain didn't get on it, she forced herself to open it slowly so it didn't rip. Damp edges had seeped inward, blurring the last digit, but she could still read it with some effort. She gave a long, loud, shuddering sigh. The area code was one she didn't recognize.

Now to find a phone somewhere. She couldn't call from this town. She had to get far from here—quick as she could—then call and pray Sheldon was there and knew what to do. Still, how could she get out? She didn't have a car. What if she talked one of her friends into giving her a short notice lift, to Northampton, Keene, wherever? What if the killer caught up with her while she was with them? Hell, if the killer had Sheldon's abilities, they must be hot on her trail either way, leaving her little enough chance as it was.

"What should I do, Mom?"

Mom didn't answer. Janie shifted, checked, and found, yes, she still had her wallet. How much money was in her bank account? She'd saved plenty working this summer, money she'd thought was for community college or moving away or something. Now she'd make for the bus station, stop to make a big ATM withdrawal on the way, then pay cash to the driver of the first bus to pull in, then she'd try to reach Sheldon. What if Sheldon wasn't there, or whoever answered wouldn't let her talk to him? Never mind! She'd figure it out as best she could, when she could.

Once the rain let up a little, Janie edged the rest of the way down the embankment. She headed towards Main Street, walking as fast as she could without attracting attention. She didn't run into Mom's ghost. She didn't run into Rose, or Becky, or Liam, or Allen, or Ashley, or Ashley's evil drug-dangling stalker, or anyone else she'd probably never see again.

Just remember somethin', honey.

Janie was busy trying to get downtown without getting washed away. Mom's comings and goings were getting annoying. "Sure, what?"

I told you, don't take that tone with me. Anyway, you find the little brave, just remember—He's a warrior. He knows what's goin' on. You don't. He's built for this shit. You ain't…and that's fine, baby.

"Nothing about this bullshit's fine," Janie said through clenched teeth. Pouring rain flowed between her lips.

Just sayin', Janekins, whatever you find when you find him, remember your mama didn't raise no wimp. 'Cause in the times comin', he's gonna need you just like you need him right now. You don't gotta be a warrior, but you still gotta be brave…and just as tough.

"You sure picked a weird time to give me a lecture on social equality."

Mom didn't answer.

CARVING OUT ROOM

ONE

The further they traveled, the smaller the forests got. Actually, no, there was plenty of forest. It was civilization as he knew it that shrank, because fewer and fewer Crimbone stayed discreet. His pack kept running into other, less organized bands. In a way, there was more wilderness than ever, even where there was still urban sprawl. When animals ran out of stores to raid for food, they reverted to true animalism, hunting and killing their food, which included the cops and soldiers who tried to stop them. Sooner or later, you either got the hang of it, or got eaten by someone who had. No one had dropped bombs on his pack from the sky, so he guessed someone had eaten the guys who knew how to fly those planes. Or those guys had decided it was more fun to hunt and kill and eat on foot. Probably a combination of the two. Either way, it was fine with him—except it took longer and longer to walk away through the trees from the damn *noise* of it.

No woods seemed deep enough anymore. It hadn't gotten too weird, relatively speaking, 'til this particular Arkansas forest. From one direction flickered a campfire, while the light of a house came from another. A yard from Rob's outstretched feet, a small stream trickled by. Frogs and toads chirped and hopped across soggy leaves. Were their slimy skins actually fluorescent, or was that a trick of the campfire's flicker? It reminded him of pictures he'd seen of those South American toads, the ones whose skin secreted hallucinogenic chemicals, used in spiritual rituals by the Shamans there. Whistling air nudged a weird agitation through the sway of the local flora and fauna, like everyone and everything—the lands themselves included—was on a perpetual bad trip.

From the campfire came noises Rob recognized. The sounds from the house might be real human voices, maybe a TV or radio. He imagined an old married couple out drinking a few beers, listening to these same night noises. While hanging with the Carters, Rob had often pictured their porch fifty years ahead. Obviously, the Carters would be dead by then, because that's how Earth-line folks got after that many years. Maybe by then, he and Sally would be the old farts out there at twilight, nothing to do but listen to the forest and the swamp and the orange grove.

Presently, he made no more noise that anyone at the house would hear. He didn't want to disturb them. Let them enjoy their idea of how the world worked, before this New World closed in on them. He hoped for their sakes that they died of old age before that happened. Maybe he should go say hi. No, they probably had the shotgun ready in case it *was* him, or someone from his pack, or whatever the Earth-line news media painted them as by now.

Remelea was the only face he recognized back at the campsite. The rest were all local boys, from the nearest Schomite territory, or what used to be Schomite territory. Either way, they were here for the scoop. Everywhere was Schomite territory now, went the prevailing sentiment, Crimbone territory specifically. There was no more Spirelight territory. The Spirah Gods ruled Spirelight territory. The Crimbone had burned away the gods by burning down the homesteads and drinking up the glow. The homesteads were emptying, and the Spirelights all ran and fought and died in panic.

It must be worse now that the pack no longer traveled openly, no more unified collective body to identify. Had any lands still favored the Spirelights, Rob and his pack wouldn't have been able to take a piss without squirting a rattlesnake and getting a pair of venomous fangs stuck in the dick or the cunt. Large animals would come running into the paths of their vehicles, causing mile-long pile-ups. Policemen would clear their holsters at all the distance they needed, and the Crimbone would die bullet-riddled, their weapons half out of the scabbards. Last time the Earth-line law had tried anything, some cameramen from that TV show *Cops* had ended up getting stomped. Rob felt bad about that. Maybe his ol' lingering inner film student made him sentimental.

Either way, the lands of North America had turned their backs on the Spirelights, and at least didn't hinder the Crimbone. The rest of the pack assumed that meant the lands were actively on their side. Earlier today, Rob had been sure, too. No doubt he would feel that way tomorrow—high and frenzied again on the Spirelight glow. For now, he'd used up what he'd absorbed, along with his own energy. It left him just enough strength to stagger to where the noise didn't threaten to make his head explode. He slumped against a tree. It would be harder to get moving tomorrow. Just like this morning had been harder than yesterday. After that first slog, of course, he would blaze brighter than ever all over again, before he knew it.

Puttergong hadn't been around for almost a week, which should be a relief. The thing wouldn't give any more real help, even if it could. Rob could use one thing from the Familiar now, one answer it obviously had no plans to give: *Where the fuck is Sally?* Still, for some reason, its absence bothered Rob. If nothing else, he'd expected a visit full of taunting praise after slaughtering those homesteads.

Tomorrow, the pack would head north, because that's where Sally might be. At least that's what one Spirelight had said today, on the promise of a quick death. Rob had kept the promise, but that shit was getting old. The lands all felt too disconnected lately for one town or state to carry messages over borders to another. A flock of birds with their guiding song might fly across those borders, but apparently they no longer felt like picking up the songs they found on the other side to send those messages back. The lands led Rob only to the Spirelights, led only other Crimbone to him.

The Spirelights may or may not have clues to where Sally was, and he may or may not reach the ones who did before other Crimbone got ahold of them. If Rob could think of a better option, he might rethink things.

He and Remelea seemed to do all the thinking, them, and occasionally Joel. Frankly, Rob was amazed any of the rest kept enough presence of mind to take captives. Not for the first time throughout these nights, he thought of Jesse and Zane. Neither Jesse nor Zane would ever be so thoughtless. Most of these guys made Rob go, *Excuse me, how is it that you assholes are veterans and I'm still a fledgling?* If he'd had Jesse and Zane in his pack, they probably would have found Sally by now.

Remelea always filled the new ones in. Rob told them the new course of action, then sent word out to the rest of the pack.

When he closed his eyes, the lights from both directions burned brightly through his lids. The blood slowed through his stiff, battered body. His head swam. There came a flash of green through murky orange mist—green like the dreams he would soon be lost in within moments, dreams he never remembered as clearly as he wanted to, which never lessened the gnawing pull towards whatever he saw there. *Green…so much green…and blue!* Blue, yes, as of lakes deeper, vaster, and clearer than anyone of this world could imagine...

Couldn't he just have a few old-fashioned normal dreams? One involving a threesome with Sally and Remelea, maybe?

Yeah, he saw those lakes, dove from the cliffs above, swam through the ruined temples of the deep. He almost saw it now, was almost there—

"Rob?"

He opened his eyes and followed Remelea's voice through murk splashed in electric orange, moonlight gold and night-sky blue. No, he shouldn't be so hard on this real, waking forest. It was letting him stay here. The surrounding lands would let him fight his battles here tomorrow, might finally put him on the direct path to Sally. Except it had let the Earth-line people hold it this long, had let them slow it down, cripple it—

"How many?" he asked.

"How many what?"

Now he knew he was awake, because a third of that threesome was playing Questions and Answers with him, when she already knew the answer. Women never did that in kinky sex dreams. "Challengers," he growled.

"There haven't been challengers since Tennessee." She rolled her eyes and sat down close enough for him to feel her body heat lining up with his. That wasn't good. "The road's really dead tonight. I don't think anything's come down it 'cept wind since we set up camp."

"So, what about the motel?"

"You mean the last one we found? I didn't check it out, just watched 'em go up, the ones staying there I mean. We're the only ones there. As in, no one's even running the place."

Rob stared ahead wide-eyed. "They're open, Remelea. I passed the place with you, remember? I saw the sign. Why didn't you go check it out?"

"The boys can handle themselves. Joel can find us if there's trouble. I wanted to get back to the campsite, bring the new crowd up to speed, then make sure you're okay."

"I'm fine. You talk to anyone knows anything about this county?"

Had anyone gone exploring, he meant, and they both knew it, along with the answer. No one would go exploring 'til tomorrow. It didn't matter who they found or didn't find, what indigenous weirdness they noticed, except for Spirelights. The Spirelights wouldn't be waiting in the open anymore, but they couldn't hide the glow.

"These lands act like they love us so much," he said, "like they love me so much. You know what I'd love? More straight fucking answers."

"You can really be a whiny little bitch sometimes, you know that?"

"Try getting married, have that go pretty well for a while, all things considered, then have the Spirelights show up to fuck it all up…then go have to deal with that shit." He squeezed his forehead with both hands.

"No thanks. Okay, fine. 'Cept you're supposed to be a High Natural. Until I hear you objecting to that title, you can shove your whiny little bitch excuses up your ass. So anyway, what straight answers do you feel like these lands owe you?"

He shot forward into a poised crouch. "A straight path to *her!*"

"Yeah? So, what if the lands don't think that's what they should give you? What about the rest of us?"

"What about you?"

Rob felt her slap before noticing she'd raised a

hand. It was stronger than a lot of men's punches, enough to knock him sideways. His hands neared his blades as he righted himself. So, why didn't he draw them? Because Remelea showed no sign of drawing her hook, he realized.

Through the blades, you work the will of your purest self. The blades will never fail you, unless you wield them towards ends untrue to that self.

Judging by how many Crimbone had died with their blood-soaked black blades in hand on his watch—never mind throughout history—Rob guessed everyone slipped up sometimes. The only difference was, a Crimbone had fewer chances to say, *It seemed like a good idea at the time.* Oh, it was in him to kill Remelea if they had a big enough disagreement, but to use the blades on such a close, wonderful battle-buddy when she hadn't raised her own weapon on him…it wasn't his style.

It doesn't matter which of us is the better skilled fighter. If I broke that rule, she'd win.

They didn't go there now, though, so she was still his second-in-command. He met her eyes, left the blades in their scabbards, and growled, "Bitch."

"Yeah. So, *what about us*, you ask? We're the ones killing and dying for you. 'Cause we're all wrapped around some nutty idea that you might end this middling bullshit we've spent our whole lives in. Because that's what a Crimbone High Natural should be doing, not dragging it out and making it worse, all over something you don't realize you've lost."

Now he was ready to hit her. "I haven't lost Sally."

"Whatever. You keep sending the Spirelights the

message to give her back. After causing so much trouble—and they still haven't managed to kill you—don't you think they'd decide by now it'd be less of a pain in the ass to just hand her over? Assuming they still have her to give."

Rob's posture was calm. His eyes flashed like little spinning pin-balls. "If they don't—"

"Then they're probably scared of what you'd do if they told you."

"They should be. All of them…and I mean *all* of them."

If he'd said that when they met, Remelea wouldn't have believed him. For all his ferocious charisma, she'd still sensed too much…what was it? *Sanity* probably wasn't the word. Whatever it was, he called it "weakness". He'd obviously worked it out of his system by now.

"Ever think of asking them for something else?" she said.

"Fuck *asking*—"

"Just imagine for a second…imagine you go ahead and make things as bad as you can, make us all as bad as you…but what if you told the Spirelights to back down, stop their feud on us, to let peace start to grow."

Rob fell back against the tree and let his eyes roll. "You're forgetting someone: the Spirelights' filthy gods. Even if the Spirelight people liked that idea, their gods wouldn't let 'em. Nothing's gonna clean all this shit up. That's why all I want is to get her back, so we can leave it all behind again. I haven't done a damn thing that's about anything else. I've been pretty publicly straight up about that. People do what I say or they don't. Everyone who's been doing something else—something I didn't tell them to do—that's on them, not me."

Besides, there'll be somewhere better for us to go this time. He didn't tell Remelea that part, because he hadn't yet figured out how to find the trail to that place. *Remelea would just try to stand in your way. Been listening to her negative-nancy bullshit? She doesn't want you to get there, just like she doesn't want you to find—*

"You still think you could leave it all behind," she said. "So, what *would* you leave behind?"

"Easy. All this bullshit. It's the same shit that's been going on, and it'll keep going with or without me. It's hit me and mine just like it does everyone else. Apparently, I'm just better at hitting back than most."

"*It is not the same shit!* The Crimbone following you aren't the same creatures they were! I knew a lot of these guys before, remember? You didn't. They're nastier, more powerful as a body, and the lands don't keep them in check like they used to. By now, they're so jacked on the glow, I doubt the Earth-line police or military *could* take some of 'em down, with machine guns or maybe even a nuke. *You* sparked this change somehow, and *you* control them, give them something to focus their new nastiness—their new power—on. When you speak to them…damn you, you don't even know what that *voice* you use does to people, do you? It almost doesn't matter if it's good or bad, because without it, they'll plunge into pure chaos, and that chaos will spread."

"Huh. Maybe I just don't see it that way. Maybe I just don't believe that's true."

Remelea rolled her head limply on her shoulders. Rob wanted to say something so she'd feel less defeated. Interesting how she always referred to the pack and the changes therein like it didn't apply to her. He'd watched her fight plenty. She never showed any problem getting as nasty as everyone else. When had she decided to be his goddamn conscience? Finally, he stood and stared off at the light of the house.

Remelea looked up. "What is it?"

He'd already started towards the light. "C'mon, let's check something out."

They went silently, Rob's ears and nose flaring. Nothing moved now but soundwaves. He parted the brush and saw a cabin about the size of the Carter's place, though otherwise there wasn't much resemblance. Still, the sight sent part of Rob somewhere else. He felt all here and now less and less lately, except when the blades were drawn. Otherwise, he wasn't sure which space or time he occupied more. Then he would think of Sally, remember their love in Brattleboro, in Postville. That reminded him exactly where he was. Because Sally wasn't here.

"Deserted cabin in the woods," he sighed. "Well, let's—"

Remelea skipped nimbly up the porch steps, barely shaking the boards. Rob caught himself watching her ass. He allowed himself one thirsty snarl, then followed.

The front porch smelled like the same oak, pine, and earth as the rest of the woods. Inside was the scent of spice and many meals cooked, of clothes and furniture loved and well worn, of children born and bred, cried over when they grew up and struck out into the world. For the first time in years, Rob missed his dad. Why wasn't Dad here with him, on this trail? By now, probably for the same reason Louis wasn't. Whoever had lived and loved, eaten and slept, laughed and cried here, they'd left the porch light on…along with a radio, somewhere inside.

Rob didn't fumble for any light switches. He didn't want to ruin the perfect sightless sense of this place. There were enough moonlit windows to see how languidly Remelea swayed in it. To think, this amazing, scrappy, punked-out warrior woman had seen fit to follow a guy like him through all this bloody madness. He still knew so little about whatever she'd been through, whatever trials had hammered her into the badass bitch with whom he'd already shared so much. Either way, here she swayed, dreaming like an innocent kid who'd never even heard of such brutality. It was so gently, breezily nostalgic in here that he couldn't help falling into the spirit with her. Old Lords knew she deserved it more than he did.

The sleepy blues tunes faded for some local news. Rob followed Remelea into the next room—good thing it wasn't the bedroom—towards the radio. He knew it was an old-fashioned one before she turned the dial through so much garbled, scratchy dissonance.

Obviously, she was looking for more music. He wanted to agree with her, but he still said, "Turn it back to that."

"Really? *Really?* C'mon, man—" Her hips shimmied in the murk, so the sweaty cloth of the scanty skirt she wore clung enticingly between her legs. Didn't she usually wear jeans? Where'd she pillaged that skirt from? He asked himself questions like that, to distract himself from the urge to pillage it off her.

"In a minute." He pivoted just so she might not notice how close he was to breaking the zipper of his jeans. "Let's hear that broadcast."

Her fingertips moved the dial back without searching or faltering, stopping perfectly on the spot. Rob heard only the tail end, but it was enough. His eyes had adjusted enough to see her face. She'd heard it too.

"So, did we miss it, or what?" Of course she meant the killer storm the announcer had talked about. Local authorities were so sure it was coming, expected something so horrible, they'd decided to evacuate the area.

"We haven't missed the storm," Rob growled. "No, we haven't missed a thing."

Two

"Giddup…Huh! Giddup…Huh! Go on, go on, giddup…Like a sex-machine…Huh! Git on up…Git on up…"

That's how Rob woke up the next morning in the deserted cabin. Puttergong did a horrible James Brown impression. Well, there was that question settled, at least. Rob's whole body and mind were swiftly awake, despite the soft comfort he slept in. Remelea lay curled close to him, one arm thrown across his chest. He briefly wondered where she'd come from. Yeah, he'd definitely crawled into bed alone last night. He knew this because he'd made sure to. Before that, they were out on the porch, talking, listening to jazz on the radio. Last he remembered, she'd still been out on the porch. At least he was still fully clothed, but he wasn't yet sure about her. If it weren't for the wake-up call, it'd be way too tempting to slide his hand under the covers and check—

It wasn't just a problem of how nice her warm, slumbering body felt against his. It wasn't just about monogamy, either. He knew his wife was bisexual. If she were here right now—theoretically assuming she could get past the whole Crimbone-who-weren't-named-Rob-Coscan thing—she might be more into the fucking-Remelea-senseless idea than he was, if that was possible. The problem was, the longer he was around Remelea, the less it felt like simple lust. The confusion was the last thing he needed right now.

So, of course, that's around when Puttergong decided to show up—along with more trouble.

"Hang onto that there dream, Biter-Boy…nearly there…closer than ye think—"

Closer to Sally, or the place in the dream? The place he and Sally would go…

Everything after that had happened so fast, Rob barely remembered how he'd gotten from that moment to this. The twin blades of Magur Sevi now guided Rob Coscan's clenched fists. They pulled his whole body into the continuous marauding motion after the glow.

They were all Secret Police, naturally. More and more of those assholes showed up uninvited these days.

A whole family of them swarmed Rob and Remelea. When the Secret Police had thundered through the front door into the living room, Rob and Remelea had snapped up, grabbed their weapons, and come out to meet them. The fight splashed the living room in blood and guts, then moved to the front yard.

Where the hell was the rest of the pack, and how many of these fuckers were they dealing with? All Rob saw was the red swirl and the enemies who came blazing through it. It wasn't the whole family assaulting him anymore, which meant Remelea had taken on some of them, because he knew he hadn't killed that many of them yet.

Where the hell was she? Had she made it outside?

The younger daughter swung a two-by-four into his hip. His body whip-spasmed from the blow like a rearing, wounded snake. With a howl, he half-buckled. His left blade lashed wildly and opened her neck. The mother's foot slid on a leaf behind him. His other blade arced low and backwards. As it disemboweled her, she sunk onto his arm, pulling his spin into a sloppy stumble. While he fought for balance on his good leg, the son came in for the kill.

There'd been an older daughter, and the father. Remelea must have gotten them, wherever she was.

The boy drove a pitchfork at Rob's neck like a lance. Rob's right blade caught it between two prongs, steering it away from his face. The boy followed through the driving motion, wrenching Rob's arm nearly from the socket. The knife flew out of his grip. Frenzied, he dropped the other blade, dove forward, grabbed the boy's skull and twisted 'til the neck gave that echoing crack he'd been looking for. He went in, mouth agape to tear out the throat and taste the blood, taste the glow before it fled.

Rob dropped the body, staggered and tripped over it. He caught himself before he went spilling. Another figure came towards him, Remelea—no, not Remelea, one of the Secret Police, the older daughter. He didn't look for his knives, just shambled for her in a daze. She slashed at him with a pocketknife that opened his chest nearly to the ribs. Before the blade withdrew from flesh, he had her by both wrists. He twisted, screamed with her, and hoisted her into the air. The weight made his injured leg flare. If the bone hadn't broken, he would be damn proud. He flung her through the air, heard wood splinter as she struck a porch beam.

Remelea must be close, must have finished off the father by now. The older daughter wasn't dead, could be made to talk, take them to—

The father of the Secret Police family pitched forward through the front door. His back arched. A rocket of blood exploded from his mouth as Remelea's hook ripped out his spine. Meat dangled from the hook like ragged, red seaweed. She gave it a shake. The spine clattered wetly on the boards in a halo of spatter. She crouched over the body, ready to rip more flesh from bone with her teeth. Then she looked up, screamed, and launched herself from all fours into the air.

Rob swayed and stared. The red swirl bled back for this single, impossible image of bloody beauty. Pain sheered through his gut, eclipsing his shrieking leg. The gash tore sideways then pulled out and stabbed higher, between his ribs.

Remelea landed.

The cold steel sting became a wide, hollow sucking as she pulled the girl away.

Rob stumbled and caught the porch. Last he saw of Remelea or the Secret Police girl, a black hook was yanking at a loop of intestines that slithered out of the screaming girl's belly. Remelea's jaws shook and worried a throat that gushed all over her face.

Rough, slender hands pulled Rob up by the shoulders, yanking him from one moment into the next. For a second, he thought the whole morning was a bad dream. The slices in his guts told him otherwise.

He lurched free drunkenly and slid to the earth. The hands caught him under the armpits.

"Get up! Come on, Rob, you dumb fuck!" Remelea slapped him hard across the face.

The shock bolted him to his full height. He gripped her fiercely. "The blades," he hissed.

"Right." She met his eyes, nodded, and led him to where he'd dropped the first one. The sight burned through the red swirl as only the glow or its bearers had previously done.

Remelea was reaching for it.

Two voices echoed from years ago.

You know how good I'd be if I tried to handle those blades of yours?

I guess you'd kick a lot of ass.

I'd be worse than useless, probably cut my own dick off.

Rob screamed, "*No!*"

Remelea drew back reflexively, then met his eyes as if to say *Trust me, sweetie, I know what you're worried about. Not a damn thing you could tell me about all this.* She reached for his blades again.

"No," he repeated, growling low, then he shrugged free and slumped to the earth. She sobbed his name. He must look a half inch shy of death. He sure felt like it. He still focused all he had left on the shimmering black metal. "Let me." His hand slid feebly around the handle.

As he crawled in search of the second knife, he heard her follow.

His vision had cleared a little since retrieving the first blade. As he crawled, its edge scraped the earth.

It wasn't this forest fading from the mists before him, or even the ground beneath him.

Whispers of strength refilled him, but they felt nothing like energy or power as he'd ever known them.

Giddup…Huh! Giddup…Huh! Go on, go on, giddup…

"There it is, Rob. Go on…right in front of you."

His hand closed on the second handle. It was the most he felt of this place, of this reality, and the shimmering black metal was all he saw of it. He didn't want to see this world, didn't want to feel this body as it bled out, beaten and stabbed beyond recovery. He wanted to watch the mists clear, wanted to—

"Rob!" Remelea jerked him up so hard that he almost dropped the blades again.

"Go away. Let me go there. I can almost—" Whose blood did he taste most right now? His enemies' or his own?

"She's not there, Rob. You won't find her there.

You gotta find her *here*, in this world! Now come on, let me help you get those back in their sheaths."

At least he'd found his knives. Through the trees, midmorning sun scorched his eyes. Blood soaked him. His pumping wounds screamed and throbbed. He roared, heaving his shoulders back. Remelea stumbled away. It was funny how the knives didn't seem heavier than usual, but his arms felt like they'd turned to lead. He forced enough strength back through them to thrust both blades skyward.

Remelea had promised to stay at his side 'til she saw him fuck up with these blades. Shouldn't she have finished him off herself by now?

"I'll handle them myself." His words were a wet mumble. "The blades of Magur Sevi, Remelea...see? I can still handle 'em. I can still carve the path...carve my way...can still—"

"I know. That's not the point. Just let me—"

"No," came the fading, blood-bubbling grumble. He aligned the points with the scabbards, then drove them both down as though towards an enemy's flesh. The familiar hiss sounded as they slid home. Now he let her haul him along as best she could.

Close by, Remelea's Camaro screeched to a halt. Joel's frantic face stared from the driver's seat. The rest of the pack was coming, howling through the trees. Rob smelled Spirelight blood on many of them, felt how alive they were with freshly absorbed glows.

"Get him in here!" Joel shouted.

"There's no time," Remelea shouted back, as Rob felt a wooden plank brush his ankle. "Help me get him in *here!"*

"Huh? When did you guys find this place?"

Remelea snorted exasperation, then Joel had Rob by the other shoulder and they were hauling him up the porch steps. He sprawled limp across a bed, felt Remelea cradling his head, straining to steady her hands as she did what she could for his wounds. Far away, other Crimbone were shoving each other to get through the front door. Remelea shouted at Joel to keep them out. Farther off, the glow still pulsed strong, from sources not yet drunk dry, not even tapped. A few of the Crimbone were still off chasing those sources.

That world vanished. Rob sank for a long time before leaving behind the last of this body's pain.

That's when the mists started to clear.

PART TWO:

DISCOVERY

OLD WORLD MAGIC, OLD WORLD EVIL

ONE

Zane swam to consciousness through the murk of dreams. He didn't try to remember them. This remaining fog was bad enough, and he couldn't shake it. The groggy feeling wasn't new to him, though he couldn't remember knowing it regularly. That was too long ago for it to matter now. It was a hindrance, like the vines binding his limbs. He shook his head, shook his body as much as the vines allowed. His arms and lower legs were numb from the squeeze, his arms especially, considering he'd hung by them for—

How long *had* he been hanging here? More than a day and a night, that was for sure. Sweat saturated his clothes, so he was cold, yet he felt sweltering heat boiling from somewhere in the house.

When he'd first lost consciousness then woken up,

his head had hurt so bad that he wondered if Jesse was the only one who'd taken a good noggin-knock. It sure as shit wasn't just a hangover. Either way, his head still hurt. Someone was keeping him dehydrated, but not too dehydrated.

He recalled a small, soft, cold hand handling his junk. Whenever he had to piss, someone opened a door like they had a telepathic relationship with his bladder. He fought for coherence, but all he could figure out about the visitor was that the vines knew not to fuck with them. The hands undid his pants so his dick flopped against the inner rim of some cold metal receptacle, and it was like the metal caused him to lose bladder control. Then followed the kettledrum echo as he filled the receptacle.

Next those same hands always tilted his head back by the chin, before a glass pressed his mouth and poured some weird liquid down his throat. It tasted sort of like tea, only thicker and more bitter. He really hoped it wasn't from the first receptacle. Whenever he drank it, he lulled again. The second time he lost consciousness, it was almost willful.

Obviously, raw strength would no longer do him any good, for now. He concentrated instead on his thoughts, puzzling through all the angles and corners of his situation. It drew him deeper and deeper inward, 'til there was nothing left for the body to do but sleep. After that, he could keep his mind fully awake for a while, but eventually his brain became exhausted too. Then he started coming around, and he received another visit from the hands. Now he was fully conscious, or almost there. Pain returned, replacing numbness, which helped. His nurse must be late.

Green light flickered somewhere. Zane's eyes rolled up to see that most of the galaxy of glowing, hanging pods had withered and gone out. A few still pulsed weakly, providing what light remained, aided only scantly by new pods, freshly dropped and dangling on their spindly stalks, barely glistening. He knew that days had passed, because the pods sprouted, glowed, and died daily and nightly. His theory was that they came into full bloom by night. From the progress of this crop, it was mid-afternoon.

Zane's thick arms yanked and flexed against the vines. He pumped and bucked his legs. Fresh strain chased away the numbness. The vines tightened, threatening to crush his bones. He snarled, purely for his own spirit, though he wondered how much the vines sensed his wrath.

His nostrils flared. A rasping, inhuman laugh rumbled out of him. In this small room, the echo was unexpectedly satisfying.

These New Orleans Crimbone had funny ideas about how to treat their living legends. Just wait 'til they tasted how those legends would thank them.

Before fading out on the first night, Zane had heard them out in the hall. He'd guessed they were still cleaning up the mess, hauling away the wounded. Then one of them called out, "Would you look at this shit? It's Zane Rochester's hammer!" There came the barely perceptible echo of the hammer lightly brushing the carpet, then subtle thumps of its turning contours, as the violating whelp got hold before hoisting it.

"Fuck, this thing's heavy." Another moment—just the right moment, whenever the new wielder brought it to just the right angle—and it would be a lot heavier. *"Old Lords, would you look at it…It's beautiful."*

Nergal had shouted, "Sam, you dumb fuck, don't—"

Zane's sharp ears caught the unmistakable sound of shattering bone—a kneecap, specifically. After almost two centuries of breaking bones, you notice the different sounds they make. The floor shook, first from the hammer thudding headfirst, then from Sam crashing onto his back and rolling around, howling in the kind of agony known only to those at the wrong end of the black metal.

Nergal had yelled, "All right, leave that fucking thing where it is! Everyone out of this hall! You, get Sam downstairs." He mumbled to someone, "Might be nicer to finish the dumb bastard off."

From his prison, Zane had laughed loud, long enough for the sound to follow them out, to chase them away, to fill the ears of the stupid blasphemer who'd dared try handling another Crimbone's weapon. When he stopped laughing, the hallway was silent. No sounds from the rest of the house reached him.

At least he knew for sure where his hammer was, if he could just get to it. So where was everything else, or everyone else for that matter?

Zane recalled the fight, starting at the end, tracing how he and Jesse had slipped up, how the enemy had gotten the drop on them. From there, he worked backwards, took into account the space they'd fought in, the hallway right outside this room. He remembered the way they took into that hallway, how it connected with the ballroom downstairs, and he formed a rough picture of the layout. At the time, it had felt like some brain-twisting labyrinth.

Looking back, it was pathetically simple. His door was at the end of the hall. Under all these vines, this room must have at least one window, facing either the back yard—Talino's "courtyard"—or maybe the side of the house next door.

For an instant, Zane imagined that the whole place was this silent. He remembered Sally Wildfire's testimony, her pitiful, crumbling voice on that recording Jesse had played for him more times than he liked to remember. With all this time to hang around, he started to figure out why Jesse was so obsessed with torturing both of them with that disgusting shit. This must be how Rob's Spirelight girl—*Sally*—had felt. A little of it, anyway. There were more vines in the ballroom when she'd been here. No, not here, Zane reminded himself. A different house; the other one was abandoned and rotted by the time her family had found her.

Finally, he caught street noises—passing cars, people talking on sidewalks, the trolley tracks rumbling and sparking blocks away— but still no sounds from the house around him.

That's because there's no one in here...no one left but you and your best friend, wherever he is. He's the one who's probably got brain damage. He's probably already dead. Lucky him. So, here it is for you. These vines will hold out longer than you. They're

Old World vines, never mind what the fuck they're doing in this weak little world. They're too strong to be here. You're nothing but a sad old relic of this world, and you've spent your whole life scrapping for some foggy idea of what the Crimbone used to be. These vines will hold you for as long as they need to, then they'll rot, along with the rest of this house, along with you.

"Bullshit," he growled and yanked inward once more, with both arms. It felt like fighting solid iron, like the veins and cords in his neck would explode if he fought any harder. He kept fighting anyway. Whenever the vines squeezed crueler, they felt a little more sentiently threatening. He held the hard tension in his forearms. Somewhere, something ripped like tearing muscle.

This is it. The fucking vines are gonna pull my arms off now. Good thing so much of me has gone numb.

He'd still pull right back, for as long as he could. He heard more ripping, but there was no worse pain than he felt already. Liquid squirted on his cheek. He twisted his head to the side. Deep rifts had opened in at least two of the vines that braided to form his chains. They leaked something bubbly and syrupy. Above, the dangling glow-pods started flashing epileptically, as though in panic.

Zane roared, "Jesse! Where the fuck are you, Jesse?"

That's right, Nergal and the others had put Jesse in the room next door. Zane had seen them do it. He remembered his fear, his despair from a moment ago. He took it to heart as the spirit of the enemy he now fought. Lately, Zane had to admit that Jesse was right: the Crimbone were disintegrating from within. Honor corroded into arrogance, suckling on the corruption of the civilian Cabinets, more and more like bestial Earth-line thugs and drones. They'd never been in this world what they'd been in the Old World.

"Jesse!" he roared again, louder. "Jesse, c'mon, answer me wherever you are! We're getting the fuck out of here."

Still no answer, but he kept fighting the vines. They'd stopped tightening, he noticed. The rips he'd made still oozed, but they hadn't gotten any wider. He fought and pulled hard with everything he had left in him.

Old Lords, even the plants in this fucked-up place knew how to toy with him. The glow-pods had stopped flashing. They were brighter now. More of them had sparked up, as though his commotion had jogged them. Zane sweated and panted. His body sagged again. He collected his breath and his strength.

Keep it together. You can't do anything yet, so keep correlating what you know and accounting for what you don't. There's bound to be something you can use once things start happening. It can't be too long 'til they do. It never is.

You're Zane Thumpy-Bumpy Fuckin' Rochester, after all.

Talino had said he wanted to have his little garden tea party with Jesse and Zane *tomorrow*—a tomorrow that came and went several times over. Talino still wanted to have that conversation at some point, though obviously on other terms. Why else would they still be alive? Some new factor was at work. Talino was waiting for the right moment. Zane had been allowed to get this lucid, so he figured that moment was near.

Footsteps padded softly through the hallway,

towards his door. *Hey, what do you know!*

Somehow, Zane connected the tread with the hands that gave and took liquid from him. He watched the door. The vines had crept inward, covering its outer edges. They receded as the knob turned. In walked the girl Talino had worn on his arm like jewelry at the party. She now wore a light, flowery summer dress. Her hair was curled into ringlets, so she looked even more obscenely young. Zane knew she was far older, which made it worse somehow. At the party, he hadn't been nearly as disturbed by her as Jesse, but even he smelled something profoundly wrong.

In one small hand, she held a glass of pale green liquid. In the other, she held a big jug, big enough for his urine. So she meant to drug him again after all. Maybe this exploded his theories, except she didn't seem surprised to find him fully conscious. As she approached, he shrank as far back as he could. She lifted the glass to his mouth. He recognized her cold touch on his chin. When the liquid touched his lips, he was ready to spit it back in her face. It tasted like room temperature tap water. It ignited a thirst he hadn't noticed growing. He must have drained half the glass before she drew it away.

As he stared at her, for no apparent reason, he kept thinking of Sally Wildfire. He racked his brain over it, tried to shake it off as a delirious delusion. Too bad he wasn't remotely delirious anymore. There was some literal, physical connection between the two girls, and not for any similarity he could spot. They were both white girls, but that was about it. All the Spirelights looked like modern Earth-line white people, unless you knew what else to look for, and this girl was no Spirelight.

Zane hadn't spent much time around Sally. As a matter of fact, he'd barely interacted with her. Still, Spirelight or not, she'd been an undeniably intelligent, vital young woman. This girl was so—

"Who are you?" Zane hissed.

"I'm Kimberly."

"What do you know about Sally Wildfire?"

Kimberly twitched and cocked her head. Her eyes rolled and fluttered like she was about to have a seizure. "Sally?" Her voice trembled with mournful dissonance. "Hey, where'd she go, anyway?" Her eyes rolled up to the galaxy of pods, as if searching there. "You're missin' the party, Sally. See, I told you these guys'd be cool."

Zane recognized those words. He almost didn't hear the second set of footsteps padding near.

Talino stepped into view and leaned against the doorframe. He wore an open green silk housecoat, of the same weird material as his fancy suit from the party, and nothing else. "Good to see you're awake, Zane. Are you ready to have a civilized conversation?"

"Get this fucking thing away from me."

"Careful. That's the lady of the house who just gave you water."

"She's fucking dead!"

Talino stepped fully into the room, hands clasped casually behind his back. "If you mean she's not alive in the same sense that she was when she first entered my house, then yes. Her body died long enough to serve its purpose, and then—"

"So you and your degenerate minions could *eat*

her?"

"So we could make Sally Wildfire eat her, actually. Otherwise, yes. Kimberly served as the sacred vessel for what I needed to be put into Sally Wildfire. After I sent Sally on her way, I replaced what needed replacing in Kimberly's body, then filled her with what animates her now." Talino drew close to Kimberly. He fondled her and chewed on her ear. The open housecoat showed off how much this turned him on. "Be a bit more open-minded, will you? She's nicer to have around than you'd think."

The sweat felt colder than ever. Zane shivered violently. "Get her out of here."

"If I do, will you be able to hold up your end of an intelligent conversation?"

Zane glared and nodded.

"Kimberly, be a dear and go wait for me in the dining room."

Kimberly smiled and nodded. On her way out, she paused and kissed Talino's cheek. "Be down soon, darling."

Talino patted her ass before she left. "Now," he said to Zane, "where were we?"

"You turned Sally into what she is now. You did…something…to the flesh of that Earth-line girl, the one Sally was bumming around homeless with, so when Sally ate it, she turned into something else."

"It was a bit more intricate than that, but basically, yes."

"Why?"

"Didn't we discuss this already? To create the

perfect bride for a High Natural."

"What could a degenerate like you possibly understand about a High Natural?"

"More than you, apparently."

"Wake the fuck up! This ain't the Old World we're living in. It's this world keeps us alive, the spirits of this world we serve."

Talino chuckled. "Listen a while, Zane, and see if your eyes don't open. It's always been the Old World and its spirits watching over us. Always. It was the spirit of the Old World that guided us here, the spirit of the Old World that's grown strong here, stronger than the native spirit ever was. It's stayed alive because of *us*."

"Where's Jesse?"

"Kept just as you are. He's a little less comfortable, though. Has quite the skull, that one. But enough about him for now. Why haven't you asked me about Metaiew Coscan?"

"What about him?"

"That *is* who you came here to ask me about, right?"

"So fucking tell me!"

"Fair to say. Metaiew Coscan created the High Natural, and I don't just mean by spurting him into a cunt. Crazy old Metaiew…" Talino shook his head and *tisked* through his teeth. "That man had the luck to be born into an extremely strong Crimbone bloodline. Then he let his personal weaknesses send him running from it. Think of all the accomplishments he threw away! He won the love of the Crimbone woman who gave him his son, and what does he do when she dies at his side? He drags the poor kid off to neutral territory and remarries, to an Earth-line woman of all things." Talino paused to study Zane. "You've met his son. You already knew his father's cowardice, the birthright his father would have denied him. You scorn Metaiew for it just like I do. I suspect part of you hates him more than you hate me."

Zane didn't answer.

"You know what happened from there, don't you, from Metaiew's efforts to keep his boy ignorant, sheltered and suppressed. The spirit of the Crimbone was too strong in the boy's blood. In its fight for survival, to assert itself, it grew stronger beneath the airtight pressure, than it would have if it had flourished naturally. Ironic, right? To stay alive, to feed that strength, do you know what little Rob Coscan's spirit had to draw on?"

Zane had the answer on the tip of his tongue. He realized what Talino was waiting for him to say, though, so he held back.

"*Just to stay alive*," Talino went on, "Rob's Crimbone soul was forced to look deep into the purest blood memories, from which stems the power of your beast race. So, when the boy's nature finally found its way to the conscious surface, when his instincts pulled him forward to make his First Call…" Talino smiled. "Well, I don't have to tell you that part. Do I? You were around for it. The High Natural is the ultimate divine accident. Not that the *divine* itself was at all surprised, as usual."

"So, what made it your business to create a mate for the High Natural, out of a Spirelight?"

"To *finish creating* the High Natural. What else? That

was the second happy accident. Call it the land's intervention if you like. You wouldn't be wrong. Not so long before the Spirelight girl wandered into this swamp of a city, a certain irate Crimbone father paid us a visit. Seems his son had run away. He suspected the boy was drawn here. I heard him out, and I realized what he hadn't. He gave us less than half the trouble as you and your friend, in case you wondered. So there I was, aware that a High Natural—or the makings of one, at least— was out there somewhere, and that the forces I serve had assigned me some role in his creation. Then one day, three of my fledglings dragged in a runaway Spirelight girl and her little Earth-line friend. I acted on a moment's inspiration…for whenever she happened to run into Metaiew's prodigal son."

Zane shook his head. "I still don't get it. What's it supposed to do for the High Natural, giving him a mutated Spirelight for a girlfriend?"

"You've seen them together. Given the unique effect of her special glow, it would be impossible for him to ever really see her as a Spirelight. That's the key. Based on what word's filtered back to me lately, things seem to be working out nicely. Before long, the Spirelights and the Earth-line people will fall beneath the wrath that the High Natural has set free from within the lands. The purest glory of the Old World will be reborn, brighter than ever, here in a truly New World. You've been part of that, Zane. You should be proud."

Zane spat. "You rich, nutty old fuckhead. You *sound* like a damn Spirelight!"

"Come on. Before the High Natural, you and Jesse

were maybe the last two great Crimbone warriors who still embodied the integrity of your legacy. I know you've both sensed the wellspring that is this city, how it calls to your purest soul. Too bad Jesse hasn't handled it so well. He has too many of his own demons to accept it with a clear head. It's brought out something erratic in him, made his judgment sloppy. You've seen it. Am I right? That's why I'm having this conversation with you instead of him. So, what do you say?"

Zane hung limp, only his head raised. He stared blankly. "If you were hanging onto your own dick any tighter, you'd be your nutsack."

Talino shrugged and walked towards the door.

Zane shouted, "Hey, Talino, you know what, man?"

Talino turned back. "Yeah?"

"You got a really little dick."

Talino looked down. He shrugged and smiled. "You're still the one tied to the wall in my house." He walked out.

After a few minutes, another set of feet sounded. Crawler ducked into the doorway. The fledgling gawked in horror. "Are you hurt bad?"

Zane never expected to be so glad to hear that kid's screechy voice. He looked left and right at his restraints. "Nah. Just irritated."

"Where's your hammer?"

Zane looked and saw that Crawler had brought his own weapon. "Never mind for now. Just cut these fucking vines."

Crawler came forward. The door crashed shut behind him. He spun in time to see one of the thickest vines in the room shoot across it like a beam. More vines shot instantly into place over the door—up, down, zigzagging, nearly obscuring it in seconds. Zane spotted another vine come loose from the wall. It struck at Crawler from behind like a snake. Crawler snapped around. His black blade sang free. The lashing vine skewered itself at the end of his outstretched arm. The little bastard knew how to kill shit, Zane gave him that. The skewered vine lashed back, slitting itself up the center. The two halves flapped and smacked each other. They splattered greenish, syrupy juice everywhere. The physical trauma seemed to reverberate back through all the vines, driving them to a quaking panic.

Overhead, the budding glow-pods flashed like out of control strobe lights, brighter and faster 'til Zane almost heard them screaming. The vines slackened on his arms, like he'd been waiting for. He thrust himself forward. The restraints groaned and the ripping sounds grew louder and deeper than ever. He felt them all tearing. His limbs gained more slack.

He still felt them tugging him back. The other vines had fallen inward onto Crawler. The kid flipped, floundered and darted. Around him, his blade sang like a bolt of black lightning. It struck everywhere, cleaving anything that touched him.

"One of my arms," Zane shouted. "Free just one of my arms, and I can—"

A sea of the writhing, snaky shapes filled up the space between them. Zane thought, *That's it, the kid's dead.*

Zane threw his whole body to the right, giving one

final great wrench of his left arm, the one that had damaged its restraint the most. The vine popped loose from whatever had rooted it and slithered limply off his arm. His hand was numb, but he willed motion into the fingers as he swung it at the vine binding his right. He grabbed hold and squeezed, just as another vine lashed and tightened around his neck and jaw. It jerked him backwards, straining his neck to the breaking point. He bit deep into it. The outer layer was as tough like melon shell, dusted in prickly fuzz that cut his tongue. He dug his teeth in as deep as they would go, then he tore. Putrid, gelatinous plant blood slimed his mouth, stinging his cuts. He held on 'til he ripped out a huge chunk.

He spat it away, spat out the goo that drenched his face. The vine recoiled from his face but tightened around his neck. It forced his mouth open in the fight for air. The slime seeped between his neck and the vine. Sensing the small advantage, he pumped and wriggled his neck and shoulders. It won him only a few quick, shallow gasps, enough to let him keep fighting. Now both his arms were free. One arm actually had most of the sensation back by now. He tore frantically at the strangling cord. He looped one arm through the vine so his elbow pressed it, then he threw himself to the floor, driving down hard, squashing the vine. That freed his neck and arms. By the time he had his breath, though, the ones on his legs had climbed around his torso. His spine felt ready to splinter at the base. A chopping thud sounded.

The last vines holding Zane went limp.

Crawler stood over Zane, knife dripping, mouth

twisted in a panting snarl, body bruised and scraped, clothes torn. With his free hand, he reached down and pulled Zane up.

From there, they didn't bother with words. They crouched back to back in the center of the room. The floor around them was strewn and saturated in mangled bits. The things still in one piece slithered and coiled, drawing up for the next wave of attack. Zane and Crawler had barely thinned enough of the room to show some of the bare walls beneath. The more damage Zane and Crawler did, the harder the whole network tried to kill them in its agonized panic.

The glow-pods on the ceiling had swollen to the size of tennis balls. They started throbbing. The light churned like lava in the translucent sacks. Zane still spotted no trace of the door. He could rip the vines away from it with his bare hands, or Crawler could slice them away, but not before more got hold of them both. Zane glanced at Crawler. Everything but raw fighting, killing instinct had fled the kid's brain. He poised ready for the final onslaught, his last goal to eviscerate as many of the monster vines as possible before he and Zane were snuffed out.

Zane remembered being young and stupid like that, when he might have let go of his last trace of sanity and embraced the final frenzy. That was just one more way of pussying out, though. The flashing pods were no longer the only light source in here. Across from the door, right behind the spot where he was held, the wall of vines had thinned enough to reveal a few fragmented shafts of sunlight.

Zane pointed and barked, "Crawler, the window! Slice there!"

Apparently, Crawler had enough mind left to understand. His knife seemed to leap in the direction Zane pointed, pulling the arm behind it, the arm pulling the body into a tigerish spring.

Black metal flashed. Thick fluid splashed. More chunks thumped to the floor, revealing more glass and spilling sunlight. Now the vines would focus their attack on Crawler. Zane sprang up behind the lad, ready to catch them and tear them to shreds as they came.

Something exploded overhead. It rained huge sulfurous sparks around him. One of the sparks hit Zane's arm. A flame ignited in his flesh, bright as magnesium. He howled, swatting then clamping his hand over it, scarring his palm deep before he could snuff it.

Pop, Pop, Pop filled the room. One, then another of the glow-pods exploded, showering everything. Zane's arm shielded his eyes, as flames sprang up between the dead mangled vines on the floor. Crawler had already taken several burns. He still hacked his way towards the window. Only a few were left. Zane clearly saw the wall of the house next door. Whatever was beneath the window couldn't be worse than what surrounded him. He barreled forward into Crawler.

They crashed through together, snapping the remaining vines, then plummeted two stories. They hit rocky, grass-dusted earth in a shower of glass, then rolled away from each other. Zane regained his senses. So did Crawler, but not by much. Overhead, black smoke rose from the window. The stomach-turning smell of burning vines wafted down.

Zane spat out a mouthful of blood and plant goo. He would probably be spitting out the latter taste all day. "How'd you find me? You follow Talino?" His voice was a horrific rasp. His throat felt worse.

"My…my Familiar…said you were—"

Zane nodded, mildly amused that his body was still in one piece. His limbs still felt crushed where the vines had constricted them for days. At least Crawler had gotten the worst of the broken glass.

"C'mon, let's get back in there." Zane started around towards the front.

"*What?*"

"Jesse's still in there. So's my hammer."

Crawler looked bewildered at first. "I heard…I thought Jesse was dead."

"Who told you that?"

"My Familiar." The boy's face twisted savagely. "It said…it said Nergal…Nergal and the others—"

Zane smiled wide as the pain in his face allowed. "You think Nergal and those fuckers could kill Jesse Ripper-Man Karn? C'mon, kid, let's get back in there."

TWO

Nergal heard the commotion overhead in his sleep. Probably just Zane Rochester, fighting again with Talino's vines, wearing himself out, ripping himself to pieces bit by bit. The great ol' Zane Rochester—he'd probably never be such a heroic sight again.

In the steak house, Nergal had accepted meeting Zane Rochester and Jesse Karn as the greatest privilege he was ever likely to know. Now his proudest accomplishment in life was that he'd bested them both. No one brought up *how* he'd bested Jesse, so he didn't either. Then again, he was still loving his youth, and it hadn't even been a full week since the accomplishment.

What a week that was! His victory had earned him a longer stretch of time off than he could remember. When he wasn't partying or sleeping it off, he kept track of the news. The High Natural's cross-country campaign just kept providing more to celebrate. Last night, Nergal went for a woman in a group of tourists, which pissed off all the men she was with. His limbs were still sore from the brawl. He impressed himself over how well he could still fight with his broken arm. Getting an actual challenge out of Earth-line men was surprisingly refreshing.

His blade rested in its scabbard, on the belt that hung by a rung on the wall next to his bed. He hadn't put it back on since that night. If anyone asked why, he would say it was because it was his time off, and his knife hand was broken anyhow.

No one asked.

Of course not. They're too busy paying attention to everything else happening.

The pain in his splinted forearm had already reduced to a numb throb, one he could ignore. He blocked with the arm several times in last night's fight. He'd been drunk enough, so it hadn't bothered him much.

When he woke up, he wouldn't be able to ignore it so well, so he stayed asleep.

At first, he liked the dream he found, most of it. He was back in the Quarter, except night hadn't quite fallen. When he went through Pirate's Alley, the bar down that way was how it used to be, years back, full of enough real punks and ragers of the hardcore scene that he didn't mind all the fancy Goth types so much—before some spics bought the place out and turned it into some kind of swanky Spanish cantina bullshit.

In the dream, there was that little Spirelight bitch he and the boys had caught in there all those years back, and her drunk, slutty Earth-line friend, the one Talino had kept around as a trophy zombie—or at least a pair who might as well have been them, except they were both Spirelights.

How often do that many stupid fuckin' glowsticks bumble into this town, anyway? Don't they know who runs it? My lucky day!

Nergal's arm wasn't broken when he dreamed, and he wore his Crimbone knife. This time, he didn't bother with the drawn-out cat-and-mouse game he'd pulled back then, just drew his blade right there in the bar and went to town on the little Spirelight bitches. He barely noticed how he didn't get much of a glow-snack from either of them, was basically just working his way through lots of writhing, screaming raw meat. That in itself was a fun enough way to sleep off last night's waking revels. The bartender didn't even give him shit about the mess!

When he went out into Jackson Square, though, he kept spotting Spirelights everywhere he looked. Everyone—Crimbone, civilian Schomites, Earth-liners, everyone—saw the sopping red mess all over him, and they *did* seem to mind. In fact, a lot of them started screaming.

No, you idiots, what the hell are you freaking out at me for? Can't you see the French Quarter's filling up with Spirelights, strolling around eating lucky dogs and snapping pictures like any other tour-rons? Don't they know the Crimbone run this town?

Hey, he might as well make the most of it. It wasn't everyday you could just run howling mad in broad daylight, slashing your way through all the Spirelight glows you could drink before—

He must have killed dozens, maybe hundreds of them before he realized he wasn't tasting any glows. Because none of the Spirelights he killed were giving off any. When he turned and looked at the red litter strewn everywhere, he didn't see Spirelight corpses. They looked like the remains of many worthy, rugged foes, many still gripping their ancient weapons of black metal in their cold dead hands. Nergal looked at the one in his hand, still soaked in all the blood—*all the Crimbone blood*—he'd just given it to drink.

No, this ain't right! Crimbone don't use the black metal on each other.

Oh yeah? You sure did. On one of your own childhood heroes, no less. That's what you've been reaping the rewards of since, remember?

Yeah, but not the blade itself! I only—

Right. Just keep telling yourself that, cocksucker. You're the only one who is. You're still the one who broke that seal, and the rest of your pack saw you do it. You broke the seal, man, hahahah!

Glass shattered somewhere above. An instant later, two heavy thumps sounded outside. Nergal's eyes snapped open. After giving his blood a moment to speed up, his gaze rolled over the ceiling of his small, sparse bedroom. He sat up. The thin endoskeleton of vines on the walls and ceiling had started writhing and twisting. They smelled like they were burning. No, not these vines, but somewhere in the house—

Nergal pulled on some pants, strapped on his knife, and stormed out into the low concrete hallway. After a short set of stone steps, he followed a gilded, carpeted hallway to the ballroom, where he froze in his tracks. The house had become a quaking, churning, lashing jungle. Throughout the ballroom, five of his fellow Crimbone stood bewildered.

Since obviously no one else would, Nergal pulled himself together and barked, "Stermet, Fritz! Find Talino."

As Stermet and Fritz started forward, Hobs cried, "I've already checked his room. He's not there."

Nergal stormed to the center of the room. "Look, if he's in this house, just find him and get him out." The smell of burning vines got stronger. Nergal sniffed, looked up the stairs, and saw black smoke. When he looked back, Hobs had moved to join Stermet and Fritz in the search. "Not you, Hobs. You come with me. Gorm, Dex, you too."

Nergal thundered upstairs. He heard Hobs, Gorm, and Dex fall in behind him. Three of last night's lightpears—which should be withered and dry by now, waiting to fall and be swept away like confetti—had come alive again, so they flashed and flared blindingly.

At the top, he paused and glanced back. Stermet and Fritz had taken off in separate directions. Stermet was midway towards the same door from which Nergal had come.

Nergal was about to shout *No, not that way, you idiot,* when one of the lightpears exploded in a magnesium flash. A fireball spilled down onto Stermet's head, crushing him like a hammer driving a nail home in one strike. Flames flowed out in all directions across the floor.

Fritz hurried from it, into the lower house. Nergal darted into the hallway, his companions close behind. Up here, the vines thrashed and lashed in a more violent panic than anywhere. One of them smacked Nergal in the face. With his good hand, he ripped his knife from the scabbard and hacked it away.

Time to learn to use this damn thing left-handed, I guess. So far, so good.

In a quick dance of savage slashes, he cleared half the hallway. Dead, sticky remnants littered the floor in his wake, the walls lined in twitching, flopping stumps. The smoke was still thin here, had mostly risen towards the ceiling, but it was already stinging his eyes. He turned back to the others.

"Gorm, Dex. Guard both ways out of this hallway. Hobs, come with me."

Nergal and Hobs hacked their way down the central hallway. The vines were relatively thin here, not like they were in Jesse and Zane's rooms. Tendrils of smoke rose from the seams of Zane's door. Nergal almost tried it, though he sensed it would be barricaded by blazing vines within. Something made him pause.

The other door—Jesse Karn's door—hung open.

"Check it," Nergal said to Hobs, pointing to Zane's door just in case.

Hobs passed him, turned the knob, pushed on it. "It's stuck."

Nergal nodded, his great forked knife ready, already edging towards Jesse's room. Since besting Jesse Karn using just the pommel, part of Nergal had felt like he'd left a victory tragically incomplete. Now he stepped into the doorway, eager to remedy this. *Gonna be the one to break the seal, might as well rip it all the way off, right?*

The room was a raging, slithering green sea, the ceiling enflamed with a thousand tiny lightpears, all ready to explode, like the one downstairs had done onto Stermet's head.

Jesse Karn wasn't there.

From somewhere behind came the wet, slicing crunch of a blade chopping through meat and bone. Something rolled next to Nergal's foot. He didn't need to look to know that it was Hobs' head. Instead he turned and faced Jesse Karn. The man had just stepped out of another doorway. The door behind him was still closed, so he must have pressed himself in there very tight and still. Dried blood still crusted his bald head. His blade extended thirstily from his iron grip. There was no savage abandon in his fierce, bloodshot eyes as they stared into Nergal's, only the clear, pure glow of a hatred he would now put to work.

With his own eyes, Nergal told Jesse he understood. Their blades both flashed through the gloom.

THREE

The flame burst came so fast, so thick, so hot, that for an instant Zane and Crawler thought it had met them at the door to incinerate them. No, it had only engulfed the far right corner of the ballroom. Still, the heat was already nearly intolerable as they ran towards the left staircase. As they thundered up, two Crimbone met them halfway. They spotted Crawler and looked ready to ask him for help. When they spotted Zane, their faces contorted in understanding.

Crawler didn't hesitate, showed no inner conflict. His blade struck the nearest one, painting his hand red. The body tumbled past him, is spilt guts slithering after it, smearing the steps.

Zane ducked the second attacker's hatchet. He came back up with a lightning punch to the chin, lashing the man's head back so hard that the neck snapped. Zane trampled the body, leapt onto the landing, then halted at the edge of the hallway.

Behind him, Crawler asked, "What the fuck happened here?"

When Zane's foot prodded a fallen vine, he half expected it to still writhe like a freshly decapitated snake. "Looks like someone saved us some hassle."

With that, he moved towards the central hallway, slowly and cautiously as he dared with the fire eating up their time. The fight on the stairs had boosted his faith in bare fists, though he still didn't go as boldly as he would have with his hammer. A heavy dragging sound jolted him, then a lean, giant-framed shape lumbered into his path and fell towards the wall, catching itself on a splayed hand. Zane sniffed dried blood, as well as fresh, wet blood that didn't belong to the shape. A lot of the latter soaked both of Jesse's arms to the elbows.

"How the fuck did you get loose?" Zane asked, already slipping an arm beneath Jesse's shoulder, hoisting him.

"Not sure…I think they were keeping me drugged for a while… then the drugs wore off, I woke up with one killer hangover, then those vines got all excited and…sorta lost interest in me." He paused and looked at Crawler. "What the fuck's going on?"

"I think me and Crawler here managed to piss off the whole house."

"Yeah." Jesse sniffed, face wrinkling against the smoke. "We probably ought'a leave."

"Let Crawler here help you out. I need to get my hammer."

Zane slipped free and Crawler tried to take hold of Jesse. Jesse shrugged him off roughly, swayed then stood strong. "I can walk fine," he said, the slur in his voice burned away by something almost manic. He started towards the ballroom, then cast an eye back at Zane. "Watch your head in there, man."

Zane rolled his eyes and started into the hall. What

he saw almost froze him. Just past the sealed, smoke-leaking door he'd lately occupied were two enemies Jesse had apparently dealt with. One lay stretched on the floor, minus a head. The other hung from the high ceiling by a vine wrapped around the waist. Zane could tell the man's back was broken, bent in an almost perfect upside-down V. The vine's other end was looped through a tough cluster of growth still rooted to the ceiling. Zane drew nearer. The dangling man twitched and gurgled. Zane caught a new, rank smell, and he realized it wasn't a vine suspending the man, but rather a slimy, grayish pink cord coming out of the belly. The man's pants were partway down, and the waist wasn't the only part of the anatomy around which the makeshift cable was tightened. The dangling man spun slowly 'til Zane looked into the maddened, agonized eyes of Nergal.

"Shit, Jess." Zane smirked painfully. "When'd you get so literal?"

He stepped gingerly over the headless body, ducked beneath the hanging one, and retrieved his hammer. As he started back through the hall, he caught another glimpse of those suffering upside-down eyes. He almost used his hammer to mercifully splatter the skull like a piñata. Nah, that wouldn't be right. Poor ol' Nergal hadn't even met the approaching flames.

As he stepped back over the headless body, Zane saw Nergal's forked knife on the floor. Of course it wasn't the real knife anymore, now that its owner had held it for the last time. When Zane's foot brushed it, it crumbled to dust. Hopefully the next Crimbone to be sent that blade wouldn't be born in his lifetime.

Some of Talino's raving caught up with him, and he caught himself thinking, *But will there even be any more Crimbone after my lifetime?*

Cut that shit. You're starting to think like Jesse. Speaking of which, you'd better catch up with him and Crawler.

On his way out, a single vine of medium girth slithered towards his ankle. He grunted through his abraded throat and kicked it as he walked by. It recoiled timidly. Atop the stairs, Zane saw how fierce the fire had grown in the ballroom. He ran for the front door.

FOUR

The street filled with onlookers. Sirens blared close as Jesse and Crawler reached the sidewalk. Right when Jesse figured they could slip into the crowd discreetly, he reached up to rub his sore head. Red muck slushed between palm and scalp, and he noticed the mess covering his arms. Crawler wasn't nearly as bad off, but didn't look exactly inconspicuous.

"We should get scarce," Jesse muttered.

"What about Zane?"

"Oh, he'll catch up."

"Hey, dudes, dudes!" A mangy Rastafarian hurried towards them. "You dudes just come outta that fire? You look hurt bad! Anyone else in there?"

"We're fine," Jesse said. "We've been in a fight. Some guys jumped us a few blocks away."

"Bullshit, man! You all covered in soot! How'd you

get like that, huh? What about that fight, huh? Go all Jack-the-Ripper on some motherfuckers or somethin', use dat big gator knife on 'em?" The Rasta man pointed to Jesse's knife, back safely in its scabbard.

Jesse said bemusedly, "*Gator knife?*"

"C'mon, what's goin' on? Who else in there?"

More and more folks turned to look. Jesse took a deep breath and said, "Look, I don't know shit about that place, okay?"

"Yeah you do," chimed in another voice. "I saw you and your friend there come out! Look, the cops'll be here soon, so what's going on? How'd that fire get started?"

Crawler stepped up. "Look, that wasn't us, okay? Now we've had a really tough day. My friend's hurt sort of bad, so could someone please get us some help, get us to a phone or something?"

Jesse reminded himself that Crawler knew this town and how to use it. That's when a hulking black shape barreled through the front door, a great gust of flame billowing out in pursuit. The shape cleared the porch steps in one leap, landed on its feet, then rolled in the grass, extinguishing several small flames on its shoulders and upper back. Then the shape pulled itself up on the iron fence, coughed, hacked, and shook itself like a huge cat. It spotted Jesse and Crawler, hopped the fence, and hurried towards them. On the way, it shoved aside several horrified onlookers.

"Ah, there you guys are," rumbled Zane. "I think it's time to slip away."

Jesse was about to agree, then a figure on the corner at the end of the block caught his eye. He didn't realize his companions had followed his gaze 'til he heard Zane say:

"Yeah, I see him. C'mon, Jess, right now we need to—Jess! Hey, wait—*Jesse!*"

Jesse had already broken into a fast walking clip, no longer caring how many people he shoved out of his way, or how roughly. If he cared at all, the last of it was obliterated when he drew close enough for eye contact. The cold resolve with which he'd faced Nergal was replaced by a painful beating in his temples, igniting his blood with something more blistering and explosive than the flames. His throbbing brain echoed with the voice of a scared, scarred, teenage girl, a voice everyone else had only heard on an old cassette recording.

"Jesse, get back here!" It was Zane, trying to catch up. "Now ain't the time. We need to—"

Talino stood statue-still, his long green coat fluttering back from his gentleman's attire. His shoulders were straight, his arms clasped casually behind his back. Jesse was nearly through the crowd. Talino turned and vanished around the corner. Jesse heaved both great arms outward, scattering his final obstacles, then he broke into a run.

Zane and Crawler's footsteps echoed after him, somewhere far behind, so he ran faster. He knew he could run faster than Zane. As for Crawler, damned if some city-bred fledgling would catch up and rob Jesse of this. At the corner, he stared in the direction Talino had taken, and laughed. The fucker was trying to play it cool, standing there, then turning and walking away, as if daring Jesse to try to catch him. Now there he went in the distance, already two blocks away, running like he ought to.

Two fire trucks and a police car sped up the street and around the corner, passing Jesse.

"City, swamp, whatever you are," he growled low, "if he's the one you choose to shelter, then put him before me so he can show what he's worth!"

With that, he launched into a cheetah sprint. The burning smell was now well behind him. The rich, heady, swampy smell of the New Orleans streets filled his nose, filled his head, filled him with a wild, youthful energy that reminded him of being a fledgling. His mouth frothed and his legs pumped harder. Shops and houses sped by in a thickening blur. His scabbard swung and smacked his thigh, too heavy with the knife still in it.

A block away, Talino darted left and disappeared around another corner. Jesse veered into the street. Traffic screeched to a halt all around him. He leapt over a car half-spun to a stop. Still running, he rounded the corner. He'd lost speed in the street, but he regained it quickly. By now, he didn't have to shove anyone from his path, because they all scattered when they saw him come charging. Always he seemed to gain ground, yet his prey kept managing to keep at least a block between them. How the fuck could Talino run so fast, and for so long? No way could that indolent degenerate be in such good shape.

As they darted, wove, and barreled through block after block, the neighborhood changed. There were more and more ruins of strange, small, brightly painted box-like houses, and fewer businesses. The smell of ancient decay thickened. Ahead, the last of the houses dropped away.

The high grassy mound of the levee rose before them. Jesse skidded to a halt. Ahead, Talino slowed to a trot, then to a walk. He climbed the steep embankment, no fatigue showing. Jesse absently wiped some of the blood from his hands onto his shirt, then wiped a glistening gob of sweat from his hard, bald scalp. His palm brushed the deep, long cut left by Nergal's pommel. He grimaced. With the pain, there flickered a lucidity that faded quickly.

Lucid…lucid of what? Where the hell was he? He'd left Zane and Crawler somewhere far behind, he knew that much, but were they even waiting in a place that he could find his way back to over mere distance? This grimy, empty, glass-strewn street was less like the run-down section of a city, more like a decimated border town. The town in which he'd spent the last few days was an illusion. The pale sun had bleached it away, leaving him alone with his enemy in this empty, silent land of slithering nightmare.

Atop the levee, Talino turned and waited, done with running, though he hadn't yet led Jesse to the chosen place of meeting. Jesse started up the hillside. Talino backed away, out of sight. Obviously Talino wouldn't be in view by the time Jesse reached the top. Still, the chase had ended, so Jesse didn't run uphill.

Somewhere moaned the bass horn of a passing barge. Out across the water, Jesse saw the broken stacks of what used to be a factory or power plant. Things of modern Earth-line industry were distant. His concern waited at the bottom of the levee, somewhere through the thick brush, within the wall of trees, within the naked swamp—

Jesse sniffed and found his prey's path through the brush. His feet sank in soggy earth beneath deep shade. He expected the shade to cool him, yet somehow, the heat only thickened here. Jesse tore off the remnants of his bloody shirt and stalked silently among the low, mossy branches of the twisty, leaning trees. His hand neared his knife, fingers circling the handle but not yet touching it. It wasn't his way to lay hold of his weapon 'til the moment he drew it, and he never drew 'til an enemy stood close enough to strike.

That enemy stood ahead in a clearing. Behind the enemy lay a deep, murky patch of stagnant swamp water where some of the river had flowed in and gotten trapped. Nice strategic spot, Jesse granted. He stalked slowly inward, eyes locked with Talino's. Between their eyes, the fight had already begun. Jesse's blood pounded with the need to kill this man, superseding whatever more delicate dealings his assignment mandated. The chase had burned away the raw madness. In its place glowed the special, almost ritualistic bond known only to intimate foes. Jesse circled menacingly.

"If you ever really wanted to stop me," said Talino, "all you had to do was kill Rob Coscan when you had the chance. It doesn't matter anymore if you kill me. Not that you will." With that, Talino threw aside his long coat, revealing a jewel-hilted short sword. He drew it with a florid, theatrical motion and stretched his arm sidewise so Jesse saw the length of the blade. It had the shape of a scimitar, but thinner…forged of the black metal.

"How the hell can you handle that? You're not Crimbone!"

"I'm the only living Schomite to have mastered the Old World's free-flowing magic as it exists in this world. I think I can handle its metals."

"You ain't mastered shit. All you've done is pervert everything." With that, Jesse sprang. His blade whipped free and sailed in an arc towards Talino's chest. Since his Second Call, Jesse's instinct was never to bother with blade play. Just as he drew only at the moment of the strike, he struck only ever to kill, his body and soul all channeled to the razor-edged teeth of his knife, which was always back in the scabbard afterwards just as quickly.

In a fraction of a second, Jesse's eyes took in all of Talino, ready for the smallest movements that might force him to subtly redirect his strike. Talino's arm stayed to the right, the scimitar shimmering blackly. Had Talino drawn his arm inward, Jesse would have seen the shoulder muscles move before the rest of the motion started. Yet Jesse's blade came within a foot of Talino's chest…and clanged against the scimitar.

What the hell? No one could move that fast! In over a century, it was the first time anyone had successfully parried Jesse, the first time his knife had touched other metal.

Showing nothing but irritation, Jesse slipped the teeth from the scimitar, making to dart past Talino and sheath the knife in his heart. He carried the motion through, but there was the scimitar again, batting aside the forward-curved knife. Talino now stood several feet to the left. Jesse skidded to a halt at the edge of the bog and saw poisonous things slithering in it.

His enemy was slinking away. As Jesse had anticipated, Talino had meant for him to charge like a bull into the deadly murk. That strategy had failed, so Talino now edged backwards, scimitar pointed forward. There was caution in his movements, but no fear on his face. The caution at least was heartening, that Talino still perceived himself as vulnerable somehow. Then again, that might have more to do with minding his surroundings.

"Don't you get it, Jesse? To fight me is to fight the swamp itself."

With a ruthless grin, Jesse came in with a high strike. This time he knew to expect the scimitar to appear to block him. He already redirected the blade to go under it, a slash turning into a stab. Yet the scimitar swung from below, striking the knife so fiercely that the impact rattled Jesse's teeth.

You're making yourself too tense, too rigid. He's feeding into that, making you sloppy so his magician's tricks keep working, so he can knock you silly all over the place.

For his next several attacks, Jesse loosened up, made his movements liquid. His feints and subtleties came far easier now. He came in no less relentlessly, though, driving Talino back and back and back, the trees thickening around them.

Talino's face stayed peaceful, his body not so much retreating as gliding backwards through the mud, moss, and lichen. Jesse's limbs still burned from the run, tightening as the futile match drug on, making it harder to guide his blade or keep his footing.

The earth grew soggier, 'til they danced through shallow marsh. Jesse's front foot slid into a sinkhole, and he tumbled forward. As he fell, he saw the scimitar extended to catch and skewer him, so he flung himself sideways, splashing in the muck. He shook and spat swamp water from his face, wiping it from his eyes with his free arm. When he spotted Talino circling him, he lunged upward.

That's when his forehead smacked squarely into a thick, low-hanging branch. He'd swear it hadn't been between them when he started to rise, but it rattled his skull and sent sparks through his brain, surely as Talino's scimitar had repeatedly appeared in his path with no visible movement from the arm behind it. Jesse landed hard on his back, his knife slipping his grip and sinking in the muck.

"I told you," said Talino. "When you fight me, you fight the swamp."

Right as Jesse's hand found his weapon, his enemy's blade flashed. The point raked his chest muscles from end to end, and he let out a howl. The cut wasn't deep, yet its sting shot out all through him like electricity. He dropped and floundered, half-paralyzed, teeth clenching, eyes watering and burning.

"Apparently, you couldn't flow as one with the spirit of this place, Jesse Karn. You'll live to see what I've set in motion here, and you'll fight it just as futilely."

Talino was a fuzzy black and white shape in Jesse's

blurred eyes. By the time he blinked them clear, the shape was gone. The cut on his chest remained, though, coursing blood that dripped to mingle with the swamp water. He wiped his blade semi-clean on his pants leg, sheathed it, and pulled himself halfway up. When he reached for a low branch—maybe the same one he'd smacked his head on—his hand closed on empty air. He fell again and smacked his knee on a rock. Grunting, he squeezed his eyes shut, doubled forward, and caught himself on one hand. Mosquitoes swarmed tauntingly, darting in at intervals.

Finally, he shambled to dry land. On the soft earth in the middle of the swamp, he fell face down and passed out.

JUST DROPPIN' BY

ONE

Lilly switched off the newscast about the storms in Arkansas and hit *Talk* on the phone. She'd been keeping the TV volume low because Sally was still asleep. Part of her wished Sally would wake up so she wouldn't have to see it alone. It sounded like folks were having a hell of a time down there—those who hadn't evacuated, anyway.

"I'm here. I know Sheldon Wildfire's there, or you know where he is. *Please* let me talk to him, or put me in touch with him. Please! I'm dead if you don't!"

"Is this the person who called a few days ago?" Lilly peered through the dim, across her and Tiger's stonewall subterranean bedroom. Sally groaned and shifted in uneasy sleep.

"Huh?" asked the voice. "Who's this? Who are you people? What's going on?"

"Calm down. You talked to my husband last time. He told you not to call again."

"I know, and I'm sorry! Look, this is the number

Sheldon gave me for where he was leaving for. He told me to call only if I absolutely had to, and there's nothing else I can do. There's nowhere else I can go."

"So, Sheldon did give you the number."

When the strange girl had called and gotten Tiger, the conversation had been over by now. When he called the number back, some random person answered from a drug store phone in New Hampshire. When questioned, Sheldon asked how the hell they thought he could have gotten the number, let alone given it out to anyone. No, everyone agreed, there really was no way he could have. It wasn't like Tiger, Blix, or Claudette carried it written down. Besides, they all knew how to spot a liar, even a good one, and Sheldon gave no signs of lying. Later, though, when he thought no one was around, Lilly spied him on one of the office phones making two calls. He got no answer on the first, sighed heavily, then dialed again, waited, then spoke.

He asked for someone named Janie. Apparently, Janie wasn't around, because from there he asked all sorts of questions: did the person on the other end know where she might be; when was the last time anyone had seen her; had she told anyone about anything wrong? His voice didn't rise, though it trembled more and more.

Lilly stayed out of sight, waited 'til he left, then pulled up the password-protected record screen on the computer connected to the phoneline. Sheldon had called a couple private residences in Brattleboro, Vermont. She went straight to him about it. Instead of direct confrontation, she tested the waters through casual conversation. He was friendly as always, concerned for how she was faring these days, yet he gave absolutely no sign of the agitation she'd overheard in those two calls. He pulled it off so well, she almost thought she'd hallucinated what she knew for fact. Switched sides or not, these Spirelight Secret Police were a creepy bunch like that. Had he known Lilly was eavesdropping the whole time?

When the girl hesitated before answering, Lilly asked, "Is this Janie?"

"So he *is* there! Does he know I've called?"

"He knows, but he really shouldn't have given you this number. You have no idea how dangerous it is for you to be calling, both for us and yourself, so—"

"It's too late. I'm in Virginia. I'm right here in Skybrooks."

Lilly's frame tightened up, rigid and icy. Skybrooks. That put the girl roughly half an hour from here. "Okay...how'd you find this place, Janie?"

"I did a net-search on the number."

"This is an unlisted number." Yeah, and layer upon layer of clandestine arrangements had been made to keep this place's secrets. The girl shouldn't have been able to find out anything about it, not even with a paid background check.

"I know! I checked the area code and prefix, though, and the nearest place the bus would get me was Skybrooks. Please, tell me how to get to you!"

Resourceful little bitch, Lilly gave her that. Sheldon had probably counted on it, for whatever worst-case scenario had materialized. Lilly sighed. "You took the bus all the way from Vermont?"

"Yes! Please, I have to find Sheldon. If I don't, I'm dead."

"Who's after you? Has someone followed you?"

"No, they couldn't have. There's…there's no way. No, I'm alone, but…please! They killed my mom. They'd have killed me if I'd stayed, and I don't have anywhere else to—"

"Okay, calm down, or I'm hanging up right now."

After several deep breaths, the girl said, "Please. I'm sorry. I know I shouldn't've, but Sheldon gave me this number, then all this…Goddamnit, they killed my mom! Look, if Sheldon's there, could you please find him for me?"

The girl's desperation had bubbled to a peak, strong enough that Lilly nearly choked up while listening. "Who killed your mom? What does it have to do with Sheldon? Why couldn't you go to the Earth-line authorities?" Ah shit, she'd just said—

"You *are* Sheldon's people!"

"You could say that. How much do you know?"

"Not much."

Lilly looked again across the room. Sally's open eyes stared at her unreadably. Lilly shivered. She hadn't realized it when Sheldon first showed up—mainly since she'd been prepared to dislike him—but the sibling resemblance could be alarming. Lilly was used to Spirelights, but not the Secret Police. It was counterbalanced by what a charming little scamp Sheldon was, and the fact that Sally already felt something like a sister to her—*and be honest, Lilly, it helps that you're completely hot for the girl.* Yet Lilly could never be completely comfortable with anyone who hid their mind like Sheldon. Now she had to wonder what cards Sally was keeping off the table. "Okay, Janie, where in Skybrooks are you?"

"At a little general store. The bus dropped me off here. Just a second…it's the Gray Mill General Store. You know where that is?"

Lilly listened, but paid closer attention to Sally's expression. "I might. Skybrooks is a ways from here. Listen, Janie, did anyone else get off the bus at the same stop as you?"

"No." From the prompt response, Janie had clearly been on just such an alert. When it came to Deschembines, it sounded like she knew more than she thought she did. "Now can I please talk to Sheldon?"

"Not quite. Janie, sit tight. I might call you back."

"Wait, lemme get you the number to this—"

"It's the Gray Mill General Store in Skybrooks? Just hang tight there."

Lilly hung up. There, she'd gone and escalated this shit, hopefully before it escalated itself in a worse direction. Sally had sat up sharply, the covers falling from the flimsy T-shirt and boxers she'd stripped to. Lilly walked over, trying not to let this distract her.

Since the news of the slaughters had hit, Sally had pretty much abandoned her own quarters for Tiger and Lilly's. Tiger generally didn't mind a third body occupying the bed on the other side of his wife, or that said wife and said body had enjoyed quite a bit of each other on a few occasions after quite a few swigs of Jack Daniel's. It helped that Tiger and Sally got along quite well. Lilly figured it was also because her husband found Sally hot too. The only reason he hadn't joined in was because Sally wasn't comfortable with that.

To some degree, Sally needed the comfort Lilly gave, though she only ever let things go but so far, which would have frustrated Lilly up the wall if it hadn't been for Tiger. Lilly never asked if it had to do with Sally's ideas of fidelity, or Rob's, or some combination of the two. Either way, it was just as well, since Sally had plenty to talk about, things she desperately needed to tell *someone*. It was generally after Sally got worked up telling Lilly these things, when comforting segued into something else before either of them quite realized it.

Sally talked a lot about what Rob was like in Florida, and in Vermont when they first met. Yeah, Lilly had to admit, the guy sounded incredible. Plenty of girls still liked to think of their guy as a heroic Knight in Shining Armor on some level, and many a guy truly in love probably wanted to be just that for his lover.

'Til recently, Sally hadn't been forced to think about the other side of him. She never said one way or another how she felt about him now. Lilly didn't ask. Now the guy was out there somewhere leading an old-fashioned no-tech war party, running circles around the Earth-line authorities, soaking the earth in Spirelight blood wherever he went. Everyone else here—Spirelight and Schomite alike—seemed convinced that Rob and his band would show up eventually, and that he would treat this place like he treated those homesteads. Their adoration for Sally got overwhelming fast, so she stayed indoors as much as possible. When she wasn't here, she was in Sheldon's room, or so Lilly gathered.

No doubt Sheldon told his sister many things he wasn't telling anyone else.

Lilly sat, placed her hand over Sally's, and said gently as possible, "You were listening. You can guess what's going on. What do you know about this girl Janie?"

Two

The pay phone went dead, setting off a two hour stretch of pacing and fidgeting in the blistering heat. After twenty minutes, a scratchy, nasal voice went, "Y'waitin' for som'n'?"

Through the front of the general store stretched a long, burnt, leathery neck with an Adam's apple that bulged like a tumor, beneath a nonexistent chin and a white walrus mustache that made the head look like Albert Einstein wasted by cocaine, moonshine, and inbreeding. Pale, brown, bloodshot eyes bugged out at Janie beneath the freakishly long bill of a goose cap. There was paranoia in those eyes, probably constant. For some reason it seemed to perk up for Janie like a twitching hard-on.

"Huh?" she asked.

The neck extended further, 'til a pair of billiard-ball shoulders jutted out behind it. Those shoulders probably looked as tumorous as the Adam's apple beneath the sweaty, striped shirt. "Y'jus' got off the bus, right?"

Janie had spent the last three days scurrying around with her head low, shoulders drawn inward, unable to sleep, nerves sizzling through a body that felt increasingly nasty in the only set of clothes she had, the ones she'd run off in, which were soaked by the rain at the time. Whenever she'd stepped off the bus at a rest stop or change-over, her eyes had darted everywhere as if in a frantic dream, expecting to finally see the shapeless horror she'd felt watching from the shadows of her own house. She'd never stopped feeling it, any more than she'd stopped seeing Mom's slashed throat, or the lake of blood on the table.

Unlike that image, though, Janie was less and less sure that the looming, stalking shadow was a memory, that it wasn't physically with her, just beyond her line of sight, occasionally flickering in her peripheral, through every shade or patch of night she passed. This parking lot was all lumpy barren dirt, with some gas pumps stamped in the middle. This narrow porch with its gray, warped boards was too dead for stalking ghosts. She'd be damned if she let some hick clerk scare her any lower than she felt.

"Yeah," she said in a dull, irritated voice. "Now I'm waiting for my ride."

"That who you was jus' talkin' to out here?"

"No, I was calling the people back home, letting 'em know I got here okay."

"Didn't soun' like it."

"My ride's on its way, or they will be soon."

"Better be. The boss don' like people loiterin'." He ducked back inside.

Janie rolled her eyes, sort of hoping he saw her do so. She got a soda from a drink machine. After drinking half of it, she went in for a pack of cigarettes. The clerk was glued to a chair in front of a TV news report about the rainstorms tearing Arkansas apart. More than half the state was practically shut down. Meteorologists couldn't make heads or tails of the storms, or where they came from. They started calling them a "freak of nature", like some impossible inland hurricane that swept over all radars, bypassing every coast. Since no more sites of mass murder had turned up, the storms became the latest national news craze. No one mentioned how the last flickers of clandestine cult warfare had happened in Arkansas.

Today on the bus, someone sitting next to Janie had talked on a cell phone to a relative who lived in New Orleans. One of those big, fancy eighteenth century houses had burned down, right in the relative's neighborhood. When the passenger got off the phone and started talking to Janie, he said it sounded like the mob or something. Apparently, the forensics investigation had found something strange about how the fire had started. Examining the burnt-out wreckage, it seemed an excess of some highly flammable fluid had fueled it—not gasoline, but the juices of some plant life no one could identify. After half joking, *maybe it was those crazy cultists again*, he let Janie change the subject. Janie hadn't heard anything about it since, so she guessed no one else thought so.

Unless she was mistaken, New Orleans' hurricane season wasn't due for another month or so. Folks there were probably thankful this natural phenomenon had spared them for a change. The clerk's TV kept comparing the Arkansas storms and Hurricane Katrina, though it was repeatedly stressed that this was a far different meteorological beast. Analysts kept tossing around the word *phenomenon*.

Now and then, Janie heard fellow passengers talking about those *strange people*, either the ones they noticed in the place they just left, or those they were hearing about from people they were going to see. The word spread here and there, through a few scattered whispers. Janie thought back to Brattleboro five years ago. She'd been thirteen. Why had everyone else taken so long to notice? The rumors had gotten weirder, too, like autopsies done on the victims in Tennessee had revealed some completely alien internal organ system. When people en route weren't talking about all that, they kept bringing up solar flares.

"Yeah," the last guy who sat next to Janie on the bus had said, "it's what the scientists call it when there's a big flare-up of radioactive energy on the surface of the sun, gets so hot that it messes with radio transmissions down here on Earth and stuff. I saw a special about it on the History Channel. The biggest one on record was, like, back in the middle of the eighteen-hundreds. They say it, like, turned the sky bright purple all over the Western Hemisphere for a few hours, and it was messin' hard-core with the telegraph wires, like makin' 'em catch on fire. Those telegraph offices, they were catchin' on fire so all the power lines had burned up, but the radiation was so strong that the telegraph messages were still comin' through and the machines just kept spittin' 'em out like they was possessed. Those scientists they interviewed were talkin' about what it'd be like today. I mean, pretty much everything we have now is run on cell phones and the internet and stuff, so if we got another solar flare that powerful, it could shut the whole world down, y'know?

"Now the scientists have been watchin' the patterns of the sun spots or whatever, and they're expecting us to get another really big one soon, like sometime next week maybe, like the biggest we've seen in a long time. Crazy shit, right? Like all that happenin' right as there's these storms, when we've had all these devil-worshiper bikers an' hippies an' shit, all *those strange people* runnin' around killin' each other, like it's the end of the world upon us or somethin'."

Now here in the middle of nowhere, Janie's only hope was that those *strange people* were on their way to get her.

The clerk carded her for the smokes, probably mostly out of pettiness, annoyance at being pulled away from the boob tube by actual work. His latent paranoia was awake and active, though no longer pointed at her. Given her own state, Janie couldn't blame anyone for acting edgy, even this jerk. Lord only knew, her manner during the trip had probably turned its share of people off. Now she had cigarettes, which might help her nerves a little. She didn't even feel guilty about it. She'd smoked heavily when she was sixteen, and halfway through year seventeen, and was damn proud of herself for quitting. On her eighteenth birthday, she'd gone into a store to buy a snack, saw the rack of smokes behind the counter, thought of buying her first legal pack, and was even prouder when she didn't. At every stop, people stood around outside sucking back smoke, and she hadn't bummed one.

Now that she finally broke down, all she felt was cold, sick relief. Outside, through the rest of the waiting, she smoked a third of the pack.

The Gray Mill General Store in Skybrooks, right? Just hang tight there.

The woman's tone hadn't sounded completely convincing. Had she just said that so Janie would stop calling? How long did she expect Janie to linger before figuring out that no one was coming, that she'd been left to wait for the horror to come out of the shadows to claim her? Why would someone do that, though? Because if they did take her in, she'd bring the horror to the woman and her husband, or to anyone else who was on the other end of the phone with Sheldon.

Only a few people had stopped at the general store since the bus dropped her off. It had been at least an hour since the last one. Janie stared off across the dirt lot, across the dead road to the thick forest. Was that where the horror would come from when it finally decided to grab her? If Sheldon had abandoned her, maybe she should finish this cigarette, then go right out to meet it.

Janie chucked the butt, stepped off the porch, and made it as far as the pumps. Then something in her recoiled, so she stopped and dug in her heels. Over the trip, she'd counted Sheldon as her one hope of a safe haven, had built her mother's killer in her mind into some nearly omnipotent evil. So, how full of hot air had she filled those delusions? What if it was all nothing but bullshit, this whole time? Mom's ghost hadn't talked to her since she left Brattleboro, as if Mom had decided to stay behind with Sheldon's ghost-buddy from the bar. Either way, it was time she got it together and took more initiative.

Now that her brain was clearing, it seemed less and less possible that the killer could know she was here, at this random little place probably not even on the map. No one else back home could find her, either. Someone must have found Mom by now. The report would read something like, *Middle-aged single mother found dead in home, daughter missing, possibly abducted by killer.* She'd made her last big ATM withdrawal in New England, had lived off the cash since, so there'd be no useful account activity for the police to trace.

For all practical purposes, she stood in a different world now—Sheldon's world, she guessed, though maybe she was equally cut off from him. If so, fuck it. There had to be more around here than this store, better people than that hick clerk. As she started towards the road again, a loud engine rumbled in the distance.

Up the road zoomed a battered purple station wagon, running faster and smoother than it looked like it had any right to. Janie jumped back as it swerved into the lot, screeching to a halt a few yards past her. The left rear door swung open before it reached a complete stop. Out sprang a slender, limber shape with scruffy blond hair. The shape stumbled only slightly from the stunt, then ran and grabbed Janie into the most powerful embrace, not to mention the hungriest, most savagely loving kiss she'd ever had. For a second, she worried Sheldon would start ripping her clothes off right here in the parking lot. Then the kiss ended and they hugged each other just as fiercely.

When he drew back, his eyes looked as dazed and bewildered as she felt. "Holy shit, Janie, where'd you come from? Goddamnit, Janie, you're fucking insane! Goddamnit, you're so fucking wonderful!" He hugged her again and buried his face in her neck.

She ran her hands up and down his tough, narrow back, then squeezed his tough shoulders. Nothing felt any less like a strange dream. Except suddenly, it was a *good* dream. Janie squeezed Sheldon as hard and close as she could, trying to make herself wake up. She wanted to feel this moment as reality. The strangest thing was how happy he seemed. How could he not know how fucked-up everything was?

Because this is his world. It's always this fucked-up. He's used to it, and I just got here.

"I don't wanna be a bitch," said a soft, even voice, "but we should probably get moving."

From the driver's window peered a woman with short, auburn hair and a heart-shaped, freckled face with wide, doe-brown eyes. Her voice managed to be gentle and soothing, yet strong and stern all at once. Janie recognized the voice on the phone. She immediately sensed something off, almost alien about the woman.

She's like Sheldon, only not. No, I've seen others like Sheldon—that woman who came and took him away in Brattleboro, for instance. This woman's something else, but she's different than most people in the same kind of way you can't quite put your finger on—

Sheldon was tugging Janie into the car. She sensed these folks feared the same thing she'd been running from, so she scooted quickly into the middle of the back seat, between Sheldon and another woman, one who was like Sheldon. In fact, they looked a hell of a lot alike, though this one was older, probably mid-twenties. Sheldon slid in, slammed the door, and said something Janie couldn't hear because the driver had already stomped the gas. She circled the lot in a swinging screech, close enough to the pumps to freeze Janie's heart and lungs for a moment.

Once the car sped smoothly down the road, Janie shouted at Sheldon, "*What?*"

"Sorry," the driver called back. "I feel most comfortable making this quick."

Sheldon nodded, waited for the tire screech to die down. "I said: Janie, meet my sister Sally. Sally, this is the Janie you've been hearing so much about. That lady up front is Lilly."

Lilly smiled tersely and waved. Sally looked almost as rattled by the driving as Janie. Sheldon and the driver didn't look phased.

"Good to meet you, Janie," said Sally. "Didn't expect it to be so soon."

Lilly grumbled and glared through the dashboard mirror. Sheldon and Sally smirked at each other, Sally letting out a sputter. When Lilly glared harder, the siblings' eyes drifted widely in pathetically exaggerated mock innocence.

Janie couldn't help laughing with them. "Good to meet you too, Sally."

Then all three fell against each other, laughing their asses off. It felt better than Janie could have imagined, even though she was only half laughing, the other half sobbing.

THREE

Vencie walked out around the side of the general store. He stayed hidden 'til he heard the car screech in, then peered around the corner, saw Sheldon Wildfire, and noted the license plate before the car drove off. He recognized the driver's voice as Schomite. Blood pounded in his temples and clenched fists, and he hissed triumphantly through his teeth.

No, not yet. He'd found them, yet at the same time not quite. He recalled what he'd figured out about the Indian girl while trailing her and correlated it with his knowledge of the United Deschembines. Then he applied his own speculations, based on those files, of their habits before the first wave of them were wiped out. Of course, the survivors would have thickened their secrecy since those times, but Vencie could adjust accordingly. After all, he'd been right so far.

He'd known the Indian girl would get off the bus in Skybrooks, because he'd sat next to her at one point. He watched her check her ticket over, and saw the final destination printed at the bottom of the schedule sheet.

That was the most fun so far on some level. Of course she'd been growing a sense of how to spot Deschembines, and he saw her looking around everywhere for his kind. He even struck up small talk with her, then watched her dismiss him as the most boring, forgettable sonofabitch she met on her journey.

At the next changeover, he switched clothes in the men's room, then bought a ticket to the same destination. At the start of the final hour, the driver had rattled off a string of destinations that ended somewhere in Georgia. Vencie had known the Indian girl would be looking over her shoulder 'til she got off for good, so he moved to the rear, the better to see every passenger's head.

When the driver mentioned Skybrooks, everyone getting off there had made at least some slight responsive shift, whether they knew it or not. The last stop before Skybrooks was a rest area half an hour beforehand. When they reached that rest area, Vencie made sure that no Skybrooks-bound passenger got back on, except for the Indian girl. After hiding three bodies, he bought a map, found a car he liked, stuffed the driver in the trunk, and drove to Skybrooks ahead of the bus.

Once he scoped out the stop, he parked half a mile away, walked back to the convenience store, and waited. Now that he was in the United Deschembines' rough vicinity, it would take three days at most to locate them. It would be within an hour's drive, somewhere still predominantly rural.

Vencie went inside and talked to the bug-eyed clerk for a while, asking general questions about the area. At first the old bastard was suspicious and vaguely hostile. Once Vencie wrapped his head around the broken cracker English, it was only a matter of asking the right questions, stirring the man's pathetic regional pride, 'til it would be next to impossible to get him to shut up. Vencie half-listened, the rest of his mind elsewhere, ready to snap alert if the man spouted anything useful. Some offhand remarks clued him in that the town was Lepod territory, of which the old bastard was naturally ignorant. That might come in handy later.

Fifty miles south, the old man rambled, some folks had once tried opening an amusement park of all things. Some place called Renaissance Kingdom. This got Vencie's attention. Yeah, the man said, sort of a third-rate hybrid of Disneyland and King's Dominion. It had lasted about four years, then closed something like ten years ago. The bad location had killed it, too remote for a tourist attraction. Apparently, the managers used to buddy around with renfest reenactment groups, had come into some inheritance, and decided to try to put their next-to-non-existent little Podunk community on the map.

The sad bottom line was, those guys were just flat out incompetent businessmen. They blew the last inheritance in a final effort to save the place with some broader, more aggressive marketing. They probably would've gone right back to squalor, except someone had bought the property at a hefty price. Some rich weirdos from the Midwest, rumors went. For a while, there was talk of the park reopening, revamped by more capable hands. Nothing came of it, and the grounds were left falling to ruin out there in the woods, just off the interstate. If you drove that way and looked off to your right, you'd see the big white spikes of that Disneyland-style castle, still sticking up from the trees.

"Cute," Vencie muttered, then lifted one finger. "Just a moment."

He walked to the cooler at the back, hoping listlessly that the store carried some wine befitting the occasion. There was nothing but beer and cheap wino-wine, so he shrugged and walked back to the counter. Surely there'd be someplace with a proper selection between here and Renaissance Kingdom. He asked the clerk again how to find the place. The clerk kept giving him the strange eye, but didn't lie, so Vencie wouldn't need to torture him. Instead, he thanked the old grouch then hiked back to the car. He hadn't ruled out all other possibilities, but this felt in his gut like the right lead. After driving halfway, he checked into a motel. He hadn't slept since Vermont, and he hadn't enjoyed a full night's rest since setting out from the compound. By now, no one could tell him he hadn't earned it.

Before bedding down, Vencie called the compound. The Official would expect him to gloat and boast pettily, so instead he simply said, "I've found them."

"Found who?"

"Sally Coscan and the United Deschembines. Who else?"

"Where?" The eagerness in the Official's voice made it hard—oh, so hard—for Vencie to hold his own dignity.

"Virginia."

"Where in Virginia?"

"Now, now." Ashwin had specially rewired Vencie's pirate-registered track phone to make tracing the location next to impossible. "Things aren't ready for you to send the cavalry charging in."

"What the hell are you talking about? What about Rob Coscan?"

"That's the one detail that's not quite ready."

"Yeah, I'll bet. Because you don't know where he is."

Vencie glanced at the motel room's TV. The set was off, though he remembered recent conversations and news snippets, so he had an idea of what he would see if he turned it on. "Don't worry about that. It's mainly a matter of getting word to him."

"So you say."

"So I say, so it'll have to do for now."

"Or you walk?"

"You *are* getting good at this."

"What's your plan?"

"In three days, assemble all field agents in Skybrooks, Virginia."

"So that's where the United Deschembines are hiding."

"Don't expect me to make it that easy for you to sweep in and steal the credit. No, that's where you're going to have the agents assembled. I'll be in Skybrooks, at a location of my choice. I'll call you from there, give you that location, then you contact the agents wherever they've gathered, and tell them to go there. None of them will see me before the assembly. I'll lead them to

Coscan, and the United Deschembines."

Vencie hung up. That was enough prattle for one evening. The Official would comply. Three days was more than he needed, but Rob Coscan's timing had to be perfect. That would be tricky, particularly getting the word to Coscan. Vencie already had an idea on how to do that, involving yet more useful inside information the Tribunals didn't have. He still hadn't mentioned that Sheldon Wildfire was in the picture. The Official would have checked over the files Vencie had pulled, so the evidence would be fresh in the Tribunal's face to figure out, but he doubted they would. Either way, it would just be one more victory, when he handed them Sheldon Wildfire's corpse along with Rob and Sally's. He would think it over more after he rested. For now, he lay down with dreams of glory among the Spirelight Secret Police.

FOUR

"How long did you know?" Deacon barked in Sally's face.

Sally said calmly, "He told me about her. Sure, he mentioned giving her the number, and yeah, I know he tried to call her because he was worried about her. I didn't know she was coming here."

"Did you know she was *Earth-line?*"

Sheldon lunged in so his face stopped inches from Deacon's. "Don't get started on that after that happy-horseshit peace-and-love speech you gave your little followers the night I got here."

"What are you talking about?"

"Well, there you go then." Sheldon settled, holding Deacon's eyes long enough to deliver one more bright flash of contempt. He looked around at Claudette, Lilly, and Tiger. "See folks? Here's your spokesman for unity in these troubled fucking times, scared of letting one little Earth-line girl in on the mix."

"Don't you dare judge me," snapped Deacon. "You're a boy who understands nothing, least of all what you've done."

"If I've put anyone in danger here, it's her. Now that she's here, she's my responsibility." Sheldon walked back and put an arm around Janie. She didn't cuddle up to him like he'd hoped.

"She's not all that's your responsibility now, boy," said Deacon.

Before Sheldon could answer, Claudette stepped up. "I'm afraid he's right, Sheldon. How'd you get the number you gave her?"

As Sheldon explained, Sally couldn't help smiling.

Tiger threw up his hands. "Hey, whoa, look, I didn't know shit about that!"

"Tiger didn't know anything about any of this," Lilly said. "Hell, *I* wasn't sure 'til Janie called a few hours ago."

Deacon turned to Lilly, but didn't speak so aggressively, probably because Tiger stood behind her, hands on her shoulders. "You still went out to her, still let yourself and *them* be seen picking her up!" He pointed at Sally and Sheldon.

Lilly rolled her eyes. "I decided it'd be less risky to bring her in, instead of leaving her floundering this close, probably calling over and over, knowing as much as she does. Hell, who knows how much she might have been shouting her mouth off to anyone who'd listen?"

"I didn't tell anyone anything," Janie said in a small voice.

"What's everyone so afraid of?" Sheldon blurted.

"They're scared of whatever killed Mom," said Janie. She looked around. "You shouldn't be. It hasn't followed me. I'm pretty sure it tried, but I lost it somewhere. No one else got off the bus with me."

Sheldon and Sally exchanged looks. Janie had just finished telling her story when they'd pulled in. Sheldon was still trying to process the news of Annie's death. Then Claudette, Deacon, and Tiger came to meet them. Of course Deacon barked at them before anyone else could say anything, then Lilly relayed Janie's story. Next thing Sheldon knew, he was in the middle of this clusterfuck. Now the details connected in his mind. The dread that gripped the others seeped through him.

"You were followed, Earth-line girl," said Deacon. "Trust me. You have no idea what you're in the middle of."

"That's right," she snapped, "'cause no one's bothered to explain it to me!"

"I doubt we could. We'll be lucky if we have time to even start, because soon——"

Claudette clamped a hand on Deacon's shoulder. "Deacon? Hon? Shut the fuck up. Lilly, you made the best call you could under the circumstances, but you should've consulted me first. Sheldon, whatever you were thinking, whether you should've known better, is irrelevant. You know as well as I do, this has Spirelight Secret Police written all over it. Whoever the agents are, they clearly knew how to predict and gamble on both your actions and Janie's. If they don't know we're here, they will soon enough."

Janie wanted to know, who where the Spirelight Secret Police? For that matter, what where Spirelights? "Great. So I've basically fucked everyone over."

Before Deacon could answer, Claudette said, "Like I said, who's to blame for what is irrelevant. It was inevitable, from one set of enemies or another. We're not fucked yet. The Secret Police haven't struck. They probably don't even know our exact location. Once they do, it'll take their agents a while to assemble a large enough force."

"We need to evacuate," Deacon said.

Claudette shook her head. "We're more vulnerable if we do that. Here we have a stronghold, not much of one, but we know it well enough to figure out how to use it. We'll send out few enough scouts not to be noticed, but enough to cover our bases."

Deacon huffed. "Will you quit talking like some blowhard General in some Earth-line war movie? No one here's ready to fight some war."

Janie's body trembled violently against Sheldon's. When he looked, her petrified eyes said, *Everyone here's gone balls-to-wall batshit bugfuck crazy, and we're caught in the middle of it. I'm in this with you, and I have no idea what it's all about, because you've never told me. Please, Sheldon, make me understand. I'm scared, and I can't go back, so I need to understand.*

He rubbed her back, ran his hand through her hair, whispered, "Come over here. Don't be so afraid. Just take my hand and remember you've made it here. That was all you. You pulled it together and kicked ass like you had to, when you had to. You're with me now."

* * * *

He guided her away from the group, past several foundations of dismantled rides, between two buildings, to the wire fence. At first, she followed rigidly. The further out they got, the more she melted against him. Once they were behind one of the buildings, he hugged her close. When she felt guilty bashfulness from him, she grabbed him by the scruff of the neck and forced his mouth down on hers.

Eventually she whispered, "They keep calling me *Earth-line*. As in, I'm of this *Earth* and you all aren't."

"That's...about the long and the short of it."

Damn, that wasn't even the weirdest thing she'd braced herself for. "Guess that explains why you seem to have supernatural powers sometimes...*and* why you're such a weirdo. Great, I'm in love with a space alien."

"Farther away than that...and closer at the same time. More like an other-dimensional alien. I'm not even sure I can explain it in this world's language."

"Yeah?" She snarled up his collar in her fist. "So, how are we alike enough to come together like this, then?"

He rested his forehead on hers. "I don't know. I used to think I had an idea where your kind ended and mine started. We…my kind…we're supposed to have come from some other world. My ancestors…I guess they looked a lot more different from yours, but they evolved over time to blend in."

"Like how much time?"

"Like…way before the dawn of what your people call recorded history. I've lived my whole life in this world, though. There's supposed to be an Old World somewhere. Think of it like another *realm*, another reality far away through mist and time. Part of that realm still lives in us, makes it possible for us to survive here, like a dream guiding us—"

"Another dimension. Got it. Like spirits from the Land of the Fairies."

"That works. It's weird to talk about. People like you aren't even supposed to notice people like me here among you."

"Mom had an idea."

"Turns out she had more than an *idea*. Yeah, she told me that too. I bet all she was missing were the words for it."

Suddenly Janie twisted away and convulsed with sobs again. At first when Sheldon tried comforting her, she elbowed him away. Finally, she pulled him close again. "Yeah, well, I've had an idea too, for a while. I think maybe you put it there in my head, all those years ago…some combination of you and Mom."

He grimaced tearfully. "Damnit, Janie…I've wanted to tell you for so long. I was brought up to think a connection like we have was impossible. Then I met you. You're the one who made me question *everything*. Yeah, I know, it was just a few days when we were kids, but then I went back into the world as I've always known it, and it just turned into more and more of a living hell, 'til all that kept me going was the idea that somehow, someday, I'd get back to you. Now all I've done is drag you into it with me, I got Annie killed, and I just keep making things worse for everyone."

"Hey…" She pressed her palm to his cheek. "Mom and me both chose to have you in our lives. You…made me question everything, too, from where I am, in your own way. Then…things happened…and I chose to look for you."

He smiled. "I thought I was the one trying to comfort you."

"Hey, I was a lot worse off before you came jumping out of a moving car."

It was his turn to laugh in spite of himself. He cradled her more intimately, running his hands everywhere smoothly and gradually. Damn, could his timing be sillier? To hell with it. She flexed against him. His face moved over her hair and neck, inhaling audibly.

"Don't *sniff* me, you weirdo!" She slapped him playfully. "God, I must smell like I just crawled out of a dead cow's ass."

"You smell great to me." A hand slid under her shirt.

Somehow, she managed to press him back before he got inside her bra. "Yeah, you too. Could you maybe not attack me 'til I've had a shower and some food and we have some better *real* alone time?"

He took a deep breath and drew back. "Sorry…I

didn't mean to…it's just I've been—"

"I know. I didn't say it was a bad thing, but—"

"I won't let anything happen to you."

"In case you ain't noticed, we ain't the only two people on Earth anymore, hon."

Before Sheldon could think of a response, Claudette came around the side of the building.

Sheldon tried to act natural. "So, how's everyone doing?"

Janie shifted and turned, adjusting her shirt.

"Well as can be expected," Claudette answered. "Deacon is calling everyone together. There'll be a meeting in about two hours."

"Aw c'mon, do we really need another assembly? We don't even—"

"I'm afraid so."

"He gonna give another big damn rousing speech?"

"Yeah. Don't worry, he'll keep it in line with my decisions."

"Except I guess the crowd won't think I'm such a big damn star once they get the news."

"They don't need to know the details—and yes, they'll need to see you and Sally as *big damn stars* over these next few days. It's more important for them than ever." Claudette smiled at Janie. "Believe it or not, dear, your presence might just help. That said, would you excuse Sheldon and me for a while?"

"I'm not leaving her alone around here," Sheldon said.

At that, Claudette and Janie actually exchanged a slight smirk. "Don't worry," said Claudette. "Tiger and

Lilly'll make her feel at home."

"Where's Sally?"

"Seeing to things with Deacon."

"It's okay," Janie said. "Go do what you need to do."

They followed Claudette back to the open space. Tiger and Lilly stood waiting. Janie went to them.

Claudette's hand settled on Sheldon's shoulder. "Follow me, once there's enough blood flow back in your brain."

FIVE

Sheldon followed Claudette into the castle, then deeper than ever into the dank, narrow network of hallways. Rusty old pipes rattled. The string of light bulbs on the ceiling occasionally buzzed and winked. Sheldon glanced back at what little natural light spilled down the stairs after them. They turned a corner and it fell out of sight. After another turn or two, he imagined feeling his way back to those stairs if those lights failed. The deeper they went, the more old things he felt in this earth. The United Deschembines had settled on a hotspot, sure enough. When he glanced at Claudette, he got a feeling that was the idea. He also wondered where the water in those pipes was pumped from.

The overhead lights stopped atop the final staircase. Claudette didn't pause before descending, so Sheldon didn't either. The stone staircase steepened 'til it was almost more of a ladder. In nearly utter blackness, Claudette stopped a yard or so down from Sheldon. Sheldon had to press both palms to the grainy walls to keep from losing balance and crashing forward into her. She dug out a set of keys and undid a padlock that clanked and groaned.

The door swung open and a greenish light spilled out, half-illuminating Claudette so Sheldon only saw one eye arch and shift, coaxing him to go first. Sheldon took a deep breath and went on in. The walls were still all bare stone, spreading not much bigger than the average living room. At the center waited a table draped in shimmering blue tapestry. The fabric wasn't of any world Sheldon had ever known, and neither were the designs embroidered on it. It was the same material as the dress Sally had worn on the night he arrived, though the patterns here were far richer and deeper—*Fabric from the Old World…woven from pure Deschembine material.*

No one alive on this land today has set foot on Deschemb. We know that's where we come from, yet we know so little about the place, when you get right down to it. However this fabric got here, it was woven there, by the hands of people who knew the truth behind our legends as daily life.

All those tedious religious ritual drills growing up, everything in the wilderness camps…Why were there no lessons on how to read this?

Because there were no lessons for this magic, he realized as he got lost in the spill of the line work, only the experience itself. The fabric could tell Deschemb's stories, but only to those who could bear its brilliance and look long and close enough. Sheldon didn't get a chance to take that time. What lay atop the center got his attention.

Sheldon spun. Claudette lingered in the doorway. He stabbed a finger at the altar. "*I know those blades.*"

"No, you don't, trust me."

"*Try getting one stuck in your gut by one of them, bitch!*"

"I'll pass, hopefully. That said, trust me, the blades you're talking about are still a long way from here."

Sheldon looked from Claudette to the Altar, then back. "I…yeah, logically, I know that. Damnit, I know it's impossible. *Those* blades are with *him*, wherever he is, but at the same time, somehow, that's them right there."

Claudette moved forward, eyeing him with a new fascination. "You're saying you feel it in the energy they give off?"

"Yeah. I'd know it anywhere. Before you go there, one blade of the black metal ain't the same as the next. Rob Coscan was the first beast I fought, but he sure as hell wasn't the last. You ever felt the air off the black metal while a Crimbone swings it at you?"

"You mean, have I ever fought a Crimbone?"

"Yeah."

"No, I haven't had that experience," she said. "I'm telling you, though, those aren't blades of the black metal."

Sheldon stared at the altar again. *She's right. So, why is the scar in my midsection throbbing with that old rising burn?*

"I know," she went on, "they're carved identically to the blades of Magur Sevi. Or maybe it's the other way around. Could be they *are* the same, on some level. The blades you faced on Marlboro Mountain were—*are*—the twin black blades of Magur Sevi. You knew that, right?"

Sheldon nodded.

"Those blades right there are older than the black metal."

"From Deschemb…stronger?"

Claudette shrugged. "Who knows? No one really knows what these are, where in Descemb they're from, or what they're for."

"*What do you think they're for, carving a Thanksgiving turkey?* That's a pair of battle knives. Sort of narrows it down, don't you think?"

"Fair to say. Some craftsman put a lot of love into them, though, you gotta admit. Just look at them! Studied any Deschembine language much? One thing they all have in common: you almost never find two words separating the highest arts from the basest practical craftsmanship. No Deschembine craftsman—Spirelight or Schomite—builds so much as a chair or table without pouring the heart and soul into their idea, of whatever bigger picture the work is part of."

Sheldon was, of course, brought up studying both common Deschembine and the sacred, secret language of his people. Well, shit. How did he not notice that 'til Claudette pointed it out just now?

"The people alive who've looked at those blades could be counted on one hand," Claudette went on. "That includes you and me. Some say they were forged in Spiralla, before the coming of the Crimbone. Some think the blades were there for the birth of Spiralla, that they were forged in Spirah itself and were wielded by the warrior-scholar Bathshire to drive the demons of the

Dark Lands from what would become the first and greatest Spirelight city-state. Either way, they're the oldest surviving relics of the Old World I've ever seen or heard of. Far as I know, nothing else made from the metal has ever seen this world."

Sheldon's horror hadn't faded, but some other feeling pulled him trance-like towards the altar.

"Go ahead." Claudette's voice sounded far away. "Pick them up. Try them on. See how they feel. You'll know right away if they're yours."

Sheldon reached for them, then froze. "Mine? Whose are they supposed to be?"

"Like I said, we don't even know what they really are, or what they're meant to do."

Who they belong to...what they're meant to do. Only the Crimbone knew such kinship with individual weapons. A blade belonged to whoever picked it up, anyone who properly fused its physical dynamics with their own. Earth-liners made all that sound romantically naïve in some morbid way. The Crimbone had no such naiveté, which was the ultimate demonstration of their monstrosity.

Sheldon looked back at Claudette. "Why are you showing me this now?"

"Because for better or worse, your actions have set things in motion. Before, it was always your choice and no one else's when it came to us. Now there's a responsibility for you to follow through on. These blades are the means with which to meet your responsibility. I'm offering them to you, and I don't even know if they're rightly mine to offer."

Sheldon's hand slid around both scabbards. He lifted them, clamped in one fist. They pulsed with something that filled his body, chasing the clutter from his brain. Whatever it was, he no longer feared it. He still didn't think it was a good thing, either, exactly. It was now a natural part of his makeup, though. He'd never quite remember who he was before the fusion, or what it felt like to be without it. The knives still looked and felt like alien matter. Then again, he'd spent the last five years of his life feeling like a being unknown to himself. Maybe that made him and these weapons perfect for each other.

A thin leather belt strung the scabbards together. Sheldon tugged his own belt from the loops and threaded on this new one. As the scabbards settled on his hips, there came a feeling of clarity, of savage serenity. Just for a moment, he *felt* like everything was explained, though actually he was as clueless as ever. It was as if some other young man had just learned all the answers somewhere else, believed those answers in his mind, but didn't *feel* their truth. Here stood Sheldon Wildfire, experiencing that *sensation of truth* for him. The weight of the knives wasn't new to him. He'd first felt it in the Elliot Street Café, through the agonized vision that had ripped him to shreds over and over. His fear remained, though it no longer felt so much like a barrier as an odor. His hands drifted towards the handles.

"No," Claudette whispered.

Sheldon spun and faced Claudette in a motion that would normally have accompanied the drawing of a weapon. Some of the trance faded and he blinked. "I want to know what they feel like in my hands. I want to know what the metal actually looks like. I...I have to know."

"No, you don't, not yet. It's not time for you to learn what they're for, because that purpose isn't in front of you yet. Could be whatever's about to happen is just practice."

"If I'm gonna ever use them, I need to...you know...get a feel for 'em."

"Not with these blades."

Sheldon almost argued, then said, "Then can we get out of here?"

"Sure."

"So, can I take them with me?"

"If I were you, I'd be asking permission to leave them behind. The answer would be no. In other words, yes, by all means, wear them out of here. You've already picked them up. You've already put them on. They're already yours. You can't leave them here now. They won't let you."

TWO STORMS

ONE

Jesse still smelled the swamp, felt its pulpy wet heat all over him. A series of sharp, precise stings lanced and looped through his chest around the long slash, tugging the nerves awake so they screamed and throbbed. Noises blended, echoed and pulsed against his bruised skull, pounding his brain, his whole body, shaking up every injury great and small, 'til his nerves felt like a screaming chorus, taunting him with his inadequacy. Of course he couldn't decipher the noises. He'd failed to keep rhythm with the swamp, so its voice was no longer his to understand.

Now it was metal beneath his back, not earth or mud. The rumbling came from the road beneath the speeding van. Crawler crouched over him, stitching his chest. Steadily, Crawler and Zane's voices separated from the rumble and rattle.

"Okay, now his eyes are fluttering and rolling like crazy." Crawler's voice was too loud for this close space, or at least for Jesse's head. "I think he's coming around."

"Yeah," said Zane from the driver's seat, "jabbing him over and over in the chest with sharp, cold metal tends to do the trick. Except on every other Tuesday, for some damn reason."

"What day of the week is it, anyway?" Jesse asked.

Crawler's hands stayed steady. Jesse was impressed.

"Oh good, you're conscious," said Zane. "Come to think of it, it *is* Tuesday, ain't it?"

"How'd you guys find me?"

"Crawler knows New Orleans, and I know you."

Jesse smiled and looked up at Crawler. "So your city approved your switch in loyalties?"

"I haven't switched loyalties. My loyalties are to the lands." Crawler jabbed Jesse's chest again, less delicately. "And to where the blood in my veins takes me."

Jesse rolled his eyes as far forward as they would go. He saw the needlepoint pop out of his flesh. It lengthened like a sprouting stem, tugging up the skin like a tent, tightening another centimeter of flesh closed over red, wet meat. Yeah, that was definitely *his* needle and thread. How many times had Jesse used those stitches in this van, on himself or someone else? Someone else using them on him was a little surreal. It was a bit late to be shocked by anything, though, so he figured he'd just lay there and enjoy the special treatment.

"You were right, Zane," he finally said. "I didn't let myself flow with the energies of this place. I…it made me act like some crazy little fledgling." He looked at Crawler. "No offense. I just let myself get lost in it."

"Apparently," said Zane. "We're not in that crazy place anymore, just so you know."

"We might not be in it, but it's still in my head. Where are we?"

"Still Louisiana, but well out of the city."

"How's the rest of the state treating us?"

"Couldn't really say. It feels *different*—different than anything I've ever felt from any lands. It ain't hindering us, but it sure ain't sending any relief."

Jesse felt it too, though he couldn't have articulated it any better than Zane.

"Once we clear the state and you've gotten yourself together, you can tell me what the hell exactly you got yourself into in that bog."

Remembering made the pain worse. The black metal, in the hands of *that* man…it made Jesse sick. Literally, maybe, if that deep, raw burn beneath the surface of the wound told him anything. His flesh would heal, but his mind felt infected. He focused on the rage boiling his brain, felt it purging the infection as only a Crimbone's rage could. "Someone really has to kill that Talino guy."

"Yeah, no shit."

"You didn't see what I saw—"

"No, and you didn't hear what he told me. Just sit tight 'til we're in the clear."

"And then?"

"Then you tell me your story, I'll tell you mine, and maybe Crawler here could enlighten us on a point or two. Once we have a better idea what we're dealing with, we call Vermont."

After crossing into Mississippi, they rented a room and got cleaned up. While Jesse and Zane took stock of their wounds, Crawler went for some beer. Jesse was eager to fill Zane in, but Zane insisted they wait for

Crawler.

"Interesting kid," Jesse mused, watching the door. "You sure we can trust him?"

"Yeah. We're his childhood heroes, remember?"

Jesse grinned lazily at the ceiling. "At least he knows how to pick his role models."

"Obviously he didn't have much of a firsthand selection."

Jesse grinned wider. All this time, he'd watched Crawler for the slightest hint of inner conflict. He'd expect it from any of the current generation. No, Crawler had seen the truest choice to his purest nature, and he'd followed it. The evil he'd stopped serving may as well have been a dream. Yeah, the kid was Crimbone. Maybe *the beast race*, as some folks called them, had a future after all.

Bringing back a case of Heineken sure didn't hurt Crawler's case. As the beer cooled their bodies and brains, Jesse and Zane filled each other in.

As Zane related Talino's scheme, though, Jesse didn't stay quite so cool. He shook his head, almost manically. "No. It can't be that simple. There's gotta be something to it even he doesn't see, some other answer we have to find between the lines."

Zane's brow furrowed. "Except there's more to even him. Yeah, he's crazy. Yeah, he's invoking more dangerous shit than we've seen, but he's not incompetent with it. That's where we underestimated him."

"I really hate being right sometimes."

"That's a relief. What I still don't get is why none of this happened 'til today."

"What do you mean?"

"I mean Talino let us hang around in those rooms for almost a week—"

Jesse was in the middle of a deep swig. His eyes widened and he almost sprayed beer everywhere. "It's been a fucking week? Damn!"

"Yeah, and I don't think that's an accident, either."

Jesse ran a hand over his cracked scalp. "I plead brain damage. You think he meant for us to escape?" Jesse looked at Crawler. "You got any light to throw on this?"

"I wish. What I can't figure…my Familiar, wherever it is—your old Familiar, right, Zane?"

Zane smiled. "Thing's a pain in the ass, ain't it?"

Crawler laughed. "Sure is!" He went serious again. "It led me to you, so I could help you guys escape. Still, if it was really guiding me in the right direction, why did it wait for *Talino's timing?* Hell, why'd it…Damnit, if that's how it is, why the hell did the swamp let me waste so much time doing the wrong things for the wrong people?"

"'Cause that's where the lessons you needed were," said Zane. "You'll know for yourself when it's time to apply what you've learned to the right things, in your own way, whatever that is. I don't know what shitty things you've done with Talino's goons. It doesn't make a squirt of piss worth of difference now. At least it had better not."

Jesse stared at the floor and smirked. "As for Talino, no matter how big an evil dickhead he is, the lands have shown him every reason to believe whatever he does is right, just like they've given us. Just like they've given you through your Familiar, Crawler. It's— Wait a second…Talino's timing? Sounds right there like you did know something."

"They never told me directly," said Crawler, "but they didn't exactly hide it either. To tell you the truth, this explains a lot of— Oh, shit…you guys don't know, do you?" Crawler gave them the rundown on the recent national news. Jesse's head hung lower and lower as he listened.

* * * *

When Crawler finished, Zane stood up. "That's it, I'm phoning in with all this." He dialed the Cabinet office in Barre, Vermont.

A moment later, a high, tense male voice said, "Speak now."

"Byron, this is Zane. Listen, you guys are not gonna believe—"

"Zane Rochester? Holy shit! Is Jesse Karn with you?"

Zane perked up. Byron was a twitchy one, but he'd never called them by their full names. No one in Barre did. "Yeah. Look, we're—"

"Where are you guys now?"

"In Mississippi. Things got completely fucked in New Orleans. The local charge, Talino…I don't even know how to describe it. The guy's off-the-map clownshit insane. Metaiew Coscan did go to New Orleans, ten years ago. Talino—"

"Save it. We know about New Orleans, and what you've done there."

"Huh? How? Who from?"

"Your attack against Mister Talino and the New Orleans pack will be discussed when you get back. The Cabinet has decided to keep you on this assignment, because it just got easier and you happen to be conveniently located, lands and Old Lords be thanked. We're giving you this chance to redeem yourselves, partly because of how little chance you have at this point of screwing up again without getting yourselves killed."

"Byron, what the fuck are you talking about?"

"You guys are aware of the business with the High Natural… right?"

"Yeah."

"Well, the good news is, we know where he is. He's in Arkansas."

"After all the shit that's been going down? *How did you not know where he was?*"

"You think the Cabinets are in on this? While you've been making your little mess in Louisiana, Cabinet rule's been dissolving left and right all over North America because of the High Natural…or this insane fledgling who's got everyone *thinking* he's a High Natural. Last I heard, we're one of the last eight major holdouts. He's inciting Crimbone everywhere to abandon local charges and stations and follow him. If they can't find their way to him, they just tear around wherever they go like mad dogs off the leash anyway. It'll only spread if he isn't subdued."

"So, who told you he was in Arkansas? Same source that told you about New Orleans?"

"Not that it matters, but no."

"Who, then?"

"Another source. Look, the High Natural is in Arkansas, and the tainted Spirelight girl is in Virginia."

"What the fuck's she doing there?"

"Being held by the United Deschembines, our source tells us. Obviously, the High Natural assumed it was the Spirelight Secret Police who grabbed her."

"So, what do you want us to do about it?"

"You're his friends, right?"

Zane looked at Jesse, who stared on. "Last I checked, yeah. That was a while back, though."

"You'll find out soon enough. He's in Arkansas. Go fill him in, then go with him to—heh—*rescue the girl.* Once we have both of them, we can finally move all this forward productively." Byron gave the location of the United Deschembines as his *other source* had given to him.

"If you know where they both are, why don't you send another party to get Sally while we collect Rob?"

"*Because we need his trust.* He's already thrown up a big *fuck you* to established Schomite authority. If he thinks we're holding the girl as a bargaining chip, he'll turn his pack on us, or worse. Hey, Arkansas is a big place, with a shortage of clear roads at the moment. Everyone agrees, if the place likes him and he feels the bond towards you guys like it sounds like he does, you stand the best chance of reaching him. If you two join with him, as fellow Crimbone, fight with him for his goal, you'll be his brothers-in-arms."

"So how do we find him? Arkansas's big."

"Just get there. It shouldn't be hard, unless you've completely lost touch with the lands."

Zane let the receiver fall back into the cradle and slumped into a chair.

"What's going on?" Crawler asked eagerly.

Zane kept his voice dull so it wouldn't tremble as he filled them in.

"They can't be serious," Jesse said through gritted teeth. "Old Lords, when did they…Zane, how long have we been out here, taking their orders, while *this* has been what's going on behind our backs?"

"Doesn't matter now. Guess we better hit the road."

Crawler snapped to his feet as if on cue.

Jesse looked around, still in shock. "Hit the road?"

"Yeah. Time to go find Rob."

Jesse stood and faced Zane. "We're not giving him to *them*."

"No? What do you say we do instead? Join his little rape-and-pillage anarchy party?"

"Don't you get it, Zane? They don't represent what we fight for—what you and me, Jesse and Zane, have always fought for together. They stopped sometime when we weren't paying attention. If we run one more errand for them, we might as well go back to New Orleans and get in line to suck Talino's cock."

Zane was calm, but his eyes blazed as brightly as Jesse's. "Yep, and if we turn against them now, we're alone in this world, all three of us. Byron's right about one thing: last time I checked, Rob respected you and he respected me."

"Yeah, then he snuck out on us."

"He followed the voice in his blood. Maybe he still

does. Sometimes a fledgling just needs the right advice, from the right friends, to know how to walk his blood's trail, so it leads properly to the will of the lands. And hey, he just went and set fire to everything the rest of us have been settling for…including everything the Cabinets have been lying to us about this whole time. That's gotta count for something, right?"

"Yeah," said Jesse. "Something. That's for damn sure."

Finally Crawler said, "So, are we off to see the High Natural or what?"

Two

The land of Deschemb sprawled in mountains and oceans, a young world that would one day be remembered somewhere else as the Old World. He lived his life in that other place, but his blood had always been pulling him towards Deschemb. Deschemb waited patiently. Then he was cut open, deep enough for his blood to flow from its deepest source, letting out its purest call. Deschemb had answered from across the dark ocean, letting itself into him so it could draw his spirit back—

Yes, so he could do what he'd been groomed to do.

He knew this as he leapt and glided along mountain ranges. The time of the Old World had come and gone, as had that of the refuge world. Still, he moved ahead of everyone else, saw what they would all soon pass through. By now, it had led him around to the beginning. Soon, he would show others what he'd found. He and his queen would guide them back into the rhythm of its winds, would open its voice to them as the Old Lords had in the first days of the refuge world.

For now, he simply explored, losing himself in what he had found. It was one of the highest mountains—maybe *the* highest mountain—through which he bounded, leapt, and soared, for it seemed he could see all other summits and all oceans, even through the mist that surrounded the peaks. Above the mist, the sky was as clear as the oceans. When he stood on the banks of those oceans, dove into them, he saw all the way down through their depths, saw the ruins of many a fallen glory. When he swam down to them, they rewarded him with even greater wonders.

Scattered through the mountains and low hills, he saw the great dwelling halls of his people: glorious, maze-like architecture, as had never been carved from stone or steel, but pulled from the earth, vines, stalks, and trunks, molded and entwined by Schomite sorcery. Far beyond, there stood the silver domes and towers of Spirelight civilization, long before blood spattered the stones of every road between them. He never looked down as he made his way, nor had he trod this ground before. Yet his feet knew each spot, each indentation of stone, earth, water, wood, grass, before touching down, because his consciousness flowed as one with the winds of this world. His body moved as one with them, as his heart beat in tune with the greater rhythm. All things flowed as one here, flowed with a grace that could rip your heart to shreds with its beauty. Each tree, each blade of grass seemed to live, laugh, cry, die, and grow again, grander than ever in their countless shades and hues, many times over within the brief flash of his passing eye.

Here a kingdom could rise and fall in a day. In that day might live as proud and sprawling a history as the scrolls of the millennia. Here he was king of those millennia, king of all that came and went within them— as he would be to those he must lead back here. First, though, he must go farther through it himself, amongst the people who'd originally lived here, as the man he was in the days when madness shattered the great, harmonious flow.

No, this harmony was eternal, encompassing whatever the creatures within brought with their actions. For a first great age, the creatures understood this. Then somehow, something trickled through the ages on a flow of blood.

At first, the blood flowed only from the natural struggle for survival that is part of every world's rhythm. Somehow, though, an infection spread through it, causing the people to stumble out of step from the land's rhythm, so the voice echoed ever fainter. It was in this turmoil that the wars and feuds caused the bloody river to widen and deepen past all reckoning.

So the world sped up, or so it seemed to the people. Different races tried different ways to survive, invented new ways in their own minds of comprehending the situations.

When the Schomites ran out of explanations, their sorcerers led them to the farthest shores of the farthest, coldest land. Those who survived the journey looked out from those shores, across a deeper, darker ocean than any other in Deschemb, shrouded in clouds so low and thick, a stone ceiling seemed to block out the sun.

They sailed this sea to the shores of a world that moved slowly enough for them to survive, though too slowly to ever completely *thrive* in. Only two of the refugees could hear and feel that yes, this world was alive with its own spirits, with their own voices. Those voices were weaker than the great voice of Deschemb, but still full of this world's own rhythms and tolls. Once the two leaders had led the people as far as they could, they abandoned their corporeal lives, never again to be reborn in flesh. They fused with the spirits of this refuge world, so those who listened might hear the voices of the lands and be guided by them. Perhaps in time, some would even learn to thrive here in whatever small way they could. The Schomite people never dreamed that the enemies they'd left in the Old World would follow them across the dark ocean.

The explorer had once been Rob Coscan. Somewhere back in the refuge world, his queen still waited for him, held captive by the descendants of those enemies. She'd been born of those people, yet she'd transcended them. Together, he and his queen could continue to transcend what their people had degenerated into, to accomplish something beyond the dreams of even the Old Lords.

Once they lifted the fog from the dark ocean, the great Deschembine spirits would flow across, bringing all life back within this sublime synergy of old. That time was near.

He needed to go back to the refuge world, of course, to again flow within its sick, slow, polluted rhythm, heed its faint voices, find his queen and destroy those who'd taken her from him. First, though, he had to flow deeper and farther here, had to fight his way through the wars of the Old World, had to find where the infection had come from.

As he ran on, the world darkened and grew old.

THREE

Remelea smelled meat cooking. Her empty gut crawled and burned eagerly. The rain beat the roof so hard, she wondered if it had turned to hail. She glanced through the nearest window. No, still just rain, though it came down thicker and harder. She almost wondered how anyone had found an animal in the deluge out there, let alone managed to kill it and haul it back. *There by the love of this land,* as always. None of the edible vegetation out there was any good right now, that was for damn sure.

This was the strangest love she'd ever known, not to mention one of the stranger lands. What was with the water, anyway? Did it have something to do with those little neon-colored frogs she kept spotting hopping and swimming through it? The higher it rose, the weirder her dreams got, and the less she managed to shake them off. It had reached this point over several days, and she'd stopped marveling that it hadn't risen and drowned them all.

Obviously, the land didn't want them to drown, any more than it wanted them to starve, so it would absorb as much downpour as it had to, or take the flow somewhere else. Maybe this cabin was located just so, the better to survive something like this, and that's why the land had led her and Rob here. So, what would eating meat from around here do to her mind? Either way, whoever had found it, hopefully they had the sense to leave it good and rare. After this past week, overcooked meat might just do her in.

Somewhere, a door flew open and the wind rushed in, straining the walls, rattling furniture and hanging decorations. Joel's voice sounded, "Holy shit, you seen the road?"

"What road?" someone else answered.

Only a few of them stayed in the cabin, which was more than a good thing, though Remelea wondered how everyone else survived out there. Some came and went, bringing news: some had drowned, while most stayed at the motel. Remelea's one real concern lay stretched on the bed, still as a corpse, save for his labored breathing. The stillness wasn't because of his injuries. Neither were the harsh, growling breaths. She'd pooled her medical knowledge with that of a couple others in the pack. Someone had brought a medical kit from their car. That was around when the storm first broke, before it reached its pitch. By now, likely as not, most of the pack's vehicles had floated away. They did what they could for Rob's injuries, and it wasn't enough. His heart wasn't pierced, though, so it kept beating.

Something just wouldn't let the life leave his body. Remelea let the others believe the crude, frantic first aid had saved him. Now she stayed at his side, forcing food and water down his throat periodically, cleaning him when he needed it. Once she no longer needed the others for medical assistance, she kept them out of the room. Damn them! They'd doubted him when he was here to lead them, before he got his dumb ass stabbed, leaving her to shoulder that weight on top of looking out for him. No way in hell was she letting them near him in his indignity! Last time someone had tried to intrude, she'd threatened them with her hook. When she left the room to eat, she kept one eye on the door in case anyone approached it, a hand ever near her weapon. She still felt his mind and soul in there, though she remained cut off from both. Maybe she always had been.

So yeah, Rob Coscan was a High Natural. If his twin blades—now lying in their scabbards, wrapped in his belt, placed reverently at the foot of the bed—didn't prove it, his beating heart and the wounds she couldn't have otherwise saved him from did. So did this storm, probably.

For a long while, Remelea hadn't known or cared if Rob Coscan was actually the High Natural. It was enough that someone broke the stasis, heedlessly brushing aside the hypocritical barriers, showing them for what they were, *forcing* the rest of his kind to see the truth and follow his example. What kinds of men or women would they be, after all, to linger behind fallen barriers?

Remelea had never had much use for the barriers herself, even in her cast-off days before the Calls, or what she remembered of them. She'd had less use for the Earth-line foster family, or their fanatical, caging, abusive ideas on how to raise her. There had been a foster father who'd tried to rape her, so she'd broken his neck. When the foster mother had tried calling the cops, Remelea had left her on the kitchen floor in a bubbling lake of entrails. After that, there was life on the road and on the streets, 'til the night of her First Call. 'Til then, she guessed she'd known as little as most fledglings about what it was all supposed to amount to. The world had a spirit with many voices, and her fate was in the hands of that spirit.

Among the people, only the Crimbone were privileged to hear those voices, or more specifically to be able to make sense of what they were hearing. Yet it was the tradition to mask their nature, to blend in with those of the *Earth-line*. With only the fledgling's faint ear for those voices, she'd followed her instincts, indifferent to Earth-line social mandates designed to hinder her on the trail. Fate rarely punished her, at least through that society, so she guessed the lands had better things to do. When her First Call came, she expected to finally be given a worthwhile use of her instincts. Her Familiar had filled her in like it was supposed to, guiding her through all the usual adventures, broadening her context accordingly.

She'd lost count of her years as a full-fledged Crimbone. When the threat of Spirelights came, she used her Crimbone weapon and drank deep of the glow. Killing people who hated her for not being a slave to their gods, getting livelier and stronger from their life force—what wasn't to like?

Whenever she asked the lands about any larger reason, all they showed her was more of the same. She might start her own fight for something higher, if she'd seen a damn thing anywhere worth stabbing for.

Then one day, she found herself in the Pittsburgh headquarters, staring across the conference table, at the headless body of the local charge, and a mad-eyed fledgling with two blades, telling everyone he was the heir to Magur Sevi.

She thought of all kinds of little things about him, like his frustration at not knowing the ancient Crimbone language. At one point, he'd asked her to teach it to him. Oh, she could adequately sum it up in words he knew, explained basically why he couldn't yet know that ancient tongue, why neither she nor anyone else could teach it, how he would learn it before he knew it, once he was ready. What use was *adequately summing it up* in Earth-line speech? She thought again of his voice in the conference room, at the homestead, of its distilled power over everyone. Old Lords, was he already speaking the language of the Crimbone without even realizing it?

Leaning close, she listened to his heartbeat. "Damnit, Rob, can't you hear the world out there? It's going crazy around you because of what you've stirred up, just like I told you it would, because you've stopped doing anything with it. So it just builds and builds. It can't stop 'til you either die or wake up and do something with it again. You've left me in charge of the people who were following you. What the fuck am I supposed to do?"

She was supposed to kill him, of course. That's what she'd promised if he fucked up with the blades. Even if she brought herself to do that, though, what would happen to the movement if he wasn't there holding the center? Before him, she'd never questioned the killing, but she'd also never killed a Spirelight who wasn't of the Secret Police. Since this started, the glow had faded time and again, and she'd found the blood of whole civilian families dripping from her hook. They would have willed nothing better onto her, she reminded herself. Old Lords, though, what was he turning her into? What was he turning them all into?

Remelea eased her cheek away from Rob's chest. Her hand crept towards her hook. She noticed how much his hair had grown since they'd met. A few scraggly strands had fallen across his closed eyes. Before she realized it, her hand moved away from the hook and brushed them back. She stroked his eyebrows, and her face lowered towards his. Her mouth paused an inch from his parted, slumbering lips. She kissed him on the forehead instead.

Is she really worth all this to you, Rob? When I try to think clearly about you, it seems you really shouldn't be worth it to me. Yet here I am. Old Lords, I hate her. Old Lords, I want to hate you.

Had the rain tapered off a little? She listened close, peered hard out the window, and saw a little more clearly beyond the glass than before. In the next room, the voices of Joel and the others were less muffled. Apparently, they noticed it too.

Remelea looked back at Rob. His eyes had snapped open. For a second, she didn't recognize them.

"Is that meat I smell cooking?" he asked.

She didn't recognize the voice, either.

Four

"Rain's letting up," Crawler announced.

Jesse couldn't tell. This was his van, but Zane's mechanical mind and hands had tricked it out in a million and one ways he'd never wrapped his brain around. All he needed to understand was that the Big Red Beast could plow through all of this and worse like a battleship. They both knew how to maneuver that ship. Right now, Zane was steering it.

For a while, Jesse had sat up front. Then they'd passed into Arkansas. He'd climbed into the back after spotting his fourth floating, drowned body. Now he and Crawler leaned against the sides of the van, facing each other. Outside, the tires kicked up two perpetual waves. The metal rippled against Jesse's back. He glanced to Zane in the driver's seat. Zane didn't look back, couldn't have seen him through any of the mirrors, but he nodded confirmation on cue.

"Good," Zane said. "Arkansas favors us, or at least favors Rob enough to let us reach him."

From the reverberations of the world outside, Jesse was amazed the van still ran, that the engine hadn't been waterlogged, with or without Zane's tinkering. He shrugged. "Seems like the lands favor everyone these days. We sure didn't get clued in on what's been going on behind our backs this whole time. Makes me wonder about everything Talino said…about Old World energy taking over here—"

"It's our own damn fault we didn't see what was happening with the Cabinets." Zane's eyes stayed forward.

"We didn't listen close enough to our own blood, you mean."

"So that's what's wrong with them in New Orleans? That they don't listen to their own blood enough?"

"That ain't obvious?"

"Right. So, why's the swamp keep favoring Talino? Unless he's right and that really is where this world needs to go? Have we really lost that much touch with what we're naturally supposed to be, that when we actually run into a glimpse of the real deal, as it was in the Old World, it looks that warped? Is that really what we've been holding onto this whole time?"

Zane sighed. "If Talino's really tapped into the Old World magic flowing through this world, it's not because he's the most fit to. It's because he's the only one—or the first in a long time—who followed through on it. Either way, what's started is a reformation of everything. Our conflicts are part of it—not just with the Spirelights anymore, but between everyone, in figuring out who we're really supposed to be."

"So the world's pitting us against each other, making all sides feel supported, just to see who comes out on top."

"Maybe," said Zane. "While you've been back there belly-aching, I've paid real close attention to these lands...or this ocean, whatever the fuck this is we're driving through. Either way, that helps with not getting washed away."

Jesse stretched and resituated himself. "I'm all ears."

"These Spirelight states Rob's been raiding, they all spent a long time with their spirits sewn together with poison Spirelight magic, right? Sort of like a chemical addiction." Zane glanced at his pack of smokes on the dashboard. "Heh. So Rob's been just waltzing in and cutting 'em free, just like that. Leaves a void, you know?"

"So you're saying the lands are going nuts from withdrawal, 'cause Rob's been making 'em quit Spirelight cold-turkey, and that's why they're dumping this mess on us."

"Pretty much."

"You know, Zane, the more you're right, the more I wanna punch you in the head. Where the fuck are we, anyway?"

Zane peered through the windshield and shrugged. "I've just been turning onto whatever roads are left. The deeper we get, the fewer there are."

"So, when was the last time you saw a road sign?"

"One I could still read, or in general?"

Before anyone answered, Zane steered up a rocky incline. As the van lurched and shook, Crawler planted himself firmly. Jesse climbed up front. They pulled into a motel parking lot, or what was left of one. There were four or five two-floor strips. Figures passed each other on the upper level of the nearest one. The rain had lightened enough that Jesse recognized his own kind by their movements. Their apparel and surroundings were a dead giveaway…yet so much more so than he was used to. There were so many youngsters here, not bothering to hide what they were.

The storm had blown a lot of brush, branches, and vines over the structure. Even the most haphazardly strewn of it looked at home there as organized decorations. Still, the storm hadn't pulled down the curtains from all the rooms within, or torn out the carpets and slung them into the nearby dumpsters so the fire pits still glowing through open doorways could be hammered and dug out of the floors. The storm hadn't hung fresh meat and drying pelts in those windows. It wasn't what had let the torn-up brush grow fresh roots, fuse with its brethren and start climbing over the structure's sheltered spots in nearly sentient patterns.

Zane parked in front of the stairs. Crawler shifted into a battle-ready crouch.

"Easy there, kid," Jesse said.

They climbed out, Jesse and Zane through the front side doors, Crawler from the rear, hands on their pommels. Down the stairs came a tall, dark man wearing nothing but old-fashioned buckskin pants and the belt holding his Crimbone knife. That buckskin smelled fresh. How the hell did the guy manage to tan leather in this weather? His pale, dilated eyes would have looked stoned if they weren't so sharp with all sorts of awareness that was new to him. He probably still couldn't have described it, even in the Crimbone tongue. Those eyes peered with tentative welcome.

In the shadows of the stairwell, three more Crimbone crept midway down and waited. Jesse, Zane, and Crawler all noticed, of course, but only Jesse and Zane recognized the threat in the smoothly feral movement. Everyone in this crowd was freshly blooded, stinking of so much Spirelight death, there was no counting their kills over the last few weeks. They contained themselves well, considering how palpably thirsty they all were for more. For the first time in the better part of a century, Jesse and Zane felt outmatched among their own kind. If either of them showed that awareness, they would be fucked.

Zane stepped forward first. "Good to see you. My name's Zane Rochester. This is Jesse Karn. The fledgling is…" Fuck, he didn't know Crawler's last name.

"Call me Crawler." Crawler sounded a little impatient.

The dark man smiled.

Zane blinked away his embarrassment. "Who's the local charge?" He saw the shadowed Crimbone tense up.

"There's no charge here," growled the dark man. "We don't answer to the Cabinets."

"Then you're friends to us," said Zane.

"I hope to be, if you're friends to the High Natural."

"Oh yeah, we go way back. So you know where he is?"

"In body, yeah. You'd best just go see for yourselves. I'll give you directions."

"Why not just take us to him?" Jesse asked.

"If you're his friends, you'll get there fine on your

own. It's not far. If not, the forest will drown you on the way. If I lead you, I'll be drowned with you."

Crawler puffed up. "Do you even know who you're talking to? This is Zane Rochester and Jesse Karn!"

From the stairwell, other Crimbone moved forward, naked except for their scabbard belts. Crawler tensed cautiously but didn't back down. Jesse and Zane stayed cool, though their fingers touched the handles of their weapons.

"I caught their names the first time," the dark man said.

"We don't have time to fuck around," said Jesse. "If the woods let you come and go around him, it'll sure as hell let us find him."

"Check it out," Crawler added. "The rain's really letting up." He was right. It had reduced to a light shower.

The dark man peered around. It looked like an enormity that was beyond the four of them had settled on his consciousness. "Okay, fine. I'll take you to him." When they started forward, he added, "Just you two. The fledgling stays here."

Zane put a hand on Crawler's shoulder. "We're all on the same side. Hang out. Hang loose. Talk to these folks. Get a sense of what's going on."

The dark man led Jesse and Zane around the side of the building, to the back of the parking lot, to a fallen wire fence half buried in washed-up leaves. They stepped over into the woods and followed what was left of a path.

The soggy debris was thick enough that Jesse felt

like he was back in the swamp. Only the smell reminded him where he really was, that the life here didn't bubble, churn and swelter so much. No, here was the clear, light, vibrant scent of a normal forest after a rainstorm. Well, not quite normal, but the storm had truly moved on. It still rumbled in the distance. By now, the only drops splashed from heavy leaves above. Those leaves had grown thin for this time of year, and the sun shown brighter through them. From the floating fallen ones, a chorus of dissonant croaks mingled with tiny, echoing splashes.

Glancing around, Jesse saw more and more huge black eyes blinking at them from little amphibious neon bodies, perching and hopping on fallen leaves that floated like lily pads. "Zane, you realize this muck we're walking through…the water, I mean—"

"Yeah, I know. What, it making you feel any different?"

"Nah, just pointing it out. You?"

"Not really."

"Okay, just checking."

Their boots were soggy by the time they reached the cabin. Smoke billowed from the chimney. Jesse smelled fresh meat cooking. He realized he'd barely eaten anything solid since before hitting Talino's party. As they drew nearer, he smelled the still raw and bloody flesh, which made him even hungrier.

A young Crimbone man ran out onto the porch. "He's awake!"

The dark man froze then looked back at Jesse and Zane. "I guess you weren't lying."

Jesse and Zane both shrugged and walked past him.

As they climbed the porch, the young man stepped into their path. "Who are you guys?"

Jesse shoved the man aside, sending him stumbling several feet to the left, 'til he hit the railing. Inside, a kitchen adjoined a quaint living room. An old-fashioned open fireplace marked the break. The kitchen's gas stove looked functional, but the meat smell came from the fireplace. Two more Crimbone men tended it. On the floor opposite the fireplace, the remains of a slaughtered buck lay spread on a sheet that used to be white.

In a doorway at the far end of the living room, a Crimbone woman with a fox-like build stood ready for anything. Her savage green eyes fixed on Jesse and Zane. Jesse drank in the sight of her, and he knew she wouldn't be such a pushover as her companions.

Before either of them could speak, he spotted a wiry, scraggly shape moving in the room behind her. It lurched and sagged on one side. In the dim light, Jesse saw only the eyes clearly, for they seemed almost to glow. They were the eyes of a creature who looked around at profoundly alien surroundings…a creature come straight from the bloodiest fields of the Old World itself.

The shape slid past the girl into the living room, still buckling a pair of blood-crusted jeans. "Jesse…Zane…"

Jesse almost said *No, that's not him. There must be some mistake.* Surely this man—this creature—was too old to be Rob Coscan, older than Jesse or Zane, and many times stronger. He wasn't even at his full strength, thanks to the deep, broad wounds on his bare torso. That he'd survived those wounds at all, even in the care of the girl, was more than testament to that strength. Still, Jesse stared hard at the map of scars that made up the face.

When was the last time he saw Rob, the last moment they stood before each other and exchanged words? On Marlboro Mountain where Jesse and Zane had hidden him and Sally before driving back to Barre, to plead the kids' case to the Cabinet. At the time, Jesse had still seen a pair of scared kids when he looked in their eyes.

The last of that kid was cut from Rob Coscan's face, replaced with livid scar tissue. His eyes held even less evidence that the kid had ever been there. When he finally spoke again, there was a little bit of it left in his voice, or at least Jesse hoped that's what he heard:

"Where'd you guys come from? Where's Sally?"

"Sally's not here, Rob," said Zane. "We're here to help you find her."

Rob started sharply forward. His face contorted in agony and he grabbed his stitched side. He didn't double up, fall, or go to sit, as someone normally would from such pain. When the woman caught his arm, he seemed oblivious.

Jesse couldn't help thinking, *Whoever this woman is, if Rob's brushing her off, he really* must *love Sally.*

Neither Jesse nor Zane moved, still trying to figure out what they were looking at.

"Find her?" Rob forced the words out. "You mean take me to her."

The woman said, "Rob, please, sit down first! You're in no state to—"

"Fuck off." He wrenched away so sharply that she

stumbled back with a shocked cry. The more pissed off and anxious he got, the less debilitated he seemed. He stared at Zane. "You were about to say?"

"Your lady friend's right," Jesse said. "We need food, and it looks like you could use some too, so let's all sit down and get some of that meat in us first."

Rob nodded. "Fine. Talk while we eat. My *lady friend* here's Remelea, by the way. She's my second-in-command. That means she outranks you here, by the way."

Remelea clapped the other pack mates to attention. "You guys head back to the motel."

"Yeah," Rob added. "Get everyone ready to move."

The pack mates cut portions of meat for themselves, then hurried out and disappeared through the woods. Jesse, Zane, Remelea, and Rob sat around the small kitchen table. They ate quickly while Jesse and Zane took turns telling their story. Finally, Zane repeated Byron's news.

Rob stood, leaving his meat half-eaten. "Okay, then. Let's get moving."

The only pain he showed was a slight grimace. Remelea didn't try subduing him anymore. The agony that should have paralyzed his body was on her face. Whatever he'd brought back from the edge of the void—whatever now fueled him—wasn't confined to his body.

Zane said, "There's more going on, Rob. Things've—"

"Fine. Tell me on the way."

With that, he stormed into his room and came back wearing his knives and boots. He was halfway into a long bloodstained duster coat, which he yanked on over bare shoulders. His three companions followed him outside. Dusk was bleeding out as they reached the motel parking lot.

"Fellow Crimbone, we know where we're headed now. Soon your blades will drink deep of the glow again!"

The voice—*the unearthly sound*—that came from Rob hit Jesse and Zane like a tornado. For a moment, they kept looking back and forth, from him to each other, just to make sure they'd both heard the same thing, that it had really come out of his mouth. If they hadn't come with their guard up, neither could say they wouldn't have fallen in step with the *fellow Crimbone* he addressed, before even realizing it.

As the bloodthirsty rally filled the lot, a high, scratchy voice sounded from the motel roof. "Hoool' on there, lil' sailors! Don't get too glow-horny just yet."

Everyone froze, turned, and stared up at the shape.

Jesse leaned in and muttered, "Zane, what the hell's that damn thing doing here?"

"I. Don't. Know."

All things considered, the last thing Jesse or Zane would have noticed was that Rob was still technically a fledgling…that he hadn't somewhere made the Third Call, banishing the Familiar back to its native realm in the process.

"You fuckers is headin' to the right place, but ye're off to kill the wrong folks, and get a hefty helpin' of yourselves killed while you're at it. The right folks need killin', that's what they's countin' on ye doin'."

Rob staggered forward, staring up into his Familiar's

eyes. "I won't fall for your bullshit this time, Puttergong. We're headed to get Sally and kill the bastards who snatched her."

Puttergong's body ruffled violently. Apparently, even the Familiar was caught off-guard by the change. It still held eye contact. "Hehehehehehe. Tha's what you think, Biter-Boy! I'd like to sit back so's I could see the look on yer face once you realize you've made such a jackass outa yerself like you's about to. Thing is, though, shit's finally rollin' good an' forward, an' I don't feel like riskin' you fuckin' it up."

"Fine. Spit it out. We're in a hurry."

"That's your fuckin' problem right there. While you been dancin' 'round in dreamland or wherever, Biter-Boy, I been hoppin' all over the damn place, gettin' the real scoop. Looks like someone beat you to it, see. 'Cause the folks yer Sally-Poach is layin' low with, they ain't the ones snatched her from ye. Them Urinated Deschembine folks, they rescued her an' are holdin' onto her for safe keepin', is all. Trouble is, the same sneaky ol' glow-cop that snatched her found her again. Only this time, he's settin' a trap for you. It's him put the word out where she is, so's that word would get back to you. He means for you to show up an' charge in, while he holds his troops back an' waits for the fight to get goin' good. Once your pack here an' the Urinated Deschembines has killed off half of each other, and most ever'one left is good an' tore up, that's when him an' his troops plan on rushin' in to finish y'all off."

Jesse crept to Rob's side. "It doesn't make sense. It sounds like—"

Rob turned and silenced Jesse with eyes that didn't belong to a fledgling in need of advice. "No, it makes perfect sense, actually."

"Don't tell me you still trust that thing."

Rob stared hard at Puttergong. "I do, this time."

"Why?"

"It's always about the big picture. This time, the truth just happens to be most convenient. Besides, why else would it try to talk us *out of* going on a killing spree?"

"He's got a point, Jess," said Zane.

Rob looked around. His pack stood ready for his command. Remelea stood at his side. He looked into her eyes.

"Guess we'd better get on the road to Virginia," she said dully.

"Right." Rob brought everyone to attention with a gunshot clap. "Okay, everyone with a vehicle that ain't waterlogged, divide up everyone else and stuff 'em in. We should have enough night ahead of us. Find whoever knows where the nearest car dealership is, and put 'em at the front of the caravan. Whoever knows anything about disabling security equipment and hot-wiring cars, get your asses primed. Whoever gets fresh wheels…I trust your judgment."

"Not bad so far," Remelea muttered. "So, what's the plan after that, if you don't mind my asking?"

"I'll tell you when we get there."

THE TRAIL ENDS

ONE

Vencie looked south from a high hillside, through a set of high-powered binoculars. Miles out yet, the bloody caravan roared towards its destination…towards his. First, though, he needed to rendezvous with those he would lead. Over the past days, he'd staked out the old grounds of Renaissance Kingdom. Things were shaking out just as he'd theorized. He'd already called the Official, told him to call the agents for assembly at the Gray Mill General Store. It would be roughly an hour before the Crimbone reached the ruins of Renaissance Kingdom. That left plenty of time to group up with his team, get them into position, and wait for the Crimbone to make their move. Once the chaos was underway, Vencie would make his.

Vencie reached the parking lot and spotted only two vehicles. One was the same pickup truck from days earlier, probably that degenerate clerk's. The other was the van in which Vencie had delivered Sally Coscan to the homestead. Only the grill was visible, the rest hidden by the side of the building. Vencie would still know it anywhere. Ice filled his spine and his gut churned.

He parked his stolen car near the edge of the lot and slipped around the opposite side of the building. By the time he entered the weeds behind the store, his fists and teeth were clenched, his every muscle tight. The veins in his head pounded painfully. Around the corner stood the blonde female agent, the one Amos had offered him at the homestead. In both hands, she gripped Vencie's homemade iron-pipe spear.

"I was told specifically to kill you with this for some reason." She shrugged then swung the curved two-foot blade at his head.

Vencie ducked and grabbed the pipe mid-swing. With a twist of his wrist, he wrenched it from her, pulling her off balance. By the time she recovered, he'd spun it into the old proper grip. He made no sound as the blade drove through her solar plexus, razor edge up. Her body doubled forward, hands grasping and cutting themselves at the blade's base as it pushed the air out through her mouth in a satisfying shriek. The metal of the van's rear door made an even better shriek as Vencie pinned her to it. The door's whole frame moaned as the metal strained and sank from the body's impact.

Vencie let go, stepped back, and gave himself an instant to gaze on his work. The heavy iron beam sagged so the twitching, gurgling shape slid towards him. The edge scraped faintly in the crook of the breastbone. To his left, through the wall, he heard another body bolt from a seat and dash awkwardly through the store.

Still silent, he moved forward through the tall grass,

in time to see the old clerk bolt outside, waving a giant handgun. With one hand, Vencie jackknifed himself over the porch railing. He hit the boards as the clerk aimed, cleared the short distance as the hammer drew back. Splayed palms struck the man's chest at full force, knocking him backwards into the door frame. The clerk's skull, spine, and ribs shattered. His spasming finger squeezed off one shot before the gun slipped from his grip. The crack reverberated through the porch boards and off across the barren lot. The shot blew a chunk out of a porch beam, bouncing flecks of wood off Vencie's leg through his jeans.

Vencie picked up the gun and did his best not to step on the twitching corpse on his way into the store. At the back by the beer cooler stood a dumpy woman in a muumuu, staring still and dumb from eyes that were dull like the clerk's. In the candy aisle, the woman's young daughter also stared frozen. Vencie fired two shots into the store. He was back over the porch railing before the bodies thudded.

Behind the van, the female agent had pulled out the spear, tumbled onto her hands and knees. She crawled and groped, her blond mane tumbling over her head and brushing the earth. Circling her, Vencie was impressed by how much natural grace hadn't bled out of her, even in her death slog. Somehow, she was still sexy, particularly in a crawl that set off all the right angles. Too bad. He'd have preferred other ways than this, of showing her the difference, between a renegade like himself and what the rest of the Spirelight Secret Police had become. Her hand fumbled towards the spear. Vencie plucked it up, planted the base against the ground, and leaned on it like a staff.

"The Official?"

She coughed out, "The Tribunal." Her hair hid her face. Flecks and gobs of blood spattered the grass beneath her mouth.

Vencie's foot shoved her onto her side, his heel pushing the hair away. "Those idiots!" Then in the ancient Spirelight language, "*Where are the others?*"

She gurgled what might be a laugh. "You did your part. Now you're useless. Oh well. Someone'll get around to you, once they're done with the United Deschembines."

"You stupid bitch. They *need me to find* the United Deschembines!"

Still hacking and spitting, she rolled onto her back and met his eyes. Her twisting contortions were weakening, though the mockery in her gaze stayed strong. Blackish red slime ran down both her cheeks. "Fucking idiot. We know where they are…you got us close enough. Once we were here, how hard you think that place was to find?"

Vencie grew increasingly aware of his spear back in his grasp after too long. This pathetic little agent had tried to kill him with it, so she and the rest of them could go fuck up his whole plan. Fine. He would still take the heads of both the tainted ones himself, plus the head of Sheldon Wildfire's little Indian bitch for good measure.

The spear spun in his hands. This time when he stabbed, he let himself roar and cry with exaltation. She lived through several more stabs. As he twisted and dragged the blade through the wounds, he kept his eyes on hers, watched all the pain she felt in this final moment. He stabbed and hacked 'til there was nothing to recognize in the red ruin. He shook his head, cleared his brain, and found his arms and legs thickly spattered. Well past the base of the blade, the spear dripped with thick goo and hair, bits of brain and bone. Soon Vencie would further redden it, not least with anyone else who tried for his chosen trophies.

He walked around his van, saw no keys in the ignition, went back, and knelt next to the body. After digging the keys from the pockets, he spotted something on the belt: a narrow, rectangular leather case clipped shut at the top. When he opened it, a pocketknife slid into his palm. His grandfather had worn one just like it, as had many of the Spirelight Secret Police Vencie had known and idolized growing up. It was the weapon on which all Secret Police children were trained. Many adults still carried theirs, as both a secondary weapon and a talismanic keepsake. Vencie slid the case onto his belt, then opened the dented rear van door and placed his spear inside, after wiping the blade semi-clean on his shirt.

Two

The caravan plowed along its final stretch. Rob sat in the back of the Big Red Beast with Crawler. Crawler wasn't much for conversation, mostly just stared in undignified awe. That was fine with Rob. Conversation felt unnatural right now, like trying to talk to a dull, distant painting, which was what this world felt like. He reached into his coat and pressed one of the stitched gashes on his torso. A fresh lightning bolt of pain shot through his body, so everything felt closer to real. Normally, he would curl his fingers around the knife handles. That usually sent bright, savage alertness all through him. Now it would only make him feel more disconnected, heighten his awareness of what wasn't here, what his mind flailed and grasped at futilely.

*The Old World…the power he felt there…Sally…*especially Sally, even now, even after hearing about Zane's conversation with Talino. After listening to what had happened in New Orleans, Rob sensed Jesse and Zane expecting him to rethink things with Sally, considering who'd played matchmaker. Hell, people hooked up for dumber reasons all the time, and often made fine lives together from it.

"We stick to the plan," he growled.

Only agents of the Secret Police were to be harmed. Civilian Spirelights were as sacrosanct as the girl with the altered glow. At best, they would reach the hideout ahead of the Secret Police, arrive at some quick understanding, and strike outward from there. At worst…

"They'll still obey me," he muttered. "They will. I have to lead them. We have to reach—"

"Yeah, long as you obey yourself," Zane said from up front, which seemed impossibly far away. "Just like the blades, remember?"

"Yeah. Goddamnit. Dad. You know what I kept thinking these last couple weeks on the road with the pack? *I should have taken Sally and tried to find him, back when we left Brattleboro.* I kept thinking, *Where is that old bastard? He should be here at my side helping me lead this pack.*" He shook his head, then let his chin touch his chest.

"Now's the time for you to get your game face on," said Zane. "Something you ought'a know, though. While that Talino fuck was trying to sweet-talk me, he brought up something else. Anyone ever explained to you why your dad left the trail and kept you off it?"

Rob shook his head. "Now seems like the time to spit it out."

"How much you remember about your mom—your real mom?"

"Not much. She died in a car wreck when I was—" His eyes livened. "It wasn't a car wreck, was it?"

"Hey Jesse, I believe we have comprehension." Zane said to Rob, "Jesse and I could spend all day telling you badass stories about her—her *and* your dad, together on the trail—if we had a day. 'Cept for him, right or wrong, her death was the last straw. A lot of us resented that for a long time. I sure did, but I thought it back over lately. I remember a long time ago, you going on and on like some sad sack, pussy-whipped Romeo about how much you loved Sally and how that wasn't gonna change."

"I remember," said Rob.

"I said talk to me in a week. You didn't talk to me. You just ran off with her. You ain't said much since we met back up, 'cept to rally everyone like a chief, all to go make sure she's safe. Had a look at yourself lately? I'm surprised you can even stand up. And there still ain't a doubt in my mind, you ain't gonna stop 'til the job's done. Guess you sure put me in my place over that, huh? Just like your dad did." Zane twisted around and stretched his hand towards Rob.

Rob leaned forward to shake the hand, then pulled himself up and forward on it.

"Just remember," growled Jesse from the driver's seat, "whatever's about to go down where we're going, it ain't just about you and Sally anymore. Neither is whatever comes afterwards."

Through the windshield, one vehicle ran ahead of the van: a small, white pickup truck, almost as battered as the van. Joel had snagged the truck, and Remelea had gone with him in it, because a tree had smashed her car in the storm. Rob had invited her to join him in the van. She'd peered into the space and said it looked too cramped. Joel had driven the truck out of Arkansas. The pack had stopped twice since. Peering hard now, Rob recognized the back of Remelea's head in the driver's seat. By the animation of her head and shoulders, she was obviously speaking heatedly. Joel's head nodded periodically.

"Zane," Jesse said bemusedly, "is that a mass wreck up ahead or something?"

Peering through the glare, Zane dropped hand to hammer. "Nah, just a police roadblock, I'd guess two dozen or so state troopers, all sighting down the barrels of shotguns and assault rifles at us."

"Okay. So, why's that?"

Rob said, "They're after me." He noticed Crawler shifting forward and springing onto all fours. "After the first couple massacres, I figured we'd start to stand out, so we split up and got discreet. Then you guys showed up with news about Sally. We were in a hurry, so I said *fuck discreet*."

"And now?" Crawler groaned.

"The same, pretty much."

The barricade was coming up fast. Several links ahead, the pickup screeched to a halt. Jesse hit the brakes, so everyone else had to grab something quick. The nearest two vehicles behind them swerved, grinding to a halt on either side. Over the cocking of shotguns came the blare of a bullhorn, telling everyone to get out with their hands in the air. No one budged. the bullhorn sounded again.

"What's it gonna be, Rob?" Jesse asked.

Rob felt like the bullhorn had just raped his brain through his ears, searing him like his stitched wounds couldn't do. The cop's voice was a nasal, broken twang, brutishly high on authority. Those fucking worthless, bullying backwoods bastards, thinking they were the heroes of this countryside, ignorant of how they were getting in the way of the true, rightfully favored creatures of this world. Sally was waiting, might die before he could reach her. These fucking backwater hogs were holding him up.

Rob breathed deep, focused, and looked around. The barricade sat some twenty feet from Joel and Remelea's truck, the rear of which was less than five feet from the van. In the truck, he could see both Joel and Remelea poised to spring out and charge in. The fighters in the car to the van's left were similarly poised, as was the man on the motorcycle to the right. The others behind them would also be ready.

Across fifteen feet, through a barrier of glass at either end, Remelea's eyes met Rob's, waiting for his signal. She was the most ready and willing to attack at his command. If he gave that signal, she and Joel would be the first to go down riddled. Some of the others might make it to the cops, might hit the ditch to the left or the trees to the right, move in and take them from the sides, even from behind if they were crafty and fast enough. Yeah, they would kill plenty of Earth-line cops—maybe all of them—and there might even be a few Crimbone left who hadn't been torn to shreds by bullets and buckshot by the time it was over.

Rob closed his eyes, sat very still, and became aware of his whole body, a muscle and bone at a time, 'til he felt the very bloodflow within his veins. He listened to his blood, and his blood listened to the air, to the bird songs and woodland rustles for miles around. He felt the Virginia summer heat—something he knew from what seemed like worlds and ages ago—through the cracked windows. He listened to the sky, opened his eyes, and watched birds settling on the power lines. Not all of them were birds.

The bullhorn sounded again. This time when Rob looked back at the barricade, he didn't look at the grotesque, barking hog heading the assembly.

"Rob," said Jesse.

"Wait," said Rob. "Just wait."

THREE

Among the staties training guns on the pack were two rookies, a young man and a young woman. Now they both looked away from their gun sights, up to the same flock of birds Rob Coscan had watched settle on the powerlines. Like Rob, they noticed that four of the shapes up there weren't birds, looked more like large bats with floppy, dog-like ears and long, horse-like snouts. Two of the interloping critters stood out to the young officers, specifically the ones on the right. The man most noticed the inner one, the woman the outer one. They'd been on intimate terms with the creatures for a while, unbeknownst to their Earth-line superiors.

Their Familiars hadn't told them to expect this today, but had explained and hinted at enough so the fledglings weren't surprised. It had been a year since the man had made his First Call, a year and a half for the woman. The Familiar to the left of the woman's also stood out. It was larger and more gnarled than its companions. Its gut drooped heavier, its talons longer and more cruelly hooked. Its razor saw-teeth gleamed more prominently, even at this distance.

The man was tall, stocky and hawk-featured, eyes dark and calm, and he moved with the deceptively lazy grace of a panther. The woman was also toughly built, even for the police force, though her large, bright eyes, moon face, and general nonchalance were deceptive. Energetic bubbles rose in their guts as they spotted their Familiars, blooming into a sensation that consumed their whole bodies for an instant.

When the consummation passed, it had burned something away within them. In its place was clarity, and with it came the second wave, this one from without, as if in response to what they'd released. They lowered their guns, turned from their posts, and walked back to the patrol car they shared as partners, so smooth and silent that their fellow officers didn't even notice at first. The choice was so clear that neither of them would have consciously called it that. It wasn't without sentimental pangs that they abandoned their Earth-line duties forever. They opened the doors to the cruiser, set their rifles across the seat, removed the belts with their sidearms and placed those next to the rifles. Then they reached to the floor and picked up their new weapons, which hadn't been there when they got out.

The man's blade was forged around the handle, the upper blade running nearly two feet in a scimitar curve, the lower half a foot long, with a flat inner side made to rest comfortably against his forearm. When he drew away the scabbard, he found waving flames etched from tip to tip along the razor edge. When he swung the blade—as he would soon see—the carvings seemed to become real flames in the instant before the edge cleaved its target.

The woman's weapon was a jewel-handled axe, roughly the size and shape of a tomahawk, the head capped in three wavy spikes, same shape as the man's flame etchings. As they stood, they heard the chief turn from his bullhorn and bark at them in furious confusion. *Get back in formation,* he shouted, *before those freaks saw weakness in the ranks. Goddamnit, if the two of them didn't get back in formation, he would shoot 'em himself!*

As they walked back, the chief obviously didn't see the new gifts they carried. Some of the other officers noticed, though, the ones for whom this unheard-of new dissension was too much, overruling their programming, drawing their eyes from their targets so their guns relaxed. The man and woman circled their chief, each boring one eye into him, the other cast out at the vehicles of the gang, the caravan…the pack.

"Officers Cash and Summers, get back in fuckin' formation, 'fore I arrest y'all right along with them out there!"

Past the line of shotguns, behind the white truck, Officer Sam Cash looked through the windshield of the rusty red van. A shadowy, scarred face gazed back at him, eyes ablaze with fire fueled by something not of this world. In that fire, Sam Cash recognized the essence of what had ignited him and his partner.

The man in the van with the blazing eyes made a hand signal, one the driver of the truck must have seen too, because that's when everything happened at once. The truck's engine gunned and it shot forward. Officers still minding the pack squeezed off a panicked volley. Metal screeched as two police cars were bulldozed sideways like parting gates, crushing and splattering several gunmen.

The chief pointed his shotgun at Anya, just as Sam's blade made its first strike, skewering him through the heart from behind. From both sides, the nearest officers still standing turned guns on Sam and Anya. They both spun, ducking and sliding forward. Sam's blade sheared through calf muscles. A man fell away screaming, blood spouting from both halves of a leg severed at the knee. The spikes on Anya's axe tore out her would-be shooter's groin, so his gun flailed back and let off a wild burst. The stray shots went between the four Familiars, all of whom had taken flight, soaring down on the melee, shrieking and cawing. Sam and Anya's Familiars attacked throats with teeth, as did the smallest, left-most one. The big, gnarled one sank its talons into a man's shoulders and soared high above the powerlines. A shrill wheezing cackle echoed down, mingling with its victim's screams. The claws snapped open, and the body dropped right on two other officers, breaking one's neck, fracturing the legs and lower spine of the other.

The rest of the pack were already leaping out and charging in. Gunfire lit up the highway, blowing chunks of meat and bone out of some of them in their tracks. Some dropped from their injuries. Others didn't. The sight of the latter still charging and roaring was enough to make plenty of gunmen lose their shit, either to turn tail or stare in disbelief like deer in headlights. The Crimbone reached the fray, springing onto the cars and pouncing on the troopers. Everywhere, Old World metal rose and fell, 'til the space behind the formation became a soupy lake of shredded flesh and entrails.

The leader moved in slow and ghostlike, his twin blades lowered but ready. The otherworldly inferno of his eyes had faded to a slow burn, but it was still the heart and soul of everything those eyes scanned, everything he authored.

For a mile around echoed the howls of the

Crimbone. In the short time of the slaughter, then in the following minutes, the countryside spoke only in that cacophony.

FOUR

"He's on his way here, Sally."

Sheldon's voice was calm, but it somehow reminded Janie of that day in the Elliot Street Cafe. That hadn't even been so long ago, had it? She looked at the twin short swords strapped to his belt—short swords, or long knives, or whatever they were. Over the last few days, she'd hardly seen him without them. For whatever reason, though, they kept reminding her of that episode he'd had in the diner.

It had something to do with Sally's husband, the one Sheldon had fought on Marlboro Mountain, the one who'd given him that nasty black scar on his midsection, when he was eleven years old.

Rob Coscan, Wing-Nut Liam's old fencing buddy who'd gone missing, the guy these people called the *High Natural*.

What fucking world is this? Janie kept wanting to scream.

Sally sprang to her feet. Several conflicting shades of excitement danced through her eyes. "How do you know?"

Almost apologetically, Sheldon tapped the scabbard on his left hip.

Claudette placed a hand on Sheldon's shoulder. "He's drawn his own blades, hasn't he? Is he coming to use them on us?"

Sheldon furrowed his brows and shook his head. "I can't tell. It doesn't work that way. It was just…well, he's close, though, and he's already using them."

"Who on?" said Claudette.

"I don't know. Not the Secret Police."

Claudette gulped. The four of them stood in the deep cellar room that had once held the knives Sheldon now wore. The lights now burned evenly and naturally, with no lingering aura of what they'd once held in sanctuary. Heavy furniture had been moved into the room, on Sally's insistence. She planned to shove it all up against the door, once everyone else was out.

As soon as everyone knew an attack by the Secret Police was inevitable, Sheldon had been ready to leave and take Janie with him. When she refused to dive back into the wild without a safety net again, he was stuck in a Catch-22. Then Claudette offered this cellar as a place to hide her during the fight—the deepest, safest place on the grounds.

The catacombs were where they stashed everyone too young or untrained for what was on the way.

"Fine," Sheldon finally said. "I'll stay down here with Janie, then. Last line of defense."

"You don't have that option anymore," said Claudette. "You're gonna be up there with the rest of us, on the *first* line of defense, against this situation you've helped create."

Sheldon clenched his teeth, got right in Claudette's

face, and snarled, "I'm staying with Janie, one way or another. You motherfuckers take it or leave it. You don't let us stay together? We walk. We—"

"Sheldon," Janie tried to cut in.

He spun and stared at her pleadingly. "No, love, please, you don't get it. I'm sorry, but if we stay here, we'll—"

After watching and listening all the while, Sally stepped up and said, "Little brother, I love you, but for once, please, will you shut the fuck up?"

Sheldon blanched, scowled, then looked at Sally quizzically.

"I'll stay with her here," Sally continued. "Anything that makes it down those stairs has to get through me to get to her. Okay?"

Before Sheldon could answer, Deacon shouted, "Is everyone's brain leaking? We can't spare an able-bodied fighter to guard one little Earth-line girl."

"Exactly," said Claudette, glancing at Janie. "She's our one Earth-line member. Good call, Sally."

"Sally's Secret-Police trained," said Deacon. "That's half our *fight fire with fire* power right there, and the half I trust with my ass more in pitched combat. Sheldon's so googly-eyed over the little Earth-line bitch, let him stay down here and protect her."

"For once, I like the way you think," said Sheldon.

"Hey," said Deacon, "if the little Earth-line bitch is that important to you all, fuck it, I'll stay down here and keep her safe." He glanced at Janie, as though expecting her approval.

"Right," said Sally, sneering. "Nice try, you sleazy,

handsy prick."

"*Shut up, all of you*," Claudette shouted. "Sally, Sheldon, I can't risk losing both of you in this fight."

"Why not?" said Sally.

Claudette's eyes narrowed. "Whichever of you survives—assuming any of us do—you're our future. So is Janie. Sheldon, you're the one who picked up those blades and strapped them on. One of you has to survive this fight."

"What if no one survives?" Janie heard herself whisper.

"Someone always has, so far," said Claudette. "Everyone has to hang onto something, right? Otherwise, what's the point?"

From there, they set about moving heavy furniture into the room to barricade the door. That's when Sheldon had his strange episode, when his link to Rob Coscan ignited.

Sally drifted towards the door. "He's coming. I have to go to him."

Claudette stepped into her path. "No, you have to stay here with Janie. You just pledged yourself to it, remember?" Sally tried to shove past, but Claudette grabbed her shoulders. "He's still a ways off. Our enemies—the ones we *know* are enemies—have already surrounded us. You couldn't get through them to him if you tried. Let's give these kids a second."

Once Sheldon and Janie were alone, he asked, "How you doing?"

She dropped her eyes and spoke slowly. "I'm in the middle of the woods, in a state I've never been to before, surrounded by everything I never knew was there in the world. Everything Mom always saw finally makes sense, and it's coming to kill us all. I haven't even had a chance to let myself settle down and grieve for Mom. You're all I have left."

"You're all that matters to me in the end," he said. "Do you love me?"

"Yes."

"Good. I'll see you soon." With that, he hurried out, pausing in the doorway to flash her a last, boyish smile.

FIVE

Sheldon found Sally at the top of the stairs. She looked calmer now, more resolved to the arrangement.

"Just in case," he said, "you're armed...right?"

She rolled her eyes. Her hand darted in and out of her pocket. The blade of a large pocketknife flipped open and closed. In any other hands, that knife would look pretty silly. Sheldon knew the lethal grace with which Sally handled it, though, so he smiled.

She yanked him into a fierce, quick hug, then hurried back downstairs.

Outside waited Tiger and Lilly. They both wore authentic Japanese swords on their belts. At first, Sheldon blinked incredulously at the sight. Neither of them had exactly struck him as the fighter type 'til just now. He peered at their eyes and posture. Had either of them ever faced anything like this, what was about to happen?

Hell no, he realized. *For that matter, neither have I. Fuck.*

Of the grounds' population, about a third went about outside. They appeared to stroll casually through their daily outdoor activities—mainly farming and building maintenance. Everyone else waited in their dark dwellings, ready to spring. Everyone outside carried some kind of weapon close to their sides, from archaic Earth-line battle blades like Tiger's and Lilly's, to farm equipment like axes and scythes, to plain, heavy-duty machetes. Some carried strange, ugly, homemade implements—raw beams of metal wrapped in leather or cloth at one end, chiseled to points at the other, edges sharpened on rocks, or welded, bolted creations made from spare parts gathered from this place. Some were children, both Spirelight and Schomite, some younger than Sheldon had been on that first family trip to Brattleboro.

No one carried firearms. Sheldon remembered, Mom had always carried a Glock, not that it had done her much good in the end. Firearms had never done much good against the Crimbone, and besides, they'd spent millennia perfecting the craft of keeping their feuds private from the Earth-line people. The noise of gunshots tended to put a damper on discretion, not that discretion would mean much from this point forward.

Most folks held their weapons competently enough. *Of course they've learned how to fight*, Sheldon realized. *They all started out as outcasts from their coteries, for one reason or another, running for their lives. Just like me. Just like Sally.*

How many Secret Police agents were about to swarm this place? A whole hell of a lot, that's all he could be sure of, a lot more fighters than Claudette had here. Sheldon's betrayal of his upbringing now felt complete. What other fundamental assumptions were left to shatter? A few people watched him, trying not to be obvious. The hope he saw in their eyes only made him more nervous. He turned back to Tiger, Lilly, and Claudette.

"So, where's Blix and Deacon?" he asked.

"Blix is watching the front gates," said Tiger. "Deacon's walking the west fence."

"Everyone in place on the other two fences?" said Claudette.

Tiger nodded and named off who was in command at those points. Sheldon didn't recognize the names. He was glad for that. Those minding the fences would likely die first, without warning. Most of these people, no matter how diligently they patrolled, probably wouldn't see the Secret Police 'til most of them were over the fences into the grounds. Those hiding in wait were the most important. If they tried a visible, ready stand, no matter how well they'd covered their bases, the Secret Police would fuck them from behind a lot harder and faster.

This whole mad gamble was Claudette's idea. Deacon had first proposed for everyone to stay inside and wait to ambush the intruders. No, Sheldon and Sally had assured them, the Secret Police would smell that quickest of all. Going out to meet the enemy head on, of course, would be suicide. Claudette had crafted the best defensive strategy possible on the fly, with Sally and Sheldon as consultants.

Once the attack started, everyone outside was to meet the Secret Police on the outer fringes of the grounds, get the fight going strong, then fall back into the center, drawing them inward 'til they were as surrounded as possible by the dwellings. Then those within would make their move. The buildings were tightly packed enough that the Secret Police would get congested while swarming between them. Once that happened, once the hidden fighters sprang, numbers would matter less. The more Sheldon thought about it, the more the situation felt about as rickety as the remnants of the old rides still hanging and strewn about.

When the throb of fear threatened him again, he reminded himself, *It'll work or it won't.* It was easiest, reduced to that cold simplicity.

Sheldon strolled towards the west fence, over dry grass and cracked sidewalks. The makeshift dwellings had all once been shops and concession booths. He passed the rusted skeleton of a Ferris wheel and thought, *This place was built in these times, during my lifetime, by Earth-line hands for Earth-line frivolity, a symbol of the modern world as they've shaped it…now it's the grounds for an ancient fight, fought in an ancient way.* When he looked around, though, he saw the most rust on the Earth-line trappings. The knives on his belt felt heavier than ever. He thumbed one of the pommels, eager to draw. *Not yet.*

Ahead, Deacon leaned against a pole, gaze trailing up and down the fence. He looked like a young man enjoying the sights, sounds, and smells of the forest in the late afternoon. Maybe that's what he still was on some level, drinking it all in deeply for the last time. Sheldon paused and drank it in with him. Rural Virginia was quite a marvel after all, even through the fence of this rusty makeshift fort. The air was rich with moss and fertile earth, and the green of the tall pines had gone deep in the red glow of the low sun.

As he gazed, Deacon leaned on the pommel of a katana that matched Tiger's and Lilly's. Sheldon walked up and looked out through the fence with him. He hadn't forgotten how much he disliked Deacon. He wasn't even sure why he chose to come wait with him. It would probably be easier to watch Deacon die than one of his friends. Shouldn't something about all this be easy?

Deacon looked at Sheldon. "You know, none of us have seen those blades out of their sheaths. We don't even know how strong the metal will be."

Sheldon half smiled. "How'd Claudette find 'em, anyway?"

"I'd tell you what I know, but even that takes some telling. I have a feeling we'll be interrupted soon."

"Yep."

"I was afraid you were gonna say something like *sooner than you think.*"

Sheldon suppressed a chuckle. He'd thought about using those exact words, actually. Gazing through the fence, in fact, he was surprised the Secret Police hadn't struck already. He considered mentioning that the Crimbone were close too, but Rob Coscan's pack was a ways off yet. Everyone needed to think about the enemy at hand. It bothered Sheldon more and more that said enemy kept hanging back. They were waiting for something specific. So he walked to the gate, drew one of the blades, and was blinded for an instant as it caught the sun's glare. The knife's haft and weight were perfectly familiar to him. So was the action as he drove it through the wire mesh, into the throat of the man crouched on the other side.

Deacon cried out and sprang forward, his sword leaping free. The shadows of the forest bolted forward in a body, scaling and leaping over the fence. Sheldon leapt, freeing the second blade. He spun in the air as the shapes descended in a silent avalanche. He caught them from below with the two spinning beams of razor light, his muscles moving with what seemed a faint memory, a revelation just now consciously dawning. Then again, less and less of his mind was consciousness, giving way ever more to a coldly lusting instinct. The blood of his former coterie showered him. Of those he didn't kill before they hit the ground, half seemed to come back at him. The others swarmed on Deacon.

Yeah, Deacon knew how to use that sword, it turned out. No wonder Claudette had warned Sheldon not to pick a fight with the sonofabitch! Of the Secret Police already in, half seemed taken off guard just to get such a strong fight out of anyone.

All through the grounds rose the clangor and shrieking of fighting, and the rising stench of death. There'd be nowhere to fall back to where the air was free of it. Many folks here would die quickly by surprise, but not nearly as many as had the Secret Police not been jolted into action, had they been allowed to strike according to their own timing.

Sheldon's back was to the fence. His kills piled into a fort, some of them still writhing and squirming and groaning as they bled out. Fresh enemies scrambled over, stumbling on slip-sliding corpses so they tripped forward onto his whirling blades. The knives were perfectly weighted to his hands, absurdly perfect even—as he guessed he'd known they would be—enough that he himself was almost thrown off balance by a degree of effectiveness he'd never thought possible in a weapon. *They felt like they* wanted *to do what they were designed for,* cutting through everything they touched, including other blades that rose to block them.

He put full force into every stroke, shearing all the way to empty air through the toughest hide and bone. One enemy fell away in two halves as his left blade continued forward. Sheldon sailed with it into an over-extension. Someone's knife gashed his shoulder. The arm shivered, fingers wanting to spasm open, so he willed his grip tighter on the handle. His right lashed around, the edge and tip not so much guided by his arm as pulling it. He skewered one attacker's skull, then slid free in time to sever the head of another.

"Sheldon, get out of there!" It was Deacon, waving wildly for Sheldon to follow him towards the center.

Thanks for the help, asshole, Sheldon thought as he leapt and bounded over the sprawling heap he'd made, feet sloshing in gore. When his soles touched the earth, it was already soggy. He ran from it as more living enemies swarmed at his back. When he caught up with Deacon, they turned to face them together, falling back steadily towards the center.

Out of the corner of his eye, Sheldon tried to see how well things were working.

Spirelight Secret Police agents swarmed like hornets through the grounds. All of them must be in by now. Several yards off, Deacon cut down his fair share before vanishing, engulfed as though by a sea of piranhas. Of the United Deschembines who'd stayed outside, something like two dozen still stood, surrounded. With each of them Sheldon saw fall, the thought pounded harder on his brain:

I've fucked them all over, just like Deacon said. I've brought the Secret Police here, and I've given them victory, as surely as though I'd led them like I was raised to do.

He went faster and fiercer, rage and self-loathing fueling a new, unimagined coordination. *You don't need to imagine it, though, do you? Nah, every muscle in your body knows this feeling, with these blades…well, not these blades and not your body actually, not that it seems to matter.* The battle fatigues they wore shouldn't even have camouflaged them half as well as it had on the other side of the fence, but for their just-so, hide-in-plain-sight attunements. *I didn't even know we had this many, back when I was one of 'em!* Good thing most of them were bred more for quick, intimate assassination than pitched broad daylight combat.

Years of homeless hardening, without the off duty comforts they took for granted, had made the adjustment more natural to him. That didn't mean they made it easy for him. His body had become a burning machine, spinning, lashing, leaping, no longer making a series of attacks, but one continuous lightning swirl, destroying anything that moved too close. In the enemies surrounding him, he saw a great collective manifestation of what his life was meant to be—all he had known for so long, the inescapable shadow over everything he'd tried to be since, made flesh in a sea sent in to overwhelm him. The only thing left to live for was to kill it a piece at a time, 'til either he or it was extinguished.

The physical world was a sticky, muscle-burning, bone-straining, nerve-scraping blur, punctuated by hot crimson splashes, 'til his clothes sopped pungently like he'd just gone for a swim in a stagnant pond. He spotted Lilly with her back to the castle wall, eyes wild and desperate, blade flailing at the three agents she fended off. At her side, Tiger was on his knees, his red arm pressed to his midsection as though holding in its contents. Through Sheldon's madness flashed the memory of why he was here, what he hoped to protect. The ones inside hadn't come out yet. What the hell were they waiting for? There were hardly any fighters left out here that he could spot.

"Spring the trap, damn you! Now or never, spring the fucking trap!"

The Secret Police paused and spun. In the space of a finger-snap, their foes had doubled, tripled, and they were the ones surrounded. In that one startled moment alone, quite a few were cut down, caught off guard. After that, they gave back harder than ever. Most of the United Deschembines were less than a match, though the agents still seemed thrown off by the fact that their targets put up any fight at all. The numbers had evened out, diminishing on either side, though that advantage quickly fell back to the Secret Police.

Sheldon had paused in his rampage to shout the command, and his brain had cleared some. Weaving back through the chaos, he hacked agents from his path, not caring whether or not they saw or engaged him. Soon, though, they would notice his energy starting to lag. At that point, he wouldn't last long.

By the time he reached Tiger and Lilly, only one of her opponents remained, though she was fading quickly. She bled from several shallow wounds, the worst being a slice to the forehead that had soaked half her face. Sheldon slid into a crouch, and swung his right blade to the left, shearing through hamstrings, scraping bone. As he rose, the man screamed and fell to his knees. Sheldon's hips twisted. His left blade drove through the crown of the skull. He sheathed both his blades, not bothering to cleanse them of the thick, clotting gore, so it bubbled around the hilts.

"Tiger," he shouted, stretching out one red hand.

Tiger looked up with bleary, shaking, agonized eyes, face bled pale, then swayed as if to roll onto his side. Sheldon and Lilly caught him by the shoulders. Lilly reached in to grip his arm, to keep it pressed to the gut wound. They hoisted him up.

"In here," Sheldon yelled, and guided them beneath the castle archway.

He led them to a secluded side door, tried the knob with his free hand, found it locked. With a growl, he kicked savagely, splintering the wood around the knob. The door flew inward, smacked the wall, hinges straining. In the bare room, he helped Lilly ease her husband down against the wall.

"Stay here with him," said Sheldon. "You've done your part out there. Barricade the door if you can."

Lilly nodded. Sheldon ran back into the hallway. At the end, framed in the glow of the archway, four agents broke into a silent, synchronized sprint towards him. He sprang to meet them. He drew his blades again, and the synergy with the weapons told him he still had some of that inhuman strength and coordination left. The agents hemmed him in. Four machete blades flashed in from as many directions, all at different heights and angles. He wove through the gauntlet, dodging two swipes, striking the others aside with a pair of clanging crashes that echoed deafeningly in the close space.

One man fell disemboweled as Sheldon stabbed another through the heart, ripping the blade free in time to slash the throat of a third attacker. From behind, a line of pain shot across his ribs. The fourth machete had cut deep into his side. In the blur, he saw his enemy's foot shift on concrete. He drove his own heel down, splintering metatarsals. As the agent bolted backwards howling, Sheldon stabbed him repeatedly with both blades, roaring as he gored chest, stomach, and throat wider and wider, 'til the body hit the floor with a heavy, wet plop like a ruined piece of fruit.

Staggering through the door, Sheldon looked out across the fight. In the sun's red glare, all he saw were bodies lunging at each other, killing in the purest, most graceless, undignified, murderous abandon. His own brain had almost cleared, but the madness that had held him was still there, everywhere he looked. From it all, two friendly shapes ran towards him.

"Claudette, Blix!" His voice was hoarse, his throat almost too raw to get it out.

He'd nearly reached them when a great call of triumphant malice sounded across the grounds: *"Sheldon Wildfire!"*

Claudette, Blix, and Sheldon all skidded to a halt and stared together.

"Sheldon Wildfire! Sally Coscan! Sheldon Wildfire! Sally Coscan!"

Sheldon's first thought was that it was Rob Coscan, the High Natural. No, there was a horrid smoothness to the voice, even at its great pitch, a formality to the declaration, even in its madness—the voice of a Spirelight Secret Policeman. Far on the other side of the fight, a new chorus of screams rose and mingled around the source as it thundered closer.

Around the marauding, approaching center, fighters on both sides were hacked away indiscriminately by a shooting, spinning, slicing black beam. Wielding that beam was a tall, pantherish shape, long, lean, hard, and swift as the great swinging instrument with which it killed. Finally, the fighters on either side made way, and the spring-steel juggernaut barreled forward along a clear path.

Sheldon, Blix, and Claudette exchanged nods, then they ran synchronized at the monster. Sheldon ran as fast as his companions, then two more agents closed with him from the left. He barely spotted them in time to pivot, deflect their strikes, and give back. By the time he finished with them, Blix and Claudette had closed the distance with the unstoppable force of nature and its spear. Blix went into a sliding crouch, swinging low from the left. Claudette came in high from the right, bringing down a forked hatchet.

The black iron spear flashed once in a straight line, then in an arc. Blix died instantly on his feet, pierced through the heart. Claudette's head flew from her shoulders before the former's body hit the dirt. The nightmare righted itself, gripped his weapon with both hands, and met Sheldon's gaze as the corpses thudded around him.

Sheldon ground to a halt so fast, he almost lost footing and toppled backwards, momentarily paralyzed by grief and terror. The nightmare stood three yards away. Sheldon didn't know the nightmare, but he saw in those eyes, in the pure, mad determination and anticipation, that the nightmare knew him.

Well, of course he knows you on sight. You're the tainted one, *remember? You're half the reason all this is happening.*

Sheldon launched himself forward. The nightmare man turned sideways, aimed the spear like a rifle, drawing back and driving it forward with his left hand, the beam sliding smoothly over his right palm. Sheldon nearly ran headlong onto the jutting point, then struck it aside with his left blade, while his right flew up in a moon-shaped arc.

The nightmare man stumbled sideways, then recovered as Sheldon closed in. He ducked, and the beam caught both of Sheldon's legs from behind, full-force. Sheldon rolled forward with it, his feet leaving the ground. He crashed on his back. In a daze, he saw the spear drive downward towards his face. He rolled out of its path towards the wielder, planted his rump and feet, then put the force of his whole body into his left shoulder, which he rammed into his enemy's knee.

The enemy staggered. The spear's tip ripped from the earth as he went, then swung like a pendulum at Sheldon's face. Sheldon batted it aside and rolled away. As he rose, the razor tip touched his cheek. He darted back, wiping blood from his face with the back of his hand as he found his footing. He went into a defensive stance, then nearly fell as the crippling pain set into his legs. His teeth clenched. He blinked hard against the sweat that stung his eyes.

The nightmare man limped too, but only on one leg. "You're too bled out, Sheldon," the bastard rasped. "You didn't save enough of yourself for me. It's time for me to show your head to the Tribunals."

"Think I'm too bled out for you? Come on, then, I'll take you with me!"

"It doesn't matter now." The bastard grinned deliriously and shook his head. "They'll be forced to acknowledge me for this." The voice trembled, with more than the pain of his injury. His spear would be quick and dead-on as ever, but his eyes were pale and wide with desperation, fueled by the pain. "I'll be remembered as the hero *you* should've—"

This time when Sheldon flung himself forward, it was with his upper body first. He forced his failing legs to carry him into it. His knives found their way back into their single, continuous spinning attack. He sidestepped the next spear thrust, caught it at the welded, bolted base in a scissor hold between the flats of his knives, and made a full-body wrench that jerked the shaft from the man's grip.

Before he even raised the knives again, though, the nightmare man lunged in barehanded and slugged him full in the face. Sheldon staggered away blinded. Blood from his broken nose filled his mouth.

Footsteps dashed sideways, obviously to retrieve the spear. Sheldon would never know how he found the sightless reflex that saved him. When he chopped furiously and blindly at the sound, his knife struck metal. He dashed backwards, blinking desperately.

Blurry vision faded in. The spear point came in rapid, taunting jabs, driving him farther and farther backwards. He struck it aside madly, again and again with both blades, each time feeling it coming closer. The icy, metallic tip plucked at him, opening his chest a bit at a time, in ever wider and deeper gashes. He backed into a tree and rolled aside so the blade drove into the wood and got stuck for a moment. Sheldon went in to seize the advantage, but the nightmare man ripped the spear free and swung, bashing Sheldon's already injured shoulder.

"Keep on going as long as you can." The nightmare man closed in. "*Yeah, that's it, that's it, yeah!* Bleed to death fighting on your feet. You'll still be dead, and so will your sister, and so will your little Indian bitch!"

Something broke in Sheldon's brain, letting something else come together. He willed himself forward with a failing growl, his left blade parrying the spear with an inward, downward sweep. He led with his right. When the spear dipped low, it made a deep slice across his upper right leg.

Sheldon's knees smacked the ground. His arms dangled at his sides, fingers holding the knives feebly. The flats tapped the earth. His eyes rolled upwards, and he saw the spear rise high in one hand like a harpoon. Sheldon's knuckles tightened and he drove his left blade up between the nightmare man's legs. The nightmare man gave a high, moaning wail as the air left him, eyes bugging and tearing up. Sheldon pistoned himself up on his left leg. His battered left shoulder screamed as he shoved the pommel, driving the blade through the pubic bone. His right blade swung up, hewing the spear arm from the shoulder like a stalk. Now it was the nightmare man who fell to his knees, so he landed on the pommel of the knife in his crotch. It drove the blade in to the hilt with a wet crunch.

Sheldon wanted to fall over now, but he hobbled in place. His face quivered with agony and loathing. His enemy sat bobbing and twitching in shock. The enemy's head lulled backwards and his eyes rolled up, meeting Sheldon's.

"You're the one who killed Annie, aren't you?" Sheldon said in a trembling hiss. The one who'd known about Janie, knew to drive her here, to set this whole mess up.

The only answer was a gurgling mumble.

Sheldon was about to use his remaining knife to finish the nightmare man off—*not so nightmarish now, pathetic fucker.* Then he noticed something on the man's belt, beneath the dripping stump. He wiped his blade semi-clean on his left pants leg, sheathed it, then reached down, snapped open the leather case, and drew out a pocketknife with a three-and-a-half-inch black grip, and press-down lock mechanism at the base. Sheldon flipped open the blade. It was good steel. He waved it in the man's face.

"You know, I used to have one just like this."

Sheldon gripped the man's scalp, yanked his head back, pressed the edge beneath the jawline, and jerked sideways. The throat opened ear to ear. He shoved the spurting corpse away, then tossed the knife aside. It stuck in the ground beside the dangling head. Sheldon hobbled away, then collapsed on his side.

It seemed he still heard the fighting somewhere, but it might only be echoes in his head. Bodies ran back and forth. He couldn't tell over what. The ground rumbled with the approach of many heavy vehicles. A hand gripped him by the scruff of the neck—a woman's hand, he figured out absently—and dragged him up. Through the blur, at the other end of the arm, he saw Lilly's face.

Crazy girl…I told her to stay with Tiger! Tiger must be dead. Good for him. I'm pretty sure we all are.

A Spirelight voice—maybe United Deschembine, maybe Secret Police—shouted, "Ah, holy shit, where did the Crimbone come from?"

SIX

Four vehicles, including the Big Red Beast, were left to come tearing into the Renaissance Kingdom parking lot. Within, a total of seventeen Crimbone remained to leap out, hands on weapons. The other vehicles had mostly been totaled in the fight with the troopers. Few Crimbone had died during the fight with the staties, though quite a few could see death from where they were, once the battle joy wore off and the extent of their injuries became impossible to ignore. A division was left behind, led by Joel, to get the wounded off the road.

Make camp in the woods, Remelea had told them, and hide well. They would regroup later. Once at the destination, Rob was the last out of the van, after Jesse, Zane, Crawler, and Remelea. Through the gates, the fight looked nearly over. Out blazed the glow, not quite as strong as at the homesteads, but enough to madden him, so his mouth watered and his hands itched to clutch the blades.

"*Remember,*" he roared, "*no matter how much the glow draws you, only kill the Secret Police! If you kill others and I'm not alive later to punish you…Remelea, Jesse, or Zane will be.*"

With that, he jolted forward, then halted and staggered as his stitches stretched and his innards contorted. The ground rumbled and thumped around him as the others broke into a charge. He made to push himself forward, then Remelea's arm slipped around his shoulders, steadying him.

"I'm fine," he whispered. "Go on."

Her hands lifted, but hovered. When he started forward again, screaming wounds sent lead weights through his limbs. She went to support him again, but he forced his hands to find his knives and clenched his fists around the handles. With a roar, he ripped them from the scabbards, flinging his arms out and upwards, stabbing at the sky. Remelea jumped back with a cry. Rob's stitches strained again. Something inside uncoiled and pushed at his ribs. Several thick, hot streams flowed down his side within his duster coat. By the time he reached the turnstile, he was walking upright at a maniacal clip.

A dying battle spattered the earth between him and his goal. He strode past and between the fighters, as he would the last dancers at a music festival in the cool, drunk early hours. Everywhere the Spirelight glow raged and flared, as his brothers and sisters of the pack tore open the vessels and drank deep. His blades were ready at his side, but they weren't the means by which to taste the glow he sought. Yeah, he tasted it—tasted *her*—still vibrant and strong, waiting for him…but where? So many glows, and oh, they always burned brightest and hottest and sweetest just before they were cut free for someone to drink down, making it harder to know where one ended and another began.

One enemy glow came in on his left. His blade licked out and slashed it in two. It screamed and its vessel thudded at his feet. He walked on, not bothering to taste it. Before him loomed a tower, gates wide. Was *his* glow waiting in there, or was it out here somewhere? Still too many of them! Two more ran screaming at him, but they weren't his, so he cut them both down. The second to fall got caught on his blade at the base of the neck and hung there twitching and struggling.

Rob strode on, eyes forward, arm outstretched to the side, walking the dying Secret Policeman along like a struggling dog on a leash. The fleeing glow coursed through the blade, up his arm, into him. As it ran dry, he flicked his wrist and cast the body away, then he walked into the castle.

Yes, Sally was in here somewhere…but where? She was, but she wasn't. Damnit, the inside of this castle was nothing but one great hallway lined in doors! "*Sally*," he roared earth-shatteringly.

Behind him, one of the doors burst open, set deeper in the wall than the others. More of the enemy glow exploded forth. It jabbed at him with a knife, which one of his own blades slashed away, along with the hand that clutched it. His other knife continued to pull him forward in a sweeping semicircle. His shoulder followed, then his torso twisted into it. For an instant, he felt ripped in two, so he screamed along with the Spirelight. That Spirelight lunged, spouting wrist and all. Their heads and shoulders collided and shoved like two enraged bulls, and they careened back through the doorway into darkness. The Spirelight kept punching Rob's face and chest, both with the remaining fist and the spouting stump. The rough, meat-encased end of a severed wrist-bone scraped up his face. He stabbed the man repeatedly in the sides and thighs 'til the floor dropped out from under them and they went crashing down a flight of stairs together. At the bottom, they rolled across concrete. Rob grabbed the dying Spirelight by the scruff of the neck and slammed the head against the stone wall 'til the shattered skull sagged like a sack of broken clay.

Now there was no glow, none but those far off.

Rob groped his way painfully up the side of the wall in the darkness. He only had one blade in hand, so he reached down to grope for the other. After yanking it from the dead Spirelight's ribs, he sheathed them both. Sally was down here somewhere—Sally, and no other Spirelights. Rob groped through the darkness along the walls, then turned one corner and found his way to another.

Yes, now he didn't need to kill anyone else, because no one had killed Sally before he could reach her. She was close, so close! He shouted her name over and over, hoping she heard, hoping there was enough of him left, just to see her clearly.

SEVEN

"You hear anything up there?"

"You kidding? I can't hear a damn thing."

Those were the last words Janie and Sally had exchanged, maybe several minutes ago, maybe an hour. There was no time inside a small, barricaded room this deep underground. For a while, they crouched together in a corner holding each other. Sally figured she'd put her time in comforting the Earth-line girl, but she herself wasn't one for huddled, cuddled cowering. Finally, she shrugged loose, got up, and set to pacing. A while after that, somewhere faint and far off, but definitely down in these halls, there came a series of heavy crashes between intervals, drawing steadily closer. Sally and Janie froze as the sound neared their hallway.

A set of whispering feet glided across the stone, one only Sally could hear. Poised near the door, she flipped out her pocketknife, despite the heavy giant cabinet and sofa barring them in. From further off came some other, less distinguishable noise. The footsteps paused, then hissed off back the way they had come. Sally let out a big sigh. Her knife arm relaxed a little.

"What do you think's going on up there?" Janie was still curled in the corner.

Sally gazed down at her, partly with shared fear, partly with pity, partly with annoyance at the useless, helpless rhetoric that comes with Earth-line panic. "I have no idea." Hopefully only the compassion came out in her voice. "Either our side wins and they'll be back down here for us soon, or—" She saw that Janie got the idea.

From far away came more commotion, more violent, loud enough that Janie heard it, so she perked up then shrank tighter inward. A wild, monstrous roar echoed through the hallway. It drew nearer, calling Sally's name. In her bewildered terror, she spun to face the door, her knife going up and stabbing the air.

"*What* is that?" came Janie's hushed cry.

Sally didn't answer, because she had no idea, except that the sound was of a creature never heard in this world, something from the deepest nightmare corners of ancient stories from her childhood. It got closer, calling her name over and over—

"It's getting weaker," Janie said, and it was. Not fainter, not further away, nearer than ever in fact, but the power was bleeding out of the voice with each exclamation.

Sally blinked and shook her head. Her ears must be playing tricks! As the monstrous, otherworldly thunder drained, she heard a voice she recognized beneath it. She started shoving the couch out of the way.

"Help me," she shouted at Janie. "He's out there!"

Janie stood, but just looked more scared and confused. "Yeah, I noticed, whatever he is…you wanna let him *in?*"

"We have to. It's Rob. He's hurt."

"Sally…" Janie's voice seemed full of some sad resignation, one she expected Sally to figure out.

"Fine then." Sally gave the couch a powerful shove. It smacked the wall so hard that the frame let out a crack. She gripped the cabinet by the sides, and with a savage heave sent it toppling and smashing. Janie screamed and jumped back. Sally bent and pulled the remains aside by its stub legs, then pressed her palms to the door and shouted, "Rob, I'm here! Rob, this way!"

"Sally!" The last of the thundering menace was gone. The door thumped as he fell against the other side.

Sally yanked, but the door was bolted from the outside. A chillingly familiar sound rang out, of metal chopping metal, and the padlock clattered on the floor. She jumped back as the door flew open. In shambled, not Rob, but the creature that had let out the nightmare roar. Janie screamed. Sally whipped her knife back out, drove it at the thing—and saw its eyes just as the point was about to strike home. She barely checked her hand, and the knife hovered near the creature's neck. A scarred, blood-soaked hand fell lovingly on her shoulder, then he slid towards the floor. Sally saw deep into his eyes, and she cast her blade away.

"Good," he said with a delirious smile, "you're safe. You're okay." He fell at her feet.

BLOOD WRITES THE BOOK

ONE

For the second time, the rusty red van pulled into the Renaissance Kingdom parking lot. This time, only Remelea got out. She'd left Joel and Crawler at the camp, fifteen miles south. When she opened the door, the smell assaulted her strongly enough that she almost couldn't climb out. She wrinkled her face and hopped down anyway.

Motherfucker, it was gonna take forever to scrape the Renaissance Kingdom off her boots! Most of the bodies would be dealt with by now, somehow, though the smell would stick around for a while. It would still be here when these people hit the road, which had to happen soon. She didn't want to imagine how they'd have to pacify with the locals between now and then. Thank these lands, that wasn't her job. Hell, at this point, what was funnier than worrying about Earth-line public relations?

The smell of death was nothing new to her, though

she'd never had to linger near it so long. She'd never even known the lives that had ended here, and she should have been the one to kill half of them. At least she used to think so, 'til she met a crazy, courageous guy named Rob, and he told her over and over all about this wonderful girl named Sally. Since last seeing Rob up and about, it was hard to think of him as an inspiration *not* to kill.

Since the last time she'd seen him at all, it was hard to imagine him killing or saving anyone or anything, ever again, harder than before to comprehend how his body clung to life. At least she'd finally met Sally. They spoke briefly. Yeah, Remelea looked at that girl, heard her voice, listened to the few words she spoke, and she understood what all this was for. Like Rob said, there was something of the Crimbone in the one they called the tainted Spirelight girl. It was weird, how tiny the girl was in the flesh. Remelea wasn't large, yet she felt like some ungainly giant, towering over that buzzing, defiant little frame, gazing down into those reddish copper eyes, like Goliath trying to stare down David.

We're not trying to stare each other down. We're in the same boat, like everyone else here, shoved into it by that same asshole she and I are both still so hung up on.

Who cares anymore, who either of us loves or hates? Not these lands, that's for damn sure.

When Remelea encountered the other Spirelights here, the back of her brain still felt the destructive tug towards their glow. It was easier to suppress than she'd ever thought possible. Clearly, it had to do with Sally's presence…*her unique glow.*

So, did that make it all worthwhile? Could anything justify what had happened, in any reality outside of Rob Coscan's insane heart where nothing mattered but Sally? Either way, the proof would show up. This was nowhere near over.

At the turnstile, Jesse and Zane waited for her. Aside from herself and Rob, they were the only two Crimbone still here. Sending the others back was Jesse's idea. With Rob out of action, without the grip of his command, it was safest for this uneasy arrangement. Given what she'd felt from Sally, Remelea didn't think the split was strictly necessary. Still, just in case… Apparently there were two official leaders here, one Schomite, one Spirelight, both of whom had been reported dead. Two younger Schomites also helped run things, mostly with morale. One of those had been confirmed dead. The other was barely alive, hooked up to machines or something. So Jesse and Zane ended up pulling and holding everyone together. If anyone felt uncomfortable under Crimbone leadership, they dealt with it silently.

They'd arrived to find thirty-five Secret Police agents still alive. None lived to take Crimbone life. The Crimbone had glutted their thirst and spared as instructed. Eighteen United Deschembines still lived. Eleven were Schomite, seven Spirelight. Everyone had wounds that needed seeing to. Miraculously, only a few survivors were badly hurt. Some of those were expected to live.

Among the worst off, word went, was Sally's younger brother. From what Remelea understood, these people held both him and Sally in some mystified reverence. Apparently, he shared his sister's unique glow. Remelea hadn't quite wrapped her head around that. From what she understood, Sally's only brother had tried to kill her and ended up—*surprise*—gutted by Rob. Remelea shoved it out of her mind. Old Lords knew, she might as well get used to shit that made absolutely no fucking sense.

She found Zane smoking. "I bum one?"

He produced the pack with a wrist-flick. A single cigarette slid up halfway. By the time she had it between her lips, his lighter was raised and ready.

"Thanks," she said through the first exhale of smoke.

"How's everything at camp?" Jesse asked.

"Better than I expected. First I meant to leave Joel in charge, but those two fledglings from the trooper barricade, Sam and Anya…they've pretty much assumed command. They're both from Earth-line military background."

"So, how are they adapting," said Zane, "to the new instincts of this new structure?"

"They've taken to it just fine, from what I can tell. Why? Is that surprising?"

Jesse and Zane exchanged a look. "You've never been in the Earth-line military, have you?" said Zane.

"Uh, no."

"They'll be fine," said Jesse. "They're not fledglings, you know."

"Huh?"

"What they did," said Zane, "that choice they had

to make for us, on the spot…that was the Second Call *and* the Third Call for them, in one shot. Those cops who died in that fight, they were those kids' brothers and sisters in arms, sure as their Crimbone brethren now. They might act like it was an easy choice, but it wasn't. There's no going back from it now, so the pressure's on their own conscience, to make good on what they've committed themselves to, hell or high water. In the eyes of the lands, not much makes you a fuller fledged Crimbone than that."

That took Remelea a moment to process. "Well. Fuck me. Hey, good for them. I like breathing. Has that ever happened before…I mean, two calls at once like that?"

"No," said Jesse, "but I expect it'll happen more and more, everywhere. Watched the news lately?"

She patted her hook handle. "Bitch, I've *been* the news lately."

"Yeah, so have I. Notice how local it's gotten?"

"You think I've had time to sit down to watch fuckin' TV since—"

"Well, we've caught moments to glance around."

"And nothing—I *mean* *nothing*—outside the continental US is making the news," said Zane. "Even overseas, Internet communication is garbling like you wouldn't believe. Cell phone signals, too. You name it. Earth-line folks who pipe up—say, families of soldiers overseas…well, their government's been shutting them up pretty quick."

"They're panicked that bad?" Remelea blinked rapidly. "What the fuck's going on over there?"

"Probably about like whatever's kicked off here," said Jesse. "The lands will arrange more and more tests like that for fledglings like Sam and Anya, only it'll make their choices a lot nastier."

"Just like we'll see a lot more twisted weather patterns," Zane added.

"You guys don't sound that surprised."

"We've had time to adjust to the idea," Zane answered.

"Since when?"

"Since first meeting Rob, five years ago."

"So…how is he?"

"Most of those who seen him don't think he'll wake up," said Jesse. "He took some nasty internal damage. That last run he made didn't exactly help. Me, I give him about a week 'til he's back on his feet." He glanced at Zane for affirmation.

"Maybe two weeks," Zane said.

Remelea's eyes drifted. She spotted awkward glances between Jesse and Zane. They were debating whether or not to tell her something. "What else is up?" she demanded.

Zane cleared his throat. "He'll be waking up in restraints."

Remelea wasn't sure what to call the present arrangement between the people here and the pack. Something between a truce and an alliance? Whatever the hell it was, it wouldn't last long once word of this got out. Her eyes and voice flared. "You guys allowed this?"

Jesse answered, "It was our decision."

TWO

All day, he and the pack scaled the mountainside. Spirelight Police met them at every step. The sopping splashes thickened under their boots the higher they ran through soggy red grass. Then the dome came in sight, the sky behind it like a solid sheet of white-hot tin. The sun scorched him, boiled the blood in his veins, even as it flowed freely from what seemed like countless wounds. Still, he fought higher and higher, springing and biting and tearing as one with the pack. Together they cleared the slope and plunged towards the ivory-painted glass dome, howling as one as they slaughtered and feasted. By the end, though, he alone entered the temple. Outside, the others still fought and drank deep, the mountain howling with them, blessing their victory.

Now he stood alone in the center of the temple, staring down at the altar, at the book he'd come here to find. It lay open before him. Maybe he should be dead after this much blood loss, yet he no longer felt the wounds, here at the altar. Looking down, he saw the words on the right page, the picture on the left.

The temple was dark, but he saw it all clearly. It was the drawing Louis had done of the Old World, of Magur Sevi emerging from the valley, the sea of mist rolling back behind him to reveal the deadly path through which he'd prevailed. The effacing page tried telling the story in words.

Rob looked back. "Louis? Louis, where are you?

You gotta come see this, man!"

Louis didn't answer, because he hadn't been in the battle, hadn't scaled the hillside with Rob today. Louis had died a long time ago. That wasn't Louis's drawing Rob found in these ancient pages, nor in the story the drawing depicted. He'd already seen these things. He flipped back through the pages, skimming quickly. Somewhere, here, were the answers he'd come for…to lead him forward, so he could lead others forward.

Some words caught his eye. He read closely 'til he found his way back to the page with the drawing. More confused than ever, he flipped back further and further. Several times, he reached that same page. *Magur Sevi, and the mists rolling from the deadly valley. Before that, he beheld a life he knew all too clearly, a life of—*

"Louis…you never told me any of this. If you had, I'd have done so many things different. *Everything* could be different, better, right here and now, if you'd just…"

Again, Rob reached for the edges of the book, this time shoving back a massive clump of pages. It opened much further back than he dared look. He still started reading again. The words made him jump back. He spun 'round, eyes darting frantically through the chapel, and he shrieked, "*Sally!*"

That's right, he hadn't come here looking for this damn book. He'd come looking for his wife. What was he doing here, on this mountain, in this temple? Looking for the answer, that's what, for why all this had started, for the source of the infection that had caused the people of the Old World to lose touch with the rhyme and rhythm of its lands. The answers were here, yeah, but

Rob didn't dare read another word.

"Louis, you knew," he shuddered. "You knew every Goddamn thing, from the second you first saw me, and you never told me."

Of course not. Because Louis had assumed it wouldn't make a difference. Rob had to get out of here. He had to find Sally. It was too dark to find his way out of the temple, to see anything but the words printed in the ancient book. Through the darkness, only one voice echoed back to him, a voice that wasn't Sally's and wasn't Louis'.

Postville didn't betray shit, Biter-Boy, didn't I tell you? Nah, that lil' town never sent a damn thing your way you didn't want it to. Thing is, you wanted some trouble to find ye there. Naw, you never said it to the place—but the place heard you screamin' it loud an' clear…felt it bubblin' up in ye, ready to explode. You needed out'a there, but you wasn't gonna make yer move so long as you had yer Sally-Poach there safe an' sound. Hell, that town hadn't brought you what ye really wanted, sooner or later you'd'a flipped out an' sliced up ev'ry livin' thing in sight. Well, it sent ye what ye needed, didn' it?

An' don't tell me it ain't felt great, swingin' an' hackin' with them blades again, grabbin' this world by the balls an' tellin' it what's what. That's what you told that shithole town ye wanted, 'cause that's what the blood in your veins said you wanted. Like I always tol' ye, Biter-Boy…"

THREE

Propped up in bed, Sheldon ran his finger back and forth over the line of black bristles holding his right leg shut. The spear had barely missed the femoral artery, Lilly kept cheerfully reminding him. Now she sat next to him, between his bed and Tiger's. These United Deschembines were better stocked up medically than he would have guessed.

Claudette really did think of everything, didn't she?

Claudette had had a good head on her shoulders, as the saying went. Sheldon squeezed his eyes shut, trying to black out the image of that head flying from those shoulders, to roll across the ground somewhere like that basketball he and Janie had shot hoops with when they were kids. The image still didn't leave him alone, so he opened his eyes again.

This subterranean stonewall chamber had become quite the makeshift hospital room. In the far upper corner of the left wall, sunlight spilled through a small window, so he knew this was one of the dugout lodgings around the grounds, not one of the rooms in the castle cellars. At least he wasn't hooked up to all those tubes like Tiger over there.

On the other side of the bed sat Janie. She snatched Sheldon's hand away from his stitched leg, wove her fingers with his. "No. You can't have your hand back."

She smiled much more often and willingly, since he'd told her Annie's killer was dead. Apparently, Sheldon and Sally's beast had *just missed* each other. Now people said Rob Coscan's pack had won the fight for them. At least now they had someone else to force their hero-worship onto. Except now, the beast was somewhere else on the grounds, worse for wear than Sheldon, maybe worse than Tiger.

Sheldon pulled Janie inward. Her mouth covered his. His free hand slid up her arm, then up and down her body. It was the most he'd used his left arm in days. The shoulder wasn't broken, but the muscles were pulled all to hell, the bone bruised, so the whole arm blazed when he moved it. Janie pressed herself into his touch. When his hands tried his luck, she eased back. He followed her gaze. Lilly eyed them sidelong without embarrassment. Oh well, more motivation to get well quick, he supposed.

Sally came in and said to Lilly, "You want me to watch these boys for a while?"

"Nah, that's fine," said Lilly. "I'm enjoying watching the antics of this one here." She nodded at Sheldon. Janie's red face went redder and she hid it in the crook of Sheldon's neck.

"Well, don't let him give you too much trouble," said Sally. "That goes for you too, Janie."

Janie looked up. "I think we can make him behave, between the two of us."

Sheldon's hand snuck to Janie's ass. "You're both welcome to try."

Sally smirked at Janie. "You have my permission to beat my brother."

Sheldon saw his sister trying not to look sad. He knew why. Much as he hated himself for it, that still complicated how he felt about her. He didn't want to deal with it now, though, so he nuzzled his face in Janie's hair instead.

FOUR

Down the hall, Sally found Remelea waiting.

"How're you holding up?" Remelea asked.

Sally started several answers, then blurted, "They won't let me see him!" Her voice broke into sobs. "I ask everyone, and they won't tell me shit. They won't even tell me where they're keeping him in this fucking place."

When Sally fell forward, Remelea embraced and cradled her, letting her get it all out, loving and hating this strange girl, in a way not so far from how she loved and hated Rob.

Part of Remelea's brain recognized Rob Coscan as bad news, something both her and Sally would be better off without. That same part saw Sally for the good person she was, Spirelight or no, someone she'd have been honored to call a friend, if so many things weren't so fundamentally fucked about this reality they shared.

Something else in her kept screaming, *This little bitch could never handle it in the long run with the Rob I know, the* real *Rob I've come to know on the trail. Why the fuck does he keep wasting time, pretending he belongs with her?*

Instead, she whispered, "Follow me."

FIVE

Moments later, they hid together, pressed far into a doorway towards the back. Sally couldn't see anything, couldn't hear much beyond the usual footsteps coming and going. When a door opened somewhere, Remelea peered around the corner. Sally moved to look too, but Remelea pinned her in place for nearly a minute.

Finally, Remelea stepped out and looked back at Sally. "Come on."

Claudette had cut the lights in the cellar via some main power source before the fight, but they now burned brightly again. Remelea led Sally down the stairs, then through the winding passages. Down another set of stairs was a familiar door.

The one place I didn't think to look, Sally mused. *They sure do mean to get all the mileage they can out of this room.*

Remelea stepped aside. Sally crept through the door, and all her thoughts were replaced by heart-rending horror. Rob lay on his back, bound naked to the kind of table Sally had hoped never to see again. For a heart-stopping moment, she was sure he was dead. Then his chest rose and fell. She ran to his side, calling his name. Even up close, she barely recognized him, so covered in stitches and bruises that he looked like the Frankenstein monster. Finally, she looked back at Remelea.

"I know." Remelea's eyes were as bright with tears as Sally's. "He's been like this since that day."

"Why are they keeping him like this?"

"It has to do with how he was acting, with

the…vibes we were getting from him. When he first came out of a state like this, after he first got those wounds."

"*Vibes?* You're keeping him strapped to a fucking table, when he's like this, because of some fucking *vibes?*"

"It's not just that, and you know it. It's what he's done. What his…voice makes other people do…other Crimbone do."

"Don't give me that shit," Sally shouted.

"Keep your voice down," said Remelea.

"Yeah," Sally hissed, "I've heard all about what he *made you all do. Made you*, my ass. You think I don't know your kind? What you're capable of?"

Remelea shrugged. "He's still the one who told us to, led us to it…all for you."

"*I* didn't make him—"

"No, that's right, you didn't," whispered Remelea. "So what gives you the right to condemn all of us except him?"

Sally still didn't have an answer for that one.

"It's not just that," Remelea went on. "It's because of what Jesse and Zane found out. Apparently they were down in New Orleans—"

"*New Orleans?*"

"Yeah. Some stuff that ties in with our legends, matches up with what we've seen in him since…what having him around did to the other Crimbone, including me, even when he was comatose…hell, *especially* when he was comatose."

"From who?"

"Huh?"

"Who'd they learn it from?"

"I don't know."

Sally leaned close over Rob, ran her hand over his body. Yeah, he was alive…but he felt so cold, colder than it was down here. His wounds were healing fast, much further along than they should be.

Now would be a good time to run like hell from this room, forget Remelea had ever led her to him. How often had she thought things like that about Rob, thoughts she'd never followed through on, because they always turned out to be stupid, things she'd been weak enough to let others plant in her head about him? Wasn't she stronger than that by now? When she bent and kissed his forehead, his eyes opened.

"Sally…" It was the low, monstrous voice she'd heard roaring her name in the hallway, and it was also Rob's voice—*her* Rob, soft and imploring.

Behind Sally, Remelea started forward, then held herself back.

Sally placed her hands on Rob's cheeks. "I'm here, Rob. Please, you stay here too." Her hands fumbled at the strap binding his right wrist.

He sighed. "No…no, I can't stay here. Sally, I have to go away."

She started back at his binds. "Yeah, we both do. Just hold still for a second. We're leaving. We'll leave today."

"Not this time." His voice broke, stayed broken. "No, you have to stay here. I…I need to get as far from you as I can."

She drew up sharply. "What are you saying?"

"I bet they've told you shit about me lately. It's all true, and it's worse than any of them know. I love you, Sally. I love you so damn much…that's why."

Sally looked back at Remelea, pleading for help.

Remelea lowered her eyes. "I'll give you two this time. I'll be back after you've left, Sally." With that, she turned and walked out. Sally looked back desperately, pleadingly at Rob.

"I'm not Rob anymore," he went on, voice trance-like. "I still am, but not like you used to know me…still myself, but different, too. I don't understand it…I'll go away. I have to go away. I don't know where yet. Please, Sally, let me up so I can go. If I stay here—"

She cut him off with a slow, deep, desperate kiss. When she drew back, she'd undone his restraints. The sobs didn't break full force 'til she found her way into the room she'd first stayed in when she got here. She spent the next few hours hiding there, from the world.

FIVE

When Remelea came back, Rob was on his feet, leaning wearily against the table. Over one shoulder she'd slung his duster. Bundled under her arm was a pair of jeans and a shirt. Her other hand gripped his knives in their scabbards, wrapped in his belt. She held them out respectfully at arm's length. He took them unceremoniously and started to dress.

"Can you walk far?" she asked.

He nodded as he buckled the jeans, not meeting her eyes.

She amended, "Quickly and quietly?"

He pulled the shirt over his head and nodded again.

"I have a car waiting."

He was busy looping on the belt. "Good."

"The pack's about fifteen miles from here."

He buckled the belt, the scabbards slapping then hanging against his hips. He pulled the duster on over them. "We're not going back to the pack."

EPILOGUE

ONE

On the day of the fight on the grounds of the Renaissance Kingdom, the Earth's sun let loose the most massive solar storm on record in over a hundred and fifty years. For over an hour, the sky worldwide bled red, then purple, then finally pulsating green. Floating snakes of light drifted across the heavens like the northern lights had split free and circled Earth like the rings of Saturn. Throughout the heavens, satellites shorted out and fell from orbit in flaming chunks that sizzled in lakes and oceans, and set trees and pastures ablaze.

Internet server farms combusted, setting off infernos that raged out through cities and country sides alike. Of course, with all the failing internet and cell phone service, fewer and fewer people and businesses had any idea of what the hell was happening.

Wherever Earth-line wars were fought, Crimbone fledglings on either side set down Earth-line weapons, picked up their Old World weapons, and crossed battle lines to form new packs. When their Earth-line commanders and comrades tried to stop them, the earth and skies opened, engulfing them, wars and all. Old, dead volcanoes erupted, while new ones sprouted fresh to drown towns and cities in fire.

In Schomite strongholds everywhere, weapons of the black metal poured in by the dozens from the ephemeral realms, almost too quickly for the Crimbone elders to prepare and perform the adequate rituals, so all the weapons could be sent off again to their fledglings. Crimbone packs ran openly on their warpaths. When what was left of Earth-line law crossed those paths, it always ended the same way. Infrastructures and technological networks were sabotaged, shorted out inexplicably, or simply seemed to reprogram themselves to let slip what came rising through the cracks.

Earthquakes and killing storms happened where they'd never occurred before—with unprecedented ferocity—as if strategically placed to most disrupt the flow of Earth-line civilization and communication.

Throughout the wilderness, life churned, bubbled, and began to grow out of control, finding its way into new, strange forms that the Earth-line botanists were at a loss to categorize. At first the Earth-line people went on through their daily lives, the failing of their support systems coming so gradually, it seemed like steadily mounting inconveniences, even as the crumbling of their governments trickled increasingly onto their heads. In those governments, strange figures hitherto unseen stepped further from the shadows, exerting their influence more openly.

Long before these figures would speak the names of

their coteries openly, it would be the derelicts of cross-country bus lines and ramshackle railroad cars who began to whisper the words *Schomite* and *Spirelight*, *Crimbone* and *Secret Police*, and finally *High Natural*. Of course, it really started in the rural places, the border towns and smaller cities, in swamps and forests and mountains whose spirits hadn't suffered so many Earth-line illusions to borrow space, where this new energy gathered strength and seeped slowly outward.

No one tried to name what was seeping through, for it only paved the way for whatever would emerge when the barriers truly fell.

Two

As they passed out of Virginia, Remelea asked, "So, where am I supposed to drive, anyway?"

Rob leaned the passenger seat back halfway. The minute he'd started up the cellar stairs, he'd realized just how weak he still was, how much pain his guts still gave him. By the time he'd reached the car, he doubted he could have taken another step. Thank fuck for Remelea, keeping her head about her and her eyes peeled, or they never would have reached the vehicle undetected. At least there was a long drive ahead. He could do most of his recovery while she drove.

A flock of birds soared out ahead. One of them wasn't a bird. Rob thought about Remelea's question, while he sorted through everything Jesse and Zane had told him.

And through what he'd read in the great old book…

What book? The one on the altar, in the Spirelight temple, of course. By now, though, the more he tried to consciously remember what he'd learned there, the less he could anchor himself anywhere. He knew only whom he loved and what he saw reflected. For the sake of one, the other now had to go on alone.

No, damnit! What was he doing, running out on Sally, over something he read in a book in a dream he couldn't even remember? Several times he almost told Remelea to turn the car around. If she refused, he would get out and walk back if it killed him. He would tell Sally he made a mistake, beg her forgiveness. It didn't feel real, letting himself end things between them, climbing voluntarily into the car that now sped him farther and farther from her.

No, he hadn't given up. He was moving forward, on the only trail left. It would be true soon enough. That's when the real pain would come. Weren't this Talino guy's revelations confirmation enough, even if the man was crazy?

No. Whoever made the connection between him and Sally possible, it was the two of them who'd always filled the space together. How else could it leave such a cold, sucking pit in him now? Part of Rob felt like his soul had crawled into that pit and died. He wanted nothing more than to pour enemy blood into it, even if it was too deep to ever fill. There was more to Rob Coscan than that, though, a part that still dreamed, against all odds, of sitting with his queen on the throne of a world reborn. That side of him needed answers. He knew where to start looking.

Rob looked at Remelea and smiled for the first time in days. Okay, so he wasn't completely alone. He still wondered what screws were loose in her head, but what better living friend or fighting comrade could be so loyal to a fault?

"Hey, Remelea. Ever been to New Orleans?"

"No."

"It's a fun place. Let's go. I'll show you around."

"So, what's the plan there? Don't you dare pull that *I'll tell you when we get there* crap!"

Rob gazed up through the windshield, at the bat-like shape soaring above the treetops, ever just ahead, ever in sight. "I'm afraid I have to. I know about as much as you at this point."

THREE

The survivors stood waiting in the Renaissance Kingdom parking lot. Most clustered close together. Few spoke. Only two figures stood apart. Back by the gate, a tall, bald, powerfully built man watched the crowd. Out near the road, a slight, caramel-haired woman stared off, her back to everyone else. Sometimes the big man gazed at her, but never for long. It was easier to look at the crowd. From one cluster, a teenage boy limped towards him. Usually the man could only stare at the twin scabbards the boy wore. It was just too damn surreal a sight, on too many levels. Now, though, there was a strange purpose in the boy's eyes and walk…a sad, awkward purpose, but still strong.

The boy dug something from his pocket. "Mister Karn—"

"Call me Jesse."

"I'm sorry I didn't do this earlier. Someone asked me to give this to you." He handed Jesse a folded piece of paper.

Jesse peered over the boy's head, back towards the crowd.

"No one here. I've been carrying this for a while. I just…I didn't realize 'til recently, but I'm pretty sure you're the one I'm supposed to give this to."

Jesse unfolded the paper and stared in silent shock for a while. Finally, he looked up. "Where'd you get this?"

"In Vermont. From your…from someone who says he never left the place. He said…he said he hoped when you saw it, maybe it'd help you understand something."

Jesse almost hounded the boy with all sorts of questions. "Thank you," he said instead, then folded the paper and slid it into the left breast pocket of his shirt.

A rumbling sounded through the trees, somewhere on the winding road ahead of them all. It turned out to be a strategically scraped chunk of metal on wheels, big enough to sit the small refugee band. Maybe the scraped-off stenciled letters used to spell "Greyhound," or maybe the name of some touring band that no one remembered from the '80s. Zane sat in the driver's seat.

"How the hell did he get a bus?" asked Sheldon.

"You don't wanna know," said Jesse.

Zane pulled to a stop in front of the crowd, unnervingly close for some tastes. Some of them felt less like pissing themselves when he handed the keys to

Lilly—those who hadn't seen her driving, specifically. "All yours, lady, if you can keep her from killing everyone."

Sheldon limped back towards the crowd. His Earth-line girl stepped forward and let him lean on her.

Zane cast them a brief glance as he walked up, then said to Jesse, "You know, the pack's still camped out a ways from here."

"Thinking of joining up with them?"

"About as much as I'm planning on reporting back to the Cabinet, ever."

"Aw, c'mon, they ain't *that* bad a bunch of youngsters."

"Not for right now. Then again, they're taking some downtime. Hell, they've earned it. So what, were you thinking to group up with 'em?"

"Actually, I was thinking of tagging along with this bunch for a while. Ought'a have someone around to look out for 'em, don't you think?"

"*Jesse Ripper-Man Karn and Zane Fuckin' Rochester, brave defenders of the United Deschembines.*" Zane lit a smoke. "Hell, why not? Sounds about as sane as any options we've got left. Which is to say, completely clownshit insane."

"That, and I gotta admit, I'm curious as hell about those blades that kid's carrying."

They chuckled heartily together, clasped hands roughly, then they headed for the van parked across the lot from the bus. By the time Jesse climbed into the driver's seat, his face was grim again. "You sure we shouldn't try to find Rob?"

"I'm sure we will anyway, eventually. No sense

rushing things."

Meanwhile, the United Deschembines loaded up. Sally walked back from the edge of the road, loaded her small amount of luggage underneath, got on last, and sat in the back. Only a few seats ahead, Sheldon put his arm around Janie, kissed her forehead, and smiled comfortingly. She kissed his cheek, then rested her head on his shoulder.

Up front, Lilly helped Tiger get situated. Then she climbed into the driver's seat and guided the bus out of the lot. Close behind trailed the rusty red van. The plan was to head for Canada. Word had drifted in of some spots up that way that sounded less crazy than everywhere else. They would take the long way. Then again, any road would be the long way by now.

Matt Spencer is the author of seven novels, two collections, and numerous novellas and short stories. He's been a journalist, New Orleans restaurant cook, factory worker, radio DJ, and a no-good ramblin' bum. He's also a song lyricist, playwright, actor, and martial artist. He lives in Vermont with his girlfriend and two cats. Check him out online at http://mattspencerauthor.wordpress.com, on Twitter at @MattSpencerFSFH, and on Facebook at Books by Matt Spencer.

Thanks for reading, folks. Hope you enjoyed the ride. Now don't forget to go to let everyone else know what you thought! Be sure to pop over to Amazon, Goodreads, your blog, and whatever social media you frequent, and drop a short review (or a long one, if you feel like it).